DARKWINDS

Graham Watkins

BERKLEY BOOKS, NEW YORK

Lyrics from *"Strange Days"* and *"When the Music's Over"*
written and composed by Jim Morrison, Ray Manzarek,
John Densmore and Robby Krieger.
© 1967 Doors Music Company.
All Rights Reserved. Used by Permission.

DARK WINDS

A Berkley Book, published by arrangement with
the author

PRINTING HISTORY
Berkley edition/June 1989

ISBN: 0-425-11609-3

A BERKLEY BOOK® TM 757,375
Berkley Books are published by The Berkley Publishing Group,
200 Madison Avenue, New York, NY 10016.
The name ''BERKLEY'' and the ''B'' logo
are trademarks belonging to Berkley Publishing Corporation.

PRINTED IN THE UNITED STATES OF AMERICA

10 9 8 7 6 5 4 3 2 1

DARK WINDS

At a southern university, a man studying perception dreams of an impossible fate—a captivating woman—a gruesome ritual he cannot resist . . .

DARK WINDS

In New York City, a dazzling prostitute waits for her chosen lover. A teenage runaway sees visions of blood. And a sadistic killer stalks his latest victim . . .

DARK WINDS

In a timeless world of darkness, passion is the ultimate terror. And fate is the oldest, most inescapable evil of all . . .

DARK WINDS

Prologue

Briefly, he wondered at how much he'd changed in such a few short weeks.

Three months ago he would have vociferously defended anyone's right to life, under any circumstances whatsoever; as far as he had been concerned, the death penalty was just state-sanctioned murder, not deserved by the worst mass-murderer. Now he found himself clinging to a fire escape on the side of a building in New York City. Below and behind him, a steep slope led down to the Hudson River and the George Washington Bridge. He glanced at the cars moving on the street, just a few blocks down. How little those drivers knew, he thought, of the world around them and what it contained. Then he turned, looked back through the window he was crouched in front of.

Inside, a man whose back was to him was just removing his undershorts and socks. Beyond him was a stunningly attractive woman, already nude, smiling at the man undressing. She didn't know what was about to happen—quite certainly she thought the man was merely going to have intercourse with her—but the watcher did. A few minutes from now—maybe seconds, he wasn't sure—this man would attack and murder the woman.

The watcher lifted the revolver in his hand and glanced at it; so easy to stop it. But he would not. He would stand there and watch, a silent observer in the night, until the woman was quite dead. Then, and only then, would he step in and kill the man with the gun he held. That the police might catch him did not disturb him at all; it hardly mattered. All that made a difference to him now was that neither of these people leave the room alive.

1

He knew he'd enjoy killing the man. The woman—well, that'd be a quite different matter.

He looked at the two inside. The man was putting his hands on the woman's shoulders, pulling her toward him. Outside, the watcher noticed for the first time that the window was latched from the inside. He had a strong desire that it not be so; and he gazed intently at it as the latch rose, cleared the tang that locked it. He pushed the window a trifle, wanting it to be soundless. It swung open an inch or two, and there was no sound, even though the hinges were tight. He looked through the glass again, watched the two kiss.

And he waited.

1

Just an old, faded photo. Black-and-white, turning yellow with age, a few fine cracks in the once-glossy surface. The late afternoon sunlight caught the face of the girl whose image was entrapped on it, made it seem as if she had moved her dark eyes, as if she were looking out over the dappled ocean in the background. Wearing a modest two-piece bathing suit, one hand tangled in her curly black hair, she had been captured sitting on a piling at some dock somewhere; there was no information as to the location. The only comment on the back side of the picture was the statement, "Nikki—1942."

Elliot Collins let the hand holding the old photo drop to his lap, leaned his head on the back of the even older easy chair he was sitting in and closed his eyes.

With extreme clarity, he could remember the first time he'd seen this picture; he'd been about thirteen, rummaging through some of his father's things one Saturday afternoon when he'd found himself alone in the house. Once, during such a search, he had found some pictures of Polynesian women in various stages of undress, and for him at the time, that had been extremely exciting. Hoping to find more, he'd looked forward to those times when his parents were absent; when they were, he'd spend his time searching in places they would not have expected him to look. But he'd failed to find any more such treasures; instead, he had found this picture, tucked in a velvet-covered folder as if it had been precious to his father. And, with the swiftness and intensity not uncommon in young teenage boys, he had, in a way, fallen in love with the image. For hours, he'd stared at that picture; to him, the girl was so pretty that it hurt him somewhere inside his chest. He'd been certain that she was as generous and loving as she was beautiful, that she was in every way a Perfect Woman. The fact that he was but thirteen—and as the year was 1956, she had to have been at least thirty or more—bothered him not at all. Perfect Women were, in his mind, eternal.

But his fantasy affair with the photo had been doomed to an early end. Somehow, his father seemed to have known that he'd looked at the picture, because when the next opportunity came, he found it missing from its hiding place. Exhaustive searches of the house had failed to turn it up, and gradually it faded to a sweet, nostalgic memory. Never had he seen it again; not until this day, a sad day in 1969.

That morning, he had buried his father, placing him alongside his wife, who'd been waiting some five years. The fact that his mother had died in her late forties, his father at age fifty-two—both of circulatory disease—did not bode well for his own longevity, as he was well aware. Not that his medical checkups had ever revealed anything ominous; he'd always been told he was healthy as a horse. But then again, his parents had been healthy too, right up to the day they died. Stroke for his mother, sudden congestive heart failure for his father, the coroner had said. In neither case had there been any warning at all. And Elliot was quite aware that such things had a tendency to be inherited. Still, there was little he could do about it. He tried to put it out of his mind, get back to the business at hand.

As their only child, he'd inherited everything, such as it was; his parents had not been rich. So he'd found himself in the house where he'd grown up, beginning the task of sorting through things, trying to decide what to keep, what to dis-

card, what to sell. In the first trunk full of Aaron Collins'
personal things, he'd found the photo.

Without lifting his head, he raised the little paper square
and looked at it again. Strange, he thought. Almost always,
things you prized at thirteen simply don't have the same
effect after another thirteen years. But if anything, the effect
of the photo was even stronger. He had never seen any
woman even half so attractive, at least in his eyes, as the
mysterious "Nikki." Looking at her still provoked a pain in
his chest. Just as he had done twelve years ago, he wondered
who she was. Nineteen-forty-two would have been just before
his father had met and married his mother. He figured that
since she looked about twenty in the photo, she would have
been born about 1922, which would mean she would now be
about near fifty. He sighed; sad to think about this woman
becoming fifty. Meant he couldn't trust her, he thought,
allowing himself his first grin of the day. Wasn't it common
knowledge right now that you couldn't trust anybody over thirty?

With another deep sigh, he sat up in the chair, eyed the
still-full trunk on the floor in front of him. This would take
days. And he just didn't have time; the psychology department at the University of North Carolina would not allow a
junior staff member to take a sabbatical of weeks and weeks.
And there were important matters to be attended to. The
house had to be sold, the oversized Buick out front had to be
disposed of—he wasn't going to drive such a monster—and so
on, and so on. He could have shipped the trunk back to
Chapel Hill—no way was it going to fit in his VW bug—but
his apartment was small, and cluttered enough already. Still,
it would have been impossible for him to throw it out before
he'd at least gone through it cursorily. Refusing to be intimidated by the stacks of papers, he dug into it again, trying to
at least glance at everything.

And after two hours, he'd not found another thing of any
interest whatever. Oh, there were a few things he'd save, just
as mementos, but nothing that spoke to him like the pallid
photo, now resting against a lamp on the little antique table
alongside the easy chair.

The light was fading at the windows, and he'd turned on
the lamp; the new angle of the light seemed to shift "Nikki's"
eyes so that now she was looking at him, rather than out over
the sea. Periodically he stopped and looked back at her, and

whenever he did, she smiled. He could not shake the impression that she was smiling at him. Stupid, he told himself with some irritation. She was smiling at the photographer, his father or whoever it had been. Moreover, her smile was older than he was.

Eventually, he left the trunk and its contents, went out, ate his dinner, and came back. She was still sitting under the lamp, still smiling. Still had her absolutely perfect leg curled against the piling for support. Her small but perfect breasts still strained at the top of the swimsuit.

Elliot leaned on the chair and studied her; he realized he could look at the picture for a very long time and not get bored. But he forced himself to be content with an occasional glance, as he worked another inch or two down into the trunk. Finally, he could no longer keep his eyes open, and he went to bed. And in his dreams, the girl in the picture did smile, just for him.

It was well after ten o'clock the next morning before Elliot finally got back to the old trunk. Even though he'd gotten up quite early, he really hadn't slept well, hadn't wanted to get up when he did. For one thing, the dreams were too pleasant; he had too much of a sense of loss when he left them. For the other, the house and the town of Eddieville, Illinois, had too many memories for him. After all, he'd grown up here; and in spite of the fact he'd been gone only seven years, with many visits in the meantime, his childhood seemed very distant. The seven years had been long enough for him to get his doctorate in psychology—though he rarely used the title outside the university—and to secure the position of assistant professor at UNC, a position he'd only held for a year. His college years had been full ones; while he'd been studious and hard-working, he'd also been heavily involved in the activist movements on the campus, and he still was. He was quite familiar with the effects of a number of hallucinogenic drugs—though he didn't use them all that often—and he had a small scar on the back of his head, a reminder left by the club of a Chicago policeman only a year ago, during the Democratic convention. That was a bitter memory; all his work for the McCarthy campaign down the drain. When the election had come around, he'd voted for Eldridge Cleaver, and, along with many others, was even further embittered by Nixon's victory. And nothing had changed. The Vietnam war dragged on, people in stores and shops still not uncommonly made fun of his dark, shoulder-length hair, his beard. Sometimes he considered going to Haight-Ashbury, just forgetting about it. But the rapidly increasing sentiment against the war—at least on campus—kept him going, kept his spirits up. Plus, it had to be admitted, the fact that by now he was one of the veterans of the movement, and that had its advantages. Especially with a certain undergraduate woman.

These thoughts made him turn his eyes back to the picture, stare at it for a while again.

Had she gone to college? he wondered. What had been her major, her sign? How did she feel about the war? Probably, he told himself, she would support it, like most people her age did. She couldn't be blamed, he supposed. Just a function of the way she had grown up.

He sighed again—something he was doing frequently today, he realized—and turned back to the trunk. Soon, the real estate agent would be here, and he would have to deal with that; but for a couple more hours, he could pore through his father's things, pick out some more memories, file them away. The first object that came into his randomly grasping fingers was a Purple Heart, won by his father in France in World War II. That brought back memories of the violent arguments about the war in Vietnam, and those he preferred not to keep. He glanced at the medal, put it in the pile of things he would leave for the auction. Again, the hours drifted by, and though the trunk was gradually becoming empty, little else of interest was emerging.

Down near the bottom, his hands found a sheaf of letters, bound together with red rubber bands, which crumbled as he tried to take them off. He glanced at the envelopes; letters from his grandparents, his uncle, from his mother—Paula Graves before she'd married his father—and from a variety of other people. At random, he pulled the paper from inside one. Utterly uninteresting; it referred primarily to trivial events around 1941, and whatever minor fascination they might have held then had been lost by the passage of twenty-eight years.

He was about to throw the whole sheaf on his "discard" pile when one caught his attention. Not really believing he'd seen what he thought he had, he extracted the envelope. And stared at it. It was; it was different from the rest. His father's name and address was nestled in the upper left, and the envelope was sealed, the stamp uncanceled. A letter never sent. But the addressee took his breath away. It was

Miss Nikki Townsend
491 Cabrini Blvd, Apt. 9C
New York, N.Y.

Obvious what it was, he told himself; a letter never sent. But was it the same Nikki as in the picture?

His fingers trembled as he started to tear open the envelope, and he realized he might not like this. The girl in the picture was a complete fantasy, a fantasy which could not be violated so long as he knew nothing whatsoever about her. But this letter might change that.

Nevertheless, he had to see what was inside. Had to.

But just as he started a tear in the paper, he was interrupted by a knock at the door. Annoyed, he put it aside, and went to answer the door, nearly stumbling over the cuffs of his bell-bottom trousers as he went. As he'd expected, it was the real estate people, and the rest of his day was taken up by showing them the house and signing endless documents, most of which he didn't bother to read at all. Even before they had left, a representative of the auction house came by, full of condolences for his loss, hands stretched out for money. The business of caring for the remains of the dead in a pecuniary world dragged on and on.

And he never did get back to the letter, not that day, not that visit.

It, along with the precious photo, was packed into his suitcase as he made the long trip back to Chapel Hill. In fact, once it had been packed away out of sight, he really didn't think about it too much more, at least not during the remainder of his stay at the house. Those hours he devoted to memories of his parents, his father especially, concentrating on the good times as much as possible. It was true that they'd disagreed about many things, but from time to time they'd been very close. And in spite of this closeness, there were many things Elliot had never understood—would never understand, now, he told himself—about his father. Much of the time, Aaron Collins had seemed restless or distant in some odd way, as if he were only partially there; yet no one could have accused him of being emotionally cold. It was, Elliot had thought, as if a section of the man existed elsewhere, was not living a mundane life in small-town Illinois. There'd been a time—when he was about fifteen—when he had asked his father rather directly about that, about his moodiness and his penchant for staring into space for long periods. On that occasion, he'd wondered if it was in any way related to Aaron's ability—noted by many of his acquaintances, and often thought somewhat uncanny—to anticipate events, to keep himself and his family out of the way of anything unpleasant. But he'd gotten no straight answers, and gotten a decidedly negative response to his suggestions that any "psychic" abilities the man had might well be used to better their financial position. Aaron had delivered a lecture instead, about the responsibilities and troubles that came with large fortunes, and pointed out that they had always been comfortable in that respect.

At the time, Elliot hadn't taken that very well, but later had himself scoffed at the notion of his father's abilities, having come to a purely intellectual opinion—one he still held—that psychic phenomena were virtually all explainable in terms of error or fraud. In his father's case, neither needed to be invoked, for the man had claimed no special abilities of any sort. And yet, a little over five years previously, he'd made a near-hysterical demand on Elliot to make a visit home. When he'd arrived, he'd found his father in a depressed state, his mother a bit bewildered; and Aaron had taken him aside, lectured him on the fragility and uncertainty of life, how it was so very important to say the things that, once a person was gone, you would wish you had said. Perhaps somewhat shaken by Aaron's unusual behavior, Elliot had showered affection on both of them, and later he was grateful; his mother's sudden death had occurred less than a week after he'd left. Then, too, there had been a surprise phone call from Aaron just two days before his own death, a call in which he and Elliot had made peace concerning many of the issues that had divided them in the past. And now he too was gone.

As far as Elliot was concerned, he was leaving Illinois behind forever; there was truly nothing left for him there. That made him a little sad; but he knew his life was in Chapel Hill now, and he was eager to get back to it.

2

Just after sunset, Elliot's red VW puttered along Franklin Street, up the gradient that led into Chapel Hill proper. Looking at it, it never looked like much of a hill; but the VW's undersized engine always wanted to argue about it— nothing like the way it hated the hills around Fancy Gap, Virginia, on the way back, but it complained, nevertheless. And Elliot was tired. Two days driving in the cramped front seat had left him in no mood to be tolerant of the car's quirks.

A right turn off Franklin, another left a little ways down, and a short drive among Chapel Hill's convoluted residential streets put him in front of a duplex, the right side of which he called home. The curtains were open, and he could see movement inside; as he'd hoped, Melissa was waiting for him. He saw her peek out, then come out the front door. She looked good, he told himself. A welcome sight. Long, slim legs under a tiny miniskirt. Long, silky blonde hair trailing down her back. Long torso, long nose. Everything about Melissa Wallace was long. A long cool woman in a blue dress, to paraphrase the Hollies' song.

He started to tell himself that she didn't compare very well to Nikki, but mentally bit his lip. Unfair, he said firmly, silently. Nikki was a fantasy, Melissa was real. Moreover, Melissa was twenty-two years old. It might be crass, but it made a big difference.

"Hi, El," she said, giving him a warm hug even before he'd thoroughly disengaged himself from the confines of the VW. "You're a little earlier than I expected. But that's cool."

"Good to be home, I'll tell you," he commented, fiddling with the always recalcitrant handle of the trunk. It resisted just long enough to irritate him, then popped open with a bang, just missing his head. More than once it had clipped him.

"So, did you get everything done?" she asked, helping him pull his suitcases from the trunk and backseat of the car.

"Yeah. There'll be an auction soon for the house and car and stuff. I didn't feel like I needed to be there for that. Sorta freaky, watching somebody sell your folks' things."

She hugged him again. "Anyway, I missed you," she said, running her fingers up into his long hair. "Besides, I need you to help me cram for that exam in biochem," she noted practically.

He looked at the back of her head as she picked up two of the lighter cases and carried them inside. Certainly she was a practical girl, he reflected. He wondered, not for the first time, if she had hooked up with him because she was attracted to him or because he could help her in her courses. Not being sure left him in the position of not knowing if she'd be around after she graduated next June. Idly, he thought about sabotaging that graduation; he easily could, by distracting her from schoolwork rather than helping her. Melissa, though very bright, was not exactly the world's best student. And he knew one of her soft spots. Liberally provided with Thai sticks or some good Colombian and a few records by the Doors or the Jefferson Airplane, she'd forget about college altogether. He grunted, picked up the heavier suitcases and went inside, dismissing his incipient plot as unworthy. It was just that he hated to see a lover leave; you never knew when you'd find another one. At least, one that was acceptable.

They put the suitcases down pretty much at random in the midst of the chaotic clutter that filled his living space, and he flopped onto the couch, avoiding the broken area in the middle. Melissa went back and closed the door, smiled at him.

"Got some wine," she told him. "Celebrate your getting back, okay?"

"Far-out."

Sitting two glasses on the industrial wire spool that served as his coffee table, she poured two full glasses of a cheap California sauterne, handed him one. Moodily he sipped it, staring at the red and black image of the Che Guevara on his wall, but not really seeing it.

"Elliot?" she asked him, touching his arm. "Are you all right, hon'?"

He looked around at her. Her green eyes were fixed on his, and they were just a little glassy, a little watery. She'd been hitting the stash already, he knew. She'd be really beautiful if her nose wasn't so Goddamn long, he thought for the thousandth time. And if her eyes were larger. And her mouth less tight. And if she had a little more chin. Mentally separating the parts of her face like that, she momentarily looked awful to him; it seemed as if she had the face of a mule. He blinked, reassembled her, realized again that while she would never be a beauty queen, she was really quite attractive. It was just that by comparison with—

Really annoyed with himself now, he angrily cut off the thought before it had fully formed. "Oh, I'm cool," he told her, not really meaning it, but not wanting to share anything deep with her. "It's just that, well, you don't go bury your dad every day."

She looked solicitous. "I should have gone with you, biochem or no," she said, wringing her hands. It was a habit he despised.

"No, it's okay. I needed to be by myself. Just bad vibes, being in that house again, knowing the folks were gone." He took a healthy gulp of the wine, kicked off his Hush Puppies. One of them rolled onto its side on the floor, and he stared at it. Uniform, he thought. Badge of office. If you were a prof, you wore Hush Puppies. Unless you were uptight, of course. Jesus, they all acted like such sheep, so much of the time.

Melissa went over and turned on the stereo, volume down low; Donovan's voice filled the room, telling them about Sunny Goodge Street, about the magician who sparkled in satin and velvet. Sitting down across from him, she stretched out her long, slim legs, bounced the left one in time with the mellow jazz flute break in the song. Couldn't complain about those legs, he told himself, staring at them unabashedly. Beautifully shaped, beautifully tanned. Almost as good as—

"God damn it!" he snapped aloud, then bit his lip.

Melissa jumped. "What is it?" she asked him, leaning forward.

"Oh, nothing. At least nothing important. Just some old memories, that's all. Can't get them out of my head."

"You want a J?" she queried, her face a little too eager.

Though he smoked too, what he felt was her excessive use of the weed was a constant dissonance between them.

"Dope is about the last thing I need right now," he growled, finishing off the wine. "I just need to relax, unwind. That's all."

She refilled his glass. "You eat any dinner on the road?"

"No, I thought I'd wait."

"Good," she said, flowing easily into the housewifely persona. "I didn't think you would. I got a casserole in the oven."

"Casserole?" he asked, dreading the response.

"Yeah, it's far-out. A recipe Linda gave me. Bean sprouts, soy beans, and brie. I haven't tasted it yet, but I'm sure it's gonna be great!"

Inwardly he groaned. Lord God, why can't the woman cook a simple steak? More, why the hell couldn't Linda mind her own Goddamn business?

Around two A.M., Elliot woke up with a start. At first, he had the distinct feeling that something was terribly wrong, that something or someone required his immediate attention. Perhaps part of a dream, he told himself groggily.

He glanced over at Melissa, sleeping peacefully beside him. As always, she slept with her mouth wide open, the covers thrown off and her nude body sprawled over fully three-quarters of the bed. He remembered their earlier love-making and smiled; she was a first-class lover, no doubt about that. And her body, especially now, seen in the subdued light that filtered in from the bathroom—she always insisted that a light be kept burning somewhere—looked very good indeed, in spite of her somewhat awkward sleeping posture. Except that her breasts were a little overlarge and slid off her chest to the sides a bit. And the boniness of her hips. And the sharpness of her elbows. Not at all like—

I have to quit doing this, he thought. Not only is it unfair to Melissa, but I'm going to go absolutely crazy here!

He remembered the photo and the still-unopened letter, both tucked into his large suitcase, sitting in the front room. Fighting down a strong impulse to go get them, he tried to force himself to go back to sleep. But for a long while he didn't; he kept opening his eyes and looking at the clock, seeing that impossibly long ten-minute intervals had passed.

After a while, though, he did drift off. Several times, in

fact. Repeatedly he was jolted out of a transition state between waking and sleep by some bizarre or disturbing image; the only one of these he could remember was that of a monstrous snake lunging out of a suitcase far too small to hold it. This image still vivid in his mind, he looked at the clock again: three A.M. Having decided to give it up, he gingerly crawled out of bed, being careful not to wake Melissa. After pulling on a bathrobe—an old habit, hard to break—he wandered out into the front room and sat on the couch. Leaning his head back, his gaze fell on the suitcase.

More than once he started to open it but didn't allow himself to do so. His eyes wandered up, to the red and black poster of Che Guevara. He imagined being in the forests of Cuba or Bolivia with Che; it was all very romantic, but the hard fact was, he wasn't a Marxist. Still, this was an enjoyable fantasy. He allowed it to proceed, visualizing a tropical forest around Che's image. After a while, he allowed his eyes to wander away from the poster and decided that he'd dozed off while gazing at it. Since the room didn't seem to be there anymore.

He found himself in a dark jungle place, steaming with humidity, foliage so thick he could see neither the ground nor anything else more than a couple of feet away from his eyes. Vietnam, he told himself lucidly. Wouldn't be the first time he'd dreamed of it. He had some guilt about using his student deferment to stay out of the draft, though after he'd graduated he was promptly declared 4-F because his blood pressure had been high at his draft physical—which had itself been peculiar, since it had not been before or since. Still, a kind of survivors' guilt bothered him periodically; he was safe at UNC, while his friends went to war or fled to Canada. This, he told himself, was a guilt dream of that sort. Then he realized that too was peculiar; he never knew he was dreaming inside the dream. This time he did, but he couldn't wake himself; he just had to go with it.

Carefully he pushed his way through the dense forest, expecting to see the Viet Cong or a division of NVA regulars at any moment. Or perhaps he himself would be cast as Vietnamese, and be attacked by U.S. soldiers. After all, he was wearing a bathrobe; weren't the Cong usually described as wearing pajamas? Close enough, especially in a dream.

But when he finally broke into a clearing, he saw something completely different. A snake, huge, coiled on the ground in front of him. Python? he asked himself; but the creature raised its rattled tail and lashed it from side to side a few times, making a harsh clicking sound, and identifying itself unequivocably. Yet it looked like no rattlesnake he'd ever seen. It was a golden brown, diamonds outlined in black down its back, two long dark stripes on its neck behind the flat, triangular head. And impossibly big; its slightly ridged back stood some three feet off the ground, and the head was as large as Elliot's torso. He tried to back away, but the forest resisted him, branches snagging into his bathrobe. Still, he didn't seem to be too afraid. The snake wasn't moving toward him, wasn't attacking.

It was moving, though, piling itself into a heap with its head atop a number of symmetrical coils. The sides of the piles of coils made even angles up to a flat top formed by the head. A familiar image, but he couldn't place exactly where he'd seen it before. He was still trying when Nikki stepped out of the forest beyond the snake.

Looking even more alluring than she did in the photo, she smiled at him as she walked toward the coiled reptile. No longer clad in the '40s swimsuit, she was wearing a scarlet robe, simply cut, that fell to her ankles. She pushed it aside, exposing one leg almost to the hip, and sat down on the lowest coil of the snake, leaned back against it. Its black tongue flicked around her hair, and she caressed the line of its jaw with her hand, looking at Elliot the whole time.

"At last, Elliot Collins," she said.

He looked confused. "I don't—" he started to say.

She laughed at him, a wonderfully musical sound. "Oh, of course—you think this is a dream. But I tell you, Elliot Collins—it is not. I have been waiting for the right time to bring you here—and it is now that time!"

"Weird dream," he said in a firm voice, and she laughed again. "But I gotta get out of it. Gotta quit this. I'm a psychologist, I know an obsession when I see one—"

"Well now," she said, leaning back against the snake in a most seductive manner, "I suppose you could rationalize this as just an ordinary dream. You go ahead; far be it from me. But, if you don't—then come to me. That is your *tonalli;* that is what you were born to, my lord. You come to me, let me show you your destiny!"

"Oh, man," he said, not looking at her. "This one beats all. Can't believe I'd do this to myself. Probably just the strain and all, Dad's death, so sudden. It's understandable."

She laughed again, jumped up off the snake and ran to him, her hand outstretched. Mechanically, he held his own hand out, but he wasn't thinking about what he was doing. He was too busy looking at her beautiful body; her robe was not tied in the front, and it swept open as she ran. She wore nothing under it, and he watched her come to him, felt the touch of her fingertips on his outstretched palm; her touch was like electricity, almost painful.

"You'll see, Elliot!" she cried. "I don't think you can deny me. Remember when you were five? Before you ever saw the photo? Think about it, Elliot!"

With that, she turned and ran gracefully back into the forest, her scarlet robe flaring behind her like a cape as she went. Slowly, ponderously, the big snake uncoiled itself and followed her. He watched until the rattle vanished among the leaves, then discovered that he was again looking at the Che Guevara poster on the wall of his own apartment, barely visible in the near-darkness.

There'd been absolutely no sense of waking up, no transition at all. Somewhat shaken, he sat straight up, looked around. A dream, he told himself firmly. Really a very strange one, but just a dream.

He let out a long deep breath and returned to his bedroom, sliding silently in alongside Melissa. She smiled in her sleep as he put his arm around her, and the rest of the night was relatively peaceful for him. One thing bothered him: that word, "*tonalli*." He could not remember ever having heard it before. If it was not a real word, then it must symbolize something personal to him, he told himself; but that was something he could go into the next day.

3

Chapel Hill in August is a relatively quiet little town; the permanent population is not very large, though it burgeons whenever the regular school session begins in September. But now, as Elliot crossed Franklin Street on his way to his office, it could almost be taken for a sleepy New England village. Most of the businesses in town were located in the few blocks along Franklin, which clings to the north side of the larger UNC campus; a variety of restaurants, two small theaters, some import shops, and a little post office, this last being a common scene of demonstrations by the students. The tallest structures in the immediate vicinity were the churches, the majority of the other buildings being two stories or less; trees dominated Chapel Hill's skyline, and the majority of the permanent residents liked it that way. A perennial controversy existed between those who wanted to maintain this village image and developers who wanted to convert it to a thriving— and profitable—city.

Elliot, however, was not paying very much attention. His mind was elsewhere; try as he would, he could not entirely exorcise last night's dream images. In fact, he was surprised when he looked around and realized he was already on campus, crossing through the Arboretum. He could not remember passing by the post office, could not remember crossing the street.

He slowed down his rapid walk, nodded to a couple of gaily bedecked students who often lounged in this parklike area, tried to get himself back to something resembling a normal frame of mind. He was acutely aware that he couldn't keep this up, but he rationalized away his mounting anxiety by telling himself that it had only been a couple of days. And he'd been under considerable stress.

16

Perhaps he should have his blood pressure checked, he told himself, particularly because of his father's death. But it had never given him a problem.

He suppressed a grin, remembering the draft physical. He had not been exactly eager to pass it with flying colors but had thought he was doomed to 1-A during the hearing test, when he had feigned almost total deafness and passed anyhow. He'd told them he had a family history of hypertension, and, exaggerating, that he himself had had some problems with it. When they'd taken his blood pressure, he had worked himself into such a state that they actually considered sending him directly to a hospital. But that had ended any problems for him personally in terms of the draft, though he remained a vociferous opponent of Selective Service. Once again he was aware of the guilt he felt; but mostly he was able to rationalize it away. He could do more in his current position than he could have in jail or as an expatriate in Canada, choices he would have made rather than allowing himself to be sent to Vietnam. His opposition to the war, he often told people proudly, went far back, back to a time when such opposition was not popular. These were average, commonplace thoughts for him, and right now he was actively encouraging them. Gradually, he became a little more relaxed, went on to his office, tried to plan his day.

First things first, he told himself firmly. He had one class, a summer session Psych 1, and they were expecting the results of an exam. Due to the unexpected trip to Illinois, he hadn't quite finished grading the papers; he threw himself into that with an almost ferocious intensity and after a while began to feel even more normal. Everyday life: test papers, trivial research, departmental politics. Sometimes it irritated him, but right now it was what he wanted. Stability. And this type of exam could be graded without requiring too much of his thought and effort. Fifty multiple choice—multiple guess, students usually called them—questions, answers A through D on a master sheet he'd made up along with the questions. Mostly easy, this quiz was really only designed to encourage the students to keep up.

At two that afternoon, he waited in the classroom with a stack of papers as the twenty or so students taking the course filed in, took their seats. After they'd settled down, he passed out the exams, watched the faces, the disappointment on some, the glee on others.

There was one girl whose face he watched rather closely. Pretty, with close-cropped black hair and dark eyes, she reminded him of Nikki, though there was no similarity whatsoever in their facial features. She was holding her paper up and studying it, as if she was displeased by it. Several times, he saw her eyes flick up to his face. He wondered what the problem was but felt that to ask was not proper classroom protocol. If she had a question, she should ask him.

He kept his head down, but his eyes were up, glued to the girl as she shifted uncomfortably at her desk, swinging her legs—almost completely exposed by her tiny miniskirt—out into the aisle. It seemed to him like a long time, sitting there waiting for the students to ask questions; and he found himself fantasizing about the girl he was watching. He knew who she was, of course; her name was Eileen Cates, she was a freshman anthropology major. But he didn't know her personally and felt he might like to.

She stretched her left leg straight out, tightening the muscles and creating a vertical crease down the center of her thigh. Elliot could not take his eyes off the display. He found it intensely attractive, and somewhat lost track of his surroundings.

Somewhere, somebody was saying something. "Professor Collins!" the voice came again, louder and more insistent.

"What?" he said, jerking his head up and looking around. The students tittered, and he felt a surge of embarrassment. The fact was, he didn't even know who had spoken to him.

"Over here, Professor," said the voice. He turned his head, saw that the speaker was one of his male students. The boy's name was—damn, he thought. Don't remember. He'd have to wing it.

"Yes?" he asked.

"I have a question about number nine," the boy said. "On the test. You know, the one you just gave back to us?" Again, a rustle of laughter through the classroom.

He ignored it, glanced at the master sheet. "Yes, the question about aggression. What about it?"

"You've got circled here, 'C'—frustration. Right?"

"Right."

"You really believe frustration of desires is the only cause of violence?"

Hardy, that was the kid's name. Thankful that he'd remembered it, he addressed the question: "Well, I think you're pushing it a little far there—to say that only frustration is the cause of all violence. But I'd certainly say frustration causes some."

"What are some others?"

He stopped and thought for a minute. "Well, the first example that comes to mind is violence in ideological wars."

"Aren't most wars economic at the bottom?"

"Probably—at least I'd agree, but that's really a question for the sociologists. But there are probably some fought on purely ideological grounds. Religion or political differences."

"Well, is that all? Is that the only other one?"

He sighed; the student was trying to lead him, and it could go on for a long time. "Mr. Hardy, what answer did you put down?"

"Uh—'A'."

He grinned. "Libido?" he asked.

Now Hardy turned a little red. "Well, I'm sure there are some examples—"

"Were you thinking of your own approach to the opposite sex, Mr. Hardy? That isn't normally what we mean when we say aggression!" The kid was squirming, and the class was laughing with Elliot now, not at him. "Sorry, Mr. Hardy. No half credit."

Hardy sank back into his seat, looking sullen. Elliot could not restrain a little pride; he considered himself a master at verbal dueling. It was seldom he came out second best, seldom that he could not talk his way out of a bad situation. Forcing himself to keep his eyes off Eileen Cates's legs, he dismissed further questions and returned to his class schedule. But Eileen had set him off, and thoughts of Nikki kept intruding on his mind, becoming more and more insistent.

After his class had finally ended—and it seemed to him that it took forever—Elliot started across the campus toward his apartment. It was true that he had more work waiting to be done in his office, true that his day was not over. Those ideas never even crossed his mind. He was utterly focused on the apartment, the suitcase, the letter still inside. No more delays; he had to read it, had to read it now.

Back on Franklin Street, he walked alongside the stone wall that flanked its east side; as usual on a nice day, dozens of the people the media would have referred to as "hippies" had congregated here. Elliot gave them only passing glances, being surprised as usual at how young many of them were. Normally he didn't feel old, but afternoon walks out here could sometimes change that. Even distracted as he was today, he turned his head to stare at a girl in a vaguely Indian outfit; she could not possibly have been more than twelve or so.

"Brother!" a voice screeched right in front of him. "I have to talk to you!"

Startled, he looked up. A very raggedly dressed young man had jumped from the wall to stand right in front of him, waving his arms almost frantically. Behind him stood a similarly dressed girl, a vacant expression on her face, chewing gum. Elliot didn't want to be bothered right now; he started to go around the couple, but the boy blocked his way.

"Brother!" he yelled again, right in Elliot's face. "The Lord God Jeeesus has commanded me to talk to you! You have to listen to me, it's your immortal soul that's at stake! The Lord God Jesus—the Superstar—has given *me* the word! *Me*! And I have to save you sinners from yourselves, I have to—"

Elliot sighed and gazed at the boy's face. Tolerance in all things, he told himself patiently. After all, he hated it when people shrugged him off when he tried to talk about racism, or the war, or the military-industrial complex. He could spare a few seconds, even though . . . he . . . was . . .

Something seemed to snap in his head, and he looked directly into the boy's eyes. "Get out of my way," he said, in a low, menacing tone. "Get out of my way or I'll kill you." This last was delivered in a flat, emotionless voice. A serious voice.

The boy stopped waving his arms and stared; the girl behind him was wide-eyed, her mouth hanging open. Elliot could see the wad of chewing gum stuck on her teeth. For just a second, no one moved or said anything. Then, like crabs scurrying to one side, the two cleared the sidewalk. Elliot glanced at them as they vaulted over the wall, picked up the stack of religious literature that was lying there. He was aware that other people in the street had stopped what they were doing and were staring at him, but he didn't care. Not looking back, he continued on down the street, crossing to the other side and disappearing into a little alley where a number of women always had tables set up, selling flowers. On any normal day, he would pause here, admire the colors and aromas, perhaps buy something for Melissa. Today, he didn't even glance at them.

He had only one thing on his mind.

About fifteen minutes later, he reached his apartment, went inside. Melissa wasn't there, but, then, he hadn't expected her; it was likely that she was over at the "pit," a sunken area in front of the Student Center, which was a common meeting place for the counterculture types on campus.

Slipping the screen door latch into place so that she could not walk in on him unannounced, he sat down on the couch and opened the suitcase. He was not surprised that his hands trembled as he held the photo and the letter in them once more. After gazing at the old picture for several minutes, he carefully put it down on the table and opened the envelope. No great surprise; a letter from his father to someone named Nikki, almost certainly the woman in the picture. His doubts about the wisdom of doing so gone, he read the letter:

My dearest Nikki,

I just wanted to let you know that I am going to marry Paula. Then, at least for twenty years or so, I'm going to try to live a normal life. If that's possible anymore, knowing what I know, knowing what I've done, what you've made me a party to. I know what you'd say if I was saying this to you in person: nobody twisted your arm. But you know that isn't true, Nikki. It's funny, isn't it? That I should be so concerned over a person who doesn't even exist. To have these regrets even before anything has happened. And yet, even now I don't think I could refuse you anything you might ask me for. I just cannot stand thinking about what you are, and I cannot stop thinking about you. Quite a problem. I guess it's just that I love you so damn much. If you'd have me, you know I'd come back. Ten years from now, I'd come back. You know I'll never forget you; for me, you'll always be the girl on the beach. I'm not sure I can ever go to the beach again.

All my love,
Aaron

At the bottom, it was dated Sept. 16, 1942. Elliot read it through at least four times before he put it aside. There could be no question that it deepened the mystery of Nikki, though it seemed to confirm that she was indeed the girl in the picture. But he was already sure of that anyway. It did give considerable insight into his father and why he had been as he was throughout his life. Nikki, not his mother, had been his True Love, apparently; and as far as Elliot knew, he'd never seen her again. This letter had an air of finality about it, and it, of course, had never even been sent. Elliot found himself speculating on the nature of their relationship, on the meaning of the cryptic "what I've done" and "what you are."

Useless, he thought. He'd never know; his father was dead, and Nikki had probably married someone else and had grandchildren. If indeed she was alive. Probably was; she wouldn't be all that old.

For a minute, he put his hands over his face and rocked back and forth on the tattered couch; he had to quit obsessing over the girl, she was not real! But when he uncovered his eyes, she was again looking at him from out of the old picture, from out of time. Emotionally, he just couldn't admit that she might now look old. An utterly irrational part of himself demanded that she be eternal, that she exist exactly like that right now, somehow. He wondered if perhaps he should seek some professional help; this was really getting out of hand. After all, he told himself, he was one of the few psychologists or psychiatrists he knew who was not in therapy. Seemed to go with the territory.

The screen door banged against its hook, and he heard Melissa call out to him; quickly he put the photo and letter back in the worn velvet folder and put them in his desk. Only then did he unlatch the door and let her in.

"Why'd you latch the door, El?" she asked him.

"I dunno. Didn't realize I did."

She let it go, though he saw her glance around the apartment surreptitiously. Probably she thought he had another woman here. "There's a party at Linda's tonight," she told him in a conspiratorial tone, her voice lowered as if the police were listening outside the window. "She says she got some fine Colombian. Can we go, El?"

He started to say no, but shrugged, told her it was okay

with him. Perhaps, he thought, it would take his mind off things. He needed to be distracted.

"Want me to start some dinner?" Melissa asked then.

"Oh, no," he said, almost too quickly; she looked a little hurt. "You relax, read your biochem. I'll do it tonight."

She seemed to accept this as altruism on his part and bounced off to her studies. Elliot started rummaging through the refrigerator and soon was thinking about nothing except the magnificence of his Western omelets. With plenty of ham, of course.

Elliot and Melissa arrived at the party a little after eight that Friday evening; she was in high spirits, he drifted through the door almost like he was sleepwalking.

It just wasn't going well, he told himself. Constantly, all the way over here, his mind drifted back to the photo, back to the enigmatic letter. He almost turned the wrong way down a one-way street.

He was, after all, a psychologist; he knew an obsession when one was staring him in the face. This couldn't be very healthy in the long run. After all, what could events in the 1940s possibly have to do with his life now? The answer, of course, was nothing at all.

Trying to take control of his thoughts, he demanded of himself that he stop thinking about Nikki and the letter, start thinking about the party, about trying to have a good time. He was still trying to convince himself when they went inside Linda's house.

Low lights—mostly black light—wall-to-wall people, and an already-pervasive scent of cannabis greeted him. Almost immediately he became somewhat paranoid; sooner or later, he thought, one of these parties was going to get busted. If he got caught up in it, the department would not be amused; and he didn't have tenure. But in the end, he just shrugged, hoped this wouldn't be the night.

A girl with long, red hair disengaged herself from the crowd and approached them, greeting Elliot first.

"Hi, Linda," he said without enthusiasm. Hands in his pockets, he watched Melissa for a moment as she engaged Linda in a lively discussion about the godawful vegetarian recipes. The kinds of potential problems he was thinking about never occurred to either of them, or never bothered them if they did.

"Why the long face, Elliot?" Linda asked him, trying to draw him into the conversation.

"He just got back from his father's funeral," Melissa said, answering for him. "It was a real downer for him."

"Oh, sorry, Elliot," the red-haired girl said. "I didn't know."

"It's cool," he told her mechanically. He wasn't really listening; he was examining her freckled legs, the curve of her hips inside her shorts, the pale skin visible alongside the halter top she wore. He'd always thought Linda was a sexy girl, but she didn't compare well to—Goddamn it!

Linda became aware of his blatant staring and grinned at him. It was just a hair away from being seductive, and it earned her a glare from Melissa. None too subtly, the blonde steered Elliot away from her, into another room where the sounds of the Jefferson Airplane filled the air. Here, a cardboard tube with a rolled joint sticking through a hole at one end—a "bazooka"—was being passed around. Melissa took it, put her hand over the end nearest the joint, the other end to her mouth. Inhaling deeply, she filled the tube with smoke, then removed her hand, evacuating it. Choking back a cough, but smiling, she passed it to Elliot, and he repeated her action.

"So, Elliot, what's new with you?" came a voice from behind him, accompanied by a rather heavy hand on his shoulder.

He turned, looked at the man. Jim Cardwell, anthropology graduate student, a man who owned the reputation for having done more drugs than the rest of Chapel Hill put together. He weaved a bit, running his hand over his prematurely bald head, almost knocking off the Ben Franklin glasses. Normally, Elliot did not like to talk to Jim too much. He did not seem capable of discussing anything other than the latest drug he'd taken, and he insisted on trying to describe his experiences; always they were "out of sight." But right now, there was no avoiding it.

"Not much," he said, having no desire to discuss anything even remotely personal with this man. "You?"

"Oh, man, I just been studyin' the Book, you dig? Man, it's far fuckin' out, isn't it?"

Elliot heard the capital letter, but he didn't know what Jim was referring to. "The Book?" he asked.

"Yeah, man, Don Juan."

"Don Juan?" he repeated, thinking of the Spanish Casanova.

"You know. Casteneda?"

"Who?"

"You mean you haven't read the Book yet, man?"

"I don't even know what you're talking about."

"Oh, man. Oh, shit. Far fuckin' out. I thought everybody had read it by now!"

"Well, I haven't. Why the interest in a book about—"

"It isn't about Don Juan chasin' girls, man. Don Juan is an Indian brujo, a sorcerer. Casteneda—he wrote it—is this grad student from UCLA that went down to Mexico and studied with him. Took peyote with him, man. It's far-out."

"Well, I've done peyote too, and it was—"

"Hey, man, not like this. Don Juan, he's a guide, see? Guides the trips. He's really cool. You gotta read it, man. It's far fuckin'—"

"All right, all right, I'll read it," he said irritably, cutting the other man off. Jim looked hurt momentarily, and Elliot regretted taking out his frustrations on him. Damnation, people had such fragile egos these days! "What'd you say the title was?"

"The Teachings of Don Juan: A Yaqui Way of Knowledge."

"Yaqui?"

"Yeah, man. They're desert Indians from Northern Mexico. Shit, they were still fightin' wars with the *federales* this century! Man, the Indians are where it's at, man. They're far fuckin' out. Close to nature and all. We gotta lot we can learn from them. Had great cultures until the white men fucked them over, man. Never fought wars, never hurt each other, lived in harmony with nature, man."

"Seems to me I've heard some tales about Indians fighting wars the whites had nothing to do with," Elliot said, peering intensely at Jim. He'd taken two more tokes from the bazooka as it came around, and it was getting to him; Jim's nose looked peculiar, and the glints of light in his glasses were downright fascinating. "And a few stories about human sacrifices?"

Jim looked as though he'd been hit. He was forever promoting the Indians as archetypical hippies, and he didn't like facts that spoke otherwise. This, Elliot was well aware, was a source of difficulty for him in graduate school, since he was given to construct theories out of virtually nothing. "Well, I guess some of them—but, man, the Hopis and Zunis are as near a perfect people as you'll ever see! Hell, they never hurt anything!" Jim leaned forward as if he was going to start a long discourse, but to his credit, he saw that Elliot was not really listening. Reluctantly, he wound down. "But you gotta read Casteneda, man," he repeated. "Magic and drugs and shit. It's really far-out."

"Yeah," Elliot told him, "I'll pick it up." He had to admit that it did sound interesting. Graduate students were doing some odd things these days, but hauling off to the desert to take drugs with some old Indian, that was unusual. Much like Timothy Leary going out and discovering the much-touted magic mushrooms. Or actually rediscovering; the Indians had never forgotten about them, still used them.

The effects of the marijuana he'd smoked began to come on stronger; Elliot had the sensation of "rushing," which he well knew could be a prelude to passing out. To avoid it, he laid back on a pile of cushions, a few of the many Linda had scattered around the almost unfurnished room. Jim stared down at him for a moment, realized he'd lost his audience, and wandered off somewhere.

Elliot glanced over at Melissa; she was sitting on one of the cushions with her eyes closed, her body rocking back and forth as Grace Slick sang of multiple lovers. He smiled; the gestalt of the times, he told himself, and he really liked it. A kind of sensory overload, the loud music in the oddly lit room, the aromas of patchouli and burning hemp. Watching Melissa, he wished momentarily that she would take off her clothes; yet he knew that even in her drugged state, she would be aghast at the idea. The media painted a picture of the counterculture, the "hippies," as free-spirited, free-loving. Perhaps they were, in Southern California; he didn't know. In Chapel Hill, for the most part they weren't. In spite of what they might say, they had basically the same hang-ups, the same inhibitions as anyone else of their generation. Regrettable, he told himself. We move so far and get nowhere.

Looking away from Melissa, he focused his eyes on a crack in the plaster of the wall across from him. At the moment, it was quite fascinating, the way it curved and twisted on its path from ceiling to floor. He studied it, tracking it with his eyes, for quite a long time. Most interesting. At a point about eighteen inches off the floor, the crack intersected with another, this one running horizontally. His eyes narrowed as he looked at it; the wall had settled here in such a way that the lower part protruded a little, forming a tiny ledge under the crack. Now he followed it along with his eyes, left to right, seeing it as a roadbed along the face of some huge cliffside in the Alps or Himalayas. As the drug effect became stronger, the fantasy became more intense. He mentally converted his imaginary trail to a railroad bed, visualized a tiny train chugging along there.

"Choo choo," he said very softly, and giggled to himself.

He had an impulse to share the fantasy with Melissa but was still rational enough not to. Dope fantasies are very personal; they don't transfer from one person to another easily. So he kept it to himself, sat cross-legged on the floor and enjoyed it.

His imaginary train went behind a chair, and he waited patiently for it to come out the other side. And sure enough, it did. Grinning like a five-year-old, he kept his eyes fixed on the slow-moving train. It went behind a male chest in a blue shirt, then behind a female chest in a plaid blouse. Then another female chest—a very nice one, he told himself as an aside—in a green workshirt, the ends pulled up and tied to expose the stomach. Now male again, a red shirt this time— all the colors were so incredible! he told himself—and in behind a silky-looking bright red sleeve. His gaze tracked across the almost painfully intense red, encountered two spectacular bare breasts. And there it stopped.

Knowing his eyes were wide enough to show white all around the irises, he let them rise, passing a slender neck, finally coming to rest on a face. Black hair, almost black eyes. Nikki.

The game with the train forgotten, he looked around the room rather wildly. No one else was paying the slightest bit of attention to her, and even in his current state, he knew that wasn't right. There was no way in the world a woman who looked like that could sit in this room bare-breasted and not be the total center of attention. At least from the males. She smiled, hooked a finger at him. Again he looked around; nobody seemed to see her.

Hallucination, he told himself. Evidently the grass had been spiked with something. You just didn't get hallucinations like this from pot alone.

Across the room, Nikki appeared to laugh, shook her head. With a fluid motion, she came to her feet. She modestly closed her robe, held it with her hand as she walked across the room toward him. He was unable to tear his eyes from her face as she came and sat beside him. Her long slim fingers rested on his shoulder; they felt very real to him.

"Enjoying the party, Elliot?" she asked.

"You aren't here," he told her firmly. "You aren't real."

"Partly right. I'm not here, but I am real!"

"No . . ."

"Oh, yes. I just thought I'd visit you while you're—ah—shall we say, receptive!"

"Why?" he asked inanely, fighting the urge to try to touch her.

"To remind you, Elliot. There isn't a lot of time left. You need to come to me."

"I can't! You aren't real!" he insisted, his voice getting louder.

"I think you know that I am," she told him. "Or at least a part of you does. That part will get stronger in coming days, Elliot. And you'll come. You have to, you know. And the sooner you do, the more time there is for—pleasantries."

"Pleasantries?"

She released her robe, allowed it to fall open. Her body was exposed down as far as the top edge of her pubic hair. "Pleasantries," she repeated, with a seductive smile. Her fingers twisted his hair, traced over the top of his ear.

"Elliot?" came a different female voice, speaking into his other ear. "Who are you talking to?"

He turned, looked at Melissa. "Uh—" he said lamely. His head swiveled back: Nikki was still there, looking just as real as Melissa did. Like a man watching a tennis match, he moved his head from one to the other.

"Are you freaking out, El?" Melissa asked, concern in her voice. In an equally audible voice, Nikki laughed. And to Elliot's total shock, Melissa turned her eyes away from him, in the direction of the laughter. "What was that?" she asked.

"What was what?" he asked her in turn, a slight tremor in his voice.

"That sound. Like a woman laughing, right here on top of us!" Nikki giggled again, stood up. "There it is again!" Melissa cried, her own eyes getting wide.

"Dope's laced with something," Elliot mumbled, trying to convince himself as well as Melissa. But he was watching Nikki. She waved at him, walked across the room to a spot in front of a bare wall. There she raised her arms in a rather theatrical gesture, and Elliot watched a mist form in front of the wall, as if it were afire and smoking. As soon as its density obscured the wall behind it, Nikki stepped into it, disappeared from his sight. Then, very rapidly, the mist faded and vanished. Nothing was left except the wall, looking very ordinary.

"The dope's laced?" Melissa asked him shakily. "With what?"

He shook his head. "I don't know. Something. I've been having some wild hallucinations."

"I guess I was too," she said. "Oh, well. Try to enjoy them, I guess!"

"Yeah, sure," he said. But he'd never had hallucinations quite like that before, not even with LSD.

He reached for Melissa, pulled her close to him. She laid her head on his shoulder, and for a while they just listened to the Airplane. The hallucination began to fade into memory as his mind found other things to occupy itself with, such as the warmth of Melissa's body against his. In spite of the proximity of the vision, he was not having difficulties with comparisons; for once he seemed to be able to appreciate Melissa purely on her own—not inconsiderable—merits. He was still appreciating when a loud banging at the door startled everyone, but he was forced to stop when the door was suddenly smashed open.

He jumped up, shook his head to clear it; Melissa was looking up at him with frightened eyes, and he yanked her to her feet. Through the doorway, he could see what looked like an endless stream of police rushing into the house. Among the party guests, chaos had erupted as everyone tried to head for the nearest exit. Elliot was no exception; holding Melissa's hand tightly, he made for the kitchen door, hoping that the police had not sent part of their number around back.

He was not nearly so stoned that he didn't realize that one of his worst fears had been made reality.

By comparison with the black light elsewhere in the house, the brightly lit kitchen seemed glaring. He blinked his eyes rapidly a few times to adjust them, headed for the door. Not too many people had come this way; only about four were ahead of them, Linda herself in the lead. Just as she threw the door open, a uniformed officer rushed through it, screaming at everyone to halt where they were. But everyone scattered, and he immediately began swinging his club. Linda was unfortunate enough to be the nearest target.

"Wait—" she cried, holding up her arm. But the cop couldn't hear her, probably wouldn't have stopped if he had.

He smashed the club alongside her head, and she crumpled to the floor, her red hair now stained with even brighter red blood. A young boy—someone Elliot didn't know—slammed a Coke bottle over the cop's head from behind, and he too went down. Naturally, this act made him the focus of attention for the five or so other officers pouring in the back door; Elliot and Melissa, along with a number of others, were able to slip out unnoticed. Not slowing down at all, they ran across the backyard and into the next. He was forming a vague plan of getting to the next street, then circling back to their car.

And it worked out. He'd parked almost a block away, and none of the officers paid any attention as he pulled the VW away from the curb. People were still spilling out of the house, running in all directions, cops chasing them. As they drove past, they saw at least two more go down under the swinging clubs. Nearly a full-scale riot, he thought. Over a few joints at a private party.

Melissa was crying as they got back to Rosemary Street, turned in the direction of home. "You don't suppose Linda is dead, do you, El?" she sobbed.

He shook his head, felt his own memento of the Chicago riot. "No, I've seen a lot of people get clubbed, none of them died. That's not her problem. She's busted, and that's a real bad trip.''

Melissa sobbed some more, leaned her head against his shoulder. By the time he'd gotten back to the duplex, her sobs had become near pants, and her hands were all over him. They ran inside, his fly already unzipped and her shirt unbuttoned, paused only long enough to lock the door. Then she was out of her clothes and down on the living room floor, and he didn't wait long to join her. As she was soaking wet and he already erect, he entered her immediately, feeling her fold her long legs across his back, listening to her moan. It didn't last long, but it was intense and extremely satisfying; afterward, he remained coupled with her for a few minutes, then rolled over on his back on the floor, exhausted and still stoned. But he'd loved it, and he was not unable to admit that to himself. Twice before, he'd seen this effect; the sudden, overwhelming rise of sexual passions following violent confrontations. He kept insisting to himself that he hated the violence, but he was forced to admit that the aftermath of it was most pleasant. But now, he glanced over at Melissa with real concern. As far as he knew, this was her first time, and it could be distressing.

She sat up, hugged him. ''Oh, El,'' she said, with only a trace of a quiver in her voice. ''It's so important to—to— uh—to be *loving* after such a horrible experience, isn't it?'' She stopped, looked at his face, her eyes showing doubts. ''Isn't it?''

''Sure it is, honey,'' he told her, folding her back into his arms again. ''Real important.'' He marveled at the speed with which she'd come up with the rationalization. But then, he'd always known she wasn't stupid. He cuddled her, mentally reviewing the scene at Linda's, and felt himself getting erect again. He touched her breast and found that she was more than willing.

5

New York City

The man with the silver ring sat on the curb on a street in Greenwich Village and held his head in his hands. The pavement was still hot, the cement reluctantly giving up the heat it had gathered during the unbelievably uncomfortable day.

Saturday night, he told himself. Another Saturday night, and things were no better than last weekend, or the one before that. He was alone, had no friends at all. Though in reality, the only thing that was important was that he had no female friends, or at least none willing to be intimate with him. And that was what he needed now, more than anything else. It had been that way for quite some time; too long. It seemed to him that he was slowly coming apart under the stress.

He knew—or thought he knew—exactly when all of this had started. Seven months ago, a cold, snowy February day in the city, when he had met that pair from North Carolina. The boy had jumped in front of him, screaming about Jesus, about the Bible, and about his own divine mission. He had tried to pass the boy, but the boy had kept jumping in front of him, yelling and screeching, waving a Bible. Finally he'd decided that it was less trouble to just sit and listen for a few minutes. Perhaps, he told himself now, that had been a fatal mistake.

Initially, the boy's spiel had sounded like total gibberish, but after a few minutes, it had begun to make a weird kind of sense to him. The boy had told him that Jesus could take care of him, help him make decisions, that his life would have direction, be meaningful. He'd been in the city for the better part of a year, wandering aimlessly, trying to be part of Greenwich Village street society and failing miserably. When the boy began to convince him he could be a part of something—that he could finally belong—he started to listen. Eventually he had gone away with the ragged boy and his girlfriend, stayed with them for a week in the pad they had shared with a dozen others. After that, they had left, returned to their native North Carolina. But he had stayed on, surrounded by the commune members day and night. They talked about nothing but Jesus, the Bible; he was never allowed dope, ate sparingly, and slept little. And eventually it seemed like something inside him had just snapped. From then on, up until a few weeks ago, he had been theirs. He had talked their line, basked in their approval; he had followed all their rules, and after only a few weeks had become a fully trusted member of their group. That is, insofar as anyone was trusted; no one was ever left alone. The prohibitions—no drugs, no smoking, no alcohol, and no sex—were to be rigidly adhered to at all times. If one was alone, they explained, there would be possible opportunity and therefore temptation. So they always stayed in groups of at least three. Especially when they were out begging in the streets, or trying to get new recruits. Sadly, he had not proven to be particularly adept at either. And so he had remained, just one of the flock. But he was happy; he belonged, he didn't have to think for himself. At first, he had had no problems.

Time had passed; and only one thing really bothered him. He'd not been a smoker, never overly fond of drugs—they frightened him, mostly—and only an occasional drinker. But the absence of any sexual outlet at all—that was bad. Women had always been the essence of the problem for him, ever since he'd first become aware of his sexuality. When he'd arrived in the city, he'd been a virgin; but he'd brought some money with him, and it had opened a few doors, at least in the beginning. Money brought drugs, and drugs were an entry into certain circles where he'd been introduced to a couple of young girls who were not discriminating about their sexual partners. Those times he looked back on with nostalgia; they'd only lasted as long as his money had, and his eviction from these circles had readied him for his blind acceptance of the cult, though he wasn't really aware of that. When he was in the commune, he felt as if that time had been some kind of golden age.

And in the end, it had been the cult's prohibition of sex—

except for fund-raising purposes—that had driven him to try to leave. When he mentioned his desire to go, he had received a shock—he had been told, in no uncertain terms, that nobody left. It was the will of the Chingon—the leader of the church—that no one, once saved, should be allowed to backslide into the arms of Satan. If anyone tried to, then it was their holy responsibility to deliver that soul to Jesus while still in a state of grace.

They regaled him with stories of the people who had tried to leave; some had been caught and killed in the streets, others brought to the church headquarters on Forty-fourth Street where the Chingon himself would oversee an execution by decapitation. He had been given to understand that numerous young people had lost their lives in this way. Then, paradoxically, told that almost no one ever tried to leave the church, that it was unheard of. In either case, what was stressed most was that no one ever escaped; all backsliders were inevitably caught.

He had believed these stories, and they'd caused him to change his attitude. Feeling even more strongly that he had to get away from them, he'd naturally refrained from saying anything further about it. At last, after a particularly tiring day, when everyone else had been sleeping soundly, he'd slipped away. He'd known that they'd be looking for him, so he hadn't returned to his old haunts immediately. But he'd also known that they wouldn't keep up the search for very long; and eventually he'd found his way back to Greenwich Village. So far, so good, he remembered telling himself a few days after returning; only a few people in the church knew him at all, and he'd shaved, changed his appearance somewhat. But even now he didn't really feel safe from them.

Free from the commune, he'd immediately discovered that he was no better off than before; in some ways, things seemed worse.

Many of the few casual friends he'd had had disappeared, left for other parts of the country. Others, knowing who he'd gotten involved with, had been afraid to associate with him. And as always, his luck with women was virtually nonexistent; he had no idea how to relate to them. He found himself still celibate, weeks after his escape. Of course, he could masturbate now, and he did, but he found it small consolation. Sitting here on the hot curb in the early evening, he briefly toyed with the idea of going back to the church. But he couldn't—he was too afraid they'd kill him.

A hand touched his shoulder, and he heard a voice. "Hey, man, it can't be all that bad!"

He looked up. An almost pretty girl was leaning over him, smiling at him. "Who . . . ?" he mumbled.

"My name's Jeanne," she said. "You look like a man who could use a good time!"

"What do you mean?" he asked, giving her a blank look.

She winked at him. "You know, man, a party. You got any dough?"

"Sure, yeah, a little—"

She took his hand. "Then you come with me. I'll take that frown off your face!"

She led him around the corner, to a stair, which led up the side of a narrow brick building. Climbing them, they entered an apartment like so many others he'd seen, run-down, chaotic.

"Make yourself comfortable," she said as she closed the door behind them.

"Comfortable?" he said awkwardly, feeling confused.

"Man, you are uptight!" she commented. Standing on tiptoes, she kissed him quickly, then started to unbutton her shirt. He got the idea, started to grin. "Twenty-five bucks," she said, and immediately his grin vanished.

"I don't understand—" he started.

She held out her hand, palm up. "Hey, man," she said, "we've all got to make a buck, dig?"

"But I thought—"

She laughed. "You thought I brought you up here because you turn me on? Come on, man; you drop some bad acid?"

He started to get angry. "Look, you asked me to come up!" he snapped.

"Well, now I'm asking you to either give me the bread and get on with it, or leave!" she told him, an angry expression on her face. But almost immediately she calmed down. "Come on, man," she cajoled. "Just gimme the money, and I'll show you a real fine time, just like I promised."

"You just told me I was repulsive!"

"No, no. I didn't mean that. You aren't—it's just that, well, I can't afford to get burned, you dig? Like I said, we all need bread—"

"I don't even have twenty-five dollars," he growled.

"How much do you have?"

"About six bucks."

"Shit! Will you just get the fuck out of here, dumb ass?"

In spite of the fact that she was making him really furious, he didn't want to go; he kept staring at the center of her chest, the narrow strip of skin visible when she'd started to unbutton her shirt. It had been too long for him, and he didn't want to get this close and let the opportunity slip away.

"No, wait," he protested, his voice taking on the pleading tone. "Look, I'll give you the six bucks now and the rest later, okay? I can get some bread from—"

She gave him a scornful glance. "Are you kidding?" she jeered. "If I worked on credit, I'd sure as fuck be starving! Look. You get the bread first, then come back. Okay? I'll be around."

"No, I want—"

"Everybody wants, asshole," she said coldly, walking toward the door. "I gotta get back out there, find somebody who has some money. You better be gone when I get back!"

Her attitude was making him more and more angry. "No, you wait just a fucking minute!" he snapped, grabbing her arm.

"Let go of me!" she yelled, slapping at his hand. He tried to grab her free hand, but she avoided him, swung at his face. And connected hard.

"Bitch!" he snarled, and slapped her back, full in the face.

"Goddamn you!" she shrieked. Breaking away from him, she bolted for the kitchen, which was merely a tiny cubbyhole off the side of the room they were in. Seconds later, she stood in the doorway with a totally ineffectual-looking paring knife in her hand. "Now you get the hell out of here, you bastard!" she commanded.

The knife looked so small and fragile in her hand that he now laughed at her, and some of his rage began to dissolve. But the underlying current—the feeling that most all women thought he was some kind of a bad joke—had been aroused, and his laughter had a dark tone to it. Nevertheless, he was able to manage a conciliatory tone.

"Now, look," he began. "Don't you think this is all getting a little out of hand?"

But she took it the wrong way, advanced on him a little, the knife pointed at him. "You bet it got outta hand, buster," she raged. "Now that I got this, you wanna talk. But I want you to get the fuck out of here! Right now!"

His fury started to come back. "I think you better put that away," he said, taking a step toward her.

Unexpectedly, she slashed at him with the knife. Actually, she caught his hand pretty good; if the little blade had been sharper, he would have had a deep gash. As it was, his skin was only scratched.

"Goddamn it!" he bellowed. His hand whipped out, grabbed her hand and the knife together. Unaware that he was twisting it backward, he jerked her toward him with his other hand. She grunted, but he still didn't realize what had happened. Not until she pulled away again, and he saw the bloodstain on the side of her shirt, saw blood on the little paring knife.

"Oh, you motherfucker," she said rather quietly, looking down at herself. "You cut me, Goddamn you! Look at that, I'm fucking bleeding here!" She started to pull her shirt aside to see the extent of the damage, and the knife fell to the floor between them, unnoticed by either one. But her inspection was cut short when she suddenly choked and coughed, and a mass of blood fell from her mouth. "Oh, my God," she whispered, staring at it.

He backed away from her, confused. He hadn't really meant to hurt her, he told himself. Just get her under control, get what she'd invited him here for. Now, he didn't know what the hell was going on. She'd been pricked by that damn knife in the struggle—there was no way, he told himself, that it could possibly have been more than that—but why was she spitting up blood?

He started to tell her that it'd be all right, he'd take her over to the free clinic, but she didn't seem to hear him. She just stood there, her eyes wide, wiping blood off her mouth. And the stain on her shirt had become a long streak, extending down to the top of her skirt.

Then, abruptly, she started to scream, an ear-splitting sound. Panicky, he jumped to her, tried to put his hand over her mouth; but she bit him, started screeching again. She was flailing at him with her hands, her fingers curved so that her nails were like claws. Without his ever deciding to do it, he became aware that his hands had found her throat, and he started to squeeze.

Suddenly the sound was gone. She jerked and struggled,

and then crashed to the floor. But he never relinquished his grip; with a peculiar abstract detachment, he watched her eyes snap open and close, watched her face turn dark and swell. Her lips and eyelids were puffing up, and her mouth was slightly open; to him it looked pouty. It crashed in on him that the overall effect was, to him, intensely erotic—their position, the expression on her face. But she was spoiling it by beating on him with her arms, and he squeezed tighter to make her stop. Within her throat, something gave way under the pressure of his fingers. It felt a little like a plastic tube of some kind. She stopped flailing then, and he let go of her throat; but still she could get no air. To him, it was like watching a movie.

Bent over her, he stared into her terror-filled eyes, kept staring until she lay dead.

It was only when her pupils had expanded to almost fill the irises that he realized how enormously turned on he really was. Frantically, he tore at her skirt, then at his own pants. His intercourse with the corpse was the most satisfying he'd ever had; for him, he could see now so clearly, the Perfect Woman was a dead one.

It was sad, he reflected when it was over, that they could be used only once. But the solution was so obvious.

Feeling the same as he had when he'd accepted the church's doctrine, he cleaned up and left the apartment. It wasn't until hours later that what had really happened sank in; and by then, his mind had fully accepted a new avocation.

6

For the next couple of days, Elliot had very little time to even think about the photo and letter. The morning after the party, Jim Cardwell had called him, enlisted his assistance in raising bond and lawyer money for Linda and some of the others who had been arrested. Cardwell also tried to involve him in another matter, as well—how the police had known about the party. Jim was convinced, and Elliot inclined to agree, that they had an informer in their midst. Without substantial advance notice, there was no way the police could have known about the party in time to set up such an elaborate raid on it.

But Elliot told him firmly that he wasn't about to help them conduct a hunt. Perhaps, he suggested, knowledge about the parties should not be spread far and wide; it was just possible that there was no informer, that the wrong person had simply overheard something; it seemed that half the campus knew about these parties, and well in advance. Under such conditions, leaks were inevitable.

His refusal angered Cardwell, but Elliot didn't care. He had quite enough problems of his own; the image of Nikki was very clear in his mind, superimposing itself on any work he tried to do. After a while he surrendered, gave the day over to the fund-raising effort. That, at least, was successful.

On the way back from his office, Elliot stopped off at a bookshop on Franklin Street and was directed to the paperback section, which was upstairs. He was a little suspicious of any literature Jim Cardwell recommended, but he had made a mental note to pick up the book he'd referred to. As he climbed the narrow, unfinished stairs, he wondered if it would turn out to be worth the effort. In a section containing mostly books on philosophy and drugs, he found it. The clerk looked at him a little oddly as he laid it on the counter and paid the ninety-five-cent purchase price. To Elliot, the clerk's expression made him feel as if he were the only person in town who didn't own a copy. Well, he told himself, you cannot expect to keep yourself up-to-date on absolutely everything. There simply weren't enough hours in a day.

When he got back home, Melissa wasn't there yet; she'd been working on raising some funds for Linda as well, and he figured that she was still hard at it. He settled into the corner of the couch and opened the book, began to read.

And was not at all disappointed; two hours later, when Melissa came home, he was still engrossed in the text. She interrupted him to tell him that they'd uncovered the informer who'd reported Linda's party to the police.

"Oh?" he said, without much interest. He wasn't in the habit of talking much about such things. Still, he reminded himself, it was important to know.

"Yeah. You know Andy, that guy who just got into town a few days ago? The one who dresses like a biker? Turns out he's a cop, would you believe. From Winston-Salem. Exchange, or something."

"Are you sure? Who came up with that?"

"It was Linda's lawyer," she said in a conspiratorial tone. "He recognized the guy."

"Wouldn't you know it?" he said. "That bastard has talked about nothing but dope ever since he hit town. And he does as much as any ten people! I don't know how they can live with themselves, busting people for doing the same things they do!"

"What can you expect from the pigs?" she asked with a shrug. He shook his head, watched her disappear into the bedroom, and returned to his book.

A little later, he was still immersed in it; he could hear Melissa in the kitchen, doubtlessly concocting another disaster for their dinner. But he paid very little attention. Though in fact he was sitting in a run-down duplex in Chapel Hill, in spirit he was in the Mexican desert with the characters in the book; though it was by no means the best-written book he'd ever read, he could appreciate its impact. The subject matter was strong, fascinating; he could see the desert sunsets, feel the hot, dry winds. It made him feel nostalgic for something, and he couldn't identify exactly what that might be.

It was a short book, only 198 pages excluding the formal "structural analysis" in the back, and he wished it was longer. He didn't want the adventure to end. In particular, he was spellbound by the image of the character "La Catalina," presented as a threatening bruja—a sorceress—opposed to the main characters. La Catalina was never really described in the text, but Elliot kept visualizing her as looking exactly like Nikki. He kept telling himself that that had to be wrong; Nikki didn't look at all like a Mexican. But the image persisted. There were other oddities, too; he kept seeing Don Juan as surrounded by fire, when nothing in the text suggested that. He was completely engrossed in it when, gradually, Melissa's voice cut through his fixation, brought him fully back to Chapel Hill.

He looked up; she was sitting across from him, looking at him intently. He was aware of the smell of cooking vegetables filtering in from the kitchen.

"What's wrong, Elliot?" she asked him, a slightly wistful note in her voice.

"Nothing—really, it's nothing." he told her. But he didn't look her in the face when he said it.

"Elliot, I know you. Something is bothering you. I wish you could share it with me."

"No, there's really nothing," he insisted. "I guess I'm just not quite over my father's death, that's all."

She thought about that for a few moments, then nodded. "Okay. If I can help, you let me know, okay?"

"Sure." Seemingly satisfied, she returned to the kitchen, finished preparing dinner. As Elliot sat down to eat, his thoughts were still of La Catalina and Nikki. Choking down a few bites of an oversalted mung-bean concoction Melissa had come up with, he reviewed the conversation briefly. It was obvious to him that Melissa was beginning to pick up on his obsession with Nikki. This had to stop, he told himself; but it just didn't seem like he could really keep his mind on anything else. He took another forkful of the green gruel on his plate and glanced up. Melissa wasn't eating; she was just staring at him.

"What?" he asked her, then put the loaded fork in his mouth.

Her lip trembled. "It's awful," she said, indicating the food. "I put way too much salt in it. How can you eat it?"

He couldn't tell her that her cooking in general was so abysmal that he couldn't tell the difference. Think fast, Elliot, he told himself. "It's not that bad," he said gently, but with an inflection in his voice that indicated that it really was.

"Yes, it is!" she said, her voice breaking a little. "And you weren't going to say a word about it!"

He watched her carefully. What to say now? He didn't quite know, so he just shrugged and took yet another bite. Tried to look brave.

"Oh, Elliot!" she cried suddenly, getting up from the table. "You are so sweet! You just didn't want to hurt my feelings!"

He accepted the hug, smiled. That went okay, he thought.

"I swear, I love you!" she said, sounding like she meant it.

7

Dragging himself out of bed Monday morning was not an easy thing for Elliot. Once again, he had dreamed about Nikki, and even though he couldn't really remember the dreams once he was up, he knew that he hadn't wanted to leave them.

Melissa was already up, and in the bathroom. He staggered into the kitchen, saw that she hadn't yet made coffee—a far more important commodity to him than to her—and with a sigh, did it himself. Instant coffee would be so much easier, he told himself as he dumped the old grounds into the garbage, rubbed the stains off his fingertips. The problem was, he didn't like the taste of it.

Melissa was in the bathtub when he came in; the old duplex

didn't have a shower. Her face was covered by a washcloth as he went by, pulled his toothbrush from the rack and squeezed a string of white cream onto it.

"Sleep well, El?" she asked when she finished with her face.

"I suppose," he said noncommittally, ramming the toothbrush into his mouth. He really didn't want to discuss the dreams with her at all. Melissa was the kind of woman who'd be jealous of a fantasy lover, of that he was sure. Vaguely, he wondered how he'd feel if the situation were reversed. He liked to tell himself that he wouldn't be jealous if she had a real flesh-and-blood lover, but he wasn't so sure of that. Non-possessive and not jealous were the ideals, and he surely would expose them to anyone who would listen. But he was aware that for himself personally, many of these things had yet to be tested.

"I had some weird dreams," she said.

He turned, the toothbrush still in his mouth, and watched her wipe the soapy cloth down across her large breasts. They were nice now, he thought. But as she got older, they'd sag—just a matter of gravity. Unlike Nikki's smaller ones, doubtlessly still firm after all these years.

Annoyed with himself again, he ripped the toothbrush out, spat in the sink. "What'd you dream?" he asked when his mouth was clear.

"It was about you. You were in terrible danger, I was trying to save you. Real scary."

"What kind of danger?"

"Well—dreams sound so silly in the light of day, dig? But anyhow, there was this bitchin' snake after you!"

"Snake?"

"Yeah. But bigger than any snake I ever heard of. The dream was in color, too, Elliot, and most of my dreams aren't. This snake was a rattlesnake, but it was colored—I don't know, for a while it was a kind of a gold color. Then later, it was white, and I think it had feathers or something sprouting out from its head!"

Strange, he thought. The first description—the gold color—was so much like the snake he'd seen in his dream of Nikki a few nights previously. "Well, snakes in dreams are usually phallic," he pontificated, dismissing the similarities as coincidental. "What else happened?"

"Not much. At least not much that I can remember. But the strange thing was, you didn't act like you were afraid."

Nice, he thought. She thinks of me as heroic in the face of danger. It was silly, but he felt pride. "So I fought it?"

"Oh, no. It wasn't that you were being brave, it was that you were being, well, stupid!" she said, deflating him. "You wanted to go to the snake. It wasn't coming after you, it was more like it was calling you. And you were going right to it. But it was going to kill you, Elliot, and you were walking right up to it anyway. I tried to hold you, but you pushed me aside, said 'You just can't compare to her' and went ahead. I woke up before it—she, I guess—got you."

For a minute he didn't say anything. That was really strange, he thought; not only the same dream snake, but the identification of it as female, and the line she'd dreamed coming from his mouth. Although he'd not articulated it even to himself so bluntly, he couldn't deny that it was the sort of thing he'd been thinking. "Well," he said at last, leaning against the sink, "what do you think it means?"

"You're the psychologist, El. You tell me."

"I can't—dream symbols are so personal. Take it apart, element by element. What do you associate snakes with?"

"I'm not sure I really know. I'm not afraid of them, but I'm not overly fond of them either. I'd certainly respect a rattler, especially one that big! I suppose dangerous, threatening. Maybe with a sense of lying in ambush, as opposed to rushing to attack like maybe a jaguar."

He keyed on that. "Jaguar? Why jaguar?"

"Just a big cat—you know, something that can attack you, but wouldn't—I don't know—" She seemed a little confused.

"But why a jaguar?" he persisted. "Isn't a lion or tiger more obvious? Or a wolf, or bear?"

Her brow furrowed. "It just seemed," she said carefully, "that there was some proper association between that giant rattlesnake and a jaguar. The snake with feathers makes me think of a jaguar. I'm not sure why."

He found he couldn't come up with a good answer to that either, and changed his tack. "Okay—how about this? Let's get back to the giant snake. Assume it is phallic. Big snake, big penis. That ring any bells?"

"No. You don't have an especially big penis, Elliot—"

He knew he shouldn't, but he always felt slightly insulted

when she made a remark like that. Even though she'd said many times that she had no hang-ups about size. He stuffed his wounded ego down, went on. "Okay, but still—it might be. It's threatening me, right? Maybe some other man? Who has, or it seems to you, should have, a big penis?" That in itself started him wondering. Did she possibly have another lover, one better endowed than he? And was she considering leaving him for this man, hence the threat? Suddenly he felt uncomfortable and anxious, wondered if he should be pursuing this.

"No," she told him firmly. "I just can't think so. Like I said, the snake was female. I kept thinking in the dream you were going to her. I can't believe the snake represented a penis."

He was not convinced, but he let it go by. "Okay, so the snake is a dangerous, bushwhacking female," he said lightly. "Why is it white? Or rather, why gold and then white? And why feathers?"

She looked helpless, lifted a leg and started washing it. "Gold—means precious, I suppose. White—good, clean."

"White is good and clean as opposed to black or yellow?"

She glared at him, picking up the thrust of his question instantly. "I'm not a racist, Elliot," she snapped. "At least, I do my best—for someone raised in white America. You know I've had black lovers—"

"Yes, I know, I know," he said, not really wanting to be reminded of it. "And how you act isn't the point. We're talking about a dream, unconscious ideas coming up. You can't do anything about those symbols. They may have been with you since you were a little girl."

She calmed down, scrubbed her foot. "Okay. But I still don't think the white has anything to do with race. It doesn't feel right."

"So what does it have to do with?" he asked, pressing her.

"Knowledge, wisdom, power," she blurted, then looked very confused. "I don't really know why I said that—"

"We're getting somewhere now, though," he said, leaning against the sink. "It looks like your gold-white giant snake represents something like—uh—precious dangerous knowledge?"

"That could be right, I suppose. It sounds a little silly to me."

"Well, let's go on, then. In the dream, it's something I'm trying to go toward, and it'll kill me. That right?"

"Yes. But you can't understand that. Or maybe you do, and you want to be killed. Or whatever you're going to get from it is worth being killed for. One of those, anyway."

"Which?"

"Like I said, I don't—"

"No, I mean choose one. Without thinking."

"The last," she said with no hesitation at all. "It's going to kill you, but you want it so bad it doesn't matter to you."

He nodded the way he always believed a therapist should. "Want what?" he asked.

Melissa turned wide blue eyes up to him. Suddenly she looked very vulnerable, sitting there naked in the cooling bathwater. "Want her," she said in a low tone. "The woman in the red robes. Her."

His knowing smile vanished; he knew he was staring at her with consternation. But his mind was reeling, there was nothing else he could do for a moment. "What—who do you mean?" he managed to sputter after a few seconds. "You didn't mention any woman—"

"You told me just to talk, without thinking," she said. "I don't even know what I'm saying. There was no woman in my dream."

"Yeah—uh—good," he said, not quite knowing what else to say. All he knew was that it just wasn't possible for him to proceed with this, at least not now; it had gone beyond the realm of coincidence. "You better get out of that water," he told her, turning back to the mirror. "You're getting wrinkled."

"Elliot?"

"Yes?"

"Is there a woman, Elliot?"

He stopped combing his hair, stared at his own image in the glass. "No," he lied smoothly. Then, truth: "If you mean have I been seeing someone else. Absolutely not." He listened for a response, but there was only a little splashing as she stood up, stepped out of the tub.

"I didn't mean that," she told him after a very long pause. "I meant, is there another woman on your mind? Maybe an old lover or something?"

For an instant he considered telling her about the picture; maybe they could both have a good laugh about it. Maybe it would help exorcise the ghost from his mind. But in the end, he decided not to. It was simply so much easier to lie. "No, no old lovers," he said, regaining his composure. "And no new lovers, either. When we got together, we promised to tell each other if something developed with somebody else. I'm planning to stick with that agreement."

She gave him a deep hug, kissed his neck. "I'm glad, Elliot. So am I." She left the bathroom, and Elliot watched her go; she definitely looked splendid from the back, he thought. And not half bad from the front, he snarled at himself. Trying to dismiss Nikki and the odd coincidental dreams from his mind, he went back to his morning bathroom ritual. By the time he'd finished, he had come up with what he was sure had to be the answer; he must have talked in his sleep about his own dreams, thereby subliminally influencing Melissa's. Having solved that, he had only to solve the increasing obsession with Nikki. Then things would be back to normal.

Later that morning, in his office, he found himself unable to concentrate on the work he should have been doing. He had brought the Casteneda book in with him, and he spent a considerable amount of time rereading some of the passages in it. It was so unsatisfactorily short—left him wanting more. He could easily understand why it had become such a cult hit in such a short time.

He was still reading it when there was a knock at his office door. "Come," he yelled, expecting a student.

But the man who came through the door was a deliveryman of some sort. He carried a package and a clipboard with some forms on it. "You are Dr. Elliot Collins?" he asked formally.

"Yes," Elliot replied.

"I have this for you. It was sent special delivery from First Union Bank of Eddieville, Illinois."

"What is it?"

The man glanced at his clipboard. "Contents of a safe-deposit box your father held, sir. Would you sign here, please?"

Elliot signed the form, and the man sat the package on his desk. "I didn't know there was a safety deposit box," he said.

"No, sir, thank you, sir," the deliveryman said formally.

He took the clipboard and left, leaving Elliot to pick up the package, roll it over in his hands.

Finally he felt he'd stared at it long enough. He tore it open. Inside, there was no money, no previously unknown family jewels—just a stack of papers and letters. Curious, he took the first one off the stack and unfolded it. It was a letter, signed by his paternal grandfather, Norman Collins. It wasn't addressed to anyone, nor was it dated. It said:

> "Somehow I know now that it will happen just as she said it would. Truly, I have known it for twenty-six years. I just did not wish to admit it to myself. How can a man live for twenty-six years after he is dead? But that was her promise, and if I am alive just one week from now, she will have kept it. It is so amazing to me, the things I have passed through unharmed. On the other hand, I can never forgive myself for what she made me do. What we do to ourselves is one thing. What we do to those not yet born is another. Yet I could refuse her nothing. And if she came to me today, I still could refuse her nothing. Perhaps that means I am a weak man. I just feel there was never anything I could have done about it. With such excuses do I console myself in the eleventh hour of my life."

Elliot read it twice. It made absolutely no sense to him at all, in any way. Peculiar, he thought. Some of the coincidences were just now hitting him. Not only had Norman, like Aaron, died of congestive heart failure, they had died at exactly the same age—fifty-two. But this document—whatever it was—had no relevance to any of that. For all he knew, it had been written when Norman was forty. In fact, he told himself, this didn't bear any relationship to anything. He read it again, wondered if old Norman had been a little off center when he'd written it. Still, there were some haunting similarities in some of the lines—"what she made me do" and "those not yet born"—to some of the lines in his father's unmailed letter to Nikki.

Another quick read-through, and he put the note aside. Perhaps there was something else in here that would tend to explain it, he thought. He took the next paper out of the box, unfolded it and looked at it. This was not particularly interesting to him; it was in the nature of a will, Norman bequeathing all earthly properties to Aaron. It too went aside, and he dug on down through. Most of the stuff was typical of what someone might put in a safe-deposit box: birth certificates, deeds to property—all of which he knew about, and all of which had been superseded—and so on. Scattered among them were several pieces of paper that made very little sense, though nothing like the first one. Most of these had a single name and address written on them, none of which were familiar to him. Some of these were in Norman's handwriting, some in Aaron's, and some typed. Doubtlessly important to someone at some time, but meaningless now. A few were people he could not really visualize his father knowing, or Norman either, given what he'd heard about the old man. One, for instance, was a Juan Reyes, with an address c/o a restaurant called Alejandro's in New York City, in his father's handwriting. Though he'd never considered his father a racist, he'd also never known him to have any black or Hispanic friends to speak of. Maybe, he thought, this had been a business contact? Didn't really matter, he told himself, putting it aside. Just glancing at the majority of the papers, he dug on down through the box. There were only a few papers left when he found something else strange. An envelope containing about eight slips of six-by-nine paper, evidently torn from a diary. The handwriting was Aaron's, and the pages had dates from the autumn of 1942. Elliot spread them out, arranged them in order, and started to read.

"October 7. Been over six weeks since I've written anything. Time to catch up, but where to start? The last six weeks would fill a book. I shall have to be content for now to say that I have met the most appealing and intriguing woman on earth. My problem is, what shall I say to Paula when I see her again? Already I have been away so long I might not have to worry about it."

"October 10. Last time I wrote that the previous six weeks would fill a book. The last three days would fill another. It isn't easy to think about it, much less write it down. I can hardly bring myself to believe that such things are possible, that they ever existed on this earth, much less to accept that they exist now, in New York."

The page had been written in ink, and the remainder of it—a lot of text—was faded to the point of being unreadable. The next date, October 12, was wholly unreadable, as was the next, October 13. On the fifth one, October 17, he could read a couple of lines in the center of the page:

". . . that procedure. Unbelievable. I just cannot bring myself to accept that human beings are capable . . ."

And down just a little further, a few words that made his heart jump:

". . . but Nikki tells me that they can . . ."

He stared at the words for a few minutes, drumming his fingers on his desk. He'd been sure these pages had to do with Nikki after the first entry; they'd probably been put here so his mother would never see them. It was so tantalizing, and so frustrating, since most of it had become unreadable with time. He turned to the next page; the printed date was clear, October 18, but this page looked almost blank. Just a trace of writing, nothing readable. The next, October 21, was the same, but the last one, October 26, had some readable material in the center:

". . . and for better or worse, it has been decided. I will go through with it, not because I want to—I find I rather hate myself—but simply because she demands it, and in the long run I cannot say no to her. Yet I know I will lose her anyway, no matter what I do. Soon afterward, she will send whatever is left of me away, and again I will not be able to argue. If it happens as I expect, there will not be that problem! But she says no, and there will be the pain of a separation. I know I shall never be the same again. Certainly I will never view the world the same again. My biggest regret is that I have condemned it—"

He swore at the pages, straining his eyes to read the next word but failing. He turned the pile over, read through them again, trying to pick up a few more words, but got nothing else. This was so frustrating he almost wished he hadn't found it at all. More than a little irritated, he put the diary sheets back in their envelope, laid them aside. The next document was Aaron and Paula's marriage license; that was of no interest. Then, right on the bottom, another envelope. Not expecting much, he flipped it open. Caught by the edge of his thumb, the small item inside popped out, fell onto his desk. With the envelope still in his hand, he sat transfixed by the small square of paper that lay there, perfectly centered in front of him.

There was no doubt; it was another picture of Nikki, again in a swimsuit at some beach, but the style was even older than in the previous photo. Leaning over, he looked at the face. Though this was a sepia-tone—looked quite a bit older than the picture he had back at his apartment—she looked exactly the same; the pictures could not be far apart in time. Carefully putting the envelope down, he picked up the picture, turned it over.

On the back, in his grandfather's hand, was the legend: "Nikki, 1916."

The rest of that day, Elliot didn't accomplish a thing. He spent every spare moment in his office studying the strange documents. He realized that his problems were now even more profound; not only was Nikki haunting all his dreams and interfering with his perceptions of Melissa, but now she was a woman of mystery as well. And as such, an object of intense curiosity. Double trouble without a doubt, he told himself; she was even more on his mind than ever. Through his lunch hour, through the early afternoon, he thought about nothing else, and as a result he went to his two o'clock class quite unprepared, had to wing it. And didn't do very well at all. Again he kept staring at the freshman girl whose hair and eyes reminded him of Nikki's, and this time he was sure she was not unaware of it. He also felt she was displaying for him somewhat, repeatedly extending her leg into the aisle, stretching back in her seat so that her breasts strained against her blouse. It was a long fifty minutes, and he was relieved when the time was up. Returning to his office, he promised himself he would not reread the documents from the safe-deposit box any more that day. But he still found it impossible to work, and instead he picked up the Casteneda book again. That didn't get Nikki off his mind, but at least, he told himself savagely, it was not related.

He was reading a section in the book concerning Casteneda's drug-induced vision of a cactus-man with pools of water for eyes when there was a knock at his door.

"Come," he said, as was his habit.

He looked up to see the freshman girl, Eileen Cates, enter. She looked shy and doubtful as she came over and sat in the chair in front of his desk. Then she saw what he was reading and her eyes lit up. "Are you just now reading that?" she asked in an enthusiastic voice.

"No," he told her, stuffing a bookmark into the thin volume and closing it. "Rereading. Memorizing, just about. Interesting stuff."

"It sure is," she told him. "That's the area I'm going to be majoring in!"

"Psychotropic drugs?"

"No—well, not specifically. American Indian culture and religion. I've been especially interested in the Aztecs and Mayans. Ever since my daddy took us on a vacation to Mexico five years ago. We went to the pre-Colombian museum in Mexico City, and I just went crazy over it. Their art, maybe—it just kind of speaks to me, has an effect on me."

"I've never been there."

"You should go some time. It's far-out. The images in the sculptures and so on are so powerful," she enthused, as if she were glad to have this topic to discuss. "The plumed serpent, the smoking mirror—"

He'd really been only about half listening until she said that. Then he perked up. "Plumed serpent?" he asked, remembering his dream image, the one he'd apparently passed to Melissa.

"Oh, yes. Quetzalcoatl, the plumed serpent. One of the major gods of the Aztec. You've never heard of him?"

Something like that was coming back, now that it was placed in context. "Yes—seems like I do recall. Didn't the Aztecs think Cortez was that god when he showed up?"

"Yeah. 'Cause he was supposed to be bearded, and there was a legend about his returning. And you hear it said that Quetzalcoatl was white—that's only partly correct. White was his color—it symbolized knowledge, wisdom, and power of a priestly kind. As opposed to Tezcatlipoca's power—physical energy, war, leadership."

He hesitated for a minute while she ran on, thinking about

her words. Knowledge, wisdom, power—exactly what Melissa had said. Now that, he thought, was kind of weird. But maybe not—probably she'd learned it in some course, or read it somewhere. And it just came back up as a personal symbol for her—the white plumed serpent and what it meant. Interesting, he thought. You seldom get to see so clearly where a symbol comes from. He tried to pay attention to what Eileen was saying, but she was rattling off names he'd never heard, using jargon he was not familiar with. "I'm sorry," he told her, not unkindly. "But you're losing me completely!"

She turned red. "Oh, no, I'm sorry, Dr. Collins," she said. "I'm boring you—"

"It isn't boring. But that isn't what you came to see me about, is it?"

She turned even redder and studied something on the floor near her feet. "Uh—no—well, I don't know exactly how to—" she stammered.

Alarm bells started going off in Elliot's head. He was beginning to wonder what she had come for. "Well, just say it, whatever it is," he told her, though he wasn't sure he really wanted her to. "Let's get it out where we can examine the problem. Trouble with the course?" He knew that was unlikely—Eileen was headed for a minimum B in the course, an A if she didn't blow the final.

Her eyes came up and she gave him a direct look. "You know in this day," she said, her words tumbling over each other as they rushed out, "I believe that women can say what they want to men without a fear of being too forward, and so I just came by to say I noticed you've been staring at me in class, and well, I just wondered, I wanted to let you know that I was not put off or grossed out by it if you think—" She wound down, and her eyes dropped to the floor again.

He looked at her across the desk. This was not going to be easy. He considered what he was going to say, then began, speaking slowly, choosing his words carefully. "Miss Cates—Eileen—I won't pretend that I don't find you attractive; you're a very beautiful woman. But there's a problem. I'm a professor, and you're a student in my class. Now, I know some of the other profs don't seem to mind, but I think any—ah—involvement—is not ethical. I do try to be ethical. Okay?"

"Everybody knows that," she said, making him swell with pride. "But—uh—Elliot—I'm not a psych major. And a little over two weeks from now, this class will be over. Uh—I can wait.''

He was glad that the enormous and lecherous grin he was feeling did not show on his face as he considered the girl's words. The fact was, he told himself, her logic was undeniable. "Okay," he said in a low, almost conspiratorial voice. "After finals then, after I've turned in grades—let's talk."

Now she grinned too. "I'll hold you to it," she said.

"I hope so."

"You can count on it. And if it's our *tonalli* for something to happen—"

Again he stopped her. "What was that word?" he demanded, perhaps a little sharply.

She looked startled. "*Tonalli*," she said. "It's from the Aztec. It means, well, karma, fate. Sort of." Half out of her chair, she peered at him closely. "I just use it sometimes—anything wrong?"

"No, no," he said, with a gesture of dismissal. "I'd heard that word somewhere—can't say where—and I was just curious, that's all. You know a hell of a lot about this stuff for a freshman, you know!"

She gave him a broad grin as she left. "I've read everything I can find on it!" she informed him. "See you in class!" She closed the door and was gone. Elliot found that he was looking forward to the end of the summer session; what bothered him were the doubts he already had about the promise he'd so recently reaffirmed to Melissa. Perhaps his ethics were more those of convenience, he told himself a little sadly. Or those of reward and punishment.

8

The remaining weeks of the summer session dragged on; most of Elliot's friends were a little preoccupied with the upcoming trials of Linda and the others arrested at the ill-fated party. As a result, they didn't really notice Elliot's own withdrawn state. He'd immediately compared the two photos, sitting them up side-by-side; there wasn't a way to doubt that they were pictures of the same woman. And there was no difference whatever in the appearance of the face, even though the dates were twenty-six years apart. But it was remotely possible, he supposed; he'd seen pictures of actresses and so on who still looked youthful well into their forties and fifties. What bothered him was that there was no difference, absolutely none. There should have been at least a line or two visible. Beyond that was the natural speculation about Nikki's relationship to Aaron and his father; if she'd been a passion of Norman's in 1916, then she would have to be a minimum of twenty-five or so years older than Aaron. For a son to have an affair with his father's old lover was certainly a bit unusual, but he really didn't see anything wrong with it. He knew full well that if he were to meet Nikki looking like she did in the photos, he wouldn't have been put off by the fact that she'd been a flame of Aaron's, and perhaps Aaron had felt the same. But the 1916 photo insisted on her birth date being not later than say 1901; thus she'd have to be over sixty-five now. Even movie stars did not maintain a semblance of youth that long. Not, at least, that he knew of.

These thoughts were distracting him as he graded the final exams for the summer Psych 1 course. He forced himself to go over each paper twice, since he was making so many errors. When he finally came to Eileen Cates's paper, he was able, for a little while, to relegate Nikki to a back corner of his mind. He was looking forward to her return visit; and he was gratified to see, when he'd graded her paper, that she'd done quite well. In all good conscience he was able to give her an A for the course, and he'd have no problem defending it if any question ever came up. His concern that her grade might be marginal evaporated; it wasn't. Pleased, he finished the exams, filed the course grades for the students; only one failure, not a bad class at all. In agreement with his radical peers that there was too much emphasis on grades, he changed the *F* for that student to a *D*. This he'd done before, and he was concerned lest it give his courses the reputation for being "crip." But that hadn't happened yet—he'd worry about it when it did.

Less than a week later, as promised, Eileen turned up in his office. He was glad to see her, did not mind at all having his work on the experimental protocol interrupted. He felt it best to start things a little slowly, so he took her out for coffee at one of the places on Franklin Street. But that turned into a long coffee break—they were there four hours, talking about any subject that came up. Not once in that time did he mention Melissa. Eileen was not one of the radical students, at least not yet—many of the freshmen underwent changes not long after arrival. Despite her interest in Casteneda, she'd never done drugs, not even grass; she expressed uncertainty on her attitude about the Vietnam war. She also expressed an opinion, distressing to Elliot, that campus protest was downright foolishness. His confidence in himself led him to believe he could change that opinion, given time. And Eileen was interesting enough in other ways to warrant the time.

For one thing, she was very serious about her studies, something he felt was getting unfortunately too rare on the campus these days. That had led her to enroll in the summer session prior to her freshman year, get Psych 1 and Freshman Comp out of the way. In Elliot's view, she seemed very mature for a freshman, intensely interested in two topics: American Indians and the role of women in modern society. On either she could discourse for hours. And her opinions about women were far from conservative; she believed there should be legal and social equality for men and women in virtually all areas. When he asked her if women should be subject to the hated draft, she gave him an unhesitating affirmative.

"And they should be in combat, too, if we have to have combat," she went on. "Except for raw physical strength—not too important in a technological age—and the temporary situation of pregnancy, women are the equals of men. I believe it's time we recognized that."

"You'd have a hard time convincing most people of it," Elliot told her.

"I know," she replied coolly. "My parents think my ideas on the subject are lunatic. What about you, Elliot? What do you think?"

"What, on drafting women for combat?"

"That's a good place to start."

"I never thought about it much, to be honest," he told her. "My focus is there should not be a draft, period. For men or women."

"How do you propose the country defend itself?" she asked pointedly, though without hostility.

He went through a long speech, most of it rote, about how the country would have no problems in time of a real threat to its security; he felt people would flock to enlist, as they had in World Wars One and Two. But the standing army the draft provided, with the assurance of many more men whenever needed, encouraged foreign adventurism like Vietnam. In talks like this, Elliot carefully avoided the currently chic cliches, even the ones he agreed with. Terms like "military-industrial complex" and "imperialism" never entered his arguments. In talking to people like Eileen, his purpose was to convince, to win a convert. Not to put someone off with hollow dogma.

And by the end of the discussion, he felt he was gaining ground. She was quick and intelligent, asked incisive questions, but his arguments had been carefully thought out, and she brought up no issues—other than women's rights—that he had not already thrashed through in many other debates and discussions. Throughout the afternoon, they talked; it came close to dinnertime, and Elliot left her briefly, ostensibly to go to the bathroom. In fact, he called Melissa, told her he was tied up with work and wouldn't be in for dinner. On his return, he suggested taking Eileen for food, and she readily agreed. After they'd eaten, they went back to his office—his apartment was obviously not available, and she lived in the dorm—and made love on the couch. She did not ask why they didn't go to his place, and he didn't volunteer anything.

9

August turned into September, the students returned to the campus, and Elliot finally began his frequently delayed research. The two pictures remained in his desk, one atop the other, nestled inside of the velvet folder his father had kept his in. Along with them were the notes and diary pages from the safe-deposit box. Life with Melissa was good, at least on the surface. Though he was now carrying on an affair with Eileen—they met at least once a week, more if they could arrange it—Melissa did not seem to sense it, or said nothing about it if she did. Eileen's attitude Elliot did not fully understand. She was very passionate when they were together, but she never once implied that she might want anything more, any permanence or commitment. And—strangest of all—she never said a single word about the fact that they always went places Elliot's friends would not go, and she'd yet to set foot in his apartment. He assumed that she had to know he had another girlfriend, but since she didn't ask, it never came up in their conversations, which was strange. In some ways, Eileen was coming to know him better than Melissa did. Eileen was hardly turning out to be an average woman; much of the time Elliot felt completely off balance with her.

But the rest of his life went on pretty much as before. As to the outcome of the ill-fated party, the prosecution found itself unable to prove ownership of the various drugs they'd confiscated, and virtually all the drug charges had been dropped. A sad footnote to this affair was that the only remaining victim of the police raid was the young boy whose action had indirectly allowed Elliot and Melissa to escape; but even that hadn't turned out too badly. The boy got a year, suspended, for assaulting an officer.

But this, of course, had little direct effect on Elliot and Melissa, none at all on Eileen. Even as his affair went on, he was in the process of setting up more permanence with Melissa. Some of the money from the sale of his father's property had come in, and they'd bought new furniture together, made the duplex a little more comfortable; gone was the couch with the broken center, the wire-spool table. On campus, enthusiasm for UNC football had taken the place of the summer doldrums, and Elliot tried hard not to think about Nikki at all. Sometimes he succeeded, but not when he was with Eileen. Often when they made love, he focused on her black hair and dark eyes, pretended she was Nikki. To his chagrin, he'd even called her Nikki once in the heat of passion; he'd been immensely relieved when she seemed not to have heard it, and he was more careful after that. Sometimes he felt badly about it, felt he was using her, and almost decided to break it off. But he never did. The sex between them was wonderful, and almost as good, he had to admit, was the subterfuge, the feeling he was getting away with something. Crass as it was, he had to admit that it added considerable zest to his life. And so he swallowed his guilt feelings, went on doing what he wanted.

Aside from this, he knew that he had not expelled Nikki from his mind; he had just sort of put her on a shelf. It was, in his opinion, extremely unlikely that he'd ever get answers to any of his questions about her, about her relationship with either or both of his ancestors. And with time, it was beginning to fade a little. Because Elliot was above all a practical man.

It was true enough that he was involved in the anti-war movement, true enough that he was a hippie of sorts. But he'd never allowed any of that to interfere in any major way with the life directions he'd decided to take, and he rejected out of hand the various cultic movements, like the Hare Krishnas, that were springing up around the fringes of the counterculture. He and Melissa had played their copy of the soundtrack from *Hair* until the pops and scrapes drowned out the music; after that, he'd bought another copy. He loved the music, but he didn't believe that the Age of Aquarius was dawning. If the consciousness of the students on campus now projected to a more responsible politic in the future, that was good enough for him. And, he thought, all that could be expected.

Somewhat at variance to this was his attitude toward Casteneda's book. He steadfastly refused to take any part in the cult that was rapidly building up around it—refused to talk about it with people like Jim Cardwell at all—yet he was intrigued by it. Too much of a realist to buy into the romantic notions about Indian societies then current, he nevertheless found that the old brujo spoke to him from the pages of the book, and that what he had to say was important. Four times he'd read it through, and he still felt as if he didn't understand it very well. It was, of course, a common topic of discussion between himself and Eileen.

"I can't tell you what it means to you, Elliot," she would say, lying nude on the couch in his office. She never replaced her clothes until she had to, until they were ready to leave. "All I can say is that Indians don't necessarily think like we do. As far as I know, the psychology you teach may be well and good for civilized Americans. But I'm just not so sure it applies to tribal Indians. And maybe it's true, like Carlos suggests, that that means they don't live in the same reality."

"You can't have more than one reality," he'd point out. "Reality is absolute, independent of us."

"Don't forget that all your verifications of reality come through your senses," she'd say in return. "And then interpreted by your brain. You as a psychologist should know that as well as anyone."

"Yes, but there are absolutes—things like nuclear energy prove it—" And so they'd go, endless debates with no conclusions. But it was a very nice way to pass the time until he'd sufficiently recovered. Then they'd make love again, and finally he'd go home to Melissa. It was then that he'd wonder if Melissa did in fact suspect something; virtually every time he'd come in late she'd be feeling amorous. Concerned about her suspicions if he turned her down, he'd force himself, once in a while even faking an orgasm. Then he'd go to bed, so exhausted he'd wonder if it was really worth it.

But his research was going pretty well; that he had no complaints about. Despite all the distractions, he was making good headway in that area. And, he told himself as he left his office and headed to another session of testing, he was most eager to see the final results. Even though that was some time off. On the other hand, he reminded himself, it couldn't be too long. He had to get some material published if he expected to keep his position. That was the policy, and it certainly wasn't going to change because of him. Walking into the testing rooms on a sunny afternoon late in September, he greeted his graduate assistant, Bill Stein, and went directly to the classroom where the subjects from the pool awaited him. He didn't waste their time or his, introducing himself and Bill perfunctorily and immediately starting to describe the subject's role in the studies.

"Now," Elliot explained, writing on the blackboard, "this is what you'll need to know. First, like most psychology experiments, we will be working under double-blind conditions, and you won't be able to know, until after the experiments are over, exactly what we're doing here." He looked out over the assembled students, many of them reluctant volunteers; to get full credit, freshman psych students had to participate in departmental experimentation. After all, the department had to maintain its pool of subjects, even if the pool was unfortunately a somewhat biased one. "So. This one is really very simple; you'll go in and look at a filmstrip; Bill Stein, my graduate student here, will set it up, run it for you. Then, you'll come back out and answer some questions about what you saw, and I won't know which film you've seen until I've scored your answers. All right? Any questions?" No one raised their hand, and Elliot was gratified. It was simple enough, but that didn't usually prevent students from asking questions. It was what they were expected to do, so they did. Fortunately, not today.

He passed out cards with numbers on them to the students, then randomly picked five; these would be the subjects for today. The remainder were instructed to come back next week, same time, and allowed to leave. Four girls and a boy remained, and they moved to the front row. Only one looked even remotely interested, the others seemed eager to get it over with, get on with their own affairs. Elliot had them order themselves according to the numbers on the cards, and the first girl was sent in to see one of the filmstrips. Ten minutes later she returned, and the next one went in, while Elliot led the first off to a private room for the interview.

"Okay," he said when they were alone. "Now. Here are the questions; you saw a filmstrip of a fight, is that correct?"

"Yes," she said, crossing her legs. The tiny miniskirt was distracting; he tried to ignore it, went on.

"Would you tell me who started it?"

"The black man," she said.

"Okay. What kind of weapon was being used?"

"A straight razor, I think."

"Fine. Did either of the fighters get injured?"

"Yes."

"Which one?"

"The white man."

Elliot went on down through the list of questions, and the girl told him what she'd seen; or rather, what she thought she'd seen. His experimental protocol used several filmstrips, all featuring a sudden and unexpected fight between a black man and a white man. All had, of course, been carefully produced; the same two actors played in each one, but the weapons varied, sometimes a straight razor, sometimes a knife, sometimes a gun. Elliot's working hypothesis was that observers would tend to associate the straight razor as a "black" weapon, when in fact, films had been produced in which the white man used it equally often. But in this case, he himself had no idea which film the girl he was interviewing had seen, and would not know until later. Only the graduate assistant knew that, and he was kept ignorant of the subject's answers.

As planned, it took about seven minutes to complete the questionnaire, after which the girl was dismissed. Elliot barely had time to mark the form with a code number and file it before the next student, the boy, came in. This interview went exactly the same, though he was rushed by the next student waiting; perhaps he should try to do four of these in an hour, rather than five. Couldn't, he decided, asking the third student questions rapid-fire; he wouldn't have enough for the preliminary analysis.

By the time the last girl came in, he was feeling rather harried. She sat down in front of him, and he gave her just a little more than a passing glance as he picked up the questionnaire; she was an attractive brunette, and the inevitable miniskirt showed that she had very nice legs. But he had no time for that now, he thought. Taking this one a little slower, he started the questions, asking her if she'd seen a fight.

"I suppose," she said doubtfully.

He glanced at her. Why did she doubt it? Everyone else had given that one a categorical "yes." "All right, fine," he said. "Who started it?"

Again she looked dubious. "The man, I guess—I mean, well, okay. The man."

Peering up at her, Elliot wondered what her problem was. "The black man or the white man?" he asked, feeling that was really unnecessary.

She looked back at him, apparently more confused than ever. "The Indian," she said.

"Indian?" he echoed. "Uh—Miss—" He glanced down at his sheet. "Miss Borlyn, there was no Indian!"

"Sure there was, Dr. Collins. An Indian and a woman."

"What?"

"An Indian and a woman," she repeated. He looked at her more closely. Her eyes were somewhat glassy, and he wondered if she'd come to the session stoned.

"Miss Borlyn, there was a white man and a black man in the scenes of interest," he said firmly, deliberately reversing the order of their mention. "There were no women involved after the fight started, and there were no Indians in the film at all!"

Her face took on a stubborn set. "This is part of the experiment, right? Convince me I didn't see what I saw? Well, maybe some people, but not me. I know what I saw!"

In no way had Elliot anticipated any problems of this sort. He wondered if the girl could be psychotic. "Tell me what you saw, Miss Borlyn," he asked, resting his pen on the pad in such a way as to indicate clearly that he didn't mean to write anything. He'd already decided to discard her data.

"Well," she said, her eyes moving up and to the left, "it was a scene outdoors somewhere, and there was this temple. A woman—a white woman, that is—Spanish, I think, but I don't know why—was there. She lay down on a big rock, and this Indian stabbed her with a glass knife." Elliot didn't say a thing for a moment, and the girl didn't look at him. Then, without warning, she unbuttoned her blouse. She wore no bra, and she pulled the material aside to expose her left breast completely. "Right there," she said, pointing to a spot just inside and below her left nipple. Calmly, she tucked herself in and buttoned the garment back up. Only then did she look at him again. "You see?" she asked. "I know what I saw!"

Elliot was dazed, did not quite know what to do. "Uh—Miss Borlyn—" he said lamely.

She glared at him now. "What is the problem?" she asked. "I mean, I have to go to another class, all right?"

"Yes, yes," he said. "But—but—uh, look—I'll give you a note if necessary. Let's go in and see it again, okay?"

She looked disgusted. "I guess that's cool."

Together, they went back to the projection room, where Elliot told the grad assistant to rewind the last loop and show it again. He wasn't sure exactly why he was doing this; and as the film came up, he couldn't quite believe what he was seeing. The fight film, which he'd watched being made, began with an integrated party scene, out of which the fight developed. All the action took place in what was intended to look like the interior of a house. But on the screen was a view of the streets of a city, an intersection where a profusion of one-way signs sprouted, pointing every which way. There were no people in sight at all.

"You see?" the girl said, pointing. "The Indian, the Spanish woman?"

Elliot turned his head and stared at her, became aware that the graduate student, Bill, was doing the same.

"What are you talking about?" Bill asked. "That's a party, black people and white—"

Elliot's head swiveled around to stare at Bill, then back to the screen. "Is that really what you see?" he whispered, watching the traffic light over the intersection change.

"Dr. Collins?" Bill asked. "What's—"

"You see? You see?" cried the girl beside him. "He stabbed her, see? But why is she smiling? Look, he's tearing out her heart—"

On the screen, as Elliot was seeing it, a person finally walked into view. She stood on the street corner and looked directly into the camera, which zoomed in for a close-up. Then she cracked up, laughing merrily. At that point, Elliot could see the street sign over her head—Cabrini Boulevard.

He knew that street name well, he told himself, as he stared at Nikki's image on the film.

Elliot spent the remainder of the day virtually hiding in his office, brooding over the incident with the filmstrip. He didn't know about the student, and he was inclined to let her deal with her own problems. But for himself, he was seriously concerned with the state of his mental health. As near as he could judge it—and it was hard to assess one's own sanity—he had dealt with his obsession with Nikki only by substituting Eileen for her. And so, he told himself, it had been bubbling around down in the bottom of his mind—at all levels he was aware of the similarities between Eileen and the Nikki of the pictures, but at no level did he confuse the two—and it had erupted as a full-blown psychotic hallucination. Once again he considered seeing a therapist himself. But he had tried it once, for a brief time, and the results had been disappointing. There was no doubt in his mind that he needed someone to talk to about this, though. Bill Stein had been no help. He had just laughed the whole thing off, sure that Elliot and the student had cooked up a joke. Taking his phone book out of his desk, he looked up the numbers of several psychiatrists and clinical psychologists; but in the end it was Eileen he called.

Half an hour later, she was sitting on the couch in his office, stroking his hair. Briefly, he explained to her about the pictures of Nikki, the enigmatic notes and letters. He left out the dream, and the hallucination at the party; but he did fully describe the events that took place at the experimental session.

"Well," she said when he finished, "somebody knows a bit about the Aztec sacrifices, I can say that. Either you or the student."

"Aztec?"

"Yes, don't you see? That was what she was describing. Classic. Even the spot where she said the woman was stabbed."

In spite of his mental state, he managed to grin. "You're reaching a little, aren't you? I mean, every time somebody is stabbed it doesn't imply a connection with the Aztecs—"

"It is, I tell you," she said, shaking her head vigorously. "It all fits. Lying over the stone, tearing out the heart, the victim not resisting—the Indians believed in a divine mission, you know. They allowed themselves to be killed for their gods."

"It still seems to me you try to associate everything with those cultures! Besides, the girl clearly said the woman was Spanish, not an Indian."

"Yes, well, I'll admit that doesn't work very well. The Aztecs did sacrifice some Spaniards—especially war captives during the siege of Tenochtitlán—but I very much doubt that any of them were willing!"

"And anyway, as I understand it, the Aztec only sacrificed men—"

"Now, that just isn't true. For the most part, they sacrificed men to the male gods, women to the goddesses. With a few exceptions, of course. Like when temples were dedicated, they killed huge numbers of war captives, both the male soldiers and women civilians taken in the conquered villages. And women were sacrificed in the ceremonies honoring Mixcoatl, the god of the hunt, and—"

As she always did when discussing this subject, she droned on and on, to the point where Elliot no longer really heard what she was saying. He waited, her voice just background noise, until she finished her discourse. The fact was, he himself doubted that the imagery in the hallucinations had anything to do with the Aztecs. As he'd told Melissa when trying to interpret her dream, it was doubtless some personal symbol. Of the student's, or of his own. Very peculiar, to say the least. Both of them having hallucinations at the same time. But he supposed it wasn't out of the question. At least somewhat satisfied with that, he shifted his attention back to the girl's monologue; if he was hearing her right, she was trying to make a point he didn't want to let pass unchallenged.

"You know, Eileen, it almost sounds like you're trying to defend their sacrificial rites!" he said, interrupting her.

She shrugged. "It's just that the rites were a part, an important part, of their overall system of beliefs. A lot of people want to say they were some kind of aberration; I just don't believe it."

"If you're right, they had a damn barbaric belief system!"

"Maybe. By our standards, certainly. But still, the rites could have a certain beauty—"

"Beauty!"

"Yes. As in the sacrifice of the god Tezcatlipoca—"

"You mean sacrifice to the god."

"No. Many of the sacrifices were sacrifices of the gods. A chosen person stood in the god's place, and when he—or she—died, that person was believed to be the god. Remember, the gods had all sacrificed themselves to the creation of the Fifth World, the one we still live in."

"I get it. I guess. Anyway—about this particular god—"

"Tezcatlipoca, yes. His—image, is the best word—was treated as a king, taught to play the flute, given four beautiful women as consorts. Four around one in the center is a sacred pattern, you see. When the time came, he went to the altar willingly. He said his good-byes to his women, and broke his flutes on the steps of the pyramid as he went up. Up to the top, where they cut his heart out. To strengthen the god, you see, to strengthen Tezcatlipoca. Tezcatlipoca—and all the others—had to be strong for the earth and the sun to survive. And by extension, for mankind to survive. So he wouldn't have resisted, he'd have known it was necessary, that he was doing something beautiful, giving his life for his people. We honor people who do that, don't we? Like someone who tries to save children from drowning, drowns himself in the process."

"The difference is," Elliot said dryly, "is that we don't kill a man who survives a rescue!"

"That isn't the point and you know it!"

He shrugged. "So this god you're talking about—was he supposed to be good or evil?"

"When you're talking about the Aztec pantheon, those words just don't apply. Each one of them can act in ways we'd call good or evil, depending on the circumstances; I suppose you could call them amoral. But they have a stake in keeping the world going, so that makes them—shall we say—honorable, at least. Like I said, they gave their lives to create this world. That makes them good, doesn't it?"

"I suppose. I'm just used to thinking in terms of the good gods versus the evil demons."

She shook her head vigorously. "It just doesn't apply. Oh, maybe there was one—one they considered to be completely maleficent."

"Who was that?"

"She was called Tzitzimitl. They thought of her as a celestial demon, a creature from the stars; at one time she commanded a whole army of shape-shifting monstrosities that the Indians called Tzitzimeme, whose natural forms were always spiderlike or crablike in some way. For centuries they ravaged the earth, until finally Tzitzimitl was killed by the Four Brothers—Quetzalcoatl, Tezcatlipoca, Xipe Totec, and either Tlaloc or Huitzilopochtli, depending on whose legend you read. Her demon warriors were then imprisoned and controlled by spells cast by the sorceress Tlazolteotl, the goddess of sexual passions. According to the legends, they still are. But it's kind of funny when you think of how Tzitzimitl was viewed by the Aztecs. At a glance, you might think she was wholly good!''

''How's that?''

''She was a goddess of peace!''

''Peace?''

''Yes. But they recognized that true peace only comes about through stillness—through a lack of any movement. They called movement *ollin*, thought it was what made the world, kept it going. It fits with modern physics, you know—no movement, absolute zero. Entropy.''

''Maybe a little too much peace!''

''That's the way they saw it. Anyway, Tzitzimitl was destroyed and her warriors imprisoned, though sometimes she can reach people through their minds, especially through dreams. And it's said that she can occasionally release a demon from Tlazolteotl's spell, for a while at least.''

''I'm glad that's just mythology!''

Again Eileen shrugged. ''Maybe,'' she said enigmatically. Then she looked at him seriously. ''Anyway, tell me more about your vision, or whatever it was.''

''All I know,'' he told her, ''is that it was terribly God-damn real. And very disturbing.''

''Elliot,'' she said, ''you're the psychologist, you know. Why don't you turn this around? Assume that someone else— say me, for the sake of argument—came to you with a story like this. What would you tell them?''

''I'm not a clinician—''

''Beside the point. All you psych types love to analyze people. Even I know that.''

He considered that approach, thought about it for a moment. ''I think I'd tell them they dropped some bad acid!'' he said jokingly.

''Get serious. It's bothering you, it needs to be dealt with.''

"Well," he said thoughtfully, "I'd get them to analyze it like it was a dream. Break down the symbols."

"All right. Like what?"

"Well, I can't count what that girl saw, because she said it, not me. So all the stuff you said might be Aztec is out. And you know, I don't have much. Just Nikki, Cabrini Boulevard in New York—and that isn't my symbol, that's the address on my dad's letter—a whole swarm of one-way signs, and the red robe I always see her wearing." He caught himself on the last, it implied more than he'd told her. But she didn't seem to pick it up.

"So really only those three things. Now what?"

He shrugged rather helplessly. "Well, I guess that Nikki— since I first saw her photo when I was just pre-adolescent— maybe she represents, I don't know, primary sexuality? The red robe would fit; red as a sensual color, like a red-light district, scarlet woman. And it's always falling open in front, emphasizing that." This was, he told himself, working. It was all making perfect sense. Odd that he hadn't thought of it himself! With increasing confidence, he went on constructing his theory. "Now the one-way signs that point every direction. That could symbolize life directions, probably with respect to women, sex. A lot of ways to go, all seem like the only way at the time. Yes, that's it! The whole thing undoubtedly stems from an anxiety of mine that I have only one way to go, when in fact I probably have too many choices for my own comfort! So Nikki is just a symbol for my feeling that there is one and only one woman for me, and I have to find the one way! Damn, it's so simple!"

"And you said I reminded you of Nikki in ways," Eileen said quietly. In his enthusiastic analysis, he'd almost forgotten she was there. He started to blurt out a yes, but a faint warning bell gave him pause.

"Only in that you both have very dark hair and eyes—"

She stood up, straightened her clothes. "Did you know you called me Nikki a couple of times when we were making love?" she asked coolly. He ground his teeth; she had heard, after all.

"I did?" he asked ingenuously.

"You did. And I pretty much understand now." She walked to the door. "I'm glad you worked that out, Elliot," she said, only the tiniest crack in her voice audible. "I can live with being the Other Woman,'' she told him. ''But I can't be a substitute for somebody unavailable. I'm sorry, Elliot. I won't be seeing you like this anymore.''

''Now, wait, Eileen,'' he started. He was feeling a cold sense of loss, somewhere down in his abdomen.

''No, Elliot. I'm still your friend, but—'' Her voice cracked a little more, and she headed for the door. ''Good-bye, Elliot,'' she said quickly, and hurried out. He thought he heard sobs from the hall, but by the time he got to the door, she was gone.

Feeling absolutely rotten, he slumped back into his chair. It wasn't until then that he realized he'd been considering the possibility of leaving Melissa and asking Eileen to move in with him.

''Goddamn it, Nikki,'' he said to the door. Realizing his words, he slapped himself violently on the side of the head.

10

Greenwich Village

Just after nightfall, the man with the silver ring was back out on the streets. The shy and timorous person who had run away from the religious commune was almost completely gone; his place had been taken by a new man, a man who was in his own eyes self-confident and capable. A man who, he told himself as he watched the streetlamps come on, would no longer be contented with the dregs of the female gender, no longer be sneered at by attractive women. He thought he had already noticed a change in people's attitude toward him. More respectful. That, he thought, was the way it should be.

He stopped, folded his arms, and leaned against a lamppost, surveying his surroundings, reveling in his newfound strengths. His eyes lit on a girl crossing the street, a real beauty. She passed quite close to him, and he gave her what he thought was a sexy look; she barely glanced at him and went on.

"Bitch," he said under his breath. Didn't know how close she was to an ultimate experience, he thought. He had now killed three women—all prostitutes—and he believed that he understood a lot better what was happening. True, the first one had been very awkward, and the second not much better. But the third—now that, in his opinion, had been clean. The woman had not known it was coming until his hands closed around her neck, and she'd been so surprised she'd more or less just lain there and died. All of them—especially the third—had looked to him like women in orgasm as they'd died by his hands, and he had come to believe that they were. At first, his mission had been his own gratification; he'd gone after the second woman with that specifically in mind. But after she was dead and he'd had intercourse with the corpse, he'd been ripped by a massive wave of guilt. The first one he had justified to himself by saying it had not been intentional; such reasoning wouldn't work for the second. He had paid her knowing he'd take back his money after she was dead, walked to the room with her knowing she'd never leave it alive. All fully planned in advance. And the guilt had been so bad afterward he'd considered committing suicide, or turning himself in to the police. But he had gotten through the night. Until dawn he'd been by his bedside praying—nothing in his experience in the commune had diminished his faith in God— and it had helped him. By morning he was feeling better, and he promised himself and God he'd kill no more women. But by nightfall he was hungry again and prowling the street. That had been a bad night; the conflict between his desire to kill and his Holy Promise were shredding him. Inside a stall in a subway restroom, he prayed for help and guidance. And he'd gotten it, as he saw it. In a flash he saw the answer— though it took hours for him to fully articulate it. Those hours he wandered the street, talking to himself and out loud, drawing a few stares from passersby. But he had his solution. He thought that God had revealed to him that women who prostituted themselves—women he felt were evil anyway— did so because they'd never had a satisfactory sexual experience themselves. And though most women could not recognize it by looking at him—a blindness induced by Satanic forces, he had no doubt—only he was capable of giving them this ultimately satisfying experience. That's why they had orgasms as they died. It was all so very simple: they had to die, since nothing in their lives would mean anything anymore. And they all died satisfied. So, far from being a monster out only for hedonistic purposes, he was actually doing these women a service. It was his duty to them and to God to bring his precious service to as many of these pitiful creatures as possible. If a particular fact did not fit into this construct very well—such as the fact that he only had sex with them after they were already dead—he found he was able to just ignore it. God works in mysterious ways, he told himself; maybe they did live on in some mystical way until he'd had his climax. He didn't know, and he didn't worry about it very much. He had purpose in his life again, and it was enough for him. The spasms of guilt no longer bothered him.

Still leaning on the post, he took out the device he'd spent the afternoon making and looked at it. It was just brilliant, he told himself, a work of genius. His three victims had all been strangled by his hands, and he had numerous scratches—some of which had become infected—as a result of the women clawing at them. That, he had to stop; it was a problem. So he'd invented the solution—simple and elegant. It consisted of a leather strap sized and sewn to fit exactly around the middle of his right hand; he'd had it made to his specifications at a leather shop. On each edge, he'd had them sew a border of thick stitches, big enough to form a substantial ridge. After he'd taken it back to his room, he'd carefully cut three slits in it, each about a half-inch deep. Then he'd purchased a set of guitar strings, the steel type with the grooved ring at one end. The free end of the string was slipped through the ring, forming a noose; then the wire was wrapped around the leather, the end finally going down in one notch and back up from another. He'd practiced with it for hours, slipping the noose over head-sized objects and jerking it tight. Worked perfectly. The only problem was keeping his hand at the right angle, so that the string didn't slip off the leather; it had to be maintained parallel to the neck of the victim. But that he felt he would master with practice. Until he was ready to use it, he could keep the string wrapped completely around the leather band, unfurling it as needed.

The third notch was used to hold the end of the loop. Guitar strings were springy, wanted to straighten out if not restrained.

Smiling, he slipped it onto his hand, then back off again, dropping it back into his pocket. In only a few short hours, he'd become very adept at getting it on; he could slide his hand into his pocket and come up with it almost instantly, and only a little fumbling was required if he happened not to be wearing the pants. Which, he planned to be the case; he preferred for the ultimate act to occur after both parties had removed all their clothes. All he had to do, he thought, was be sure his pants were within reach at all times. He kept playing with it, scanning the streets. An hour he'd been looking, and he hadn't seen a hooker yet. And he was most eager to try his invention out.

Across the street from where he was standing, a car—Cadillac—pulled up to the curb and discharged a passenger. His mouth dropped open slightly; this was a hooker, he was sure. That is, if the uniform meant anything—the heavy makeup, spike heels, microscopic red skirt over black net stockings. But she was different from the usual run of street whores in the Village. She was a Hollywood-type beauty, with a mane of finely teased blond hair. He had to force himself to remain under control, not run up to her wildly. But he crossed the street quickly as she started to walk down the sidewalk, waving at the Caddy as it pulled away.

He managed to reach the curb just as she was passing. "Excuse me," he said politely. "Are you—ah—working?"

She stopped and looked him up and down. "I'm not a streetwalker," she said frostily.

"I can appreciate that," he told her, trying to keep her talking. "But—uh—I just thought, well—I have some money, and if you do—ah—work, well—"

Her appraisal grew a little more frank. "How much money are we talking about?" she asked, looking at his new, fairly expensive clothes. He'd managed to wangle a good chunk of money from his father with a story about a job that required a fee to an employment agency, and he believed that dressing well would open doors for him that might be closed to ragged jeans. He was hoping now that he had been right.

"Ah—seventy-five dollars?" he asked tentatively.

Her eyes lost interest. "I have to go," she told her. "I

have only a couple of hours off, and there's a band I wanted to hear down here—''

Uptown girl, he thought. Whore, yes—probably a call girl, working expensive hotels and the like. Slumming in the Village. "A hundred?" he persisted.

She didn't move away. "That's my usual," she said. "But like I say, I'm taking time off—''

"Hundred and fifty?"

Interest again. "So what do you want?" she asked. "Be specific. That way, I'll know you aren't a cop."

"Uh—laid, maybe blow-job—''

She nodded. "How much again?"

"Hundred and fifty—''

Finally she grinned. "If I was undercover, you'd be busted, sucker. Look, I don't usually do things this way, but I'll make an exception. I really wanna see this show, dig? Then I'll go back to my place." She stopped talking, scribbled an address. "You got cab fare besides the one-fifty?" she asked.

"Uh—I don't think so—''

She laughed. "Shootin' the wad, eh? As they say! Okay, you deduct the cab fare from the one-fifty. Don't try and burn me. I know how much it is. You get back best way you can. Be there in two and a half hours, dig?"

"Yeah, all right," he said. She nodded again, went off down the street. He just stood for a while, looking at the uptown address and wondering if this was a good idea. But in the end, he knew he'd be unable to resist.

At the appointed time, he found himself in front of a hotel in the east Fifties. The doorman gave him no problem, though he was nervous about being seen; he felt the man had hardly looked at him. Inside, he took the elevator to the sixth floor, found number 671, as specified by the note. His breath came in short gasps as he waited for an answer, wondering if perhaps she'd given him a dummy address. But as soon as she opened it, he relaxed. She gave him a totally phony smile, invited him in.

"Let's get these financial matters out of the way first, okay, honey?" she purred, stroking his chest. "Then we won't have to worry about it later."

He'd heard this before, and he just smiled and nodded, took out his wallet and gave her all the bills he had. She riffled through it, nodded. He watched as she put it in the top drawer of her dresser; he certainly wanted to retrieve it later.

"My name's Candy," she told him. "What's yours?"

Just in case, he thought. Just in case something goes wrong, don't tell her your real name. "John," he said smoothly. "John—uh—Davis."

"Glad to know you, John Davis. Want a drink?"

He was way out of the habit for that. "No, thanks," he told her. She turned to get one for herself, and his hands caught her from behind. Reaching around, he fondled her breasts roughly.

"Eager, aren't you?" she asked, carelessly feeling his torso with her hands. "Why don't we get more comfortable?" Did she think she was being clever, he wondered, with all these cliches?

She pulled away from him, turned on the stereo, and began a slow, sensuous dance. She was not a great dancer by any stretch of the imagination, and her lack of enthusiasm didn't make it any better. But her body, revealed as she stripped down, was certainly good enough to make up for it. As she undressed, he took his clothes off too, leaving his pants for last; he did not remove them until they were near the bed. When he did, he took his underwear along in one movement, tossing everything onto the bed within easy reach. Then he sat down on the edge of it, and she came close to him.

For a few seconds he kissed and roughly handled her breasts again. "How about a little head?" he asked bluntly.

She nodded, knelt in front of him. As her head dipped between his thighs, he fumbled with his pants pocket.

"Candy?" he said a moment later.

"Yes?" she responded, raising her head to look at him. As soon as she did, he dropped the wire noose over her head. "What—?" she began, glancing down. He didn't let her finish. Keeping the back of his hand facing her neck, he jerked backward. Immediately her bewildered expression changed to one of terror. As he had expected, her hands flew to her throat, to where the slender string was cutting off her air. He didn't try to prevent her body from flailing around; at the moment, it wasn't interesting to him. His eyes were fixed, unblinking, on her face. He had to watch her orgasm, that's what he was here for. He could see a little blood as the string cut into her skin somewhat; but all in all, it went perfectly for him. There was little noise except for a few thuds from her feet on the floor, no screams at all. Even after she stopped moving, he kept the pressure on for quite a while. Had to be sure. Then he carefully unwound the string, lifted her onto the bed, and completed his ritual.

Later, in the taxi headed back to the Village, he had an idea. From now on, he'd leave the string with the body. Kind of as a signature. He supposed that perhaps the newspapers would give him a nickname of some sort; he was curious to see what it might be. Besides, washing blood off a guitar string was a real pain.

11

After Eileen left, Elliot had remained in his office for some time, mostly just sitting and staring at the surface of his desk. He wished that he'd had a joint with him; although he made it a rule never to smoke marijuana in his office, he would have violated that tonight if he'd had any. It had been some time since he'd felt quite as badly as this. Not only because Eileen had broken the affair off, but also because he was aware of how unfairly he'd been treating both her and Melissa; neither of them deserved it. He considered coming clean with Melissa, telling her the whole thing. But that, he decided, was a poor idea, especially where his self-interest was concerned. What if Melissa blew up and walked out on him? Then he'd be left with no one. Thinking about Melissa leaving reminded him of his doubts about her motivations, and again he wondered if she'd be around long after her graduation. He still wasn't sure of her. That in turn led him to consider Eileen's purpose in becoming involved with him, and he drew a blank there. Maybe the women just liked him, he told himself. But the pond of self-pity he was wallowing in precluded any acceptance of that idea.

A little after ten o'clock he dragged himself out of his office and started wandering across the campus in the general direction of his apartment. On the campus itself, and in the vicinity of Franklin Street, there were many people around; it was a warm and pleasant evening. Several students spoke to Elliot as he walked, but he only noticed a few; he was too preoccupied.

He did notice, however, that after he left the business district and entered the residential areas, he saw virtually no one. That was unusual, but not unheard of, and the only reason it drew his attention at all was because the neighborhood was so quiet and still. He liked the peacefulness; it brought him up a little from the black depression he'd sunken into. Strolling along, he was able to observe the mixture of moonlight and streetlight on the trees and plants that grew densely in the yards of the houses. He let his pace slow even more, and simultaneously let his mind wander away from his problems to the beauty of nature, something he'd always appreciated but never seemed to be able to take sufficient time with.

There was some movement low in the bushes, and he peered into them. A cat, he assumed, or perhaps a small dog. He knelt down. "Kitty, kitty?" he called lightly. "Or doggie, as the case may be?"

There was no response. The bushes were quiet, but he had a distinct sense that something was watching him. Attempting to gain its trust—whatever it was—he extended his hand, held it still. But nothing came out to sniff at it, as cats and dogs often do. For a few seconds he remained motionless, hoping the creature would emerge. When it didn't, he stood up and started to stroll on. But as soon as he'd turned his back, there was a rustle in the vegetation. He turned around again, just as it stopped, and saw the leaves moving gently. Not just in one spot, but over a track some ten feet long. That he couldn't figure out.

"Damn fast cat," he said aloud. But he found that he was getting a little nervous and chided himself for it. Deciding enough was enough, he started to walk on, a little faster than before.

The slight rustling followed him, parallel to his path. It was a soft sound, so small that had there been any voices, any traffic, he wouldn't have noticed it at all. But now he was very aware of it. He slowed down; so did it. Sped up—it did too. Always staying right beside him, out of sight in the shrubbery.

"Now we'll see," he told himself as he came to the corner. No bushes here; it was either come out in the open or give up the chase. By now he was interested to see what sort of animal this was, though he was pretty sure it was a dog. This was rather uncatlike behavior. As he stepped into the street, the rustling stopped. His head turned, he walked across, watching the bushes carefully. He was a little disappointed; evidently whatever it was had given up the chase, and he hadn't gotten to see it. Shrugging, he walked on to the other side. Just as he turned his head back, there was a little scraping sound, like a tire being dragged over the pavement. He spun, looked, and caught only a glimpse of an immense dark shadow, long and slender, that rocketed across the opening. Then the rustling was again in the bushes right beside him.

Staring down at the bushes, he felt the hairs on his neck move slightly. Now he could see something. A flickering shadow, caught in a small pool of light from the streetlamp. It appeared to be cast by something a couple of feet long, slender, moving back and forth very rapidly. He couldn't understand what it might be. Then it slowed for an instant, fully extended. The tips spread, and he realized it looked like a snake's tongue. Two feet long? he asked himself, feeling cold in the pit of his stomach. Slowly, he let his eyes rise toward the light source, telling himself that shadows can be deceptive, the source can be of a totally different size. Maybe the projection of a garter snake's tongue? But he couldn't see it. All he saw were two spots of light maybe a yard apart. He couldn't figure out what they might be, stepped to the side a little to get a different view, and saw a dark vertical ellipse in each one move to follow him. Eyes, he told himself, stunned. Eyes. Snake eyes. He could hardly visualize the snake they must be attached to.

His hands irrationally extended in front of himself protectively, he began to back away. When he came to the edge of the curb, his heel caught it, and he fell clumsily into the street. He was in such a state of shock that he couldn't even get up immediately. Glancing around, looking for a possible source of help, he could see that there was not a soul in sight, nor any evidence of anyone. It was as if all the people had disappeared from the earth; even the nearby houses were darkened. His fear mounting steadily, he felt totally alone and vulnerable to whatever was lurking in the bushes.

His paralysis broke, and he scrambled to his feet, backed across the street. The eyes moved a little, and he could no longer see them. His stomach churned, expecting to see it emerge from the shrubbery, come for him. But there was nothing. If anything, that made it worse.

"Don't run," he told himself frantically. "Don't run. That'll only make it worse." Clenching his hands together, he tried to get hold of himself. "There just cannot be a giant snake in the shrubbery," he said aloud. "It isn't possible, it isn't there. You saw something else, made a mistake—"

Still talking to himself, he started off in the direction of his apartment. Instantly there was movement in the bushes, the scraping sound again. A glimpse of a massive black shadow, and now the bushes were moving again, on his side of the street! All his control disappeared. He ran, faster than he had in years, the sound of his heart louder than the slap of his Hush Puppies on the sidewalk. Out of the corner of his eye, he saw that the shadowy shape in the bushes was effortlessly maintaining the pace, staying right beside him. He was sobbing from terror, a pain ripping at his side, and his legs began to feel like they were made of lead. But he kept running, pumping away madly. He could not have stopped if he wanted to.

Finally, his apartment came into view, the friendly light beside the front door beckoning to him. He crossed the street, saw the shadow cross behind him, and ran for the door. His red VW was between him and the shape as he streaked up the walk; he turned his head and looked, just as he got to the door.

And for the first time, he could see it clearly.

A mouth six feet across was open wide, the yellow eyes visible above it. He could see all the details in that stark instant; the golden scales, the tongue just barely extended from the fleshy sheath on the floor of the mouth, the two eighteen-inch fangs erect, pushing out of soft pink sacs. Coming straight at him. Through the VW. He could see the car through it. Right on top of him now. He screamed, closed his eyes, and felt a rush of hot dry wind, knocking him off his feet. Folded up on the walk, he kept his eyes tightly closed and howled; that was how a stricken Melissa found him.

He opened his eyes and looked up at her. He was lying on

the couch; obviously she'd managed to get him inside somehow. And apparently, she'd been talking to him for some time.

"I wish you'd try to make sense!" she was saying as she wiped his face with a cold cloth. "What did you take?"

"Take?" he asked stupidly.

"Take, as in drug? Whatever it is, it's sure sent you off on a bummer!"

"I didn't take any drugs," he mumbled. "What's happening?"

"That's what I'm trying to find out! El, you find somebody curled up on their front walk screaming, usually they're on a bum trip—"

"Didn't take any drugs," he repeated. Then he stopped, thought about it. "None that I know about, anyhow."

"You mean somebody slipped you something?"

He pulled himself to a sitting position. He didn't really feel bad, no headache or anything. Only his legs hurt, from all the running. "I don't see how," he said after a pause. "I didn't even eat dinner, just had coffee. From a machine, by myself."

"Not with Eileen?" she asked. He didn't see her bite her lip after she'd said it.

"No, she'd already left," he said without thinking. Then what she'd asked hit him, and he turned his face up to stare at her. "You know about Eileen?" he blurted carelessly, not yet enough in control to try to bluff through.

"We've talked. Several times," she said, not looking at him.

He continued to stare at her, astounded. All these weeks he'd been priding himself on putting something over on these women. And all the time, they'd been getting together and talking about him. It was so unbelievable to him he forgot all about the snake. "You've talked?" he asked weakly. "But how—"

"It isn't very hard to find out where a professor lives, Elliot. She came by. I didn't believe her at first, but—anyway, then I was mad. I was going to leave, but she talked me out of it. She said there was something weird about your relationship with her, and she didn't know what it was. She convinced me to wait, said sooner or later you'd make a choice. But it's been a bummer for me, El. I mean, I try to be liberated and all that, but maybe I'm just not that good. I don't know. I thought—well—I don't know what I thought. That I could be everything for you, I guess. Real idealistic. Anyway, I'm kind of glad it's out in the open."

"It's over, too. Between me and Eileen."

"Your choice?"

"Hers."

"Oh." She looked sad, stared off toward the kitchen for some reason. "You should have told me, Elliot," she said after a while.

"I know. There's no excuse."

"No, none."

"Look, Melissa—"

"Let's not talk about it anymore right now, okay?" she asked, looking back at him; her eyes were wet, her nose a little red.

"But I need to know—"

"Well, I don't know!" she yelled suddenly, jumping to her feet. "What do you want from me, Elliot? Guarantees? You've left me hanging on a thread for weeks, you son of a bitch! And now you get your choice made for you, and you want a guarantee? Of what? That I'll be available to warm your bed? Well, I don't know! I just don't know!"

He was not so far out of it that he didn't know when it was prudent to keep his mouth shut. He did, looking as contrite as he could manage, hoping the storm would pass. Melissa continued to yell at him for a while, waving her arms and occasionally stamping her foot. Most of it amounted to name-calling. There was nothing he could do but endure.

At last she calmed down, sat in the chair and sobbed for a while, her shoulders heaving. That too passed, and she was under control when she spoke again. "You still haven't told me what the hell happened to you tonight," she said finally, her voice more than a little cold.

That he didn't know how to talk about. Certainly it was not a good time to mention Nikki, or tell her about the experiment. "I thought," he said carefully, "that I was being chased by a monster. A giant snake."

She looked at his face for a long time. "You remember my dream?" she asked him.

"The one about the feathered white snake? Yes. But this snake didn't have feathers, and it wasn't white."

"Was it golden brown?"

"Uh—yeah, I guess it was."

"I've had that same dream three times more," Melissa told him. "I didn't mention it because I thought Eileen was the snake. Maybe the snake's in your head, Elliot. You believe in telepathy?"

He shook his head. "I've never seen good solid evidence for telepathy. I've read a lot of Rhine's stuff, and it looks weak to me. Besides, this snake sure as hell wasn't something I'd want to get close to! I was running like a madman!"

"I have a feeling that's good. You should run from it, Elliot. Stay away from it."

"I'll do my damndest! But you've got to be right about it being in my head, Melissa. I mean, it's ridiculous—at the end I saw it come through the car, and it wasn't even completely material! I'd have to call the whole thing a psychotic episode. I think I'd better see somebody."

"Maybe so. But if the somebody says get close to it, get over your fear—don't you listen. You stay away."

"But—"

"Stay away from it, Elliot. You may not believe in things like psychic dreams, but I do, and I'm sure. If you get close to it—and I feel that it does exist, somewhere, somehow, but maybe not here and now—it'll kill you, Elliot. It'll kill you, and there'll be nothing you can do about it!"

12

After a very poor night's sleep, Elliot awoke the next morning to face a gray, dreary day. He and Melissa had slept in the same bed, but for the first time since they'd been living together she wore a nightgown the whole night. And she slept on the far side of the bed, carefully avoiding touching him with her body. All in all, a very stiff and unpleasant evening. And it was continuing; she refused to get up with him, saying her first class was not until ten and she was going to sleep in. He didn't argue. The limited time he had that morning was not the time to try to iron their problems out.

And it only got worse. By the time he was ready to leave, it was pouring rain. The sidewalk he'd been lying on the previous night was now a shallow pool. He decided to take his car rather than walk in, and he managed to stay relatively dry as he got into the little vehicle. He then had trouble starting it, and his problems continued when he was unable to find a parking place anywhere near his office. Forced into a lot halfway across campus, he swore at the parking system as he trudged along in the rain; by the time he reached his destination, his pants were wet to the knees, his hair was wet and hanging in strings, and he was in more than a foul mood. He didn't bother to go to his office but went directly to his morning class. Many of his students were as bedraggled as he was, and it ended up being pretty much wasted time; he was not able to concentrate well, and the students were no help—as if they ever were, he snarled to himself cynically. It didn't seem like anyone was interested in learning these days; Eileen had been the first serious student he'd met in some time. The thought that his own professors might have said the same of him eight years ago crossed his mind, but he rejected it.

When the long hour finally ended, he went to his office and sat behind his desk, his head in his hands. Everything was such a mess; it was as if his wet clothes, the puddles of muddy water on the floor, fitted right in. Eileen gone, Melissa probably going, and he was going crazy. He raised his eyes, looked at the telephone. Who to call, though? Melissa, no. Not time to try to talk to her yet. Eileen? Maybe. A shrink, set up an appointment? That was probably the best idea of all.

With a long sigh, he picked up the phone and dialed. After passing through a receptionist and a nurse, he got to a friend of his, Dr. Charlie Gordon.

"Hey, Elliot, whatcha doin'?" Gordon answered in a jovial tone. Gordon had a weight problem, and his manner was always jovial. It had always seemed to Elliot that it was a little too much, a little phony.

"Problems, Charlie," he told the man. He briefly explained without going into detail, saying only that he was obsessional and having hallucinations.

"Drug flashbacks, ya think?" the psychiatrist asked bluntly. Elliot would have preferred he not broadcast such information like that. But he persevered.

"I think there's more to it than that," he insisted.

"Well, there's someone over here"—meaning, as Elliot knew, Orange County Mental Health Clinic—"that might be able ta fix ya up. I can set up a time now, if ya wanna."

"Sure, Charlie. That'd be good, soon as possible."

"We can fitcha in today, if ya wanna."

"Today?" He was surprised; things didn't usually work like that. "Well, okay, why not? I have classes at eleven and two—"

"Works out. There's a free space at twelve-thirty. Good 'nuff?"

"Good enough. Who do I see?"

"Her name is Cecilia Nesbitt. I'll brief her, she'll be lookin' for ya."

He was a little taken aback. "A woman?" he said weakly.

"Gotta problem with it?" Charlie asked almost sharply.

"Oh, no—no. It's fine. I'll be there. Thanks, Charlie."

"Sure 'nuff," Gordon replied, the " 'nuff" fading as he hung up the phone. Feeling better at having at least initiated a possible solution, he was able to return to preparing for his next class. It went considerably better than the nine o'clock.

As it worked out, he was just a little late for the appointment; there'd been an accident in town, the traffic had been tied up. But Charlie Gordon had been good as his word, and Dr. Nesbitt—a clinical psychologist, it turned out—was waiting for him. He sat in an overstuffed chair in her office as they went through opening preliminaries. Cecilia—as she'd asked him to call her—was a little older than he was, a woman who might have been attractive if she hadn't made herself look so severe. Her brown hair was in a tight bun behind her head, and she wore heavy-rimmed glasses, through which she often peered owlishly. It was impossible to tell whether or not she had a good body, he thought, because of the oversized sacklike dress she wore. But her manner was friendly and open.

"Okay," she said when they'd finished the paperwork, "tell me about your problem."

He did, in concise form—but leaving out nothing that he could think of. It took about twenty minutes.

"Okay," she said when he'd fallen silent. "Okay. So. Uh—" She hesitated, looking over at him, and he returned her gaze. Seconds passed, and the silence went on. At last he began to get a little impatient; he knew these things usually started slow, but this was getting ridiculous. They looked like two statues, he sitting in the chair, and she sitting at her desk staring at him. "So tell me what happened when you were five," she said, her voice sounding quite different than it had previously.

"What?" he asked, bewildered.

"You said, in one of the dreams, the woman told you to remember what happened when you were five. What happened when you were five?"

Vaguely, he now remembered that Nikki had said something like that in the dream he'd had soon after his return from Illinois. But he'd forgotten all about it—it hadn't been included in his summary.

"How did you know about that?" he asked.

"You told me, of course."

"No, I didn't—"

"Yes, you did."

"I didn't!"

"You did! How else could I know?"

He fell silent; how indeed. He tried to compose his thoughts, consider what he himself had meant by putting that statement in his dream. He became aware that Cecilia was looking at him rather pugnaciously, and he wondered why. "I don't quite know myself," he said after a pause.

"All right," she told him, folding her hands in a classic gesture. "What can you remember from that time?"

"When I was five? Not a lot."

"What?" she demanded.

"What comes to mind," he said carefully, "are some talks with my dad. I remember some long talks that I didn't understand a word of at the time. And I guess I forgot most of them."

"How was your relationship with your father?"

"Oh, we were real close. Up until high school—then we started having some disagreements. Usual generation gap stuff. You know, the war and all."

"You were close to him, but you paid so little attention you forgot about those talks?" Cecilia asked, sounding at that moment remarkably like his mother. "Didn't you realize how important that was to him?"

He turned and looked at her with a startled expression. This certainly wasn't standard in therapy. "Uh, doctor—" he started.

She leaned farther forward onto her desk and transfixed him with the owl look. "Think, Elliot!" she demanded, cutting him off.

"Uh—sure, all right, be cool, okay?" he responded. "Let me think! It's been a while since I was five!" He turned away from her stare, closed his eyes and tried to remember. One day in particular was coming back to him, by bits and pieces. "The first one—first one that comes to mind, anyway—Dad and I were out somewhere, in the woods maybe. Yeah, or a park—they look the same to a five-year-old. We were walking together. I remember it being fall—dead leaves all over— but hot. Like an Indian summer. I can still remember that sky, almost like a psychedelic blue. Can't say I saw one like it before or since; it made an impression. And Dad was talking about things. Jesus, I haven't thought about this for so long!

"I remember him asking me all kinds of things. What is this, what is that. Simple things, like a tree or a flower. I was always told I was more articulate than average for my age. I can remember feeling really proud. Everything he asked me about, I could give him an answer. I thought he was trying to stump me, and he couldn't. And I remember really enjoying the game.

"Finally he stopped in front of a big tree, and he said, What is it? I said, a tree. This is so clear; like I was seeing it now, like it happened just this morning. He nodded, and he said, Sure does look like a tree, all right. Anybody come along here and see this, they'd say it was a tree. I was grinning from ear to ear, but I don't know why I was so damn proud of identifying a tree. Just something in Daddy's attitude, like I'd done something wonderful. But then he said, For us, just for now, let's say this isn't a tree. Let's call it something else. I said something silly, like, let's call it a woobie. But he said, No, we're going to call it a—I can't recall—oh, yeah. Let's call it a dandelion. I said something like, okay, Daddy. We'll call it a dandelion. He went on and on. Isn't it a pretty yellow, look at the leaves down there at the bottom on the ground. I giggled; it seemed silly to me. But he said, Elliot, we've been calling it a dandelion, so that's what it is. You understand me? he asked. I said, Sure, Daddy—it's a dandelion. He said, If it's a dandelion we can step right over it, right? I laughed and said sure. He said—he said—'' Elliot broke off, realized he was sweating profusely. ''Uh—uh, Cecilia, I don't know if—''

''Go on!'' she commanded roughly. ''What did he say?''

''This can't be right—it's mixed up somehow—he said, I'll go first. And he did. He stepped over it. That has to be part of an old dream or something. I can remember seeing him step normally over an ordinary dandelion, and at the same time seeing his legs stretch out enormously as he stepped over a fifty-foot tree!''

''Fine, good. Then what?''

''Then he said, Now you. I said, Daddy, I can't. I remember yelling, You can't! How did you, Daddy? And he said, We made it a dandelion, remember? Nothing to it. You step over dandelions all the time. I was screaming and crying and scared, and he pushed and insisted. Finally I tried, I tried to see a dandelion and step over it. My foot was in the air, and then I knew it was a tree but I was already over it. I fell, from over the tree—fifty, sixty feet. I remember Daddy screaming, What have I done? Oh God, I killed him.'' He stopped, wiped at his face. ''That was when I broke my leg,'' he whispered. ''We told Mama I climbed the tree and fell. But I didn't climb it. Cecilia, the broken leg was real! Oh Jesus, I sure can remember that! That was the thing that happened when I was five, I broke my leg!'' His voice was rising steadily in both pitch and volume. ''But—but by the time I was ten or so I couldn't even understand how I'd done it! Only that it had something to do with a tree!'' He stopped for a minute, folded his arms around his chest. ''Daddy—Daddy didn't want to talk about it for a while. Didn't want to talk to me at all. God, that hurt me. I thought I'd failed him somehow. And I guess I did.''

''No,'' Cecilia told him firmly. ''You didn't fail him. He believed he failed you. He thought he could show you the *way* he knew, but he didn't realize that he didn't know enough himself to teach, only to do. He was scared to talk to you, scared he'd hurt you again by trying to push you.''

''Maybe so, but I was hurting so much. The leg didn't matter, but my daddy not talking to me, that was so painful—''

"Try and understand. He was scared. He was scared all his life, even though *she* had told him not to be."

The emotional weight of the moment of nostalgia began to fade off, and Elliot started to realize what sorts of things Cecilia was saying. "She?" he asked.

"The *snake,* of course," the psychologist responded.

Starting to get angry, Elliot turned in his chair. "Now, look," he told her firmly, "I'm surely willing to let you guide the sessions, but this is outrageous! There's no way you can speak for my dead father like this and—" He stopped, looking at Cecilia's face. Her eyes were pointed in his direction, but he could have sworn she saw nothing from them— they seemed utterly glazed. He waved his hand at her—no response. Then he got up from his chair, walked a few feet across the office. Her gaze was still fixed on where he was. He noticed her hands, arched over the desk as if she were clawing it. Her whole body was so stiff he felt if he picked her up and turned her sideways, nothing would move. "Cecilia?" he called gingerly.

Her head started to move in a series of short stiff jerks until her gaze was fixed on him again, and he was sure something was severely wrong. "The *snake,*" she said in a flat voice that didn't really sound like hers. "The snake will kill you forever if you stay here. She showed you she could, last night. Go. Away from Chapel Hill, away from North Carolina. You know where. Go while you still have time!" As she spoke, nothing moved but her mouth. He stepped to the side; her eyes stayed where they were.

"Cecilia, are you all right?" he asked her. Again his fear was rising as he watched the statuelike form of the woman.

Her eyes didn't move, but her head adjusted itself two jerks so that she seemed to be looking at him again. "You are not all right, Elliot Collins. Not as long as you stay here. You must go! You must go, find your destiny! It has already been decided!"

He wavered for a moment, really unsure of what he should do. Go get help seemed the logical alternative. He went to the door, stuck his head out and told the receptionist outside to get Charlie Gordon, that there was something wrong with Dr. Nesbitt. As the girl scurried off, he turned back to see Cecilia slowly topple from her chair, rolling across the desk and onto the floor. She struck a garbage can, knocking it over and sending a hail of wadded paper across her office. As he'd envisioned, her body remained in the same posture, rigid as if she'd been cast in marble. When she stopped rolling, she was on her bent back, her legs and arms stiffly in the air, rocking back and forth gently.

Just then, Charlie Gordon thrust his bulk through the door. "What's the—holy shit!" he cried, looking at Cecilia. Almost as if the sound of his voice was a cue, she went limp, her legs and arms sprawling on the floor, her head rolling to one side. "What the hell happened?" he asked Elliot.

"I don't know—we were talking, she went stiff—"

The fat man went to her, knelt beside her. Elliot looked over his shoulder, saw her eyes flutter and open. "What—" she asked, looking totally confused. "What happened?"

"That's what I asked!" Charlie growled.

"I passed out," she said wonderingly. "He—he was just starting to tell me his problem, and I don't remember anything else!"

"You don't remember us talking about when I was five?" Elliot asked sharply.

"Not now, Elliot," Charlie said, though Cecilia was shaking her head. "I think we should get you, Cecy old girl, over to the hospital!"

"No, Charlie," she said, struggling to get up. "I'm okay—I just—"

"We dunno what ya just," he said gruffly. "You're goin', and no arguments! Elliot, I'll call you. We'll set up something else, okay? Sorry."

Knowing he had been dismissed, he left; Charlie and the receptionist were enough to get Cecilia over to the hospital. But the whole experience had hardly helped. His mind was a jumble of confused ideas as he returned to campus and tried to prepare for his two o'clock class. It, too, was a disaster.

13

For the next two or three days, Elliot was careful to get home before sunset, and there were no incidents. If he went out at night, he drove; he felt he was being silly, but he was simply not comfortable walking around the neighborhood at night. The situation with Melissa seemed to be gradually getting better, at least in a way. After almost total silence and avoidance for two days, she'd resumed talking to him, if only about matters of mutual interest not pertaining to their relationship. And that night, they'd made love again; after going to bed and not touching for a while, she laid her hand on his hip. He responded instantly, rolling over to face her and taking her in his arms. She was as passionate as ever, but throughout she never said a word. What was worrying Elliot was that they weren't talking about it. He was sure that procrastination could only make matters worse.

His therapy at the center had come to a crashing halt before it had even started. Nobody involved thought it a good idea for him to try to proceed with Cecilia; for her part, she claimed to be unable to remember a thing about the session. Currently, Charlie told him, she was undergoing tests over at Memorial Hospital. The neurologists suspected some form of epilepsy but hadn't been able to demonstrate it on EEG. There was another therapist that Gordon had recommended, this one at Duke Hospital, only twelve miles up the road; Elliot had made an appointment with him for a week later, but in his own mind he questioned whether he'd keep it or not. Elliot wanted to talk to Melissa about the incident, but he doubted if he'd get too much sympathy at the moment.

It was almost a week later—on a Saturday afternoon, un-seasonably warm for mid-October, while Melissa and Elliot were strolling around downtown Chapel Hill—that she suddenly brought the subject up.

"Have you seen Eileen again?" she asked abruptly. Nothing in their previous conversation had suggested the topic.

"No," he replied. "Haven't talked to her either." Not that he hadn't tried to call her a couple of times—he just hadn't been able to get hold of her. But that wasn't a prudent thing to mention.

"She's left college," Melissa informed him. "And left town."

Repressing a desire to ask where she'd gone, he asked why instead.

"I don't know. I talked to Lynn—one of her suitemates—and she said she'd gone. Suddenly, about three days ago."

"Was there a problem?"

"Not that Lynn knows of. She knew about Eileen's breaking it off with you, said she was bummed out for a while. But then something else happened—she didn't know what—and Eileen was real excited. Then she left. Sent her profs notes saying she wouldn't be back, and left Lynn a note telling her to forward her mail to an address in New York City."

"New York City?" he asked, feeling a little uneasy. He thought back to the therapy session with Cecilia: when she'd said "you know where," all he'd been able to think of was the city. It was stupid, he told himself—a lot of people go to New York—but it seemed to him like an odd coincidence.

Melissa looked at him closely. "I have the address," she said in even, measured tones. "You want it?"

Yes, he said mentally. But aloud: "I don't guess so, hon'. I mean, that's all over—what good would it do? The only reason I'd want to contact her is to tell her that I'm sorry things happened as they did. I should have told her I was committed to someone else, never let it get underway—" That was good, he thought. He'd been rehearsing it, and it sounded better than he thought it would.

"Is that the way you felt about it?" Melissa asked.

"Absolutely," he told her with a shrug. "Really, just a case of glands running out of control; I suppose it had a lot to do with the fact that she was so different from you—dark where you're light and blonde, and so on."

"You are a class bullshitter, El. Really. You elevate bullshit to an art,'' she told him. There was no rancor in her voice that he could detect.

"It's not—"

"Oh, yes, it is. We both know it, El. You sat around—actually I guess laid around—for weeks comparing us. Trying to decide which you might want to keep on a permanent basis. Or keep until somebody else came along.'' As she talked, she steered them onto the campus, aimed for a quiet area free from passersby. Evidently she planned a long talk, since she sat down under a tree, motioned for him to sit down with her. "You were a real bastard about it, El. Let's not try to pretend otherwise. I'm not buying heat of the moment.''

"I guess I was,'' he said contritely. "But really, I wasn't comparing—''

"I have to believe you were. Maybe not just who was the better lay; maybe who'd be better for you in the long run. I don't know exactly what men rate as the most important things. Maybe it is, in the end, who has the better tits.''

"That's pretty harsh, Melissa—''

"Maybe. When I found out about Eileen, I sat around and thought about this a lot. Then I decided to go out and make some comparisons myself.''

He felt his stomach growing a little tight, and his mouth started to get dry. "You did—what?'' he asked lamely.

She gave him a direct look, but it only lasted a moment. "Went out with a couple of other guys. Those nights you had to 'work late.' I do get offers sometimes, Elliot.''

"But—but—who?''

She shrugged. "It doesn't matter. A grad student, a prof. Both times it turned out the same.''

He wasn't sure he wanted to ask, but finally he did. "And how was that?''

She crossed her legs, shifted her body as if uncomfortable. "I meant to make love with them when I went out, Elliot. But I kept making—other comparisons—and in the end, I just couldn't go through with it.''

He felt the pressure inside himself ease off a little. Ridiculous, he thought, to get that upset over a possible one-night stand. Especially one that hadn't materialized. That crisis past, he started to chide himself for the feelings he was having. Jealousy, he told himself, was an unworthy emotion, and he would not let himself feel it. "What comparisons?" he asked.

"Just what kind of men they were, Elliot, compared to what you are. It's hard to explain. You can be a total bastard—you are a total bastard a lot of the time—but you just have a—a proper feel. Call it an aura. You are the kind of man who is right for a woman like me, and I know it. Not that there may not be other men out there who are too—it's just that these two weren't. Besides, I thought maybe my biggest motivation was revenge. And that was not a good reason to make love to somebody."

All that made Elliot feel pretty good. "They must have been disappointed!" he said, intending it to sound like a compliment. It was really more in the nature of a boast.

"Not too bad," she said. "I sucked them off." There was not the slightest waver in her voice as she made this statement.

There was a long silence. Finally, Elliot found his voice again. "You—what?" he sputtered.

She glanced up at him with innocent eyes. "I sucked them off. They weren't bad guys, Elliot. They deserved something, for Christ's sake!"

He rolled his eyes, threw his arms up. "I thought you said you didn't make love with them!" he cried.

"I didn't! I just—"

"Good God, what a definition! Goddamn it, woman, I'd sure as hell call a blow-job lovemaking!"

"Well, I wouldn't! Not necessarily—"

He put his face in his hands. An image had sprung to mind, and he couldn't get rid of it. Melissa, in a parked car somewhere, going down on a guy who persistently looked like Jim Cardwell. Whom he hated. But at least they were, in his fantasy, both clothed. For some weird reason, that made a difference to him. "Where did this happen?" he asked, his voice sounding even more upset than he felt.

"Why?"

"I just want to know."

"One, at the guy's place. The other, at ours. I'm sorry about that, I really am. There just wasn't a choice—"

"Why not a car?"

"Elliot, you can't take your clothes off in a car unless you go somewhere—"

Wide-eyed, he looked back up at her. "You undressed?" he asked incredulously.

She frowned. "Of course. We were both naked—"

He made a strangled noise. It's ruined, he told himself. He'd never again feel the same about her. How could she do this to him? "You are really a trip," he snarled, "bringing me down so hard for what I did with Eileen when you were—"

"And what did you do with Eileen?" she asked bluntly. "You fuck her? You go down on each other? Were you dressed at the time? And where was this going on, Elliot? In a car? Remember, I only did this after I knew about what you were doing! You aren't exactly in a position to criticize!"

"It's different—" he started lamely. But already he realized he didn't have much of a response.

"Why? Because you're a man, you can't control yourself?"

"Uh—well, I—"

She folded her hands in her lap and looked down at them. "I told you about this for a couple of reasons," she said. "One, so we could try to get back to someplace like we were before. Two—maybe to make you feel a little of what I felt."

He grasped at a straw. "You mean it didn't happen?"

"No, it happened," she said, erasing the hope. "But now—I hope—we at least have honesty between us again. Do you think we can keep it, El?"

"I'd hope so," he told her, feeling flat and emotionless. "There's just one more thing I need to know—"

"I'm not going to tell you who. That'd be unfair."

"Just tell me it wasn't Jim Cardwell."

She glanced up at him, then back down. Her cheeks became a little red. "I said I won't tell you who," she insisted. "If I said no, you might go through every grad student on campus—"

He moaned. There was no doubt; he knew full well that Cardwell lived in a commune-type house with a dozen roommates, a place where there was no privacy at all. It fitted. The image now changed to Cardwell and Melissa on their bed, her blonde hair draped over his crotch—and he moaned again. That one, he knew, wouldn't go away for a while.

Melissa insisted on talking about their relationship for quite a bit longer before they finally left the campus. When they did, he was pretty sure of two things: one, she was not planning to leave him—at least not right away—and two, she didn't feel much of a long-term commitment to him. Not once in this discussion did she use the term love; rather, she concentrated on things like trust, space, and honesty—nothing he could disagree with, but it made him realize that they'd never really declared love for each other. Oh, they used the words, but so casually spoken that they couldn't be taken very seriously. And that made him wonder. Did he, in fact, love her? He decided that he did but couldn't decide if he was *in* love with her or not, and therefore didn't say anything about it. The line of thought led him to a realization that he wasn't entirely sure what being in love meant. Melissa was as close to him as anyone ever had been, but it had been something that had grown out of simple lust, at least on his side. No dramatic turning point, no line he could draw between a state of sexual attraction, close friendship, and respect and a state of Love with all the baggage that term usually carried. And now, he thought, the chance for that to happen was probably gone. The image of her and Cardwell together was so strong, he could not dispel it.

But it did have an unforeseen consequence. After they'd returned to the apartment, they made love. His mental image persisted well into their foreplay, and he was concerned that it would make him impotent, but it seemed to be having quite the opposite effect. Throughout, he kept seeing it, and it was apparently heightening the experience for him. Afterward, he felt a bit ashamed of that, as if it was perverse, but he reminded himself that he didn't really believe in perversion where sex was concerned. His skill at rationalization being what it was, he finally came up with a slightly ragged theory about a kind of a defeat for the image manifested by his ability to perform in spite of it. The psychologist in him didn't really agree, but he forced it to. It was just easier that way.

14

Greenwich Village

On a corner of West Fourteenth Street, four young girls—
one of them looked as if she could not possibly be over
fourteen—stood around in a tight little knot, talking among
themselves. For October in the city, it was still downright hot
during the days, though there was an evening coolness; even
so, the girls seemed to feel that they needed no coats. They
were all dressed in low-cut or halter tops, extreme shorts or
almost nonexistent miniskirts. On their legs, netted hose; on
their feet, spike heels. And on their faces, vivid makeup. In
short, they looked almost like caricatures of prostitutes; on
the youngest, it looked ridiculous, like a child dressed in her
mother's clothes. About half a block away, two serious-
looking young men stood leaning against a wall, their eyes
fixed on the girls. After a little while, an older man in a suit
came by, looked over the group carefully. Reversing himself,
he passed them again, and a third time. One of them winked
at him, and he finally got up the nerve to approach the group.
As if by silent signal, three of them faded back as the one
talked to the man; soon she was accompanying him to his car.
Down the street, the young man jotted down the license. And
the three remaining girls kept a lookout for more potential
customers. There were many men eager enough for their
youth to ignore the absurd trappings.

On the other side of the street, the man with the silver ring
lounged against his customary lamppost and watched them,
all the while playing with the device in his pocket. For an
hour he had been there, trying to decide whether this was the

night to approach them. He knew exactly who they were; the question was, would any of them recognize him? If they did, he had problems. But he was inclined to think it was worth the risk.

The girls—and the watching young men—were members of the same cult church that the man with the ring had escaped from. Though he by no means had seen all the church members during his stay—they operated at least ten houses around the city that he knew of—two of the girls and one of the watching men were known to him, though he only knew one of the girls by name. Undecided, he waited and watched. When the girl he knew pretty well—her name was Linda—disappeared with another customer, he decided to make his move. It would be a good test, he told himself. Would they recognize him? But he was still nervous. If they did, the Chingon's shock troops would be around in force, trying to sniff him out.

He imitated the moves of the older man, passing the two girls several times. One of the remaining was the fourteen-year-old; she didn't even smile at him, just looked scared. The other was probably in her early twenties, reasonably attractive. He'd seen her around during his days with the church but didn't know her well.

She gave him an exaggeratedly lustful look as he passed the third time, and he stopped. "What's happenin'?" he said carelessly.

"Just waitin' for a party," the older girl responded. "You lookin' for a party?" ·

"Maybe. How much this party gonna cost me?"

"Depends. Ten, twenty, thirty."

"Half-and-half, twenty?"

"Right on."

"Okay. You holdin' a room?"

That might have been the wrong thing to say, since that was the term used in the church. The girl gave him a sharp glance but didn't follow it up. "Yeah," she said. "Two blocks over."

"Let's go," he told her with a broad grin. Together, they started off down the street, leaving the younger girl alone. Out of the corner of his eye, he saw one of the young men following at a discreet distance, and his grin broadened. He knew the pattern; he'd been one of the watchers. After making sure the girl and her trick were headed in the right direction, he'd circle around and beat them to the safe room. There he'd hide; if all went well, the trick would never know he was there, but the girl would. That had been a change brought about after some girl's successful escape while supposedly out tricking for the church. So for his purposes now, it was obvious he couldn't take her to the room.

One block passed; he glanced back. The boy, as expected, was gone, circling around to the safe room. He looked up at the buildings, tried to figure it. Probably he had about three minutes; then the boy would be watching from the window. He had to time it just right, and he'd already cased the area. The alley was just ahead.

As they came to it, he grabbed the girl's arm. "In the alley," he commanded.

"What are—" she started to say. He showed her his right hand, the slim shiny knife it held. Her mouth opened and closed a few times, but she went into the alley without resistance.

"I was in the church once," he told her, grinning like a wolf. "I know what's going down. And I don't wanna be watched. Okay?"

She stared at him wide-eyed. "Backslider—" she whispered.

"Shut the fuck up," he said quietly. "And understand. I'm still gonna pay you, all right? We're just gonna do it someplace else."

"You're callin' it."

"You bet I am." He took her to an abandoned warehouse a few blocks away, gave her her money. He didn't waste time; as soon as she'd stripped, he killed her, taking special pleasure in this one. After retrieving his money, he carefully wrapped her corpse in burlap he'd stored here previously for this purpose; his preparations for this had started two days ago, when he'd first seen them working that corner. As he wound the burlap on, he splinted it with wood strips. The end result looked like wrapped furniture, perhaps an art object— such things are moved about these streets with regularity. Boldly, he rolled a hand truck out of the building, his wrapped burden on it, and took it to the old hotel where the safe room was. When he was sure it was vacant—just after the fourteen-year-old and her watcher had left—he took it in, unwrapped the body, and left it on the bed. He was in high spirits when he left, rolling the hand truck with the burlap and splints its only cargo. Just so the bastards would know, he thought. Just so they'd know.

15

Monday morning after Melissa's admission to Elliot—if it could be called an admission, he thought—he walked to his office in a rather odd state of mind. He was aware of several different emotions, and it wasn't easy to reconcile them. Saturday evening with Melissa had proceeded smoothly, and Sunday as well. It looked like this particular crisis was about over, at least from her side; that made him happy. On the other hand, he knew he'd be looking at every prof he saw on campus today—even those near retirement age—and wondering if he was the one. He was sure that Cardwell was the other, and he dreaded the next meeting with the man, because he was unsure whether to ignore him, hit him, or act as if nothing had happened. That made him anxious and upset. Lastly, he was aware, at least at some level, that Melissa's extracurricular activities turned him on; that made him anxious, too, in a different way. He kept trying to tell himself he didn't feel the same about her, and there was the oddest conflict there. At one level, purely intellectually, he felt that attitude was unjustified, unworthy, and hypocritical, and he hated himself for it. At another resided the attitude itself, as if it were something he should believe, more like it was something he was being told to accept. At a third, more basic level, the whole affair seemed to have made her more attractive to him than she had been before. From that perspective, he also felt he liked her more as a person, and that completely confounded him. Why? he asked himself. Because of what she'd done, why she'd done it, or because of her honesty and openness? He kept thinking about it but found he could not answer the question. Nor could he resolve the conflicts.

Reaching the psychology department, he first stopped by his box in the main office, picked up his mail. As he went to his office, he thumbed through it, most of it junk, but a few important things. There was one that was puzzling. A note from the departmental chairman, asking him to stop by his office today. He had no idea what for, but he had the time—assuming it didn't take over thirty minutes or so. So he went there before his morning class.

"Ah, Elliot, come in," the chairman called through the open door when he came into sight. Puffing his pipe, his Vandyke perfectly trimmed, Dr. Adam Tyson looked like everyone's image of a therapist, but the fact was, he was purely a research man, had never been a clinician. Departmental politics—always a force to be reckoned with—would never allow a clinician to become chairman. Just as the opportunities for Ph.D.s were severely limited in psychiatry in favor of the M.D.s.

"You wanted to see me?" he asked. As a freshman professor the previous year, Elliot had always referred to the chairman as "Dr. Tyson," while almost everyone else in the department called him Adam. This year, he'd started doing the same, but he remained uncomfortable enough with it to avoid calling him anything if possible.

"I just wanted to tell you there's no problem with your request," Tyson said.

He was silent, racking his brain. So much had been going on lately—what request had he made and then forgotten about? Must have been a while back. Nothing came; he was going to have to ask. "Ah—request?" he said at length, immediately irritated with himself for making that kind of response.

Tyson's eyes flicked up. "Your request for leave?" he asked.

Now Elliot had no idea what he was talking about. "Leave?" he asked stupidly.

"Of course, Collins," the chairman snapped irritably. "Your request here for two weeks' leave to attend to family matters—"

"Family matters?"

"Is there an echo in here? What's wrong, Collins?"

"Uh—no, sir, I'm afraid you must have me confused with someone else, though. I made no request for—"

Tyson looked at him, a studied analytical expression on his face. "I don't get confused, Collins," he said acidly, his tone totally mismatched with the expression. He waved a memo slip. "I have it right here." He shoved the paper across his desk to Elliot. "Is that your handwriting? Does it say Elliot Collins at the bottom?"

Elliot picked up the paper, looked at it. It was indeed his writing, his signature. Requesting two weeks' leave, just as Tyson had said, to attend to "family matters"—in New York City. There were two problems, he thought. One, he hadn't written it; two, he had no family in New York. "Sir," he said, "I didn't write this. It looks like my handwriting all right, but I didn't—"

"Then who do you suppose did?"

"I've no idea. Maybe a student, as a joke."

"Hm! Yes, well, students do have peculiar notions of humor at times. Well," he said, leaning back, "we'll forget it, then." He grinned. "Consider your leave denied."

Elliot smiled back, wadded the memo, tossed it in the garbage. He got up to leave and was almost at the door when Tyson spoke again.

"Ah, Elliot," he said, "come in. I just wanted to tell you that there's no problem with your request."

Elliot turned, frowning. Who was it had peculiar notions of humor? Tyson was holding a memo sheet in his hands, smiling at Elliot over it. He didn't look like he was joking. "Sir?" Elliot asked.

"Your request. Two weeks' leave to attend to family matters in New York?"

Elliot's frown deepened. Was the man kidding or not? He laughed a little, a strained sound; now Tyson frowned at him. "Dr. Tyson, we just went over that. I wrote no memo—" he said uncertainly.

"Then what's this?" the chairman asked, pushing the paper at Elliot.

He picked it up, looked at it. Exactly the same as before. But not wadded; it was perfectly smooth.

Taking a step forward, Elliot glanced into the trash can. He felt a little dizzy; it was completely empty, not a scrap of paper in it. Yet he remembered, not two minutes ago, throwing the paper there. What the hell was this? he asked himself. Some kind of weird precognition, déjà vu in reverse? Quickly, he decided that it was not the time to try to solve it, and he explained that he hadn't written it. The same exchange about students and their sense of humor took place. This time, Elliot tore the paper in half and wadded each piece before tossing them into the empty wastebasket. After he did, he looked in to ensure they were there; they were, lying alone on the bottom. Satisfied, he turned to the door again.

"Ah, Elliot, come in," came Tyson's voice from behind him. Elliot froze, turned, and listened to Tyson tell him his request was granted. In the man's hand was a memo. Untorn. Uncrumpled. Before he answered, he went to the trash can, looked, saw that it was empty. His face took on a determined set, and he went through the same conversation a third time. When it was complete, he did not throw the memo away but kept it tightly in his hand as he walked to the door.

"Ah, Elliot, come in," he heard; it was like a tape. Same inflection, everything. Immediately he glanced down at his hand; it was empty, there was nothing in it. And Tyson held a sheet of paper again. Feeling cold inside, Elliot faced the chairman.

"Yes, sir," he said clearly. "Thank you, sir. These are matters I really need to attend to!" He turned again, and this time left the office without incident.

Somehow, he managed to get through his morning class and get back to his office. He shut the door, sat at his desk with his knuckles pressed to his temples, wondering what the hell was wrong with him, or wrong with the world, perhaps; he could no longer tell which it was. He had long since assigned the incident with the giant snake to a drug flashback; Cecilia's odd statements had been relegated to the realm of hallucination as well. Now, however, he had a real problem. If his interaction with Adam Tyson had been hallucination, he would not be expected to take a leave; but if not, he would. And if it hadn't been, then how the hell was it to be explained? It was as if he had been forced to accept a leave he hadn't requested in the first place. At least, he told himself, there was nothing forcing him to go to New York. There was a little reminder somewhere in a corner of his mind that Eileen was there, and that Melissa had her address, but he tried to ignore it. The first thing Eileen would do, he told himself, would be to call Melissa and update her. No, she was not to be touched any further—she'd already proven her fundamental untrustworthiness. And there was nothing else in New York to interest him. The same little voice now reminded him that Cabrini Boulevard was in New York, but he shrugged that off easily; he had no desire to see Nikki grown old and decrepit, whether she was fifty or seventy-five. Still, there was the matter of the enigmatic diary pages—those could be perhaps deciphered with her help. But again he rejected the idea. It was unlikely, he told himself, that she even still lived on Cabrini. Far more probable that she'd married and had grandchildren now, lived out somewhere in New Jersey. He'd never, he told himself, be able to find her. Even if she was still alive.

He shifted uncomfortably, tried to put the suddenly vivid image of Nikki out of his mind, get back to the problem at hand. Did he have a leave or didn't he? That, he told himself, was one he had to figure out soon. But, other than to just ask somebody—maybe the departmental secretary, Marge—he didn't know how. Worse, he just wasn't sure how far he could trust his senses; it was undeniable that something strange had happened in the chairman's office. Either externally strange or internally strange, he told himself; he didn't know exactly how to go about finding out which. Even if he asked Marge, there was still only the evidence of his senses. In spite of the problems, he grinned, thinking about all the coffee-house discussions about this kind of philosophical question. It was the first time he'd had to address it in his everyday life.

His musings were interrupted by the phone on his desk buzzing insistently; he looked at it, wondered how long he'd been sitting there oblivious, and picked it up.

"I have a person-to-person for Elliot Collins," he heard an operator's nasal voice announce.

"I'm Elliot Collins."

"Go ahead, please," the operator instructed. Then another voice, male: "Elliot?"

"Yes—who is this?"

"Hey, man, you don't recognize your old buddy?"

The voice sounded familiar to him, but he couldn't quite place it, Fake it through, he told himself. "The connection must be bad,'' he said. ''From this end, your voice sounds really weird.''

''It's Dave, man. Dave Jennings.''

''Dave!'' he cried. ''How the hell are you? And where the hell are you? I haven't heard from you in two years, you rotten bastard!'' At one time, Dave Jennings had been Elliot's closest friend; a year apart in high school, they had been close throughout Elliot's collegiate days, the first three years of Dave's. But when Elliot had gone to graduate school, Dave had quit; in the words he'd been so fond of using, he'd ''tuned in, turned on, and dropped out.'' Still they'd maintained a close friendship, until Dave hit the road while Elliot had been busy with his doctoral dissertation. After that, there had been a couple of phone calls—he'd been in Southern California, he'd been at Haight-Ashbury—then nothing, and Elliot had lost touch with him. Until now.

''I'm in New York, man,'' Dave said. ''The Village. And I ain't all right, man; I'm on a real bum trip!''

''What's the matter?''

''I've been busted, man. Fuckin' set up and knocked down busted.''

Elliot sighed; this was no great surprise. ''Dope?''

''Yeah, what else? Dealing.''

''You need money, Dave?''

''No, man. I got plenty of bread.''

''How can I help, then?''

''I need you to come up here, El. I sure do hate to ask—I mean, like I know you're a big college prof now and you got your own problems—but my lawyer here tells me I'm gonna do time. I can't do no time, El. I'm strung out.''

''Oh, shit, Dave,'' he said, concerned. ''On what?''

''Smack. I tried it a couple years back, and I liked it, and well, one thing kind of led to another—I tell you, man, that stuff'll get hold of you.''

''You gotta get off.''

''I know. But I can't do it in the slam, El.''

''You weren't dealing smack, were you?''

''Oh hell no. Just grass and acid and stuff like that. But they got me with fifty keys, man. They think I'm big-time.''

That sounded pretty big-time to Elliot as well. ''Well, how is my coming up there going to help?''

''My lawyer tells me if somebody tells the judge I gotta job waiting for me, and it's out of the state, I might get a fine and probation. I can pay the fine, that ain't no problem. I just can't do time!"

"But, Dave," he said, a little exasperated, "I don't have a job for you here—"

"Shit, I ain't gonna come there, neither," he told the psychologist. "I'm goin' back to the West Coast. All you have to do is say it, man. You don't have to do it."

"Damn it! I'd like to help, Dave, but I—"

"Oh, come on, El. For old times' sake—we were friends for a lot of years—"

"Dave, I just can't give you a commitment on this here and now," he told the man. "When is your hearing, or whatever?"

"Next Monday, the twentieth."

"That isn't a lot of time. Is there a number where I can reach you?"

He reeled off a number; Elliot had to ask him to repeat it. "But I ain't never here," he said. "I'll call you back, okay?"

"Okay—but give me the details, when and where the hearing is."

He did, giving a 2 P.M. time in a courtroom in Manhattan.

"Okay—where are you staying in New York?"

"It's uptown, man. Not in the Village. 491 Cabrini Boulevard, Apartment 9B."

Elliot took the phone away from his ear and stared at it for a moment. Right next door to Nikki's apartment, if he remembered it correctly; and he was sure he did. That, he told himself, was a hell of a bizarre coincidence. "Anybody I can give messages to if I call and you ain't there?" he asked, deciding against mentioning the coincidence to Dave; it'd take too long to explain it.

"Yeah, the girl whose apartment this is. Her name's Marcia. Marcia Cates."

Cates? he asked himself. But immediately he rejected the idea; that was just too much of a coincidence to be possible. Besides, Cates was not that uncommon a name. "Okay," he told Dave, "I've got it."

"Do this for me, El. I'm begging, man."

"I'll think about it. It's a risk for me—"

"Yeah, I know. I'll be talking to you." There was a click,

and the line went dead. It left Elliot sitting there thinking about it. Most peculiar, that this call should have come after he'd gotten—possibly gotten, he reminded himself—an unwanted leave from the department specifically for the purpose of going to New York.

Times like this, he told himself wryly, it'd be easier if he did believe in the occult.

16

After agonizing over it all day, Elliot decided to discuss the question of going to New York with Melissa. She'd never met Dave, though she'd heard Elliot talk about him enough. But he wondered if she'd think it was an excuse to try to find Eileen. He had a trump card there, though. He'd never asked her for Eileen's address in the city.

And at first, all seemed to go well. As was normal in their peer group, Melissa had a great deal of sympathy for Jennings; she expressed an opinion that Elliot should probably go to the city, do whatever it took to keep him from going to jail. But he was still concerned; he felt there was an imminent risk to himself. What if the judge insisted on contacting the department at UNC? That would not, he knew, be appreciated by Tyson. They ended the discussion and went to bed without his having reached a real decision; he was still agonizing over it the next morning as he walked to work—where he found another letter waiting in his box at the main office. This one he didn't understand; he looked at the address as he walked to his office. It was from a law firm in New York, one he'd never heard of. In fact, he wasn't sure he knew of any law firms in New York. Sitting at his desk, he opened it, read:

"This is to inform you that your father, the late Aaron Collins of Eddieville, Illinois, had entrusted the care of a number of potentially valuable securities with this office. As his only heir, we have determined that you are the proper recipient thereof. In order to transfer these to your portfolio, you must appear in person at our offices no later than October 31, 1969. Our offices are located at—'' It went on from there, describing the offices, office hours, and so on. Slightly befuddled, he reread the document; he had no idea that his father had possessed any securities. And if he had, why a New York law firm? Why not Chicago, which was so much closer? And why the hell would he have to appear in person?

"There's a fucking conspiracy to get me to New York," he muttered aloud. He glanced at the bottom of the letter; there was a phone number along with the address. He shrugged, picked up his phone, and dialed. Twenty minutes later he hung up again, no more satisfied than before. A Mr. Howard Nicholas of the firm had verified the letter, assured him it was to his financial advantage to appear, and further assured him—using a lot of legal jargon that Elliot didn't really understand—that it was positively necessary that he be there in person. No wiser than before, he put the letter aside. Money was important, but this—this was a little odd. He decided he'd have to speak to someone who knew something about these matters before he went roaring off. But he'd have to do it soon; October 31 wasn't that far away.

After his first class, he dropped by the main office again, struck up a casual conversation with Marge, the departmental secretary. This he'd planned; he led the conversation in a direction intended to encourage her to make some remark about his impending leave. And she did; he'd clearly not hallucinated the strange incident with the chairman, since she was expecting him to leave. In fact, she asked him for exact dates; but he put her off, told her he'd give them to her later. It was good to know, he thought as he left the office, exactly what the situation was, but it left him in somewhat of a quandary. If he hadn't hallucinated the meeting with the chairman, then exactly what had gone on in there? He turned it various ways in his mind, tried to come up with some logical solution. But he simply couldn't find any. Nothing made any sense, nothing that was acceptable to him, anyway. The conclusion he finally left it at was that there was some combination of hallucination and reality. Indeed, there had to have been a memo; maybe he'd even written it in some kind of flashback state. But the repetition—that had to have been in his mind. There just wasn't any other explanation for it. He felt vaguely dissatisfied with his conclusions, but he could find no others, and he had to leave it at that. The hallucinations themselves he attributed to drug flashbacks. That was far easier than doubting his own sanity. In this frame of mind, he made a decision; regardless of Dave Jennings, regardless of the money, he wasn't going to go to New York. Feeling the decision a victory of some sort, he smiled to himself.

He was still thinking about it as he sat down in his office once more, picked up the data sheets for his experiments and started going over them. That reminded him of the incident with the film, another one having no satisfactory explanation. They were beginning to pile up on him a little, just recently, he thought. He hadn't had an odd experience since the time he'd broken his leg. He was reviewing that in his mind when he felt the oddest sensation. At first, he thought it might have been an earthquake. The only thing he could compare it to was to a time at the beach, when he'd been standing in knee-deep surf; a wave had come in and taken the bottom away when it rolled out. He felt like that now, like the chair he was sitting in, the floor under him, had suddenly disappeared.

Alarmed, he glanced down. The floor was still there, of course. But he felt obligated to be sure, and tapped his foot on it. Perfectly solid. He raised his head, looked around, at the windows, at the darkness outside. Darkness? he asked himself. At eleven-thirty on an early autumn morning? Unsteadily, he got up and walked to the window, looked out. His eyes told him he was looking out over the skyline of a large city, most likely New York. It looked as if he was only moderately high up—maybe a tenth floor or so. Turning his head, he saw his ordinary, everyday office. And it struck him that the lights were not on, yet it was not dark inside. But outside, middle of the night. He looked down at the city street below him, at the intersecting pools of light cast by the street lamps. As he watched, a figure walked into the center of one of these pools. The image appeared to zoom closer, as if he were watching a movie, but the realism was absolute. The figure, a woman, was facing away from him. But then she turned, and Elliot could see her face. Eileen Cates.

She gave him a broad, seductive smile, made a beckoning motion with her hand. Then she turned to her left. Like an emcee on stage she gestured to the darkness, and Dave Jennings stepped into the pool of light next to hers. His appearance shocked Elliot; he was thin, gaunt, looked near death. Both hands up, he made vague pleading motions at Elliot. Eileen gestured to her right, and a man in a business suit stepped out, someone Elliot didn't know. Grinning like a maniac, the man opened a briefcase and began pulling out sheafs of money, what appeared to be hundred-dollar bills. Meanwhile, over to Eileen's left, Jennings had collapsed on the pavement.

A sound from behind him caused him to turn. Just outside his door. He listened, heard it again; a scraping sound, like a tire being dragged down the hallway. A familiar sound that put ice into Elliot's stomach. He watched, listened, heard a few rough, sharp clicks. Like the sound of the giant snake's rattle in his dream. More scraping, right at the door now, and a few more snaps. Then a gentle thud against the door, and it began bowing inward toward him.

His terror rising by the second, he backed away toward the dark window, listening to the subtle scrapings, the sound of the wood beginning to splinter around the knob and hinges. Then, when it seemed the door was about to give way, it abruptly stopped. He saw movement out of the corner of his eye, looked back out the window, at the three figures framed in light. All of them looked terrified themselves; Eileen had her hands to her mouth as if seeing something hideous. A little movement to his right drew his attention away, and he turned his head; Cecilia Nesbitt was standing right beside him, her posture rigid, her eyes staring through the glasses. He jumped so violently he almost lost his balance and fell, had to stagger for a moment to regain his feet.

"You have to go," she said in a hollow voice. "Have to."

"Have to go," he repeated numbly. A sudden bright light hit his eyes from the side, and he looked back out the window at the UNC campus bathed in September sunlight. Just as quickly, he swung his eyes back to Cecilia, who was no longer there.

Feeling suddenly weak, he sank into his chair, put his head on his desk. He had to have help, he told himself; flashbacks or no, these hallucinations were getting out of hand. Slowly, he got up and walked to the door. A few inches away from the knob, his hand froze as he saw the splintered wood around the latch, around the hinges. For a few minutes, he was afraid to open it, but finally he forced himself, yanking it open violently. On the outside, right up the center, the wood was deeply dented. As if something very heavy—or very strong—had been pressing on it. He just stared at it, felt it with his fingertips. And felt his control shatter like crystal. He could almost feel the shards flying about inside his head. Leaving everything behind, he started off for his apartment.

When Melissa returned from campus that evening, she found Elliot with his large suitcase spread open on the bed, stuffing his clothes into it in almost frenzied fashion. She put her books down near the door and came to him.

"Elliot?" she asked, sounding bewildered. "What's going on?"

"I've got to go away for a while," he said, not wanting to mention New York, not wanting to deal with it, certainly not wanting to mention his vision of Eileen. "Got to."

"There wasn't another death in your family, was there?"

He paused, looked at her for a moment. "I have no family left," he told her.

"You going to New York? To help Dave out? Maybe I should come with—"

He slammed a shirt into the case. "No!" he snapped, so violently she jumped back. "I've just got to get away, all right? I can't stay here, I'm going crazy, can't you understand?" She started to back off farther as he yelled at her, waving his arms around. "I swear to God, I just cannot take anymore! I just cannot, don't you see?"

She turned, fled from the room. He was actually pretty much unaware of her; he felt as if his mind had fallen over some kind of brink. He'd been pushed so far and so hard he felt like he'd broken under the strain. At the moment, he didn't really have much of an idea what he was going to do once he was in the city, but it seemed, in some confused way, that it was the only way, the only place, for him to find any answers. Not another thing in the world made the least bit of difference to him—not his classes, his experiments, not even Melissa. Though he couldn't say now, he believed this had started when he was five, when he'd broken his leg. It was time to end it. One way or another.

But as he closed the suitcase, with the folder with the two photos of Nikki lying on top—he didn't even think about why he was taking them—he realized for the first time what Melissa must be thinking. He cursed himself mentally. She didn't deserve this. Repentant, and hoping she hadn't gone out somewhere, he left the bedroom to search for her.

She hadn't left; he saw her lying on the couch, facedown, her silky hair billowed around her slender shoulders, hanging almost to the floor. It was bouncing with her sobs.

"Melissa," he said gently, sitting on the edge of the new couch beside her.

Unconvincingly, she tried to wave him away. But he persisted until she rolled over and looked at him with red eyes and nose, tears running down her cheeks. "I thought we'd gotten through it," she whimpered softly. "Thought it was over. I don't even know what I did wrong!" Her voice sounded almost childlike.

He pulled her up to him. "You didn't do anything wrong," he said tenderly. "It's me, not you. It was unfair for me to take it out on you just now, and I'm sorry."

She looked doubtful. "Where are you going?" she asked.

He hesitated. "New York," he said finally. He could not possibly explain fully without sounding like a lunatic. "Take care of the business with Dave," he told her, grateful in a way for the ready excuse. He waited for her response, hoping she wouldn't mention Eileen. "It has nothing to do with you."

She wiped her eyes with her hand, peered at him closely. "You want Eileen's address, El?" she asked, her gaze moving from one of his eyes to the other.

"No, dammit!" he snapped, and he immediately regretted it. The fact was, he wished there was a way he could get the girl's address—but without getting it from Melissa. "It has nothing to do with her!"

"It has to do with another woman, though," she said firmly, startling him.

"Why do you say that?" he evaded.

"I can just tell, somehow." She came up on her knees on the couch, looked directly into his face. "Vibes, okay? I just know."

"No, I—uh—"

"You don't have to lie, Elliot. Look. Let me give you Eileen's address, you can see her while you're there. I won't blame you if you sleep with her again."

He stared at her, not quite able to understand why she was

talking this way. "Why the hell would you want to do that?" he blurted.

She shrugged. "Eileen is a known quantity," she said. "Somebody else—who knows? You understand."

That sounded too fatalistic to suit him, like she was giving up on him. "No, look," he told her, shaking his head. "I don't know what vibes you're picking up, as you say. There is another matter I may look into while I'm there—and it does involve a woman." It was curious he'd be saying this, he thought. His plans certainly didn't involve looking up Nikki—he'd decided many times before that he had no desire to see her as an old woman. "But she was an—ah—an old family friend. She's—oh, I don't know—somewhere between fifty and seventy now."

Now it was her turn to shake her head. "No. Fifty or seventy or two hundred years old, you don't want to talk with her. You want to fuck her. Maybe she is old and dried up, and you want to fuck her as she was fifty years ago. But that's what you want, Elliot. Like I said, I can tell." She looked away from him, her eyes focused on some indeterminate point across the room. Finally she looked back into his face. "So. You go do what you have to. If she's young and pretty, maybe you should fuck her. Get her out of your system. And then, Elliot, then come home. I'll be waiting for you, right here. I love you, Elliot; I want to marry you, have your children."

He stared at her, speechless. Never had he heard her talk like this. This declaration of love didn't sound casual in the least, and, considering the way she'd reacted to Eileen, her telling him to go do what he wanted with some other woman sounded totally bizarre. But he found he was focused on the last sentence. Marriage had never been mentioned between them, much less children. "Melissa," he said weakly, not quite knowing what else to say.

She put her hand on his cheek. "Don't try, Elliot," she said, managing at least a partial smile. "I know you had no idea I had these notions. Neither did I, until Linda's party; you seemed like such a hero to me, snatching me up and getting me out of there. I'd have gotten caught without you, you know. I've been thinking about it ever since. Then, when I thought I'd lost you to Eileen—and later, when I was thinking about leaving—I was sure. I think it's right for me, for us."

He hadn't felt at all like a hero at the party; if anybody had been heroic, it had been the boy who'd brained a cop with a

Coke bottle. He himself had just fled; of course he'd taken
Melissa with him, but that was hardly an award-winning act.
"It seems a big jump from there to children!" he mused aloud.

"All women want children," she declared. "And they all
want the fathers to be heroes. Their own personal white
knights—and even Lancelot had an affair. We're just built
that way, what can I say?"

"Melissa, I—"

"I know you love me, Elliot," she told him, surprising
him again. He realized then he'd never been really fair to her;
she was a hell of a lot deeper than he'd ever imagined. "And
I believe you'll come back to me. So I'll wait. Not forever,
but I'll wait." She pushed her hair back, seemed to be in
complete control of herself. "Now, business. What about the
department?"

There was no way, he decided, to really explain that. "I've
got two weeks' leave," he told her. "I just haven't let them
know when I was taking it yet."

"They'll be pissed if you don't give notice," she said. He
was relieved that she didn't ask how or why.

"They'll have to be pissed."

"All right. I'll call the secretary tomorrow, tell them it was
urgent, that you got a call. That takes care of that. You've
still got some bread from the car sale, right? And, while
you're up there, you can crash with Gerald and Purple Haze—
you remember them?"

He nodded, watched her scribble a Greenwich Village
address and a phone number on a scrap of paper. "Melissa,
I—" he tried to say.

"Never mind," she told him, having taken over the situation altogether. "You just go. Take care of yourself, and
Elliot—"

"What?"

"Don't have too good a time!"

He grinned at her, got up. She even helped him load his
suitcase into the red VW, and he hugged her before he got in.
He could still feel the warmth of her body as he drove out of
Chapel Hill, and he was not at all surprised that his own eyes
were wet.

17

Out on I-85, just past Petersburg, Virginia, Elliot began to wonder if leaving that very day had been such a good idea. He'd had no chance to have the VW serviced, and in fact, little attention had been paid to it at all since he'd returned from Illinois. Now there was a peculiar sound in the engine, a constant worry for him as the evening wore on. Already it was past eleven, and outside of the cities, not many places were open.

But he pressed on, trying to ignore the odd pinging in the engine, as well as the odd swirl of ideas in his head. The engine, he was finding, was tolerable; his thoughts were far more disturbing. He tried to concentrate on the scenery alongside the highway, but weird shapes kept threatening to spring out at him from the bushes; he found himself thankful that it was an interstate he was driving on, not a two-lane where the shoulder was close. Still, it was getting more and more difficult to concentrate. For a while, he continued to tough it out but about one A.M. gave it up. Realizing he just was not in any kind of condition to try to drive all night, he pulled off at a rest stop, locked the VW's doors and settled back to try to sleep. Though his dreams were a confused welter of images— giant snakes, Nikki, Eileen, Dave, and idiotically grinning lawyers—he managed, after a fashion, to get some rest.

Just after dawn, a rapping on his windshield roused him. He opened his eyes, ran his tongue over his front teeth, and tried to look. He was hardly able to see at all; finding coffee was an absolute necessity. Be nice if he could brush his teeth, too; maybe the rest stop had a men's room. He hoped so; some of them didn't. These essential early-morning thoughts out of the way, he forced his eyes to focus on the face looking in through his windshield.

114

A clean-shaven male face, topped by a wide-rimmed brown hat. Virginia Highway Patrol. Though he was carrying no drugs—not even a stash of grass for personal use—he jumped a little, came wide awake. These days, he knew, police often spelled trouble for people with long hair and beards. Even when they weren't doing anything illegal.

He sat up straight in the seat, opened the door. "Yes?" he asked. "Is there a problem?"

"Could I see some ID, please?" he said coldly, glancing around inside the car. Elliot dug in his wallet, produced his driver's license and showed it to the officer, who looked at it closely. Then, carrying the license with him, he returned to his cruiser. In his rearview mirror, Elliot could see him pick up his radio, call it in. He felt he could almost read the cop's mind: see if the hippie is wanted for anything. Elliot knew he'd be disappointed. Minutes passed, and the officer finally returned to the car, handed the license back.

Again he looked around inside. "Where you going?" he asked.

"New York," Elliot told him, resisting the temptation to tell him that was none of his affair. That sort of attitude, he knew, could create problems.

"You carrying any drugs?" the cop asked bluntly.

Would you expect me to say yes? Elliot thought. But aloud, he said no.

"What've you got in there to—ah—protect yourself with?"

Did he mean like guns? "I guess nothing," Elliot said, throwing his hands up.

The cop glared at him for a moment. Then he looked back at his cruiser, where the two-way radio was barking at him. "It's illegal to sleep at rest stops in Virginia," he said icily. "If I catch you doing it again, I'll run you in. I suggest you drive straight on through, get your ass out of my state. Understand?"

He understood clearly: if the cop hadn't been getting some other call, he'd probably find some reason to run him in anyway. Again he bit his lip, lest he create more problems for himself, and merely nodded. The cop left, his cruiser throwing gravel as it sped past his VW. Elliot took the advice. After cleaning up as much as possible at the rest stop, he was back out on the road. He did get his coffee, but it was to go. His anger did not really fade until the skyline of New York

City came into view. There was no reason or justice to his being treated like that just because he looked different.

As he entered the city, he felt relieved in two ways: one, he'd had no more police problems, and two, the VW had survived the trip—though barely. The pinging was much louder, and periodically the little engine jerked as a cylinder misfired. There was definitely something wrong here, no doubt about it. And it was getting rapidly worse.

As the car sputtered and jerked through the Holland Tunnel, he glanced down at the scrap of paper Melissa had given him, Gerald's address on Cornelia Street. When he'd started the trip, he'd fastened it into a clip he'd long ago stuck on the dash, and there it still hung, a reminder of Melissa in the form of her rather elegant handwriting—at least compared with his own illegible scrawls. He knew approximately where it was—not far from Washington Square—and he followed Canal Street to Sixth Avenue, turned north.

The address turned out to be a second-story walk-up in a run-down Georgian town house converted to apartments. Elliot moved cautiously through the dingy hallways and up the narrow stairs. When he knocked, a young girl—she looked as if she might be as young as eleven or twelve—answered the door.

"Nah, Gerald ain't home," she told him, leaning on the peeling door frame. She was barefoot, wearing a long dress with nearly no top at all, about two sizes too large for her. "Haze is here, though. Come on in."

He thanked her, went inside. The degree of dishevelment of this apartment made Elliot's own look like a candidate for *Better Homes & Gardens*. There was only one piece of real furniture in the front room, a beaten and ragged easy chair sitting to Elliot's right. On the left, a pile of cushions, not in any way matched to each other, lay jumbled on the floor, awaiting their user's preference as to how they should be organized. By the door, a wooden crate with "Hong Kong" printed on it served as a table, and there was another in the corner; behind the cushions, the almost inevitable plank and concrete-block bookshelves. There was a rug, of sorts, though it had several holes in it and more than several frayed areas. On the walls, the faded and peeling paint could hardly be seen for the proliferation of posters, everything from a homemade collage to political rhetoric to a *Playboy* centerfold. With his

North Carolina paranoia still intact, he stared at ashtrays full of roaches, a cup full of tabs that were most likely LSD. In a back room, equally primitive in furnishings, he found the man known far and wide as "Purple Haze," after the Jimi Hendrix song. He was lounging on a bed, smoking a joint; Elliot was offered a toke and accepted.

"So, Ell-ee-ott, my man!" Haze said expansively. He looked almost exactly like one of the black characters in the Broadway production of *Hair,* and the degree to which his appearance deviated from that was purely accidental. Haze modeled his whole life on that musical, with one exception, one hangover from his earlier life on Harlem's tough streets. An example of this hangover now lay on the dresser beside the bed, and Elliot eyed it uncomfortably; usually he didn't like to be around guns at all, and the big .45 lying there looked terribly efficient. Haze loved his guns, wouldn't be without them. He always had at least three or four around.

"Good to see you, Haze," he said, shaking the black man's hand with the thumb-over grip current among political radicals.

"So, whatchoo in town for? What's goin' down?" Haze asked him. The girl came in, sat down on the bed, but said nothing.

"Business," Elliot told him. "I'll only be here for a few days."

"Dope business?"

"No."

"Politics? SDS?"

"No, Haze. Personal, all right?"

"Hey, man, 'at's cool. Cool with ol' Haze, yeah. Okay, look, you can crash in the living room, all right? We gotta 'nother mattress round here somewhere. I'll dig it up."

"Good. Thanks, Haze." The black man jumped up, went off into the front part of the apartment. Elliot was left with the girl, who still hadn't said anything.

"So what's your name?" he asked her conversationally.

"Laura. Laura Neill."

"I'm glad to meet you, Laura," he told her. "I'm Elliot. Collins."

"From North Carolina, right?" She reached over to the table and picked up a roach from an ashtray by the gun, lit it.

"Right. How'd you know?"

"Gerald tol' me 'boutcha," she said. Her voice was almost completely without affect. "You just get into town?"

'Yeah. From about Richmond—''

"You wanna get laid?"

He stopped, stared. Her question had taken him totally aback. He had no idea how to answer her, either. She was quite a pretty girl—even if her face looked a little slack—but she looked so very young! Baby fat in her cheeks, he told himself. Quickly, he let his gaze encompass the rest of her; long brown hair, soft brown, sleepy-looking eyes. Small but well-shaped breasts mostly visible above the top of the loose dress, and what looked like very fine legs, though here the dress made it hard to tell. Delicate, long-fingered hands with short nails. Everything about her appearance said "child" to Elliot. Even so, was a man ever supposed to refuse a direct offer like this? You certainly didn't get them often, Elliot told himself. "Uh—how old are you, Laura?"

For the first time, she grinned. "Thirteen," she said, drawing on the joint.

He remembered himself at thirteen, smothering the picture of Nikki in childish, romantic ideas. How the world had changed! "Maybe this is a stupid question, but you mean— I mean, by you?"

"Yah," she said, her grin gone.

He decided to play clinician; something here didn't quite fit. "Uh—you don't really want to, do you?" he asked.

She looked defensive. "Sure I do!" she snapped. "Why the hell not?"

"You just didn't look thrilled, that's all."

"Well, shit, man, I don't know you! You might be mean, might be rough, ya know?"

"So why'd you offer?"

Her face crumpled, and she looked even younger. "Haze tol' me I should ask any dude who came in here." She looked up at him, almost looked scared.

"Why?"

"Said I wouldn't be a real hippie if'n I didn't."

Elliot rolled his eyes. He'd known Haze for quite a while, and he didn't suspect the man was being malicious. Haze was simply trying to mold Laura into a classic hippie, by the media's definition. The fact that hippies might be products of the media doubtlessly bothered him not at all; there were certain advantages here for him. One, he and Gerald would have access to Laura at any time, and two, they could offer sex to visitors. This would distinctly increase their social standing in the local counterculture community and bring them more visitors. And visitors frequently came bearing free dope.

"Look," Elliot told her, "Haze means well, but you need to do what's best for you, understand? You're pretty young, after all. I wouldn't say that means no sex, but only with guys you dig. Okay?"

She smiled brightly. "Okay. Now, you wanna get laid? Or a blow-job?"

Elliot sighed. "Maybe a little later," he said, though he really didn't mean it. "Right now, I'm tired from the drive. And I'm still a little pissed about a cop that gave me a hard time for no reason. I'll just finish this roach and come down a little, okay?"

She shrugged, seemingly not offended. "Sure. Lemme know."

"Right." He watched her leave the room before he leaned back, toked the roach again.

The marijuana relaxed him too much, and he fell asleep. When he finally roused, about an hour later, he heard voices from the front room. Stumbling through the door, he tried to get himself back to full consciousness. No matter when he slept or for how long, he didn't wake up easily.

Gerald Bradford had returned, and he greeted Elliot as he came through the door. "Hey, man," he said, looking back over his shoulder. "You were pretty well zonked out in there, so I thought I'd just let you alone."

"Yeah, thanks," Elliot mumbled, plopping down on a cushion on the floor. His vision cleared, and he looked at Gerald. His slightly graying beard was over twice the length of Elliot's own, and his hair was far longer as well, tied into a ponytail in back. Several strings of love beads, in various colors, hung around his neck, and he was shod in sandals. In short, he epitomized the guru look, and he played the role well. It probably came very naturally to him; he too was a Ph.D. psychologist, and had taught for many years at NYU. But he was one of many who had taken Leary and Alpert's message to "turn-on, tune-in, and drop-out" very seriously, even if he didn't say that as frequently as Dave Jennings did.

When Melissa had introduced Elliot to him not quite a year ago—the only time they'd seen each other previously—Gerald had repeatedly pressed him to do the same thing. Elliot wanted to avoid another conversation of that sort now.

"You mind if I use your phone?" he asked abruptly, obviously cutting off something Gerald was about to say.

"No, man," Haze said quickly. "It's right over there, help yourself."

Elliot nodded, went to the phone, and dialed the number Dave had given him. It rang twice, then an operator's voice said: "The number you have reached is no longer in service—" He cursed. Dave had said he had plenty of money; why the hell didn't he pay his phone bill? That left nothing to do except go up there, and he had no idea where Cabrini Boulevard might be.

"Look," he said, addressing all of them but looking in Laura's direction, "I need to find a place here, and I have no idea where it is. Any of you guys know where a Cabrini Boulevard might be?"

Laura shook her head, and Gerald seemed to be thinking. "Uptown, I think," Haze told him. "Maybe up in Washington Heights? That sounds right. Yeah, up around the George Washington Bridge."

"How do I get there?"

"Shit, man, I dunno—I guess you can just go up B-way to like, maybe one ninety or so. It'll be up the hill, over toward the Hudson."

Elliot didn't like the idea of wandering around looking, but that was apparently all he was going to get. He thanked them, and for a while allowed himself to be occupied with small talk, the latest drugs, latest politics, latest atrocity in Vietnam. Gerald and Haze asked him how Melissa was doing, informed him that she had thoughtfully called to tell them he was coming. As they talked, Elliot found himself wondering what her relationship might have been with these two. She had always spent her summers in the city, up until this year; she was originally from New Jersey. Elliot had only seen Gerald and Haze previously when they'd visited her in Chapel Hill. Gerald, to be sure, was pretty much her type, and though he knew she wouldn't turn down a black man just because of his color—if anything, she, like many women of her peer group, might well bend over backward not to seem racist—he just couldn't see her with Haze. Though the man wore the hippie uniform, spouted lines from *Hair* as if they were his own, he sometimes lapsed into the patois and manner of the street pimp, and his attitude toward women clearly came from that side of his personality; Laura was only the latest example. It was obvious that the street kid from Harlem was not gone, just hiding. Still, it was possible that Melissa had had an intimate relationship with Haze; she'd told Elliot she'd had black lovers but had never mentioned any names. In spite of all that, Elliot liked the man, felt he could trust him. Haze was very predictable, and a very loyal friend.

At about seven o'clock, Haze imperiously but casually instructed Laura to prepare a meal. This she did without complaint, and it annoyed Elliot to see her treated like hired help. He watched her go to the kitchen, the oversized dress nearly falling off of her as she walked. A runaway, probably; he wondered what her story was. Perhaps, he mused, he'd be able to find out while he was here. Putting the strange events in Chapel Hill out of his mind as much as possible, he gave the whole evening over to relaxation, good food and some more dope. Laura's favors he declined; his life was complicated enough already.

18

As it turned out, the VW had done all it could do just to get him to New York. When he'd started out, headed uptown, the hiss in the VW's engine had become regular; he was just past 42nd Street when it gave out completely, leaving him in the middle of Eighth Avenue, blocking traffic. Trying to ignore the squalling horns of drivers stuck in traffic behind him, he got out, pushed the little car to the roadside. He'd had to leave it in a no-parking zone, and by the time he'd called for a tow and returned, he'd already gotten a ticket. When the tow driver came, he allowed as how Elliot was lucky the car hadn't been impounded. It turned out to have burned valves, timing problems, and some minor things as well; he was advised it would take at least a couple of days to repair it. Meanwhile, he was without wheels, not a problem as long as he didn't want to leave the city. A couple of days didn't sound too bad to him; it'd take that long to try to figure out what to do about Dave Jennings. By now, he'd managed to convince himself that Dave's legal difficulties and his required appearance at the offices of the law firm were the real—and only—reasons for his being here. It was so much easier to believe that, and he was making a habit of believing the easy-to-accept these days.

Leaving the VW in the, hopefully, capable hands of a West Side garage, he took the subway on up, got off at 191st. Through working-class neighborhoods with a liberal sprinkling of immigrants, he walked, trying not to be too conspicuous. He didn't like this; he preferred to have his car, explore in it rather than on foot. But the sidewalks were not crowded in this area, and he was not encountering any particular problems. Twice he tried to stop people to ask if they knew where Cabrini was, and twice he got totally ignored. He gave up that tack, remembered what Haze had said about going west off Broadway, toward the Hudson. He did that, and only a block up found himself confronted by a long flight of stairs leading up to the next street. As he climbed them, he watched an old woman coming down, cautiously negotiating every step. On each of the landings, she paused and looked around as if she expected someone to come and help her. Yet her facial expression indicated most clearly that she would be most suspicious of any help offered. Elliot figured she was probably about seventy, and he wondered if there was any possibility that she was the woman in his grandfather's picture. Most unlikely, he told himself. Just another of New York's inhabitants; there were doubtlessly thousands of such old women in the city.

Forgetting about her, Elliot ʻclimbed on to the top of the stair. Here, he encountered a quiet little neighborhood, a few shops and a plethora of apartment buildings. Ahead of him, the hill continued for at least one more block, and he could see a subway station sign down to his left. He sighed; he hadn't had to climb the stairs at all. Diagonally across was a drug store, and he went inside and inquired at the counter as to the location of the street he was looking for.

"We don't get many of your kind around here," the clerk said shortly, not answering the question. He was an older man, with thinning hair, glasses; he glared at Elliot across the counter. "Why don't you get a haircut, anyway?"

"All I want to know is how to get to Cabrini Boulevard," Elliot said, trying to be patient. It wasn't the first time he'd encountered this sort of thing, and he was sure it wouldn't be the last. But he'd be damned if he'd cut his hair or shave just to avoid it. Or to avoid harassment by highway cops.

The man glared some more, as if trying to decide whether to give him even such small assistance. "Next block up," he said finally, jerking his head up the hill.

Elliot left the store immediately; he'd originally intended to buy a snack of some sort there, but he didn't want to give that unpleasant old character his business. Up the hill, past a vegetable market and a little cafe, he found the street sign, CABRINI BLVD. For just a minute he couldn't see anything else; he felt like it was some kind of legendary place, like Camelot. Then he let his eyes roam around a little and saw something that really threw him off balance. At that very intersection, at least six one-way signs were visible, pointing in what seemed to be, from his perspective, random directions. He steadied himself, crossed the street to the other corner. And from there, it was exact. Exactly the same scene he'd seen in the film back in North Carolina. This made no sense at all, he told himself; it wasn't possible. What he'd seen on film had to be delusional, so how could it have been correct? He forced himself to think about it rationally and decided that though he'd never been here before, he must have at some point seen a photograph taken from this angle. Or something. It was just too close; he had to have had previous knowledge. A voice in the back of his head asked again why the grad assistant and the student had seen two different things themselves. He tried once more to ignore it, insisted on dealing with one thing at a time. At the moment, this was enough.

Slowly, he walked to the corner, turned on Cabrini itself. Following the numbers, he moved down the narrow street, past the cars, which were parked on one side only, past an underground garage. This area was almost strictly residential, apartment buildings rising on both sides, most of them about eight to ten stories. Beyond, the land dipped toward a collision with the Hudson River, and where there were gaps in the structures he could see the Palisades of the Jersey shore beyond, hazy because of the pollution in the air. Just after he passed one such gap, he came to a building with a small courtyard, glass doors at the end of a short walk. He'd reached his destination—number 491.

Well, he told himself, nothing to do but walk right in. He refused to consider the notion that he was as interested in Dave's neighbor as in Dave; he still insisted he didn't even want to see an aged Nikki, even on the remote chance she still lived there. But he did, after all, have to go to the ninth floor. No choice about that. He stepped up to the glass doors, pushed on them.

And they didn't open. Glancing to his right, he saw a box with a double row of push buttons, names beside some, apartment numbers by all. It was one of those doors where a resident had to buzz you into the building. He ran down the list, found number 9B—Cates, as expected. He could not, of course, help looking at 9C. But there was no name beside that button. With a little, involuntary sigh, he jabbed at 9B.

"Yes, who is it?" came a female voice.

"Marcia Cates?" he asked.

"Yes—who are you?"

"My name is Elliot Collins. Dave did mention my name, I trust?"

"Dave?"

"Dave Jennings. He is staying with you, isn't he?"

There was a short silence. "Who'd you say you were?"

"Elliot Collins," he repeated. "Dr. Elliot Collins."

"You know this Dave Jennings?"

"Yes, he's one of my oldest friends—"

"Maybe you'd better come up, Dr. Collins," Marcia told him. "I think we should talk." The door buzzed loudly; he pushed on it and found himself in a tiled foyer with an elevator off to his right. He went to it, pressed nine, and waited while it clanked and groaned up the shaft. When he got out, he was confronted by four identical doors, labeled A, B, C, D. B and C were side-by-side, right in front of him. On the door of B was the label, "Cates"; there was no such label on

C. Cursorily, he glanced at A and D; the former, which was to his left, had the name "Reyes" on it—that was familiar, he just couldn't place it—and D, like C, was unlabeled. In fact, D seemed to have been painted shut; it had a look of disuse about it, as if that apartment had been vacant for a long time. With a last glance at C, he knocked on Marcia Cates's door.

It swung open, and he was looking at a woman who was around his age—mid-twenties—who was, in appearance, very striking. She had large green eyes, a broad face, and a cascade of reddish hair sweeping over her shoulders. She was dressed in shorts—it was still quite warm in New York—and a thin cotton blouse, through which the outlines of her very large breasts were quite visible. She was pretty, he decided, though not beautiful—she missed the latter destination primarily because she was quite plump, though not to the extent of being called fat; "zaftig" fitted her perfectly. She looked him up and down, and smiled slightly; when she did, her whole face lit up.

"Dr. Collins," she said, "come in, please."

"Thank you," he said, stepping into the apartment. The rooms were quite small, and the walls and ceiling showed considerable disrepair. Her furnishings were those one might expect of an artist or painter—the place was set up more like a studio than living quarters. "Is Dave here?"

"That's what I wanted to talk to you about," she said, indicating a chair. "First—can I get you some coffee, or wine? I'm afraid I don't have any liquor or beer—"

"Oh, that's fine," he said. "Coffee'd be nice, if it's made. Don't go to any trouble."

"I always keep it made," she said, padding into the kitchen on bare feet. She returned moments later with a tray bearing two steaming cups. After giving Elliot his, she sat down across from him.

"Dave isn't here?" he prompted.

"I'm afraid, Dr. Collins," she said, sipping her coffee, "that I don't know a Dave Jennings. He isn't here. At least not yet."

"Excuse me, I don't understand—"

"I wouldn't expect you to, since I don't myself. About a week ago, I received this in the mail." She handed him a folded paper; he opened it and read:

Dear Marcia,

I will be arriving to stay at your place around the end of September. Hope this won't inconvenience you much. If my friend Dr. Elliot Collins comes by, tell him what's going on, will you? I've sent you a little something to help out.

Thanks, love you,
Dave Jennings

When he'd finished, Elliot looked back up at her. "And you say you don't know him? It's a pretty familiar letter—"

"I know. You'd think we were old buddies, wouldn't you? But the fact is, I'd never heard his name—or yours—until this letter arrived, about the middle of August. I'd kind of forgotten the names. But I couldn't forget getting that letter!"

"Why not?"

"See where he says, 'I've sent a little something'?" she asked, gesturing at the letter. "He did. A thousand dollars in cash!"

Elliot goggled at her. "You mean to tell me you got this letter with a thousand dollars from a man you never—"

She nodded. "Never heard of. Right. No return address on the envelope, no way to contact him. What you see is what I got. Weird, huh? Anyway—you can imagine that I'm dying of curiosity! And finally there's someone here to ask!"

"Well," he began, wondering how open he should be with Marcia. "To start with, I've been out of touch with Dave myself for two years. Then, maybe a week ago, I got a call from him. Said he'd been busted, for dealing drugs. I have to assume that's where the money comes from—"

She nodded. "I kind of figured," she said. "What I don't understand is, Why me?"

"That, I've no idea. Like I said, I've been out of touch with Dave for some time."

"Then I suppose we're both stuck. Until—and if—Dave shows up."

"I guess. Look, I tried to call here earlier—got a message that the phone was out—"

"Not that I know about," she said. It was right beside her, within arm's reach, and she picked it up. "It is, though. Stone dead. Shit! Now what, I wonder?"

He gestured helplessly. "Dave is supposed to have a court

appearance on Monday,'' he told her. ''I assume he'll turn up before then.'' He stopped, asked her for a scrap of paper. She produced one, and he wrote Gerald's number on it. ''Have him call me here, all right?''

''Sure,'' she said. ''If I see him. Listen, report the phone for me, would you?''

''No problem. Soon as I get back.''

''Thanks.'' She remained standing; it seemed he was being dismissed. ''Uh—don't hesitate to stop back by if you want,'' she said, a little hesitantly.

''I might do that. I may be kind of at loose ends for the next couple of days anyway.'' He put the cup down, walked to the door. As he went through it, he decided to ask her a question he'd been wondering about. ''Marcia, do you have a sister—or cousin or whatever—named Eileen?''

She smiled. ''Sure. Eileen's my little sister!'' Then she frowned. ''But how did you know that?''

He grinned, waved his hand. ''No big mystery,'' he told her. ''Just a strange coincidence. You knew Eileen was a student at UNC, Chapel Hill?''

''Yes—''

''Well, I'm a psychology teacher there. Eileen was in my summer class this past year.'' It seemed best not to mention their affair. ''I understand Eileen left school, moved to New York?''

Marcia looked surprised. ''She did?''

''You didn't know?''

''No. Last I heard, she was in Chapel Hill! You say she's here? In the city?''

''That's what I heard, yes. But I don't know where or why.''

Marcia looked exasperated. ''Well, that little bitch. If she came up here to live and didn't even call, I'll wring her neck!''

''Maybe she tried. Your phone's out.''

''Hasn't been out long—not over a week, at most.''

He shrugged. ''I wouldn't know, then. I don't even know she's here, for sure. Her roommate at school said she'd come up here. That's all I know.''

''I'll find out.'' She looked at him closely. ''Seems like you know her pretty well,'' she observed.

That, he didn't want to get into. ''She's a friend,'' he said shortly, hoping his manner would discourage further questions. It did, and he said good-bye to her, watched the door close. For just a few seconds, he stood there looking at 9C, feeling an impulse to knock on that door. So many coincidences, he told himself. In the end, he behaved in what he felt was a rational manner; he went back down the elevator, back to Gerald and Haze's apartment.

Gerald, Haze, and Laura were all home when he got there, three faces looking up at him as he came through the unlocked—in fact slightly ajar—front door.

"Not a good day, I take it," Gerald asked him, grinning benignly.

Elliot flopped down on a cushion. "The worst," he said. He hadn't realized it showed that much.

"A little dope always helps," Haze said.

He shook his head. "Not now, at least," he told the black man. "Thanks, anyway."

"What happened, man?" Gerald asked, still grinning. Like an idiot, Elliot thought, but he immediately regretted thinking it.

"Well, the first thing was that my damn car broke down. Then, after that—well, the person I came to see isn't here. More, the girl he was supposed to be staying with doesn't even know him!"

"That's a real bummer," Haze commented; Elliot was sure he'd say the same thing if he'd told them he spilled a Coke, or if he told them Melissa had died. They were all "bummers" to Haze. "But like I said, man. A little dope—"

Again Elliot waved it away. "No, really, Haze; I think I'd feel even worse if I was stoned."

"Who'd you come to see, Elliot?" Gerald asked. "Maybe I know—him? Her?"

Elliot sighed. "Him. His name's Dave Jennings; he's an old friend of mine. He called me, told me he'd been busted. Wanted me to come up and help him out. So now, I'm here and he isn't!"

"Maybe he got off, decided to split," Gerald mused. "Or maybe he's in the slam. You check on that?"

"No. But like I said, the girl he was supposed to be staying with doesn't know him! I mean, that's ridiculous! Why'd he tell me he was staying there?"

Gerald shook his head, causing the beard to wave back and

forth. "Who knows, man? People do lots of strange things these days."

"But not as strange as what the straights do," Haze put in. Everyone laughed, Elliot joining in halfheartedly.

"Well," he said, "I guess tomorrow I'll check and see if he's in jail someplace. That's about all I can really do."

"We do what we can, man," Gerald said, as if it was a profound idea.

"Look, man," Haze said, "I know you're bummed out. Like I said, I got some real good dope here. I know you'll be in a lot better shape if you do some."

Good God, Elliot thought. The man will never give up. Today had been the first time he'd done any dope to speak of since Linda's party, and he'd been a little nervous about it. But he mentally shrugged his shoulders. Why not? he asked himself. At least it would pass the evening. He grinned at Haze, nodded. The black man jumped up, ran off to his bedroom, and returned with a tall hookah, four pipes curled around the high center of it. He put it down in the middle of the floor, filled the bowl with crushed leaves, and lit it. All four of them gathered around, each taking a pipe. It didn't take long to empty the bowl; and as soon as it was, Haze filled it again. The room was so full of cannabis smoke one didn't have to draw on the hookah at all to get stoned.

Haze had been right; the dope was very good. And it hadn't affected him badly; he felt very mellow, very smooth. No disturbing visions, just the usual pleasant mistiness. Enjoying it, he just kept puffing away, only vaguely aware that he was inhaling more than any of the others. Suddenly, without warning, things in front of his eyes seemed to start vibrating. He stood up quickly, and as soon as he did, he realized that it was a mistake. The vibrating effect seemed to increase, and he fell heavily backwards.

19

Not too far from the Village apartment where Elliot lay unconscious, Art Kern, deskman at a run-down hotel frequently visited by prostitutes and their customers, was becoming concerned. One of his regulars—a girl named Vicki, he had no idea of her last name—had not returned from the room she'd gone to more than two hours previously. That was not like her; Vicki was nothing if not efficient, and it was a rare thing for her to remain in a room much over an hour. Once, Art recalled, she had taken four men up there at one time, and still she was back out on the street in less than two hours. She was a pro; and even though she'd been working the streets for at least five years, she still made good money. If she couldn't demand a very high price, she made up for it in quantity. The world was very unfair to people like Vicki, Art thought. He himself had purchased her favors on occasion, and she was very skilled, as well as a very good actress; even he'd been half convinced that she'd been enjoying herself, and nobody ever accused Art of being naive. Much better, he thought now, than a lot of the young runaways and junkies who, though they might be better looking, had no erotic skills and no motivation to develop them. They seemed to feel that their appearance alone should be sufficient, and they usually just lay there like those inflatable dolls. But they made good bucks; maybe they were right. People didn't care about artists anymore, Art told himself. That's what he thought of Vicki as—an artist of the erotic.

He glanced up at the clock, shrugged, and turned his attention back to the TV; another fifteen minutes drifted by. More and more frequently, he found himself looking up the dingy stair that led to the rooms, expecting to see Vicki come back down, smile at him, and head back out to the streets. But the stairs were quiet, except when an older man made his way back down followed moments later by a frowsy-haired girl who had only recently appeared in the area.

"Hey, Jean!" he called to the frowsy-haired girl. She stopped, turned around.

"Yeah?" she asked, blinking her eyes. Art wasn't sure she could see him very well; Jean normally wore rather thick glasses, but not when she was working.

"You see Vicki up there?"

"Vicki? Nah. Didn't see nobody 'cept the john I took up."

"Sure?"

"Sure I'm sure. Whatsa matter?"

"I dunno. It's been a long time, she ain't come down."

"Her john leave?"

"Dunno. I didn't see."

She grinned. "Maybe he's real slow."

"He'd be payin' extra, then, with Vicki."

Jean walked back over to the desk, leaned on it. Her brown hair stood out so far in all directions Art could hardly see past it. "Maybe you oughta go see, Art."

"She wouldn't like me bustin' in on her. If she's workin'," he growled.

"You could listen at the door. You know what it sounds like, Art. If it's quiet, you might need to check. I'd appreciate it if'n it was me."

Art looked up the stair, considered. Then he pulled a .38 from underneath the counter, stuck it in his belt; Art's stomach was not small, and the handle of the pistol stuck out conspicuously. "Let's do it," he said, including Jean in.

She looked doubtful for a moment, but then shrugged, followed him up the stairs. In the second-floor hallway, the dim light reflected off the peeling green paint, giving a greenish cast to their faces. They tried to walk quietly, but the planks in the floor creaked anyhow. As they came up to the door of number 242, the room he'd given Vicki, a large cockroach skittered across the floor in front of them, making a surprising amount of noise for an insect. Art put his ear to the thin door, listened for a moment.

"I don't hear nuthin'," he said in a low voice.

Jean was beginning to look a little scared. Then, resolutely, she stepped up to the door and knocked on it. "Vicki?" she called. "You in there?"

There was no answer. The two of them stood staring at each other for a few minutes, then Art pulled out his key ring, fumbled with it. Slowly, carefully, he opened the door, peered inside. Rickety dresser, rumpled white sheets on an old brass bed, window open with the curtains flailing around outside. He opened the door wide. Nobody.

"She ain't here, Art," Jean said, peeping around his shoulder.

"I swear she didn't come down," he told her doubtfully, moving into the room.

"Maybe she went down the fire escape?"

"Why the fuck would she do that? I mean, we gotta clean the room, don't we?" He moved across to the bed, looked at the wet spot in the middle of it. It stood alongside the window, about two feet of space on the far side of it. "She's supposed to pull the sheet, Goddamn it," he said with some disgust. "All you girls know that." He walked around the foot of the bed and stopped, staring.

"What's the—" Jean started to say, joining him. Then she screamed, so loudly and suddenly that he jumped.

Between the bed and the window was Vicki, her naked body in an awkward sprawl on the floor. Around her neck, a piece of wire of some sort was wound so tightly that it had cut into the flesh, and one of her stiff hands was still up as if to pull it away. Her swollen tongue protruded from her mouth, and her face was an incredibly vivid purple. The open, staring eyes caused Art to back off; he knew full well that there was no chance that she was alive.

"Oh, shit," he said, when he'd found his voice again. Pulling the .38 out of his belt, he quickly checked the bathroom and closet; nothing there. "Goddamn it, Vicki!" he yelled at the dead body. "If you had to get yourself killed, why'd you have to do it in my place?"

Jean looked at him, her eyes wild. "What we gonna do?" she asked.

"You gonna get outta here," he said, not unkindly. "I gotta call the law, I suppose. Man, there's gonna be hell to pay over this, there sure is!"

20

A cool, damp cloth was on Elliot's head when he became aware of his surroundings again. Initially, he had no idea where he was, or what had happened; but he was in control of himself enough to avoid a cliche. He felt a gentle hand touch his cheek and looked up. Laura was sitting beside him as he lay on the bed; Gerald and Haze were nowhere to be seen.

"At the risk of being corny, I have to ask—what the hell happened?"

"You just keeled over," the girl informed him. "The guys brought you in here, but they had to go out. I've been sitting with you."

He started to sit up, but a severe pain in the side of his head stopped him from doing that. "Jesus!" he exclaimed, feeling his temple. "What the fuck—"

"You sorta cracked your head on the floor when you fell. Haze thought you mighta killed yourself."

"Nice of him to hang around and find out!"

She shrugged. "He was going to, but I told him you'd be okay."

"How did you know? You a doctor? For all you know, I could've been dying! I—"

"No, I was sure. I always have feelings about these things. Whenever somebody OD's, I can tell whether they need to go to the hospital or not. I ain't never been wrong. Not yet, anyways."

"How do you do it?"

"Gerald says I got ESP. He was gonna take me down to Durham someday, get me tested at the lab there. But he didn't, and I guess he won't now."

Elliot tried to grin, but that hurt his head, too. "Why not?"

he asked. The tone of her voice when she'd made the statement had a certain finality, like she was getting too old for such things.

"Just won't happen," she said, and shrugged. Throughout the conversation, her face had been relatively expressionless, but now, with no warning at all, she burst into tears.

Ignoring his throbbing head as well as possible, he sat up, put his arm around her shoulders. "What is it?" he asked her.

She tucked her head against his shoulder, her hair tickling his neck. "Nuthin'," she said, sniffing. "Nuthin' I wanta talk about, anyways."

"Why?"

"I jus' don't." But she seemed to take no offense at his persistence.

He disengaged himself, lay back down on the bed. For a few minutes, he just looked up at her face, expressionless once more. In a few years, he told himself, this girl would be a real beauty; a lot of people would consider her one now. "What's your story, Laura?" he asked at last. "If it isn't prying, that is."

"I ran away," she said, confirming his suspicion. "From—uh—Minnesota. That's where my folks live."

"Bad home life?"

She glanced down at him. "No," she said. "I just wanted to get out, do some things."

"You had plenty of time for that."

"No, I didn't. What we got here—the scene, you know—it ain't gonna last very long. Gotta get it while you can get it, that's what I always say."

Elliot realized that he believed the "scene" would be a permanent facet of American life from now on, though he hadn't thought about it much. "Why do you say that?" he asked.

"Like I said, I just know some things sometimes. That's one of them."

"I don't really believe in ESP," he told her.

She turned her head, looked at him with a completely different face. Gone was the slackness, the mindless look; her eyes were sharp and alert. She seemed to be very serious. "So what do you believe in, Elliot? Dope? Politics? Psychology? Pretty flimsy. I'd say there were some things going on in the world you don't know anything about!"

"I'd like to say I believe in people," he said, somewhat stiffly. The turn of the conversation was making him uncomfortable; it seemed to be terribly close to the kinds of things that had been happening to him lately. Or so it appeared to him. "I feel like you mean something specific by that, anyway."

"I do. Like I said, I know things sometimes. And I can feel it. You are gettin' yourself in someplace you might have trouble gettin' out of."

"So what should I do, O soothsayer?" he asked with another painful grin.

She gave him a disgusted look. "You ain't gonna believe me—I don't really know why I'm botherin'. But—whatever it is you're headin' into—you better find a way not to. If you wanna go on livin', that is. But there's another side of it too, one I don't really follow too awful well. Like there's somethin' good you can get out of it, too. Like somethin' maybe worth dyin' for."

It was getting more and more difficult for him to take her seriously, and his face must have shown it; her own withdrew into the slack, uncaring look he'd seen before. "You ain't listenin', like I said. But you'll see, I guess." She stood up. "Now look. Right now, you just lay there, lemme go get you some herb tea. No, don't make no face. I know what I'm doin', all right?"

He gave in. "All right, okay, whatever," he said. She left the room, and with half open eyes he watched her go. An unusual girl, he decided. He didn't really know what to make of her; she seemed to have two utterly different personalities, to be able to switch back and forth with great facility. He remembered how much his last conversation with Melissa had surprised him, and he wondered if his understanding of women was even adequate. He'd always thought it was, but now he wasn't so sure.

Laura returned with the tea, left it beside the bed, and went off somewhere; Elliot sipped it, finding that it had a pleasant taste. As he did, he let Laura's predictions roll over in his mind, compared them to what Cecilia had said. Distanced from the phenomena, he found it hard to take them seriously. Yet it was true, and he had to acknowledge, that some things had been happening that were damn hard to explain. His stock answer, hallucinations, did not explain quite everything. But that didn't mean he was going to take prognostications of doom from a thirteen-year-old seriously; if he got to that point, he'd be in real trouble. No, he told himself firmly, concentrate on the realities. The law firm, the mystery of Dave Jennings, and getting his car fixed.

Slowly but surely, the pain in Elliot's head began to subside, and finally he was able to sit up comfortably. Sometime later, Gerald and Haze returned, and he reluctantly dragged himself out to sit with them. Laura had gone out somewhere; nobody seemed to know where she might be. According to Gerald, this was not an uncommon thing for her to do.

"I was a little worried about you, man," Haze told him. "You shoulda heard your head hit the floor. Sounded like a fuckin' gunshot!"

Elliot touched the back of his head; there was definitely a tender spot there. "Yah, I guess it did!" he said. "You guys were great, though. Just walking out and leaving. Shit, I could've been dying here!"

"Laura said you'd be okay," Gerald told him. "She's never wrong about things like that. Never. She's psychic, man; she's got the gift."

"Yeah, she told me. But I don't put much stock in that kind of thing."

"You just watch her for a while, and you will," Gerald said firmly. "Anyhow, I'm surprised you'd say that—you've been living with Missy, right? She's got it too. Not as strong as Laura's, but she's got it."

For just an instant he didn't know who Gerald was talking about. No one at UNC called Melissa "Missy." "She has surprised me from time to time," he admitted.

"If she's surprised you, Laura'll blow you away. When she says something like that, you can bet on it!"

"It's the truth, man," Haze put in.

"She is kind of a strange girl. How'd she end up here?"

"I found her," Haze said, looking proud. "In a Dumpster in the alley just outside. It was jus' like somebody'd throwed her away. So I tol' her, you come on up, get sumpin' to eat. She did, and she just kinda stayed on."

"You don't know anything about where she came from or anything?"

"No. Midwest someplace. Minnesota, that's it," Gerald

said. "We really didn't give her a third degree, Elliot. She was in need, and we made her welcome here."

He didn't ask any more questions. It was not, after all, the normal custom in places like the Village to try to find out about runaways; there were certainly plenty of them around. And in a way, Laura was in a better position than many; at least she had a place to live. It was just that to Elliot, she seemed so young, so vulnerable. He couldn't help but be concerned.

The evening wore on slowly; his conversations with Gerald and Haze turned to other topics. When he finally went to bed for the night—at about three A.M.—the girl still hadn't returned. But since he was bedded down in the front room, on an old mattress Haze produced from someplace, he was awakened when the front door opened. Like a ghost, Laura came in, went past him, and disappeared into one of the bedrooms. Though he was fully roused, he resisted the temptation to speak to her.

21

The next morning—a Friday—he left the apartment around eleven, planning to take care of the business with the law firm before the weekend. The address was on the Avenue of the Americas, not far from Central Park. He took the subway, had no difficulty finding the building that Mr. Nicholas had specified on the phone. A revolving door and a set of wide, highly-polished glass doors led him into an ostentatiously spacious foyer. Across from the doors were elevators, and a directory next to them. He found the suite of offices he was looking for—twenty-third floor—and took the elevator up.

Inside the front office, a blonde receptionist with thick glasses sat at her desk reading a magazine of some sort. He came closer: *Modern Romances*. She looked up, put the magazine away.

"Yes, sir, can I help you?" she asked in a nasal voice. The sentence was punctuated by smacking gum.

"I'm Dr. Elliot Collins," he told her. "I received a letter from your offices, talked to a Mr. Nicholas?"

"Who?"

"Howard Nicholas."

"Nobody here by that name, sirrrr . . ." she said, dragging out the last syllable.

He sighed; this, he didn't need. Couldn't she just look up his name in the files, or whatever? "Look," he said. "Like I told you, I got a letter from you. Something about securities owned by my father, Aaron Collins. Of Eddieville, Illinois. Maybe I got Mr. Nicholas's name wrong, I don't know. But—"

"You have the letter, sirrrr . . ." she asked, interrupting him.

"Uh—sure." He dug in his back pocket, produced the folded letter, and gave it to her. She opened it, studied it minutely for a few seconds.

"This didn't come from us," she told him. "It isn't on our letterhead." She practically threw the letter back at him.

"What? But—but it says—"

"I can see what it says, sirrrr. I wouldn't know who sent it. If we did, I'm sure that Mr. Hopkins would take appropriate legal action. But it didn't come from our offices." She reached into a drawer, pulled out a sheet of paper, showed it to him. "That's our letterhead," she told him curtly and reached for her magazine.

He started to get angry. "Look, could I see one of the attorneys, please?" he demanded.

She made a sound he supposed was a sigh—it was so vigorous it stirred the papers on her desk—and picked up a phone. "Mr. Hopkins?" she said into it. "There's a Dr. Caulkins or somebody out here to see you. Yes, sir. I'll tell him." She hung up, turned to Elliot. "Have a seat. He'll be out in a while."

After a wait of twenty minutes, a heavy-set, fiftyish man emerged, looked at Elliot. His expression was that of a man viewing something somehow disgusting. "Can I help you?" he asked, not even trying to conceal his hostility.

Elliot returned his attitude, showed him the letter. After he'd looked it over, he seemed to be somewhat mollified, and became more genial.

"I can see why you're upset, Dr. Collins," he said. "I don't suppose you have the envelope this came in?"

"No, but it had the same return address as the one on the letter—"

"Well, hmph!" He turned to the receptionist. "Miss Tuttle, make a Xerox of this, please?" he asked. The girl sighed again but took the letter and disappeared, emerging seconds later with the copy. "As Miss Tuttle told you, this isn't our letterhead, didn't come from us. If we can determine who is using our name, then we will of course—"

"But I called here! Talked to a man named Howard Nicholas—"

"Dr. Collins, no such person is employed here."

"Is this your phone number?" He held the letter up, pointed.

"Yes—"

"Then the letter came from here. Maybe not officially, but I called this number, talked to a man who said he was Howard Nicholas, and he verified everything—"

"Dr. Collins, that is just not possible—"

"Better check your staff," Elliot said, heading for the door. "Somebody's playing games!" He stomped out, tried to slam the door, but the pneumatic plunger wouldn't let him. More than a little annoyed, he took the elevator down, left the building.

Although he'd intended to go back to Gerald's apartment after leaving the lawyer's office, he decided not to. It was a nice day; maybe it'd be interesting to just wander around the city, he told himself. Maybe stop off at the Museum of Natural History, which wasn't far from where he was now. Before he did, though, he located a phone booth, tried Marcia's number; again he got the "out of service" message. That wasn't a great surprise. He shrugged, went up the street in the general direction of the museum. But he didn't know New York very well, and it took him a while to find it.

He ended up spending the whole afternoon there, eventually leaving around five o'clock. For another couple of hours, he wandered rather aimlessly, window-shopping; then he realized he was hungry, began looking for restaurants. He found one that seemed amenable in terms of clientele and decor, and tried it. The food was awful. But at least it filled him up, took care of dinner for the evening.

After the dinner rush was over, a folksinger was entertaining at the restaurant. He wasn't a bad singer, and Elliot remained for another hour or so, listening to him; mostly he did the older Donovan songs, with some original material thrown in. When Elliot finally left the place, it was almost sunset.

Once more, he tried to call Marcia, with the same results. Irritating, he thought. If he couldn't find Dave, the whole trip would end up serving no purpose at all—now that the letter had turned out to be some kind of hoax. That he really hadn't given any thought to; but it was, now that he considered it, a damn peculiar hoax. If it was funny to anyone, or gained anyone anything, it wasn't obvious. Briefly he toyed with the idea that perhaps Jim Cardwell or the prof that Melissa had gone out with had done it to get him out of the way for a while. But he dismissed that as paranoid; if Melissa was interested, he was out of the way often enough between his classes and experiments. It just wasn't necessary for anyone to go to all that trouble. Putting that idea out of his mind, he entered a nearby subway station. Back to the Village, or uptown to Marcia's? he asked himself. It was still early in the evening; he decided to go up to Cabrini, see if Dave had possibly turned up.

But it turned out to be a wasted trip, and he swore at the phone company as he rang the bell outside the building with no results. Evidently no one was there. That was too bad, he thought; maybe he could have gotten some information about her whereabouts from Marcia and Eileen. Easiest thing, he told himself, was to call Melissa, find out where Eileen was. But that, unfortunately, would be impossibly gauche.

For good measure, he punched the button once more; there was still no response. His eyes strayed to number 9C, with its enigmatic blank name card, and for just a second his fingertip played over it; but then he decided that was stupid, and he turned, headed back toward the subway station.

As he rounded the corner, under the multitude of one-way signs, he glanced quickly up and down Cabrini. Not a single soul was out in that street, and it occurred to him that that was somewhat strange; this was a residential district, and you certainly wouldn't expect the bustle of Times Square, but no one? It was almost eerie, the emptiness; there weren't any cars, either. He glanced up and down the buildings, where lighted windows formed a random abstract against the dark brick; the lights bespoke people, yet he could see no one. It was as if he were absolutely alone out here, as if he were somewhere in the wilderness. A gentle breeze blew a scrap of paper along, moved the trees along the sidewalk slowly, causing the street-lamp shadows to move. He looked up at the hazy shape of a moon just past full and thought it looked tropical. But he didn't know where that idea came from.

Trying to shrug off this mood, he walked down the hill toward the steps, idly looking in the windows of the few small shops located here. Now, finally, he saw another person on the street; a woman, walking up the other side toward Cabrini. He gave her a casual glance, started to continue on his way, but then what he'd seen registered. Stopping cold, he looked around at her. By now she'd passed him, and he couldn't see her face, but he could see a trim figure in a red miniskirt and chiffon blouse, topped by curly black hair. Moving only his eyes, he watched her cross over, start down Cabrini in the general direction of number 491. Like a windup toy, he followed her, his mind in complete turmoil.

He wasn't even terribly surprised when she turned into the courtyard in front of 491. Wasn't surprised when she took a key from her purse, moved it toward the door. But she stopped, glanced back over her shoulder. He caught just a glimpse of a smile, then she turned fully. Face-to-face, he still couldn't be that surprised. Same dark eyes, same face. Exactly like Nikki in the photographs, one twenty-seven and the other fifty-three years old.

"Excuse me," she said, her voice light and musical. "Are you following me?"

All he could do for a moment was stare at her. In a way, he was astounded that she spoke. He tried to answer, but he couldn't find his voice; nothing would come out. Finally, after much effort, he choked out a feeble no.

"I could have sworn you were," she said, putting a delicate fingertip against her lower lip. "You turned around, walked behind me all the way up here." She didn't seem the least bit upset or afraid.

"No—I—well, I guess I—look," he said, his voice dry and cracking, "would you mind telling me your name?"

She laughed, a lovely sound to him. "Not at all!" she said. "It's Nicole—Nicole Howard. But everybody calls me Nikki, okay?"

It was only with the greatest effort that he remained standing. "Not Townsend?" he asked when he could speak again.

She looked at him closely. "Townsend? Hm! Familiar name, that. But no, my friend. Howard. What about you?"

"I'm Elliot," he mumbled.

"Nice name, Elliot. What brings you up here?"

"I was looking for someone—it's a long story."

"You weren't looking for—uh—a good time then, were you?"

He stared, not comprehending. "A good time?" he said blankly.

"No, I suppose not. Okay, Elliot Collins," she said, putting a hand on her hip. "What shall we do now, then?"

"Do?" he said stupidly.

"Yes, do! You want to stand here all night?"

"No, I—uh—"

"Well. I could stand some coffee, myself. How about you?"

"Fine!" he said, almost too quickly. "That is, uh—"

"Good. I know a place a few blocks down; we'll go there." She started to walk, and he hesitated. "Come on, Elliot; what are you waiting for?"

"I don't—that is, I—"

She shook her head, chuckled. "You need something, that's for sure. You are in a sad state! Can't even talk!"

"No, I'm—wait, wait," he said, almost in a panic. "You called me Elliot Collins! How did you know? All I said was my name's Elliot—"

She looked directly into his eyes; her own were incredible to him, endlessly deep. "No," she said firmly. "You said, 'I'm Elliot Collins.' How else would I know? I just met you."

"Sure," he muttered, as he followed her down the street. "How else?" A brisk wind kicked up suddenly, stirring the tops of the trees along the quiet street; dust swirled around her feet as she walked, shadows moving alongside her. There seemed to be a little whirlwind, a tiny dust devil, right around her legs, skittering small pieces of paper across the pavement. It seemed to Elliot that it was sweeping the way for her.

They didn't talk at all as they walked to a little coffee shop and went in. As they did, he realized he had no idea whatsoever of where they were; he'd been watching her so intently he'd paid no attention to the turns she was making. Seated in a booth by the window, he watched the traffic on the brightly lit George Washington Bridge, knew he could not be too far from her apartment.

"So, Elliot," she said, after the waitress had brought coffee, "you never did tell me who you were looking for up in my area."

"Well, it sounds kind of odd. But—you do live in that building, right? Number 491?" She nodded, and he asked her if she knew Marcia Cates. He was in a frenzy to ask her about herself, but he wasn't sure how to.

"Marcia Cates—9B, right?" she asked, resting her chin on her palms. "She's a friend of yours?"

"No—a guy named Dave Jennings is. Marcia I never met until yesterday." He went on, explaining the story to her. She seemed to listen intently, smiling with her eyes, as he talked.

"Well, I can't help you, I'm afraid," she told him. "I don't know Dave Jennings either. And Marcia and I are only acquaintances." She waved her hand, evidently dismissing the whole subject. "But tell me about yourself, Elliot Collins. You aren't a New Yorker. Where are you from, what do you do?"

"Chapel Hill, North Carolina," he said. "The university— I'm a teacher there."

"Oh, a professor? Of what?"

"Psychology."

Now she looked out the window, presenting a profile to him. "The mind is a fascinating thing, isn't it?" she said. "So complicated. You believe you understand the mind, Elliot?"

The question sounded almost condescending, and he wondered if he should take offense. "No, not really," he told her, not wanting to get into a long discussion of his work. "We just study some facets of it—"

"And what exactly is it you study?"

"Oh, you wouldn't be interested in—"

"I might surprise you," she said, looking back at him. "I'm interested in all kinds of things."

"Well," he said doubtfully, his attention distracted by those incredibly dark eyes, "what I study, myself—my own specialty, that is—is perception. How people can believe they've seen one thing, when in fact what they saw was something totally different. Like an eyewitness to a crime; the courts take them very seriously, but scientifically speaking, we know they're real unreliable. Usually, what they think they've seen is so heavily influenced by their prejudices—"

"So what they see is colored by their attitudes, by what they believe to be truth?" she asked.

He stared at her. "Yes, exactly."

"How far do you think that goes, Elliot?"

"What do you mean?"

"Well, let's say that if my belief was that I was in the tropics—then when I looked out the window, would I see palm trees, plumeria flowers?"

"You might, but that would be—uh—very delusional, I guess. I mean, there's such a thing as reality testing, too. Of course, it doesn't—" He trailed away, looking out the window at palm trees, an ocean beach in the moonlight, big red flowers sprouting from the foliage. He blinked; then he was seeing the bridge again, the Hudson River. He looked back at her; she was sipping her coffee, looking down into the cup.

"I like the tropics," she said after a moment. "Sometimes I like to pretend I'm there."

"For a minute there, I thought—" Again he let his voice trail away. Once again, he attributed the experience to hallucination. That one, he told himself firmly, had to be, suggested by her comment about the tropics. "Anyway," he said in a stronger voice, "enough about me. How about you? You a born New Yorker?"

"No, I was born in Spain," she told him. "Grew up in Mexico. I guess that's where I got my love of the tropics."

"That's interesting. You have no accent at all."

"No, I've been here for a while. But, Spanish is my native tongue." As if to illustrate, she rolled it around her lips, a gesture Elliot found very seductive.

"What do you do?" he asked conversationally.

"Oh, a variety of things," she said vaguely. "I get along, let's put it that way. Nothing so interesting as studying perceptions, Elliot."

"I'd really—"

"No, no, you wouldn't be interested," she told him firmly. Skillfully she steered the conversation into other areas, trivial matters: how did he like the city, how long was he staying? As she spoke, he let his eyes wander up and down the part of her body that was exposed over the edge of the table. There were many things he'd rather talk about than this, he realized, such as, what she wore to bed.

"Are you married, Elliot?" she asked him abruptly. He was startled; the question had come off the end of a discourse on how passionately she despised the air and water pollution in the city, the dirt on the streets.

"Uh—no—"

"Committed?"

Jesus, she was direct, he thought. "No," he lied. Somehow, he felt she knew it, felt it'd be hard to effectively lie to her. But she let it pass. "What about yourself?" he asked, trying to redirect the discussion.

"Not me," she told him. "Not married, no, not me, never me." She looked away from him, out the window again, and he thought her eyes might be a little misty. "Not married, no babies, no commitments, no strings. I, Elliot, am what you would call free."

He grinned, thinking she was hamming it up; her statements sounded sort of trite. "Just another word for nothing left to lose," he quoted.

She looked back at him, and her eyes were definitely moist. "There's considerable truth to that," she said. "But I have my hopes for the future. I suppose everyone does. It just seems I've had to wait an awfully long time."

"I'm sorry," he said awkwardly. "I didn't mean to—"

"Oh, I know you didn't, Elliot. Please, don't worry about it." She lifted a slim arm, glanced at her watch. "Oh, God," she said, "I'm running late. I was supposed to be somewhere ten minutes ago. You realize we've been sitting here almost an hour?"

He hadn't realized it—it seemed like only a few minutes to him. Thinking she was leaving because he'd made a joke about something meaningful to her, he cursed his clumsiness. Desperately, he cast about for something to maintain their connection. But all he could do was sputter incoherently.

"I'm sorry I have to run," she said coolly, not appearing to notice his panic. "But I would like to see you again. If you want to, Elliot."

I'd only kill for it, he told himself. "Yes, I'd like that—" he said, his fist clenched under the table.

"Fine. Tomorrow, then; around noon, my place?"

"Sounds good—"

"I'll see you then," she said, headed for the door.

"Wait!" he cried. "Which apartment do you—"

"Oh, Elliot," she said without slowing down, "you already know it's 9C!"

For some time after Nikki had left, Elliot remained in the coffee shop, going over virtually every word that had passed between them. In the flesh, she had almost the same impact on him as her photo had when he was thirteen. That realization in itself threw him into a quandary—she didn't merely resemble the girl in the photo, she was identical to her. If he doubted that they were one and the same, he could never trust a photo to be representative again. Besides, the same address? It was just too much of a coincidence to be acceptable. But how was it possible for her to look like that? She didn't look a day over twenty-five, at the outside. It certainly did not, however, put him off; it only made her more fascinating.

Like a sleepwalker, he took the subway back down to the Village, walked through the streets without really seeing what was around him; he still could see her image in his imagination. At that moment, he felt as if he'd found the Holy Grail. He was so distracted that it came as something of a surprise when he found himself back inside Gerald's apartment.

Laura greeted him as he came in; she was lounging in the worn armchair, still wearing the outsized dress. She informed him that Gerald was sleeping and Haze was out somewhere. He nodded an acknowledgment, collapsed wearily onto the cushions across from her. Glancing up, he saw the girl looking down at him from her elevated position on the chair. Her eyes were heavy-lidded, intense, looked far older than thirteen years.

"Something's happened," she said, a statement rather than a question. "To you."

"Yes," he said simply, not wishing to encourage the conversation.

She leaned forward, studied his face closely. "You're real close," she said. Her tone was normal, but somehow her voice gave him the creeps. "Close to some kind of fire, Elliot. And you're some kind of moth. You're going to be burned up."

"Maybe so," he told her. "I don't know if I know anything for sure anymore. Tonight, I met a girl who looks twenty-five and is about seventy-five. A female Dorian Gray. What do you think of that?"

For a moment, she was silent. Then: "I don't know Dorian Gray, but—did this woman tell you she was seventy-five?"

Overcome by a need to talk to someone about this, Elliot told her about the two pictures, the letter. "So you see, Laura, I can't make any sense out of this—it just doesn't—"

She interrupted him. "I know it's strange, but—maybe there was a Nikki in 1916 who had a daughter, named her Nikki, too. That was Nikki 1942. Then she had a daughter, named her Nikki, and that's the Nikki you met today. How about that?"

He stared at her, momentarily struck dumb. Well, Elliot, he thought, you absolute jerk. Of course, that's the answer. But it had never occurred to him! Even when he himself was dealing with three generations of Collins men! He marveled at his utter stupidity; maybe it was a bit strange that the present Nikki lived in the same place as Nikki 1942. There'd been nothing to suggest that Nikki 1916 had lived there—and maybe the family resemblance was awfully close, but that was sure as hell more logical than assuming the woman hadn't aged appreciably in sixty years! He shook his head, looked up at the young girl in the chair. "Well, you can call me an idiot if you want to; I never thought of it," he said to her.

"No," she said, "you're just too close to it. Besides, maybe that isn't right; it's just an idea."

"I'm sure that is it," he said, with a weak grin. Still didn't explain the other things, but he was getting some of his old confidence back. There had to be, after all, logical explanations of some sort.

She didn't say anything for a while. When he looked back up, she was just staring at him with those sleepy, yet intense, eyes. "I dunno," she said, as if he'd asked her a question. "I don't think everything does have a logical explanation. Or maybe—hell, I don't know how to say this, even—maybe there's more than one kinda logical. You think?"

"I don't think! Logical is logical, there's only one kind—"

"I dunno," she reiterated. "Like I said before: somethin's happenin' to you. Already started, like maybe it started a long time ago. I can feel—everybody calls 'em vibes, but I ain't sure it's the same thing—I see you like a man in a whirlpool. No, that ain't right. What I said before is. Moth to a flame. Difference is, a moth don't know nuthin' about no flame. If he did, he wouldn't go near it. But you—if you knew what was waitin' for you in that fire, you'd jump right in there! Jump right in, burn up and die!"

He grinned up at her. "I'd like to think I'm a little smarter than that!" He was trying to make light of her comments, but she was still succeeding in making his skin crawl.

She shook her head. "It's a special fire. You gotta be special to jump in. If it was bein' offered to me—" Her voice faded out, and she looked away.

"You can't tell me you'd do it!"

She swung her face back. "Can't tell you I wouldn't, either," she told him seriously. "But it ain't gonna be my choice. It's gonna be yours, pretty soon now. Think about it, Elliot. It's the most important decision you'll ever make!"

22

By nine the next morning, Elliot was up and chafing. He wasn't supposed to meet Nikki until noon, and somehow he had to kill three hours. All three of the apartment's tenants had gone out somewhere, leaving him alone with his restlessness. Twice he picked up the phone, thinking about calling Melissa in Chapel Hill, but both times he decided that it just wasn't fair to her. To kill time talking to her while waiting anxiously to meet another woman? He concluded, in the end, that it was beneath him.

Behind the pile of cushions on the floor in the front room was the long bookshelf built up from cement blocks and slightly wavy wooden planks; on it was Gerald's inexpensive stereo, a large number of rather worn records, and a number of books. Elliot turned on the stereo, put on "Surrealistic Pillow" by the Jefferson Airplane, listened to Grace Slick's voice crackle and pop. While it was playing, he went through the books, looking for something that would occupy his mind for a couple of hours. But he wasn't lucky; except for a copy of the teachings of Don Juan, there was nothing of interest to him. He wandered into the cluttered kitchen, made coffee, and sat sipping it, listening to the Airplane, then to the Beatles' "Sergeant Pepper." When it had finished, his eye was caught by a guitar standing in the corner; he hadn't noticed it before. Down the back of the neck was painted in Day-Glo violet the legend "Purple Haze." He grinned, picked it up. No chance to practice his guitar lately, he thought; might as well take the opportunity. He tuned it up, played several Leonard Cohen songs that he knew from memory. Finally he tired of it, put the instrument back. Glancing at his watch, he found that he had succeeded in dispatching about forty-five minutes. His eye caught the copy of Casteneda's book on the shelf, and he pulled it out, began to reread sections of it.

Even though he almost knew parts of it by memory now, he managed to engross himself in the book to the point that the remaining time passed very quickly. When he looked at his watch again, it was after eleven-thirty. In a rush, he left the apartment and took a cab uptown, afraid that he'd be late and Nikki wouldn't wait for him.

But she did. Outside the building, sunglasses obscuring her dark eyes, she was sitting on the edge of the stoop when the cab pulled up. Before he could pay the driver and get out, she hurried up to it and got in. Although it embarrassed him even as he did it, he could not resist letting his eyes roam up and down her body. Again, her extreme miniskirt was red, though a different shade than the one she'd been wearing the previous night; and the blouse she wore today was very sheer, giving him tantalizing glimpses of her breasts under it. On her feet she wore a kind of moccasin, with thin leather straps that laced up her calves. All in all, he told himself, an exquisite picture.

Smiling faintly, she let him look before she said anything. "Let's not let the cab go," she suggested. "We don't want to hang around here, do we?"

He would have loved to, but he was willing to agree to pretty much anything she wanted. "Wherever," he told her.

She gave the driver an address somewhere downtown, and they leaned back in the seat as a rather manic ride began. "So, Elliot," she said. "How was the rest of your evening?"

"Dull," he told her, dismissing the topic. There was a matter he wanted to get out of the way first. "Nikki—uh—by any chance, does the name Aaron Collins mean anything to you? Ever hear it before?"

She looked thoughtful. "No, I can't say that I have," she told him finally. "A relative of yours?"

"My father."

"Oh." Pause. Then: "Why would you think I might have heard his name? Was he famous for something?"

"No. I just thought you might have heard his name from your mother at some time."

"From my mother?" she asked, looking bewildered.

"Yes. I do believe your mother and my father knew each other. Your mother's name was Nikki as well, right?"

She looked at him blankly. "No," she said. "It was Consuela."

Completely unprepared for that answer, he just stared at her for a moment. He'd been so damn sure! "Consuela?" he echoed.

"Yes. As I told you, I was born in Spain. Consuela's a common enough name."

"But—but—"

She took off her sunglasses, looked at him intently. "What is it, Elliot?" she asked.

He surrendered. Even if she thought him insane, he had to clear this up. Pulling the pictures out of his shirt pocket, he handed them to her.

She studied them, frowning, rolling them over in her hands. "So?" she asked, handing them back.

He held them loosely, looking at her. "So, what's the explanation, then?"

"Explanation for what?"

"For these!" he cried, glancing down at the 1942 picture as he pointed to it. "For the fact that—" He stopped, held the picture up in front of his eyes and goggled at it. The dock, the pier, the ocean, all the same, but the woman standing there bore no resemblance to Nikki at all. His fingers trembling, he rolled it over. On the back, it said: "Paula—1942." He turned it again, stared at the picture of his mother as a young woman. The other one was also utterly different: a blonde woman, and on the back, "Eva—1916." His grandmother. Gingerly, as if they might explode or something, he laid the pictures on the seat and pulled out the letter. He didn't take it out; the envelope was enough. It was addressed to "Miss Paula Graves, 1702 Lakeview Drive, South Bend, Indiana." Again, his mother. He was unable to move; he just sat there, his eyes fixed on the envelope.

Gently, Nikki took the envelope from his hand, looked at it. "Tell me, Elliot," she said in a soothing voice. "What is all this?"

He looked away from her. "I'm going crazy," he said flatly. "I would swear, in any court, that for the past twelve years— since I first saw it—that that picture looked exactly like you do now. But all of a sudden it doesn't. Also, the letter—the one you're holding—had your address on it. The last name was different—it was Nikki Townsend—but the address was the same."

"Elliot, that clearly isn't possible," she said gently. "One of these pictures is dated 1916. If that was me, I'd be—let's see—over seventy now. Do I look seventy to you?"

"No," he said miserably. "I knew that was impossible. I thought, you know, grandmother, mother, daughter—all named Nikki. Shit, I know how it sounds! It's just crazy! Just fucking crazy!" He was almost yelling now, gesturing wildly. He noticed that the cabbie was glancing over his shoulder, but he paid no attention. Nikki didn't seem at all perturbed.

"Just our *tonallis*, I suppose," she told him, giving him a smile that had a distinct calming effect.

Familiar word, that. "What?" he asked.

"It's a Nahuatl word. An Indian language, spoken in some places in Mexico. It sort of means fate. In a way."

He remembered; Eileen had used that word. "I thought it was an Aztec word—"

"You've heard it before?" she asked, seemingly surprised.

"Yes—from a friend of mine in Chapel Hill. She said it meant karma—"

"Close, yes. Not quite, but close. And the language is right, too; Nahuatl is the language the Aztecs spoke. Some Indians still speak it; it isn't a dead language. I grew up in an area where more people spoke Nahuatl than Spanish!"

"My karma is to be driven insane," he muttered.

"Now, Elliot, I think you're really stronger than that! You just take everything so seriously! Relax, try to enjoy yourself. You're here, after all. So am I, and we've already become friends. Take it at face value, Elliot. Consider it fated."

He looked away from her, out the window of the cab. They were somewhere in midtown, he couldn't really tell where. Such an ordinary world out there, all those ordinary people walking on ordinary streets. "It never has been easy for me to just accept things as they are," he told her, feeling instinctively that she was right, that they were friends, that he could open up to her. "I always have to question things, and if the answers aren't right, I have to go my own way. Even when I was a child, I did that. It's why I went into science, why I joined the protests and all. But even there, I don't fit in very well."

"Understandable," she said, her hand on his shoulder. "And I might tell you, Elliot, that independent minds are a valuable commodity in the world. There aren't all too many of them, you know."

"No, I didn't know," he said unnecessarily, still staring out the window.

"All I'm telling you to do now is let go of it for a few hours, a few days. You could use the rest, my friend."

He turned, looked back at her. "I know you're right," he said. "But it isn't easy for me."

She started to respond, but the cab was pulling to a halt in front of a Mexican restaurant. He looked around, saw that they were on Seventh Avenue, quite close to the Village. Before he could protest, Nikki tossed the driver a couple of bills—he didn't see how much—and hustled Elliot out of the cab. "For now," she said firmly, "all I want you to think about is lunch!"

She led him across the sidewalk toward two elegantly carved wooden doors under a little canopy emblazoned with the word "Alejandro's," through the doors and inside. It was somewhat dark in the entryway; all he could make out was a stucco wall on one side and a kind of decorative fence on the other. Though his eyes were still adjusting to the low illumination, Nikki seemed to have no problems. She took him straight down the hall, where they were greeted by a tall man in a costume undoubtedly intended to suggest a bullfighter.

"Ah, Nikki," the man said. "Always a pleasure to see you, my lady! And a guest? Mr.—?"

"Dr. Elliot Collins, this is Juan Reyes, an old friend of mine," she said.

"I am so pleased," Juan told him, extending his hand. Elliot took it, looked at the man. Reyes—hadn't he heard that name recently? Yes, he remembered; on one of the apartments on the ninth floor up on Cabrini. Perhaps it was Juan's apartment, he told himself. But there was something else, he just couldn't place it. The restaurant name itself was familiar, but from where, he couldn't say. Trying to jog his memory, he studied the man. He was very dark-skinned, had high cheekbones and black, unreadable eyes. Indian, no doubt, or at least in large part. He mumbled a response, allowed himself to be guided through a maze of tables and chairs inside, past a pair of saloon-type doors leading into a darkened hallway. Over the arched doorway was a sign, "The Obsidian Butterfly." Curious, he glanced down there but could see nothing.

"What's that?" he asked.

"That's the bar," Nikki told him. "It doesn't open until seven in the evenings." She and Reyes led him on, to an out-of-the-way table nestled back in a corner. Apparently Nikki was a favored customer; he would have judged this table's location best in the house.

"This is a favorite place of mine," Nikki told him. "I wanted you to see it."

He glanced around. Lacking was some of the usual decor of Mexican restaurants, the posters of bullfights, the sombreros on the walls. Everything here seemed to reflect an older Mexico: paintings of pre-Columbian pyramids, primitive but very artistic masks, a few small sculptures in glass-covered niches in the walls. They were seated under one such, a statue of a nearly naked man wearing an odd mask that looked rather like the bill of a duck.

"It's an unusual place," he told her, making a complete circle before he rested his eyes again on her face. "Not set up like most Mexican restaurants I've seen."

"No, it isn't. I've known the Reyes family for a long time. They have very little European blood; they trace their lineage back to Ixtlilxochitl, prince of Texcoco."

He assumed the first odd word was a name, but the second

was just as unfamiliar. "Texaco?" he asked. "I've never heard of it."

She laughed, a sound he was already growing quite fond of. "No, Tesh—coco!" she said, softening the "x" and emphasizing the second syllable. "A town in the Valley of Mexico, a few miles outside of Mexico City. It had a proud heritage; some called it the 'Athens of the New World.' Of course, Cortez and the Conquistadors changed all that."

"You seem to know a lot about that sort of stuff," he observed. Funny, he thought. Eileen was into the same things. Maybe it went with the hair and eyes.

She shrugged. "Like I said, I grew up there. Sort of immersed myself in the culture, you might say."

"Must have been an interesting childhood."

"Oh, it was never dull," she told him, getting a faraway look in here eyes. "I miss it sometimes, too. But New York can be exciting as well, don't you think?"

"Perhaps. I'm not really a big-city person myself. As they say, 'a nice place to visit, but—' "

"In a lot of ways, I agree," she said. A waitress came by, a quite attractive Indian girl whom Nikki introduced as Carlotta—Reyes, of course. She only nodded to Elliot, but seemed to hang on every word Nikki said. After Elliot indicated that her choice for lunch would be fine, she rattled off a few phrases in Spanish and the girl retreated to the kitchen. Carlotta was as graceful as a deer, Elliot noticed, watching her black hair, which hung past her waist, swing as she walked.

"So, as you were saying?" he asked Nikki.

She smiled at him, then looked somewhat confused. "Uh—I forgot what I was saying!" she confessed.

He grinned back, the first time he'd really smiled since he'd tried to show her the pictures. Almost involuntarily, he reached for his shirt pocket, planning to look at them again.

"Why?" she asked simply, watching his hand.

He stopped himself. "I don't know," he told her candidly. "See if they've changed again, I guess."

She shook her head. "You know they haven't, Elliot. Pictures of your mother and grandmother, that's all. Images on film don't change!"

His hand still on his pocket, he looked back into her eyes. This time, he was very sure. "I didn't tell you whose pictures they were," he said slowly.

"Again, Elliot?" she said with a little laugh. "Last night you did the same thing with your last name! If you hadn't told me, I couldn't possibly know! Unless I can read your mind. Do you believe that?"

"No, I suppose not," he said, putting his hand down. He felt silly.

"Then let's stop this. And there's no need for you to be embarrassed. Like I told you in the cab—relax, go with it! Aren't you having a good time?"

"Yes, I am," he replied, but without much animation. At that moment, he felt a little intimidated by her.

She fell silent, her eyes dropping to her lap, the smile gone from her face. "Maybe this wasn't such a good idea, our going out, I mean," she said somewhat wistfully, sounding like a disappointed teenager. "You don't seem to—"

"Oh, no," he assured her, immediately anxious that his contact with her would be broken. He babbled on for quite a while, mostly just trying to keep her attention. He told her corny jokes, and she laughed at them; he believed the laughs were genuine. It took only ten minutes before she was all smiles once more, and he was feeling downright wonderful.

Carlotta returned to their table, bearing a plate with a number of little squares of dark brown material that resembled breads, or cakes. Nikki indicated that he should try one, and he did; he found it delicious and told her so.

"It's called Tzoalli," she informed him. "You seldom see it anymore. Made from amaranth, corn, and dark honey; it was held to be a sacred food by the Aztecs."

"It really is very good," he commented. He resisted the temptation to fill up on it, and a short while later their lunches, a chili-like stew with tortillas, arrived at the table. This too Elliot found enjoyable.

"So tell me," he told her as they dawdled over the excellent coffee that Carlotta had brought without being asked, "you said you grew up in Mexico. Why'd you leave?"

She got a slightly faraway look in her eyes. "A lot of reasons," she said. "But mostly, I suppose, it was just time for me to move on, do other things."

"Sounds like you miss it, though."

"In ways, at times. For me, it's home. I never really knew Spain at all."

"How old were you when you moved?"

"About three when we left. For a while we lived near Mexico City. Then when I was—oh, I guess maybe nine—we moved to the coast. Three years later, there was an—accident. My parents were killed."

"You were orphaned at twelve?" He was curious about the nature of the accident but didn't ask. Probably a car crash or something similar; he assumed it would be hard for her to talk about it.

"Yes—at first, it was hard. Then I was taken in by a—uh—a village elder, you might say. He was family to me—the only family I had—after that."

"Didn't you have any relatives in Spain?"

"I don't know. I might have. I never bothered. You have to understand, Elliot—it might sound cold to you, but I didn't shed a lot of tears when my parents died."

Immediately, on hearing a statement like that, the psychologist in him took over. "You didn't get along with your parents?"

"Yes, I got along well enough. It's just that—well, most of the people in the village were Indians. And my parents, they were people of their place and time, which means in modern terms, about as racist as you could get. It wasn't that they didn't like the Indians—rather, they considered them about on the same level as pet dogs. That can be worse than being hated, you know. But I—I was just a little girl. And the Indian children were my friends. I didn't feel the same way. By the time my parents died, I had begun to believe it was they who were not human."

"That does sound hard," he said sympathetically.

"It was. But the old man—the one who took me in—he made up for a lot of it. He treated me like his own daughter, taught me all kinds of things. He was wonderful to me."

"I'm glad he was there for you."

"So am I. If he hadn't been, I probably wouldn't be here talking to you now."

"That bad?"

"That bad."

He'd been watching her carefully; there was some odd expression in her eyes, and he took it to indicate discomfort. He decided to shift the subject just a little, perhaps come back to these potentially painful memories later. "So what sort of things did your adopted father teach you?" he asked her.

"Oh, like I said, all kinds. Herbal medicines, all about the old legends and prophecies, about the *tonal* and the *nagual*. About life, and the world. All kinds of things."

He caught the word *tonal*, and the unfamiliar word following it. "I missed something," he said. "Nah-wal?"

"*Nagual*," she corrected. "*Nahualli*, in the old language."

"The Aztec language."

"Uh-huh. Nahuatl."

"What does it mean?"

She laughed. "You got two weeks to spare?" she asked. "It's pretty complicated. But let me try, in a nutshell. That word doesn't translate very well. It can mean "double," it can mean something like "spiritual," and it can mean something like "sorcerer." It always refers, one way or another, to an animal. An animal a person is sort of—shall we say paired with, or linked to." She paused. "Though sometimes the animal can be a person. Maybe even a bicycle!"

He shook his head. "Sorry, I'm not following you at all." Actually, he wasn't sure she meant for him to.

"Okay, start at the start, Nikki," she told herself. "First, *tonal*. *Tonal* means "fate" or "destiny"—tendency to, not absolute—in terms of someone's ordinary life in the ordinary world. So sometimes the word gets used to refer to the totality of the ordinary world and whatever is in it. You are a college professor. If you are a good one—and you don't have to practically destroy yourself to be a good one—and if you're happy doing it, then it is in your *tonal*—*tonalli*, same thing—to be one. The old man said that by consulting the ancient calendar, the tonalamatl—which is another complicated subject in itself—a skilled person could read another's *tonalli* at birth."

"Sounds like astrology."

"There are many similarities, yes. There's a belief that you can, if you want to badly enough, overcome your *tonalli*, go some other way. But the cost can be high. In opposition to all that is the *nagual*. Whatever is, and isn't part of the *tonal*, is part of the *nagual*."

"The supernatural, then."

"There is no supernatural," she said firmly. "It's a contradiction. Whatever is, is natural. I said the *tonal* included the ordinary—say that the *nagual* includes the extraordinary. That fits."

"Where does the animal come in?"

"The animal—the double—is at the heart of the *nagual* concept. The Indians believe that from birth, all of us have a spirit animal that is linked to us throughout our lives. Whatever happens to one, happens to the other. And this link is the person's connection to the—shall we say, the reality—of the *nagual*. So it's called that, too. Each person's spirit animal is called his—or her—*nagual*. And the first step in becoming aware of extraordinary things is to become aware of one's *nagual*. A person does not automatically know what kind of an animal it is, even. But if he or she can find out, it's a step toward, shall we say, spiritual improvement?"

He tried to digest all this; her animated tone indicated it was of significance to her, and he tried to take it seriously. But to him, it all sounded like garbled mysticism, complete nonsense. He didn't understand still, but he wanted to move the discussion out of this area. "Interesting," he said blithely.

"I'm boring you," she said in a mildly hurt voice.

"No, no, not at all," he said, perhaps too quickly.

"Oh, it's all right," she told him, waving her hand. "It is a lot to take at one sitting!" She saw Carlotta across the room, pointed to her empty coffee cup. The girl nodded, returned a moment later with a full pot of coffee in her hand; in the other, she still carried an equally full pitcher of some yellow juice. Nikki spoke to her in a fluid, musical language— not Spanish—and the girl nodded, smiled. She turned as if to fill Elliot's cup as well, but he started to motion her away. He didn't get the chance. She seemed to lose her grip on the juice pitcher—it held at least two quarts—and it tipped downward in her hand abruptly. The contents rolled out, started with his beard and soaked him the rest of the way down, much of it coming to rest in his lap.

Carlotta put the coffee pot and the nearly empty pitcher down on the table, a look of horror on her face. Instantly, she was mopping futilely at Elliot's shirt with her towel, a string of apologies in Spanish peppering his ears. He realized he was sitting in open-mouthed astonishment. Nikki, on the other hand, was choking back laughter. He glowered at her for a second, then caught her mood.

"Pineapple," he said, licking his beard. "I wondered!"

"We have to get you out of here," she said, getting up. "You are truly a mess!"

"I'll go along with that," he said, standing up. Liquid splashed to the floor as he did. He went to the restroom, cleaned himself up as much as possible, and returned. Nikki, Carlotta, and Juan Reyes were waiting for him. It seemed to him the women were giggling among themselves as he came back, but as soon as she saw him, Carlotta became contrite, appeared to be near tears. He assured her no permanent damage had been done, but Juan insisted on more apologies, on giving them the lunch free.

"You come back anytime," he said. "We will make this right!" Elliot thanked him, told him it was unnecessary, but he persisted.

"I have a cab waiting," Nikki said, tugging him toward the door. He was glad enough to leave; he couldn't remember ever having been quite so sticky.

Elliot had planned to go back to Gerald's apartment in the Village, clean himself up, get a change of clothes. But Nikki would not hear of it; she insisted that she had the means to get him clean and dry at her place on Cabrini, and over his objections, she instructed the cabdriver to take them there. On the trip, she snuggled close to him to keep him warm, and he could find no cause for complaint. By the time they got there, however, her clothes were wet and sticky as well.

Inside the building, the elevator was waiting, doors open, and they took it up to her floor. She fumbled her keys for a moment, but finally got the door unlocked, let him in. Forgetting about being dripping wet, he looked around the place as he walked inside; ever since he'd first seen the letter, he'd been imagining what the inside of this particular apartment might look like. In many ways, it was quite ordinary, although the relative richness of the furnishings contrasted oddly with the somewhat run-down walls, windows, and fixtures. Just like Marcia's, he thought; the landlords were apparently not too attentive to such things. As he looked around, noticing an expensive Fisher stereo on a solid cherry table, backed by a crumbling plaster wall, he wondered why she didn't move into a better place. It seemed as if she could afford it. Again, he also wondered what she did for a living. She'd been evasive about that the night before, and he hadn't gotten around to asking her again today.

She steered him to a position facing the stereo and turned her back to him; a few seconds later, Jim Morrison's voice filled the room as the title cut of the Doors' album *Strange Days* began to play. Then she went to the window, pulling the blinds in such a way as to create a twilight effect in the room. Watching her, remembering the circumstances that had brought him here, the words of the song seemed entirely appropriate:

> Strange days have found us,
> Strange days have tracked us down.

"I like your taste in music," he told her.

She turned, grinned, then looked exasperated. "Well?" she asked. "What are you waiting for?"

"What?"

"Your clothes, Elliot! You're dripping all over. I can't clean them while you've got them on!"

He hesitated, wondering if she meant that he should take them off while she was standing there watching him. "Um—I, um—" he mumbled, stalling.

"You aren't embarrassed, are you?" she asked, her hands on her hips. "I guess you are," she added, shaking her head. "Maybe this will help you along!" So saying, she stripped off her own clothes in two quick, fluid motions; panties were her only underwear, and they vanished a second later. Wearing only her moccasins, she came close to him, tugged at his shirt. "Off!" she said, glaring at him.

He was a little stunned, both by her beauty and by the suddenness of her action, but only for a second. His hands found the buttons of his shirt rather quickly, and soon he was even more naked than she, since he wore no shoes. Gathering up her clothes and his together, she disappeared into an adjacent room, then returned. She didn't say a word, just cupped her hand around the back of his head, tangling her slim fingers in his wet hair, pulling his face down to hers.

In seconds they were down on the floor in front of the stereo; Elliot had no idea how they'd gotten there. This, he told himself as he nuzzled his face into her chest, was better than he could possibly have expected.

Lyrics from "Strange Days" written and composed by Jim Morrison, Ray Manzarek, John Densmore and Robby Krieger. © 1967 Doors Music Company.
All Rights Reserved. Used by Permission.

He was aware of how rare it was that a reality can exceed the fantasies that preceded it, but he was experiencing such a case. For a short while they rolled around on the thick carpet, kissing all parts of each other; as the Doors broke into "Love Me Two Times," he entered her.

Though Elliot was not exactly a Casanova, racking up a long list of "conquests," he wasn't inexperienced, either; but Nikki was something else, totally new to him. He'd found that women who were very wild and uninhibited, while exciting, often by their very wildness caused a certain dissonance in the lovemaking itself, preventing him from ever establishing any sort of rhythm. On the other hand, the more passive women were, it had to be admitted, somewhat less stimulating mentally. Nikki managed, effortlessly, to be both. At times he was aware that she was subtly guiding him, using the music as a base, yet at the same time she seemed to be in a frenzy of passion, a wild animal. But she never caused a dissonant rhythm; all was, from his viewpoint, utter perfection.

Part of his mind kept listening to the Doors, and he knew this album well; the next song was, he hoped, inappropriate—it was titled, "Unhappy Girl." When the needle came to it, he heard a pop and skip, and as if by magic, the surreal, unmusical sounds of "Horse Latitudes" started. This piece, its subject matter being the becalming of sailing ships in tropical waters, reminded him vaguely of the Spanish Conquistadors, of the Indian civilizations they'd destroyed. He felt a poignancy for them; he and Nikki slowed down, down to a gentle rocking motion, clinging to each other. They continued this until the song finished, then became wild again as the next, upbeat song started. Elliot was completely absorbed in a way he'd never been during sex; he felt as if he were stoned. The room around him—such of it as he could see—took on an unearthly, surreal character, shadows actively moving in the twilight. Yet nothing threatened. He was safe, secure, complete in this woman's arms.

When a song entitled "My Eyes Have Seen You" started, he lifted himself up away from her, not touching her anywhere except for their connection. He looked down at her face, saw that her deep eyes looked back at his. A man could lose himself in there, he thought; lose himself and never feel the loss, never care. He searched over her body, drinking in the sight of every inch: the delicate, smallish breasts; the flat stomach; the silky legs lifted to either side; the dark triangle between them. He wanted to make sure his "eyes had seen her," all of her. As the song ended, they rolled over, she took her position atop him. It seemed to him that neither of them had initiated the change of position; it just happened.

Closing his eyes for a moment, he listened to the Doors lament "I Can't See Your Face in My Mind" and a hazy image of Melissa tried to form; but, just as in the song, he couldn't get it clear. With a start, he realized that he was crying for the blonde girl, and when he opened his eyes, he saw that Nikki was crying too, for some reason. But the song ended, he returned to Nikki fully, and the tears dried. Outside, the sun must have gone behind a cloud, because, as the Doors sang, "When the Music's Over, Turn Out the Light," the light in the room became noticeably dimmer. He was rising toward his orgasm; he saw Nikki, her eyelids and lips swollen as if he had hit her; he reached for her with all his emotional self, and they seemed to explode together. Elliot almost lost consciousness, but he was aware of a peculiar thing; he could not tell the difference between the two of them at that instant. Rolling off that incredible high, he distinctly heard Jim Morrison sing something about "the scream of the obsidian butterfly," and he knew that wasn't right, those weren't the words. He couldn't think clearly; he felt utterly drained, weak. Nikki's hands fluttered over his chest, her fingers like hummingbird wings, as he let his head fall back weakly. All they could do was listen:

> What have they done to the earth,
> What have they done to our fair sister?

No, he told himself. Not right. Mother, not sister. How presumptuous! He listened more—

> Stabbed her with knives in the side of the dawn,
> Tied her with fences and dragged her down—

With great effort, he pulled his head up, stared wildly at Nikki. "What have they done?" he shrieked. "What have they done to the Snake Woman?"

"They have stabbed her indeed," Nikki told him, her lips near his ear. "But it's all right. She comes back, she comes back. Always. Rest now, my Jaguar Warrior. Rest."

It took even more effort, but he managed to pull his arm off the floor and put it around her slender back. Then, he did rest. He could not ever remember having been so totally comfortable in his entire life.

The most peculiar scene was in front of Elliot's eyes; it seemed to him he'd seen it somewhere before, but he couldn't place it—only that it had connotations of warmth, pleasure, security. He seemed to be standing in front of a palatial stone building of some kind; in its doorway stood an odd recumbent statue, head turned to one side as if looking outward, hands holding a bowl that sat on its belly. Beyond it, inside the structure, dancing yellow lights proclaimed the fire that burned there. Behind the building, a huge monolithic, truncated stone pyramid, with some kind of pillared structure built atop it, rose high into the evening sky. Lowering his eyes, he looked at the capstone over the doorway of the palace; there was a bas-relief there, a huge serpent with rattles, diamond pattern down its back, and plumes spreading from alongside its head. He smiled at it, felt like it was an old friend. Its name—it had a name, it just wouldn't come to him—but, wasn't someone calling his name?

He awoke, looked up at the fine network of cracks covering the ceiling of Nikki's apartment. Again he heard Nikki's voice, calling to him. He focused on her as she stood by the doorway, and he smiled at her. She was still wearing her moccasins, and she had thrown on a bright red robe, which had no fastening mechanism in the front. As a result, it hung open, concealing nothing. The robe registered on his senses, but somehow didn't trigger his memory; she just looked so right in it.

"Wake up, Elliot," she was saying. "Dinner."

Glancing up at the now open blinds, he realized it was getting late; actual twilight had descended outside. He also found that he was hungry. Looking back down at himself, he saw that he was still lying on the floor in front of the stereo, still quite naked; obviously he'd fallen asleep immediately after the lovemaking, which embarrassed him somewhat. He tried to lift himself from the floor and noticed that he was, oddly, still feeling weak. But he managed, padded into the kitchen-dining nook. As he did, he wondered where his clothes were. As he did, he realized that his hair and beard, his whole body in fact, were completely cleaned of the sticky juice.

"Right there," Nikki said, as if he had asked for his clothes aloud. He looked where she was pointing; his clothes lay neatly piled on a chair, clean, dry, and pressed.

"How'd you manage that?" he asked, grinning at her. "And me, for that matter?"

"No problem," she said. "But sit down there, eat first," she told him, pointing to the chair next to the first.

He obeyed, and she served an excellent meal, though he could not identify all the dishes. He didn't care, he just ate it ravenously. It was quite surprising, he thought, that he was so hungry. After all, he and Nikki had eaten a substantial lunch at the Reyes restaurant not many hours ago, and he didn't usually eat more than just a sandwich for lunch. There was no reason in the world for him to be this hungry now, but he was. He shrugged, didn't question it much. The food was good. He felt as if he were literally starving to death, and there was no problem.

Nikki herself ate only a little, cleared the table and served coffee when he'd finished. Unashamed, he stared at her bare chest across the table; he really wanted to make love with her again, but he didn't feel as if he could, at least not at the moment. It seemed to him as if he needed to recharge himself or something.

"I've had a good day, Elliot," she said softly, breaking the silence.

"So have I. I don't want it to end."

"It has to. Not right this minute, but soon."

"Why?"

"Business, Elliot. Matters I have to attend to, tonight. Don't look so hurt, my friend. It has nothing to do with you. I'd like to see you again tomorrow, if you want."

"I do," he told her. "But to tell the truth, I'd as soon stay tonight. You can do what you need to. I'll stay out of your way."

She shook her head, looked down; but Elliot thought he caught an amused expression on her face. "No," she told him firmly. "You'll have to go, for now. Until tomorrow—pretty much anytime you want tomorrow."

He shrugged. Not what he wanted, but he'd certainly respect her wishes. "You've never told me, Nikki," he said, "what exactly your business is?"

She glanced up, then back down. "No," she said simply.

"No, you aren't going to tell me?" he asked, bewildered.

"Not now," she said, still avoiding his eyes.

"Why not?"

"Because you wouldn't understand," she said. "Maybe in a few days, I don't know. But for now, let it go, okay? What we have is good. Don't fuck it over."

"Are you a cop or something?"

She giggled a little, then burst into full laughter. "Me, a cop! Now that is a good one! Oh, no, my friend. I'm not a cop, not hardly. Look, please don't worry about it. I'll tell you, or maybe show you, soon. It's sort of practice for me. I have to do this again in a few years, in a way."

He was getting intrigued. "Your job is secret? Government?" But he could not even suggest that she might work for the CIA, FBI, or some organization like that.

"No, not government. Quit trying to guess it. Just let it go, okay? Just for now?"

He realized that there was little he could deny her, if he felt she really wanted it. Reluctantly, he agreed. She didn't rush him through his coffee, but when he'd finished it, she made a pointed suggestion that he get dressed.

Complaining all the way, he did so, and she shooed him out of the apartment after ascertaining that he had sufficient money for cab fare back to the Village. He hated to leave but soon found himself in a taxi on the way back downtown. During the ride, he was acutely aware of two things: one, he was as weak and tired as if he'd played football while out of shape, and two, he was falling in love with Nikki Howard.

23

When he reached Gerald's apartment, he was gratified that again no one was home; it gave him some time to collect his thoughts. The first thing that caught his eye was a copy of the *Daily News* lying on the chair that Laura often occupied; idly, he picked it up, looked at the front page.

The usual distressing news, he thought. Thirty Americans killed in a firefight near Da Nang; more speculations and hype about the Sharon Tate murder in California; violent confrontations between students and police at Ohio State. Of more local interest, at least to the denizens of the Village, was an article concerning the strangulation murders of four prostitutes in or near the Village area; police had no real leads but assumed that all were related, since the M.O. in each was so similar. All of the victims, according to the article, had been strangled with either a piece of wire or a guitar string. The detail surprised Elliot a little; a friend of his in the department at Chapel Hill often worked with police on such things, and he knew that they normally tried to withhold such minutiae for use as "keys," pieces of information used primarily to sort false confessions from true ones. It was, he knew, a common quirk of human nature that caused numerous phony confessions to many crimes, particularly lurid ones. In this case, though prostitute murders were not really terribly uncommon—tragically, sometimes not worth front-page mention—the fact that four had occurred in such a short time was being taken as cause for alarm; it seemed reasonable to Elliot.

Tossing the paper aside, he for the first time remembered the old photos, the letter, and he cursed silently. He had

166

wanted to keep them, and they were doubtlessly now ruined. They had been in his shirt pocket when he'd taken his shower in pineapple juice. He glanced down, saw that Nikki had apparently replaced them after cleaning his clothes, and he gingerly pulled them out. To his surprise, they seemed undamaged; but as he looked at the first, the 1942 picture, he almost passed out. Once again, he was looking at Nikki's face, not his mother's. The other one was the same, back to its original appearance. With trembling hands, he took out the letter, saw Nikki's address once again written on it in his father's rough handwriting. He closed his eyes, leaned back in the chair, and wondered very seriously about the state of his mental health.

The door opened; Elliot opened his eyes, but didn't move. Laura came into the room, carrying a grocery bag, and greeted him casually. Then she looked at him more closely.

"What's the matter with you?" she asked. "You're real pale."

"Do me a favor, willya?" he asked in turn. "Take a look at these."

Putting the bag down on the floor, she took the pictures from him, looked at one, then the other, then back to the first. "Far-out," she said, finally. "Looks like exactly the same girl. These the pictures you told me about?"

"Yeah," he said tonelessly. "It is far-out, isn't it? What do you see, Laura? Hair and eyes, I mean?"

"Looks like black hair, kinda curly. Dark eyes. Why?"

"Because earlier today, those pictures didn't look like that. The two women looked different, one was blonde."

She grinned, gave him the photos. "You drop some acid or something today?" she asked.

"No. But I'm freaking out, that's for sure."

She sat down on the arm of the chair, put her hand on his shoulder. "That girl in the picture—what'd you say her name was, Nikki?"

"Yes."

"You saw her today, didn't you?"

"Yeah. Spent the day with her." It never occurred to him to think her question strange; she was so matter-of-fact.

"Screwed her?"

He started to tell her that was none of her business, but he didn't. "Yeah," he said flatly.

Laura nodded, looked away from him, a distant look in her

eyes. "This is all related somehow," she said, her voice slightly hollow. "I just don't know how yet."

"What is?"

"Your problem and mine," she told him.

"What's your problem, Laura?"

To his surprise, her eyes filled up with tears again. "Living is my problem, Elliot," she told him. "I tol' you, I'm psychic or somethin'. And what I saw—or felt—last year, that's what made me run away, try to live as much as I could. 'Cause I don't have much time to do it!"

Really concerned, he turned toward her, looked up at her face; large tears rolled down her cheeks, dripped onto the flowered dress. "You aren't sick, are you, Laura?"

"No," she sniffed. "I ain't sick. Not yet, anyways. I don't know how it's gonna be, Elliot. But I had a dream, a dream where I saw a fire in some weird place, and the fire was my life. It was gettin' weak. Then, I dreamed it again, several times; it's weaker, smaller every time. Today, I took a nap, and I saw the fire again. It had gone out, Elliot! It means I'm gonna die, real soon now!"

He took her hand, patted it. "No, no," he said reassuringly. "We need to talk about this, Laura. Your dreams represent your fears, your anxieties. They don't predict the future!"

"Mine do," she told him firmly.

Elliot started trying to explain Freudian dream concepts to her, hypothesizing that her death dreams were simply a reflection of her insecurities, but she was adamant. He was, however, succeeding in calming her down again, getting her to talk about it.

"I appreciate what you're trying to do," she told him, "but I know! And it don't matter, anyhow. Ain't nothing that can be done about it, anyways."

"You're going to laugh about this when you're thirty," he said. "Maybe I'll come around then and remind you!"

"I wish that was possible," she murmured, surprising him. "You wouldn't think I was too young, then."

"Too young?" he asked, though he suspected he knew what she meant.

"You act like I'm a child. Maybe I am, but nobody else does. You're different, Elliot; most guys that stay here, I offer them a lay or a blow-job, and they whip it right out.

They don't give a shit. But you—you kinda wanted it, but you thought it'd be takin' advantage. You treat me like a real person, Elliot. Haze doesn't, you know; I mean, I like him and all, but I'm just a hunka meat to him. And Gerald, he spouts a lotta nice words, but deep down, he ain't no different than Haze. It's freaky. All kinda guys have come in here, and the one I'd like to do it with won't!''

Elliot found himself flattered, this on the heels of the spectacular afternoon with Nikki. He'd never thought of himself as a lady-killer. ''Don't think it's because you aren't attractive,'' he told her. ''In a lot of ways, I'd like to, but—''

''If you would, you better hurry. I ain't gonna be around long!''

That stopped him, and he felt a rush of sympathy for the girl. He hugged her, was still hugging her when the door opened again.

They both looked up as Gerald and Haze entered the apartment, followed by another man. Elliot watched him come in; he was tall, well over six feet, clean-shaven, with only moderately long, dirty-blond hair. His face was wide, looked like that of a child, including a rather vacuous expression that Elliot associated with a bit too much drug use.

''Elliot, this is Conrad Weiser,'' Gerald said, pointing the boy at him. ''Conrad, Elliot Collins.''

''Hi, Elliot,'' the boy said, raising a hand stiffly. ''You live here too?''

''No,'' Elliot told him. ''Just visiting. For a few days.''

''Oh,'' he said. Seemingly losing interest in Elliot, he stared openly at Laura for a few seconds, his eyes scanning her body up and down. He even raised himself up on his tiptoes to peer down inside the top of her dress. She didn't appear to even notice.

Elliot glanced at Gerald; the older man just shrugged. ''We ran into him in a coffee shop,'' he said. ''Seemed like he needed somebody to point him in the right direction.''

That, Elliot had to agree with. He watched Weiser as he wandered aimlessly toward the kitchen, seemed to change his mind, and returned to flop down on the pillows in front of the bookcase. Once sitting, the boy looked up at him. ''Where you from, Elliot?'' he asked.

''North Carolina,'' he replied. ''I teach at the college there— ''

"A college professor?" Weiser asked. He seemed incredulous.

"Yes, I teach psychology."

"Psychology. Far-out, man," the boy said. "I thought college professors were all dried-up old guys."

"Not quite all of us!"

"Yeah," Weiser mumbled. Again, his attention wandered, and he stared at Laura some more. "Who're you?" he asked her.

"Laura Neill," she said. "I do live here."

"Far-out." He didn't say anything else immediately, just continued to look at her. She returned his gaze, but her expression, usually blank, was mildly contemptuous. It was more than obvious to Elliot that she didn't think much of this man. Actually, Elliot told himself, there didn't seem that much there to think anything about. The silence stretched on for a while, becoming uncomfortable. Finally, Gerald and Haze excused themselves, went into the kitchen. The boy lifted himself heavily off the couch, followed them.

Laura disengaged herself from Elliot's arm, where she'd been throughout the conversation. She gave Elliot a significant glance; then her expression changed to one of resigned revulsion, and she started after Weiser. "Hey, man," she called to him, "you wanna—"

Almost roughly, Elliot grabbed her arm and jerked her back. He knew exactly what she was about to ask, and he knew she didn't really want to. When she looked at him, surprised, he shook his head, tilted it toward Weiser. The boy had apparently not realized that she was talking to him, and he disappeared into the other room.

"But—but Haze says—" she started to say.

"Not with him," Elliot told her. "And don't worry about Haze. I'll talk to him."

She looked up at him with innocent eyes. "But we've made agreements," she said. "I have to, unless—"

"Unless what?"

She smiled slyly. "Unless I'm otherwise occupied. Like for the night, dig?"

He looked down at her, sighed. "All right," he said. "All right. You are otherwise occupied for the night. Okay?"

"Right-on!" she said happily. Elliot eyed her suspiciously, wondering if he'd just been had.

Beers in hand, the three men returned from the kitchen; Laura finally picked up her groceries off the floor and went in there herself. Sipping a beer, Weiser regarded Elliot from across the room, a totally blank look on his face.

"Chapel Hill?" he asked finally. "That's where you're from, Chapel Hill?"

"Yes."

"I knew some people from Chapel Hill, once."

Scintillating conversationalist, Elliot thought. "Where are you from, Conrad?" he asked, though he couldn't possibly have cared less.

"New York," the boy said, his eyes roaming all around the room. His gaze even searched the ceiling. "Where'd the chick go?" he asked finally. Elliot wondered if he expected her to be hanging from the overhead light.

"Kitchen," Haze said. The boy was staring at something on the ceiling, and Haze followed his eyes, stared too. "What the fuck are you lookin' at, man?" he asked after a moment.

"The designs," the boy said. Now all of them looked. As far as Elliot could see, there was nothing there except a dirty white ceiling.

"I don't see nuthin'!" Haze exclaimed.

Weiser looked back down at the black man. "Ain't nothin' there," he said mildly.

All three of them stared at him for a minute. This one was living in outer space, Elliot told himself. He glanced at Gerald; the older man was smiling and nodding, as if he was privy to information none of the rest of them had.

"Tell us what you were seeing," Gerald told the boy. "Describe it."

"Oh, I dunno. Like a buncha little pigs walking along in a line. And sometimes one of them would stop and kinda roll over. They was wearing hats and little coats, too."

"What do you think, Elliot?" Gerald asked, rubbing his hands together. "A metaphor for the police, the political state, in some way?"

I am not going to get sucked into this, Elliot told himself. "I've no idea," he said, trying to put some finality into it. He knew exactly what game the older psychologist wanted to play; let's read profound meaning from utter nonsense. Not a favorite of Elliot's, by any means.

Gerald looked a little disappointed, turned his attention

back to Weiser. He began explaining his mystical, drug-centered philosophy of life. For a while, Elliot listened, as did Haze; but they had heard it all before. First Elliot, then the black man, migrated to the kitchen. Laura was still in there, sitting behind the little wooden table, looking out the narrow window. Elliot wondered what she could be seeing of interest out there; the window opened into an alley, usually filled only with trash and people so spaced-out they could not find their way home—if they had one at all.

"Hey, girl!" Haze said as he walked in. "What about our deal, huh?"

Before Laura could answer, Elliot cut in. "She's occupied tonight, Haze."

"Wit' who?"

"Me."

"Oh . . . okay, then. I guess."

Whether it was his business or not, Elliot felt he'd had about enough of this stupidity. "Look here, Haze," he told the black man, "I want to talk to you about this, anyway."

"About what?" Haze asked innocently.

"About the way you're treating this girl, dammit! About what you make her do!"

"Shit, man, whatchoo mean?"

"I mean, you effectively force her to screw every guy who walks in here, whether she wants to or not!"

Haze looked taken aback. "Hey, nobody forces nuthin'! She does what she wants—"

"No way. You've told her that this is what she has to do, to fit in! And she's young, she buys it!" He glanced at Laura, a little uncomfortable about saying these things in her presence; but she was just watching them, her face expressionless.

"No, Elliot, now wait a minute. When she came to live with us, we made a deal. We get the money, the food, the dope—she don't bring in a dime, dig? So, she's gotta do somethin', all right? We say, you be there for us and our friends, we don't need no money from you. She says okay. Besides, we're teachin' her to be a perfect woman, can you dig it? No inhibitions. Free from all the middle-class hang-ups all these other chicks have. I mean, she's got such an advantage—she's startin' out so young, her ideas ain't fixed."

"You mean *you've* got such an advantage! She cooks,

cleans, shops, and gets you off. And your friends, too. Dammit, Haze, you've made a fucking slave out of her!''

"She ain't no slave! The door's right there, she can leave—''

"And that's her only choice, right? Well, maybe she'll take it, by God!'' He looked up at Laura, his head turned away from Haze, and winked. She nodded imperceptibly. "We've been talking, she and I. When I leave, I'm going to take her back to North Carolina with me.''

Haze looked around him at Laura. ''That right?'' he asked her.

''Yah,'' she said.

''Well, shit!'' He drummed his fingers on the table. ''All right. You don't have to fuck anybody you don't wanta. Okay?''

''I'll think about it,'' she told him. He looked shocked, like he couldn't believe she'd say such a thing.

''Man, you been messin' with her head!'' he said to Elliot, accusingly.

''Maybe I been straightening it out a little,'' he told him.

It was past two in the morning before Weiser finally left. Most of that time, Elliot had been sequestered in the tiny kitchen with Laura, talking about a multitude of things. He'd discovered that she was, as he'd suspected, very bright and almost amazingly intuitive; he was almost inclined to take her claims of psychic powers seriously. At one point, he asked her point-blank why she often acted dense and was told that it was what Gerald and Haze expected from her.

''People like you better if you do what's expected,'' she'd told him. ''And I want to be liked. It's real simple.''

''But that doesn't mean you should do things contrary to your nature, to your self,'' he'd pointed out.

''I have no self,'' she again surprised him by saying. ''I haven't had time to develop one. And, if my dreams are true, I won't, ever. You and I are different, Elliot, in that way. How can I explain it? You work from the inside. What you believe in, what's important to you, it comes from inside you. Maybe I'd be like that someday, too. I'd like to think I might have been. But at least right now, I work from the outside. I'm like a pitcher—people pour things in, and I pour them back out again. You're like a spring. It comes from there, with you. But see, if you got a pitcher and you pour pineapple juice into it, people get all upset when it pours milk back out.''

"Pretty deep thinking, Laura," he said. Odd, he thought, that she should use a metaphor involving a pitcher of pineapple juice.

"Well, I sit around and think a lot. I think when I'm stoned. I even think when I'm fucking. Some of these guys that have come around here, man, there ain't nothin' else to keep a girl distracted! I just wish I had more time, that's all. I might think up some interestin' things. You believe that, Elliot?"

He nodded, his fingers buried in his beard, holding up his chin. "I think you will, too. I'm pretty sure you've got a long life ahead of you, Laura."

"No," she said flatly. "Like I told you. Days, now. Maybe a week, but I've seen my last Halloween."

"I wish I could convince you. But I guess you'll just have to see for yourself."

"I been thinkin' about hurryin' it up."

Alarm bells went off in his head, and he sat up straight. "What do you mean by that?"

She looked at him, her eyes calm. "I mean, doin' it myself 'stead of waiting for whatever's out there. There's dyin' and there's dyin', I guess. Some ways better than others. If I do it, I can choose my way. If I wait, I can't."

"You're thinking of killing yourself? Suicide?"

"Yeah. Whatta you think?"

"I think that's ridiculous!" he almost shouted. "Laura, that dream isn't precognitive! It isn't real! But damn, suicide is! I think it's a terrible idea!"

"Well, I dunno about that," she said, still completely calm, too calm for Elliot's comfort. "But that ain't what I meant, really. I meant, whatta you think is a good way to do it?"

He fumbled his words, just staring at her.

As if he'd expressed an opinion, she went on: "I thought about it a lot," she told him. "Pills, I figure that's bad. You fuck up, somebody finds you, you wind up in a hospital. And me, they'd find out where I was from and send me home. Jump off a building, no good. You might survive it, be all crippled up, and that'd be even worse. So I suppose that kind of leaves a gun, or maybe a razor or a knife. You got any other ideas?"

"If I had, I wouldn't tell you!" he said indignantly. "You

have too many damn ideas now! Now look, Laura. I want you to promise me you won't do this. Okay? Just promise me!''

"I'm sorry, Elliot, I can't do that!'' she told him, her eyes filling up yet another time.

"All right, all right,'' he said, trying to remember what little he knew about suicide counseling. "Then promise me this; that you'll tell me before you do anything. Can you promise me that?''

She looked doubtful. "If I do, you'll stop me,'' she said.

Damn straight, he thought. "No, I won't,'' he lied. "I just want to be sure you know what you're doing, okay?''

"Elliot?'' she said in a small voice. "Would you help me if I asked you to?''

He felt as if she were tearing his heart out of his chest. "I don't think I could,'' he told her honestly. "I can't stand violence, and I don't believe what you'd be doing was right. But regardless of that, you'll tell me, okay? What you've planned and when?''

There was a long pause. "Okay. I'll tell you.''

"Promise?''

"Promise.''

He felt totally drained, again. "I gotta crash,'' he said, wiping his hand across his head. "But we got a deal now, right?''

"Right.''

He left her then, staggered into the living room, arranged the mattress. It was being kept stored behind the couch. As always, he slept in the nude; so he removed his clothing, flopped down on the mat, and pulled the single sheet up over himself. In seconds, he was beginning to drift off to sleep, in spite of how disturbing he'd found the conversation with Laura.

But he didn't quite get there. The edge of the sheet rose, and another naked body, much smaller than his, slipped into bed with him. He felt small hands fumble for and find his penis.

"Laura, what are you doing?'' he asked.

"You told Haze I was occupied tonight,'' she said seriously. "You don't wanta be a liar, do you?''

"I said that to—''

"I know, I know. But, Elliot, this isn't like the others. With you, I want to!''

He stroked her hair, trying to will himself not to have an erection, and losing. "Look," he said, "I've had a hell of a day. Let's not make love tonight, okay? Let's just sleep."

"If you're tired, I can go down on you—"

"No, no. Just cuddle up to me here, let's sleep."

"That's what you really want? But you're all hard—"

"It'll go down. Sleep, Laura."

She pushed her head into his neck between his chin and shoulder, smiled, and closed her eyes. Her hand still rested on his lower abdomen, just above the crotch, and the full length of her body was pressed against his. She seemed to be content, but for Elliot, sleep now took a long time to come. And the erection took a long time to go.

24

It was not easy for Elliot the next morning, but regardless of the affection he now felt for Laura, he could not wait to get out of the apartment, get back uptown to where Nikki was, hopefully, waiting. It was equally clear that Laura, in spite of what she had said earlier, did not want him to leave. She bustled around him, pouring his coffee, asking if he wanted breakfast, trying to think of an excuse to make him stay. He, on the other hand, did not want to leave her precipitously, and more than that, he was uncomfortable about leaving her alone. First, he tried to wake Haze but discovered that either he'd gone back out the previous night or had left early; and Gerald was a slow riser. Elliot worked at it, though, and finally managed to get Gerald up and about, although he wasn't at all sure of how much use the man would be in a crisis. Haze was much more competent at such times, even if he could be, at best, insensitive.

"Laura, I have to go," he told her at last, cupping her face in his hands. "You remember your promise to me?"

"I remember," she told him, her eyes pleading.

Silently, he cursed. "You're going to keep it, right?"

She hesitated but finally told him she would. He left her at the door, waving good-bye to him as if she were five, as if he were her father. Gnashing his teeth, he went down the stairs, hailed a cab in the street.

By the time he stood once again on Cabrini, Laura was a distant memory; if he'd thought about it, he would've felt guilty. Eagerly, he pressed the button beside 9C, his heart in his throat until Nikki answered, buzzed him in. To his pleasant surprise, she again was wearing the open-fronted crimson robe; he kissed her, realized that he wanted her immediately. But she guided him to her kitchen, insisted they sit down, have coffee, talk. Reluctantly, he did so, wondering whether she had something specific on her mind.

"Something's bothering you," she said after they were seated. "Tell me about it?"

Almost as soon as these words were spoken, he did feel a surge of guilt for having largely forgotten about Laura's problems. In capsule version, he told Nikki about her, about her irrational fear that she was going to die soon, and about her threat to commit suicide.

"You say she feels she hasn't long to live? And she's—uh—sensitive?" Nikki asked.

"Yes to both," Elliot replied. "Completely crazy. She's had dreams, dreams that she interprets as foretelling her death."

"Did she tell you what they were?"

"Yes. Something about a fire in some weird place. Her fire, she called it. In the first dreams, it was getting weaker, and recently she dreamed that it had gone out."

For a moment, she stared blankly into space. "Elliot, you aren't to a point yet where you can understand this very well," she said, "but I'll tell you anyway. There isn't anything I can do about it now. I wish I could. But your little friend is quite right. Her dream is indeed prophetic. And she will soon leave this earth, this life."

Elliot stared at her. "What in the hell are you talking about?" he demanded.

"I know a few things," she said. "As I've told you. Some

things about dreams, about prophecy, and about the fires of life. I really can't explain further, you'd just shut me off. But I can tell you that she's right. You should believe her, and you should act accordingly. Quickly, I might add.''

''I don't know what I'd do if I did believe her!''

''First, make love with her. She wants that, doesn't she?''

He was astounded. ''Nikki, for God's sake,'' he said finally, ''we're talking about a thirteen-year-old here! She's just a child! Besides, I thought—well, you and I—''

She regarded him steadily across the table. ''I don't recall us swearing fidelity to each other,'' she told him, though there was no rancor in her voice.

''Well, I know, but we were so good together—at least I thought so—''

She giggled at him now. ''Oh, Elliot, you can be such a child yourself sometimes! Now your feelings are all hurt! Look, we were good together, okay? I thought so, too. And our relationship, sexual and otherwise, hasn't ended. It isn't going to end right away unless you want it to. But I fail to see how your making this young girl happy will affect us!''

''You have a unique attitude,'' he told her, wondering if she meant what she was saying.

''That, my friend, may well be true. But here I'm only being reasonable.''

''But she's thirteen—''

''So what? Child or not child is a state of mind, Elliot. This girl, by your own statements, has been around. Physically, she's an adult. Probably emotionally too. Were you that experienced at thirteen?''

''Not even close!''

''That's my point. Just because you were a child at thirteen doesn't mean she is. Where I grew up, in Mexico, girls of twelve or thirteen are considered marriageable, as a routine thing. This whole business about her age is a product of this particular society. You reject a lot of its ideas. Why do you cling so tenaciously to that one?''

He tried to answer her, but he realized that she'd already ground up most of his logic, his arguments. In a way, he thought, she was right; there was no reason not to. Still, it didn't feel right to him, and he said so.

''There's another thing, too,'' Nikki told him, her face serious.

"What's that?"

"Something you're going to like even less, but I'm going to tell you anyhow—give you the chance not to make the mistake, though I'm awfully sure you will. It's just too soon, I guess. Anyway, you told me she asked you to help her, right?"

Elliot's mouth dropped open. He knew what she was going to say; after all, it followed logically from her conviction that Laura was right about her impending death. And he had already learned that Nikki was logical. "You aren't suggesting—" he said weakly.

She nodded. "You won't. You and I both know it. But you should."

"Goddamn, woman, you're talking about murder here!"

"No, I'm not. Murder involves an unwilling victim. By definition. That isn't what we're talking about at all. This is a case of a friend helping a friend."

"I don't even believe you'd be saying this if you weren't just absolutely sure I wouldn't do it, Nikki!"

"You're wrong. I'm giving you an opportunity; you're free to take it or leave it." She sighed, leaned back in her chair. "What's sad is that, either way, you'll regret it. No way around that, either."

"Well, let's just not talk about it anymore, okay? I'm not going to help that girl kill herself, and that's that! In fact, I'll do everything I can to prevent it!"

Nikki shrugged. "Okay," she said. "I had to give you your options. Up to you, now." With that, she dropped the subject of Laura Neill, and gradually, as they talked about more trivial things, the mood between them became more upbeat.

Once again, Nikki expressed a desire to go out, and Elliot readily agreed to this; but, he told her, there was something else he wanted to do first! She knew what he meant and didn't object.

They spent the next forty-five minutes in a near repeat of the previous day, on the floor in front of the stereo. This time, the music was the Jefferson Airplane's "Crown of Creation," and once again, his experiences at each juncture seemed to be synchronized with the music, as were their movements. For Elliot, this time was, if anything, even better than the first. But there was a difference, too; when they'd finished, he was not totally exhausted as he'd been the previous day. Completely satisfied, true; completely relaxed, that too. But he didn't fall asleep. Rather, he felt an active contentment, a desire to be affectionate with Nikki for a while, a desire she apparently shared.

While she dressed, he sipped yet another cup of coffee, looked through a copy of the *Daily News* she had left lying on the table. Another prostitute murdered last night, he noticed; strangled with a guitar string. Police were baffled, and, according to the papers, major efforts were underway to track down this very active killer; he was accounting for about one per night. The location of this murder was of interest to Elliot; it had taken place only about three blocks away from Gerald's pad, where at the time of the killing, he'd been talking with Laura. He made a mental note to caution her to be careful on the streets. Even though this killer so far took only hookers, one could never tell when he might vary his pattern.

Finally, Nikki was ready; her outfit today consisted of very brief red shorts, a top that tied behind her neck and left her back bare, and open sandal-like shoes. She told him she had some shopping she wanted to do, asked him if he'd mind spending part of his day doing that with her; he allowed as how he wanted to be with her even if she was spending her day cleaning toilets. She hugged him, and they took a taxi down to the expensive shops on Fifth Avenue.

"These stores we're going to—they're open on Sundays?" he asked her.

"You haven't been in New York much," she observed, glancing over at him. "The city doesn't ever close, not completely."

"We have blue laws in North Carolina," he told her. "Stores can't open on Sundays. Guess I'm just used to that."

"Christian laws," she almost sneered. "Forcing everyone to observe their holy day. Shouldn't happen."

"I agree," he responded. The taxi stopped, discharged them in front of a clothing store, which was indeed open. They went in, ending that part of the conversation. But it left him wondering about her apparent hostility toward the Christian religions. Not that he entirely disagreed with her.

Most of what she was buying today was clothes, what might euphemistically be called "intimate wear." She constantly asked Elliot's opinion on what she'd chosen, and she appeared to be selecting things with a pronounced emphasis on sexiness. At one point, he told her that he didn't see how she could improve on the red robe.

It wasn't until he made that remark that the significance of the red robe hit him. She'd looked so right in it, so attractive, that he hadn't questioned it until now—now that he suddenly remembered that she'd been wearing precisely the same garment in the dream he'd had, back in Chapel Hill, the dream in which she'd been petting the big rattlesnake. And he remembered Melissa's remark about "the woman in the red robes." He fell silent, wondering whether to ask her about it. But what could she say? It was his dream—and Melissa's—after all. Perhaps there was something to it, he thought, maybe the dreams were precognitive in a minor way. That thought brought him back to Laura and her dreams, the way he'd ridiculed her conviction that they foretold the future. Perhaps he ought to think about it more seriously, he told himself. Yet, what could he do? He thought about Nikki's suggestions and shuddered. She could not, he told himself firmly, have really been serious about that! He dismissed that from his mind, thought some more about Nikki, rattlesnakes, and weird dreams. Those thoughts were not so easily disposed of.

"Nikki," he said, after a few moments' reflection, "I have something I'd like to do this afternoon, too."

She turned and looked at him, her arms full of packages. "Oh?" she asked. "What's that?"

"The zoo," he said, "I think I'd like to go to the zoo."

"The zoo?"

"The zoo. You know, where they keep the animals and all?"

"Really? Well, I'll be damned. We'll just have to go see, won't we?"

An hour and a half later, having dropped the packages off at Nikki's apartment, they strolled through the gates of the Bronx Zoo. She was eager and enthusiastic as always, said she wanted to see everything; it had been a long time, she informed him, since she'd been there. But Elliot was very focused. Later, maybe they'd go see lions and elephants; right now, he wanted to find the reptile house. He studied the little fold-out map, located the building and steered her toward it, wondering exactly what he expected to get out of this. Maybe, he thought, he just wanted to see her reaction when confronted with a rattlesnake.

As they entered the building, looked over the rows of glass panes inset in the walls, he watched her far more closely than he did the scaly forms on the other side of the glass. Except for her usual manner—intensely interested in whatever she was doing at the moment—he saw nothing out of the ordinary. Like any zoo visitor, she walked along, peering at the multicolored creatures enclosed in the cases, some hardly visible amid the clutter of rocks, greenery, and branches that attempted to naturalize the unnatural surroundings they were in. Cobras, pythons, boas, vipers from the Old World, all these they looked at and went on. Finally, what he'd been waiting for. The little sign above the cage informed them, "*Crotalus durissus durissus*—Mexican Lowland Diamondback." Here, Nikki did in fact stop and look more closely. To Elliot, the creature was almost startlingly familiar. In form and color, it was exactly like the snake in his dream. The only difference was size.

"I know you," she said to the snake, gazing at it through the glass. "But that isn't what we called you back home."

"What did you call it?" Elliot asked her.

"We called it *cascabel*," she said. "Oh, we were very familiar with them. Those, the *terciopelio*, and the *cantil*. You had to be aware of them, if you did any tromping around the woods."

"Are the other two rattlesnakes as well?"

"No—another viper—I think it's called a fer-de-lance here—and the *cantil* is a lot like a water moccasin."

"Oh," he said, not really too interested. He continued to watch Nikki; she did seem reticent to move away from the snake cage. But, he asked himself, what did it prove?

Watching her, he almost missed the fact that though she was not really behaving strangely, the snake was. Almost all of the reptiles they'd seen so far had ignored them quite completely, either lying motionless in their cages or gliding about on missions known only to themselves. They were completely used to visitors and paid them no mind at all. But the diamondback was not doing that. Black tongue flickering, it crept toward the glass; it was not gliding sinuously but hitching itself along by moving the wide plates on the lower part of its body. When its broad, triangular head reached the glass, it raised the forward part of its body until its head was on a level with Nikki's eyes, then tipped its snout down so that it was looking directly at her face. The rear part of its body was twisting back and forth, about two inches of what Elliot assumed to be the tail lifted, the rattle clicking occasionally.

As he watched, two pinkish structures, bulbous and covered with recurving spines, emerged from beneath the raised tail. Elliot had no idea what they might be; they looked sort of like the bases of mushrooms that had been uprooted, except for their color. At the glass, the reptile's head moved slowly back and forth, tongue flickering incessantly. A couple of times the mouth gaped, revealing the fangs in their fleshy sheaths on the upper jaw. Elliot realized that he'd seen pictures of rattlesnakes with their mouths open before; usually the lethal fangs were down, extended. This one was not doing that; the fangs were folded, at rest. Nothing in its demeanor indicated the slightest aggression.

"Oh, man!" came a male voice from behind them. "I wish we had a female, too!"

Elliot turned his head; a young man in a zookeeper's uniform was looking over Nikki's shoulder at the snake. "A female?" he asked.

"Yeah. That guy's really ready to breed, but he's the only one we got," the man informed him.

"How do you know?" he asked, glancing back toward the snake.

"You see those back there?" the keeper asked, pointing to the pinkish structures. "Hemipenes. Ah—copulatory organs. In other words, the snake has the equivalent of an erection, in human terms!" He shook his head, turned and left them. Throughout the conversation, Nikki hadn't said a word; she didn't seem to be aware that the man was there. Slowly, Elliot moved his eyes back to the snake, which was now rubbing its chin along the glass. The twin hemipenes were even larger, obviously engorged with blood; they looked almost obscene to Elliot.

"Looks like you can even turn on a snake," he said softly, his mouth close to Nikki's ear.

She looked at him, grinned broadly. "Oh, he isn't my type," she said airily. The incident didn't seem to be having much effect on her; Elliot didn't know what to make of it. He put his arm around her shoulder, started to steer her away from the cage. As he did, the snake's head jerked down into an S-shaped loop, and the rattle buzzed loudly, warningly.

"Find your own girl," Elliot said to it, leading Nikki away; she went without protest.

They spent quite a few hours at the zoo. As she'd said, Nikki wanted to see absolutely everything. She told him how much she loved the animals, wondered aloud why she hadn't come here more often.

As they walked arm-in-arm, Elliot noticed that some of the animals behaved strangely when Nikki stood before their cages, in particular a jaguar that rolled and frolicked in front of her like a kitten. Watching it, he recalled that she'd referred to him as her "Jaguar Warrior," and he asked her what that meant.

"You remember what I told you about the *nagual*, the spirit animal," she said, her eyes fixed on the big spotted cat. "Well, although most any animal can be a *nagual*, a jaguar is really a special one in Southern Mexico. It was a name we applied to special lovers: 'Jaguar Warrior.' From the ways the cats make love, you know, violently passionate. As if they had a jaguar *nagual*."

He flushed but that made him feel really good. "I'm most flattered, my lady," he said, with a little bow. "Does that mean my *nagual* is a jaguar?"

"No, it doesn't mean that; it's just a saying," she told him. "What your personal *nagual* is, well, that's something everyone has to find out for themselves."

"What's yours?"

She gave him a penetrating look. "Normally, Elliot, you don't ask that question. Juan Reyes, for example, would be very offended. But I'm not. It's just that I shouldn't tell you."

"Why not?"

"It gives you power over me, in a way. If you decide to use it, and if you know how to use it."

He leered at her. "Ah, but I want power over you!"

She laughed. "Not like that!" Then she said seriously, "Life and death, Elliot. I'd be putting my life in your hands in a way if I told you."

He became serious also, smiled at her tenderly. "I wouldn't harm it," he said, his hand on her cheek.

"No, I don't believe you would. So, my friend, I'll tell you. But you already know."

He was sure that she was right, but he waited for her to confirm it.

She did.

25

When they returned to Nikki's apartment, she immediately led Elliot into her bedroom. He realized with some surprise that he hadn't seen it before. Very functional, few frills, but her choice in furniture here was as expensive as it was in the remainder of the apartment, and just as out of place. He did not, however, have long to concentrate on it, since as soon as she walked into the room she discarded her shorts, top, and shoes, and rolled onto the bed. He wasted no time joining her there, and another very pleasant hour drifted by, this time without musical accompaniment. Once again, when they were finished, he felt none of the tiredness and weakness that he had the first time. Still, he was reluctant to get up; her body pressed against his was much too comfortable. In fact, he didn't, not of his own choice. He waited for her to initiate their separation, and for quite a while, she did not.

But finally she announced that it was time she started some dinner; she put on her crimson robe and went to the kitchen. Elliot, liking to hold on to pleasant patterns, didn't bother to dress as he walked out, sat down at her table.

"Can I help you with anything?" he asked as she puttered around the stove.

"No, no. Everything's under control. You just relax."

"Got plans for the evening?"

She turned and looked at him, leaned against the counter.

" 'Fraid so, Elliot. Just like last night. Business. Gotta pay Con Ed, you know."

He looked disappointed. "You always work nights?"

"Mostly. Sometimes on weekends, during the day."

"You still haven't told me what kind of work you do."

"No, I haven't," she said flatly, obviously intending that the subject be closed.

But he didn't let go of it. "Nikki," he said carefully, "I've got to tell you this. Not only have you got me almost insanely curious about what it is that you do, but also you're beginning to make me nervous. I mean, you said you aren't a cop, you don't work for the government. Are you into something criminal? Don't be insulted, but you're being so mysterious about it."

"Would that matter to you, Elliot?" she asked. "Don't you have friends who make their living dealing drugs?"

"No, no, of course not. I mean, yes, I have friends who deal drugs," he said, wondering if she knew that or was just surmising. "And it wouldn't matter to me if you did. But—" He tried to think of an outlandish example. "Suppose you were a bank robber? I should know, right?"

"Absolutely not! If I were a bank robber—which I'm not—then the risk inherent in that would be by my choice. I'd have no right to expose you to it, make you an accomplice, by telling you."

"Even if I asked?"

"Even then."

"So you aren't going to tell me?"

"Not tonight!"

"But—"

"Shut up, Elliot, and eat your dinner," she said, putting food on the table—roast beef, potatoes. He glanced up at her. There hadn't been nearly enough time to cook this, he thought. But he shrugged, began to eat. This time, she kissed him deeply and fully before she made him leave, telling him she'd see him the next day.

Initially, when Elliot returned to the apartment, he thought that once again no one was home. But as he glanced through the rooms, he saw Laura facedown on one of the beds. His pulse going up with every step, he walked in, sat down beside her, touched her shoulder.

To his great relief, she looked up at him. "Elliot," she said, "I'm glad you're back."

"Yeah, well, you worried me when I saw you lying there like that."

"I made a promise to you," she said in a dreamy voice, "and I always keep my promises." She rolled over, and again Elliot felt as if his blood were freezing. Clasped in both her hands was a butcher knife with a ten-inch blade; she had been lying on top of it. "I'm going to do it tonight, Elliot," she said, still sounding far away. "Are you going to help me?"

"Laura," he almost whispered. "Laura, give me the knife. Please."

"Sure," she said, handing it to him. She lifted her shoulders off the bed, pulled her dress down as far as the middle of her stomach. Then she stretched her arms out to either side. Classic, Elliot thought. "Kiss me, then do it," she told him, her eyes closed. He watched her eyelids flutter, watched her not yet completely developed breasts rise and fall. She opened her eyes, turned her head toward him. "Unless you want to get laid first," she said.

He almost laughed. "I think I'd rather have some tea," he told her.

She looked from his face to the knife, then back. "Okay. I'll make it for you." Jumping off the bed, she slipped the straps of the dress back over her shoulders and went into the kitchen.

His hands trembling slightly, he went into the front room, hid the knife in the back flap of his suitcase. Then he joined Laura in the kitchen, where the water for the tea was heating slowly on the old gas stove.

"Our deal still goes," Elliot told her, "and you aren't doing it tonight!"

"Okay," she said amiably, pouring crushed herbs into two mismatched cups.

"You have some terribly romantic notions about all this," he advised her. "Do you realize what you're talking about here? Being dead, gone? Forever? No second chances?"

"I know," she said. "Gonna happen soon anyway."

Dammit, he thought. How could he get through to her? "You didn't plan to do it tonight anyhow!" he accused.

She turned, and he could see that she was blushing. "No, I

didn't, I guess. I was waitin' for you. I thought you'd feel sorry for me, jump my bones.''

"What if I'd decided to help you, after all? If I was a little crazy?''

"You are a little crazy, but that's good,'' she told him. "And if you'd decided to—well, that would have been for the best. Get it over with. With a friend, not like in some dark alley. Or in a hospital.''

"That reminds me. You heard about that maniac running around killing hookers?''

"Yeah, I heard.''

"Well, one of the killings was real close to here. You be careful when you're out in the street.''

For a moment she didn't say anything, just stood with her back to him, her hands clenched on the counter top. Then suddenly she whirled. "Damn you!'' she shrieked. "You don't take a Goddamn thing I say seriously! If that's what's waiting for me, I can't be careful enough! You talk to me like it was just—just—'' She broke down, started crying again, but not like before; this time she gave vent to great, rolling wails, her whole body shaking. Elliot jumped up, knocking over his chair in the process, and pulled her up into his arms. But she didn't calm down quickly this time. She just kept crying, pounding on him with her fists, wailing. "I don't want to die!'' she cried, her eyes and hair wild. "I don't want to die!''

He rocked her in his arms, said soothing and meaningless things. Finally, she became calm; sniffling, she went back to finish the tea. But the water had all boiled away, and she had to start it over. This trivial disaster provoked more tears, and Elliot made her sit down, filled the pan himself.

"You see her again today?'' Laura asked. "What's her name—Nikki?''

Elliot hesitated, but decided there was no point in lying. "Yes,'' he told her, adding nothing.

"What you guys do?''

"Shopping. Out to the zoo,'' he said.

"Fucking?''

He turned, put his hands on the table. "Why do you ask me that?'' he inquired. "I suspect you want to hear me say no, but I've not been lying to you, Laura. About much of anything.''

She blushed again. "No. I wanna hear you say yes. Actually, I'd like to hear all about it. See, I imagine I'm her. She must be wonderful, like a princess. Got to be, to get you."

"What on earth are you talking about?"

She looked up at him, looking very young indeed at the moment. "Well, you only take the very best, I mean—"

"I think you have a real warped picture of me, Laura."

"Oh, no! You—you—"

He sat down, held her hand. "Laura, really. I'm not God's gift to women or anything. I've had my problems, too."

"You could have any woman you wanted!" she insisted.

"No, I couldn't. I've been lucky lately, that's all. But it hasn't always—"

Tears filled her eyes yet again. "Then why not me?" she wailed. "I've almost begged you! I didn't think I was all that ugly—"

Elliot put his head down so that his forehead was resting on the table. "Jesus," he said, more to himself than to her. After a short interval, he lifted it slowly. "Laura, there are two things. Let me tell you again. One: I'm involved with Nikki, and I have another girl—Melissa—back in Chapel Hill. I'm embarrassed to say that Melissa has rarely entered my mind around here, I've been so damn distracted. Two: you are thirteen, and that bothers the hell out of me. Whatever you think of yourself, whatever you really are, I think of you as a little girl. But, now hear this: you are not unattractive. Not at all, not in the least. Right now, you're cute as hell, and later you'll be beautiful. Give it time, honey, for Christ's sake!"

Her outburst over, her face became expressionless once more, her voice flat. "Like I told you, I ain't got the time. I wanna do any livin', I gotta do it quick."

Elliot sighed. He did feel a genuine affection for her, but he wished he hadn't been drawn so deeply into this; he would rather have devoted all his attentions to Nikki. Idly, he wondered what she might be doing right now, what her mysterious profession might be. He began running the day over in his mind, taking his time with it, savoring each recollection; not for quite some time did he realize that he'd literally forgotten that Laura was even there. Looking back at the small kitchen table, he saw one empty cup, one full cup of cold tea, and no Laura. He called out to her, looked through the house, but she'd apparently gone out, leaving him alone. That, considering her current mental state, made him nervous, but he had no idea where to look for her. He threw up his hands, abdicated the responsibility he felt, and finished the cold tea.

After sitting at the table doing nothing for thirty minutes, he decided to try to call Marcia Cates again, see if her phone was working. A pleasant surprise: it was. But she had not seen nor heard from Dave Jennings. He realized he had forgotten to call and see if Dave was possibly in jail, and made a mental note to do that the next day.

An hour later, he still wandered restlessly through the empty apartment, feeling much like the pacing jaguar in the cage at the zoo. When he could stand it no more, he went back out, telling himself he needed some fresh air. In lower Manhattan in October, none was to be had, but he paced around the streets nevertheless, looking for something to occupy his time. Then he remembered the bar—or club, or whatever it was—at Alejandro's. And he got an idea.

Was it possible, he thought, that Nikki worked there at nights? She had, after all, told him that the place didn't open until late. Maybe she was a cocktail waitress there. And maybe she was ashamed to tell him that; possibly she thought that he, being a college professor, would look down on her if he knew she was a waitress. The more he thought about it, the more plausible it became to him. He stopped on a street corner, thought about where he was in relation to the restaurant; but it was hopeless, he just didn't know the city that well. The easy answer lay in the yellow taxis cruising by. He hailed one, watched it go by, tried another. Four cabs later, he was picked up, and soon he again stood in front of Alejandro's.

As he looked at the wooden doors, he wondered if he'd made some kind of mistake; although a simulated carriage lantern burned at either side of the doorway, there didn't seem to be anyone around. Perhaps it wasn't open on Sunday nights. Well, he told himself, can't find out by standing here. He tried the door; it was open.

Inside, the restaurant area itself was dark, deserted; a velvet rope barred the way into it. But the hallway was dimly lit, and there were lights beyond the archway, which led to the club. He smiled, pushed the saloon doors aside and went in.

Immediately inside the doors, there was only a tiny room, panels painted with pre-Columbian figures ahead and to his left. To the right were stairs leading down, obviously the entrance to the bar; he took them, descended into a murky semi-darkness. As he paid a shadowy figure a dollar requested as a cover, he looked around. The place was fairly large, with a high ceiling, which he could hardly see at all. Across from him was the stage, which had curtained-off wings at both sides; it suggested dressing rooms. There was no lighting in the center of the room at all. Over the bar, there were slender strips of light, focused away from the main floor, and there were brighter lights directed onto the currently empty stage. It made the scene look rather ghostly; Elliot assumed that was what was intended. The effect was heightened by smoke of an odd fragrance—Elliot thought it might be incense of some kind—filling the air.

Almost as ghostly was the audience. Numerous small round tables were scattered about the floor, each with three or four chairs surrounding them, and a number of these were filled. But from the door, these people looked to be mere silhouettes against the light from the stage. In the entire room, the only person Elliot could see clearly was the bartender, who looked quite ordinary as he shook some kind of a drink.

"Table for one, sir?" a deep voice asked. He turned, saw the shape of a man standing beside him; in the darkness, he could not see a face at all.

"Yes, thank you," he said. "Is Mr. Reyes here tonight?" he asked as the shape showed him to a table not far from the door.

"Not at the moment, sir. Senor Reyes will be here shortly, however."

"By any chance does Miss Nikki Howard work here?"

The shape cocked its head to one side, didn't say anything for a few seconds. "Miss Howard is sometimes our very honored guest," he said finally. "But, no, she is not an employee. And I have not seen her this evening."

The man left his table, and Elliot rested his elbow on it. He was feeling quite disappointed; he'd had high hopes that his idea had been correct. But, he told himself, might as well make the best of it. It was a curious place, might be interesting to spend a little time here. From the lighting, he assumed there'd be a stage show. Perhaps he'd just come in during a break.

A waitress came around after a short interval and asked him what he wanted. He glanced up at her, couldn't see her face either. He just asked for a beer. After another short hiatus, it appeared in front of him. He passed the unseen girl a dollar, once again tried to see her face, but she'd already faded back into the gloom behind him.

Considerable time passed while he sat sipping his beer, watching the still-deserted stage. He emptied the glass and ordered another, but he had decided, as he began to drink it, that he'd probably leave soon. Reyes's club didn't seem like a very exciting place. Besides that, the pervasive smoke was getting to him a little, making him feel a bit dizzy and disoriented.

A group of people came in; Elliot realized that they were the first new arrivals since himself. Again the general darkness made it hard for him to see them, but as they moved toward a table near his, he caught a glimpse of faces. Indians, he would have judged. Probably, considering what Nikki had told him about Reyes's ancestry, Mexican Indians. The two women and two men sat down, began to talk animatedly among themselves, but in the fluid language Elliot could not understand. Probably, he told himself, virtually everyone in here was Mexican. He began to feel uncomfortable, like an outsider. Lifting his glass of beer, he saw that it was about half full. When that's gone, he promised himself, so am I.

A shadowy figure detached itself from the bar and moved in his direction; initially he assumed it was his waitress, but as it came closer, he saw that the shape was that of a man. It looked so surreal—the black silhouette gliding silently across the room—that he was a little surprised when it spoke.

"Dr. Collins," Juan Reyes said. "I am so glad you returned. We were so embarrassed by the—ah—incident."

Elliot smiled, waved his hand. "Accidents happen," he said amiably, thinking that he should thank them, not be angry. "It's forgotten."

"Not by me," Reyes said firmly. "Tonight, you are here as my guest. Anything you order is on the house."

"Well, I thank you, Mr. Reyes—"

"Juan, please!"

"Juan. But it really isn't necessary."

"Allow me to do this," Reyes said firmly, effectively closing the matter. Elliot shrugged; Juan tipped his head toward a chair at his table, and Elliot, smiling, motioned for him to sit down.

"I really was hoping Nikki might be here tonight," Elliot told him.

"Ah, Nikki. No, amigo, she is seldom here in the evenings. Unless we have a—special show. Which we do not have tonight."

"There's no show at all tonight?"

"Oh, of course there is. But occasionally we have—how shall I say—exceptional ones."

He didn't seem inclined to elaborate, and Elliot let it go. He was wondering whether to ask Juan about Nikki's profession. But in the end he decided not to. That was, it was true, something he should learn from Nikki herself. Finally, he just asked when the show would be starting.

"Any minute now," Reyes replied, glancing toward the stage.

Even as he spoke, the curtains at either side of the platform moved around a little, then opened. Four women—all dark, all with waist-length black hair like Carlotta's—walked out onto the stage. Soft music, drums and flute, started to play as they did. The women were beautifully costumed, evidently in the style of the ancient Indians: cotton shirts with flowers embroidered on them, elaborate bands on their bronze arms and legs, sandals, and paper headdresses adorned with long plumes. The plumes were in different colors for each dancer: red, blue, white, and a very dark green, almost black. Moving in time to the drums, the women came to center stage, formed a square. Then the square began to rotate, counterclockwise. Although the dance itself was not terribly demanding physically, Elliot was more than impressed with the precision of the dancers. Each step, every arm movement, was perfectly synchronized, would have looked kaleidoscopic from above. He watched, fascinated, as they continued to rotate, collapse, and expand the square.

"What sort of dance is it?" he asked Reyes.

"It is very old," the Indian told him. "The dance of the four consorts of the Smoking Mirror."

"Oh," he said, though he was no wiser than before. He turned his eyes back to the stage as one of the women, the one with the greenish plumes, broke away from the other three. With long, graceful strides she ran to the left of the stage, stretched out an arm. A man, as Indian in appearance as the others, stepped out in response to her beckoning gesture. His costume was even more impressive than those of the women: an extremely complex headdress with long draping plumes, a vestlike cloak and a kiltlike garment. At his waist, he wore a bundle of objects that looked like large darts. On his feet were sandals, but the left one, Elliot noticed, seemed to have a small circular mirror attached to it, which flashed the lights as he allowed himself to be drawn onto the stage.

For a while, he stood in one spot near the edge, while the woman danced around him; her gestures and movements were very suggestive sexually. For just an instant, he saw her hair as long and blonde, her skin as light, but he blinked, and it was back to the way it was. Another woman, the one with the blue plumes, broke from the square, ran to the man. He was thinking that her short black hair was quite a contrast to the other's long blonde, but then his vision swam a little, and they again had almost identical tresses, black and very long. He was beginning to feel confused when the other two women came forward; the white-plumed woman remained a little aloof, while the other joined the first two around the man. After a few seconds, white-plumes beckoned, and the man moved quickly away from the other three to join her. She drew him to center stage as his hands sought her body, but she only let him touch her lightly, only occasionally. The other three women followed, and when the man was stage center, they formed the square around him again.

As Elliot viewed it, it seemed to him that his perspective shifted; it looked normal, then he was seeing it much more close up. Just like the images out his window at UNC, he thought. Even before he finished the thought, there was another shift, and he was seeing from the middle of the square, from the viewpoint of the costumed man. He was looking at the woman with the white plumes, and she was Nikki.

Slowly, he turned around, saw the other three; Melissa and Eileen were very clear, but the fourth, though she looked like Laura, seemed to be behind a screen of fog. He squinted and peered at her; her face changed to Marcia's, then to Carlotta's, and back to Laura's. An absurd thought came to his mind; she hadn't fixed her identity yet. Then, before he could consider anything any further, the women's hands were all over him, even reaching up under the kilt, where it seemed he was wearing nothing. Just when he was really beginning to get into it, they all jumped away from him, moved behind him. He could only see Nikki, off to his right; she looked very sad, but somehow proud as well. Looking up, he saw a man standing before him. He stared; the man was clad only in a loincloth, and his body was painted entirely black. His hair, too, was waist-length, wildly tangled. He was holding something in his hands that Elliot could not seem to see, and abruptly, for no reason he could discern, he panicked. He had a sensation of falling, or hurtling through space, and suddenly he was viewing the scene from his table again. But he felt sick, and terrified.

Jumping up, he mumbled an apology to Juan, made for the door. From behind him, Juan was calling, telling him the show wasn't over, but he didn't feel he could stay any longer. He reached the bottom of the stair, looked at the man who'd previously taken his cover. Now, this individual looked to be eight or nine feet tall, and almost as broad as a gorilla. He was still shrouded in darkness, except for his left eye; it glowed bright blue, as if it were lit from behind.

"Stay, Elliot," the apparition said in a soft, deep voice. "The show isn't over."

"Yes, stay!" called a voice from the audience. "You haven't seen the end!"

"Aaaaaah . . ." Elliot managed, trying to edge past the huge figure. It made no move to stop him, and he bolted up the stairs, through the saloon doors, and down the hallway to the street. Only when the wooden doors had swung silently shut behind him did he stop to catch his breath.

He hadn't gone more than ten steps when he realized that even though he was outside Alejandro's, something was still very strange. When he'd arrived, Seventh Avenue had been filled with pedestrians; there had been traffic in the roadway. Now there was nothing, just empty pavement illuminated by the glow of the street lamps. He looked up and down, saw no movement at all. Worse, he found that he was unsure about which direction he should take to get back to Gerald's apartment. And there were no cabs or any other cars in the street. He looked up and down, but still he saw nothing. Stuffing his hands into his pockets, he tried to decide which way he should walk. No use; he was sure in his own mind which direction was north, but not sure which way to go.

A shadow moved behind him, and he spun around, feeling his heart accelerate. From perhaps ten feet away, a deer stood looking at him. Disbelieving it, he stared back. A deer? In the city, wandering about the sidewalks? But there it was, right in front of his face, the large brown eyes looking into his.

"What the fuck?" he whispered.

"No fucking right now," the deer replied, in perfect English. "Lesson time, Elliot."

Stupefied, he found he was unable to move. The deer made some chewing motions, blinked its eyes, turned, and walked away. He watched it disappear around a corner, and the only thought he had was that it had gone toward the east; for some reason, that seemed important to him.

He turned, looked at the restaurant again. Facing it, he was facing west, north to his right, south to his left. He had the impression that that was proper, but he couldn't figure out where these ideas were coming from; it was as if someone was speaking to him from inside his head. Or perhaps from someplace deep within his left ear, he thought. He could almost visualize a tiny little person in there, speaking directly to his eardrum in tones so high-pitched, so soft, that his perception of them was subliminal.

Without really intending to, he found himself walking along, up to the corner, north. He looked around, eastward; there was a red glow down there, softly illuminating the deserted street. A fire perhaps? He thought he'd go see, and he walked in that direction. His mental state was becoming rather detached, like he was observing himself walk rather than actually doing it; actively he tried to retake control of his feet and legs but only succeeded in causing himself to stumble.

After about two blocks, he'd reached the source of the glow, only to find that there was no source. The light, a soft pastel scarlet, seemed to come from everywhere; to Elliot, it made it look like the streets, the buildings, were covered with blood. In the center of the glow, right out in the quiet street, another odd sight in the city: a rabbit. Ears twitching, it looked up at him as he approached it. He came almost near enough to touch it, but it didn't run away.

"Well, little fellow," he said to it, "what brings you to the city? Has there been a breakout at the zoo?"

Just as the deer had, the rabbit spoke to him. "No, Elliot. I have come to show you the Direction of Rising, Land of the Red. Do you understand? Or shall I show you more?''

He put one knee to the pavement. ''Show me more,'' he breathed, no longer worried about how insane it was to be talking to a rabbit in New York City. It wasn't even a white rabbit, he told himself inanely; but it wasn't brown, either. It was red, the same color as the glow. Dawn red, it seemed to him.

It twitched its ears, turned its head, and another rabbit bounded from the shadows, joined it. Immediately, the first one mounted the second, mating with it with the energy and speed peculiar to these creatures. Even before the first—the male—had finished, he spoke again: ''Now you see? You see a part of it?''

''I see part,'' Elliot said. But he couldn't say he understood, at least not in any way he could articulate.

The male dismounted, faced Elliot again, nose twitching now. ''Watch,'' it said. ''Watch more.''

From nowhere, an arrow flew into the street, struck the other rabbit in the side. Blood spurting from its nose, it toppled over, legs kicking futilely. The other just looked at it, completely placid. As soon as the spasmodic movements stopped, the dead animal's body began to rot at a very accelerated rate; the skin fell away, the muscles turned dark, liquefied. Soon it was no more that a dark puddle on the street, surrounded by a brittle piece of reddish-golden skin.

The arrow, Elliot realized, had somehow vanished; he could no longer see it. But from out of the blackish puddle, a bit of green emerged; rapidly it surged upward, and Elliot recognized it as a corn plant. It tasseled, the silks developed, the ears filled out. Then the shucks began to peel back from one of them. Inside, instead of corn kernels on a cob, there was a multitude of tiny, bright red rabbits. As soon as the husks were gone, they exploded outward in all directions, becoming larger as they fell to the street. By the time they hit it, they were the size of the first; there was now a whole herd of rabbits there. Another ear began to open, to peel back; when it was exposed, the arrow that had killed the original rabbit fell with a clink to the concrete.

The rabbit that had been speaking to him stood up on its hind legs, nose working rapidly. ''Now,'' it said, nodding its furry head to its left, "you should go to the Land of Thorns. To the Land of Cutting, the Land of Dismembering."

"Yes," Elliot said. "South. South." He turned, looked. Down that way, a blue glow, very similar in character to the red one that had led him here, could be seen. He saw the deer again move across the street and disappear once more. Like a sleepwalker, he began to walk that way, into the blue glow.

When he reached the center of it, again about two blocks away, he looked for an animal he expected to be there, though he didn't know what it might be. But there was nothing, nothing to talk to. Did that mean that the south was empty? he asked himself. But the tiny voice told him that wasn't possible.

He heard a rush of air, of wings, and looked up. On a lamppost, an eagle was perched. The bird gazed down at him, leaning forward a bit; it had the shape of a bald or golden eagle, but in color it was a uniform sky-blue.

"You are of the south, then," Elliot said, his voice flat, unemotional.

"Yes," it told him, spreading its huge wings. Underneath, they were dark, and the movement of the feathers made it seem like he was looking up at storm clouds. Then, to his surprise, lightning flashes began to play around under the wings, dancing among the feathers. Large drops of water struck the pavement, and soon it was raining steadily. The eagle closed its wings, and the rain abruptly stopped. Elliot was startled to discover that he himself was not in the least wet.

"Proceed," it told him, "for this is not your place. You are not of the sky. Your only purpose here would be to strengthen those who are here."

"But," Elliot said earnestly, "where shall I go now?"

"West," the eagle said. "Go to the west, the Land of Descending. There will be one there who shall be familiar to you!" With that, it took to wing, driving itself into the air with such huge flaps of its wings that the rush of air stirred Elliot's clothes. For just a moment, he saw the talons hanging beneath the blue body before the bird pulled them up; they were enormous. several times larger than he would have expected for the creature's size. He watched it as it soared upward into the night sky, leaving him alone in the desolate street. He turned, looked westward, and saw a white glow.

Again he walked two blocks, seeking the center of the whitish light. When he did, the creature that was there was indeed familiar to him, at least in general. In the center of an intersection, a huge rattlesnake lay coiled, this one so large that it made the one in the zoo and the one in his dream seem tiny by comparison. Scales, rattles, and eyes, it was pure white, a snow snake; it also had long plumes trailing from the back of its head, more sprouting from the base of the rattle. The head, over a yard wide, turned in his direction as he approached, and a forked white tongue flickered at him. Prudently, he did not approach too closely; even the eagle with its huge talons had not been threatening compared to this monster. Yet, in a way, he felt no fear; he did not imagine that it meant him harm.

"Ah, yes," it rumbled sibilantly. "Another Jaguar Warrior visits my land. Come closer, little man! Come close, I would taste you!"

"Your taste might by my last experience," Elliot told it reasonably.

"Not with my mouth, O timorous one. With my tongue! If I, or indeed the eagle of the South or the rabbit of the East, had wished you any harm, you would already have been delivered to a Flowery Land! So come close. Do you not know that you have already?"

For the first time since he'd left the club, Elliot felt a real flash of fear as his feet started moving him in the direction of the massive scaly head. Though he tried to stop himself, he continued to walk until he was only a few feet from the tip of the snake's nose.

It regarded him steadily with unblinking eyes, the elliptical pupils stark black in the white head. The tongue, glossy and smooth, flowed from the perforation between its lips, flicked lightly over his face, his body; its touch was as delicate as the wings of a butterfly.

"Ah, yes," it said, withdrawing the tongue. "Yes, I can taste your past, your ancestry. It is good, O Jaguar Warrior."

"I fear I don't understand what's happening to me," he said impulsively.

"That isn't a surprise. What is a pleasant surprise is that you haven't passed out from fear, and your pants aren't soiled!"

"My pants—?"

"There may come a day when you understand that," it said, and it seemed to Elliot that it almost smiled. "But this night, you've other lessons to learn, my friend! Let me show you, let me show the poles of myself!"

So saying, the heavy body began to move, slowly uncoiling itself. When the creature had more or less stretched itself out, Elliot estimated that it must have been at least fifty feet long. And as the last coil lifted, it revealed beneath it the skeleton of a human being.

"Behold!" the snake told him. "One of your kind, one who has long since lost the breeze of Ehecatl!"

Elliot stepped up to where the bones lay on the pavement; they were not at all fresh. He lifted the skull, held it in a Hamlet-like gesture, looked at it closely. Much smaller than his own, he decided, but probably not a child's. It was so dry and old that bits of the jaw crumbled away when he inadvertently moved it.

"Put it back," the snake said curtly, "and step away!"

He obeyed, backing off twenty feet or more. The giant reptile lowered its head until it was almost touching the skeleton, then opened its mouth. Every detail was vivid; the tubelike sheath for the tongue on the floor, the erect and exposed fangs in the upper jaw. From the narrow, almost rectangular throat, a blast of heat emerged, forcing Elliot to back off even more. A brilliant white incandescence, like molten lava, flowed forth from the creature's mouth, washing over the bones. Elliot could feel the heat on his face, as if he were standing near the crater of an active volcano. But then the gaping mouth snapped shut, leaving a dome of incandescence over the skeleton.

In a matter of seconds, the heat began to fade, and the material it had expelled seemed to be evaporating. As it disappeared, the skeleton did not become visible again; instead, the naked body of a young girl lay there on the pavement. Her hair was black and long, and she looked almost exactly like one of the dancers back at the Obsidian Butterfly. She was not dead; Elliot watched the brown skin on her chest rise and fall, and in a moment her eyes, even darker than Nikki's, fluttered open. She stood up, looked around. First she saw Elliot, and she smiled uncertainly at him; then she saw the snake and gave voice to an ear-splitting scream.

Before Elliot could react at all, she ran to him and hid

behind him; he could fell her body trembling. She ran off a number of phrases in Spanish, none of which he understood.

The snake, turning to look at them once more, chuckled. "One of my cousins took her," he said, "oh, I'd say about a hundred years ago. He sank his fangs into her leg as she walked through the brush looking for a lost dog, pumped his poison into her body, and she died. She does not know by what means she lives again, here in a place of poisons! But, my friend, her importance is little compared with your understanding. Do you see?"

"I think," Elliot said.

"Do you know?"

"I know of payment, of balance," his voice said, though he was not too sure he knew what it meant.

"Yes! Then, look! See! Understand!" With remarkable speed, the reptile swung its head around, and Elliot's eyes followed it.

He saw a man walking on the street, the first normal-looking person he'd seen since leaving the club. The pedestrian didn't seem to have seen the snake; he was holding to the wall as if unsteady. Probably a drunk, Elliot thought.

The great creature flowed toward the man, the back part of its body moving considerably faster than its head, the difference being made up in an S-shaped loop that formed in its neck. Then, far faster than his eyes could follow, it struck.

The man gave one brief, weird cry as the fangs, each a foot long and an inch thick, slammed into his torso. Behind the eyes, the snake's head worked, and it lifted the feebly-moving man into the air. Even before his body was still, the creature's jaws began working, turning him around until his head was in its mouth, his body dangling free. Then, its jaw and throat expanding to account for the man's bulk, it began to swallow him. The whole process took less than a minute, from the strike until the time the man's shoes vanished down the pearly-white throat.

"Ugh!" the snake said, working its jaw back into shape. "I do so dislike swallowing clothing!"

"I believe I get your point, though," Elliot said. Behind him, the girl peeped out around his chest, made a little sound, and drew her head back.

"Good, good. Off with you then, off to your own place!"

"Which is that?"

"Which is left?"

"South is to the left," Elliot said, wondering where he'd gotten that odd idea. But, from where he was standing, it was.

The snake hissed at him. "Yes, I know! But you've already been told you didn't belong there! I meant, what remains?"

"North, right. That remains."

"Indeed. So?"

Elliot looked to his right. Unlike the previous directions, he saw no glow there; in fact, the streetlights didn't seem to be burning, either. "There?" he asked the serpent.

"There!" it said, lashing its rattles; they produced an explosive sound, like gunshots.

Slowly, Elliot started off toward the north. The naked Indian girl, her eyes still wide and her body trembling with fright—or possibly cold, even though it was a warm evening—huddled on his right side as he turned, away from the snake.

"I don't think it'll hurt you," Elliot said, looking down at her. She spoke back to him in Spanish, and he gave that up. They had no language of communication; so he put his arm protectively around her shoulder, walked down the silent streets.

After two blocks, he started looking for something, even though there was no light to tell him where it might be. In this area, all lights were out; there was only a faint, eerie light, mostly from atmospheric reflection of the city's brilliance.

Somewhere close, he thought, things must be normal; they certainly aren't here.

As he neared an intersection precisely two blocks from where he'd seen the snake, he heard a low, threatening growl. The girl cringed against him, tears of fright on her cheeks. Straining his eyes, Elliot looked into the roadway.

A big cat, apparently a jaguar, was lying there. It was so heavily spotted that only a little yellow showed on its fur; generally the animal was black. Slowly, majestically, it came to its feet, ambled toward them. Far larger than any natural jaguar, it stood nearly six feet tall at the shoulder. As it came close, rumbling deep inside itself, Elliot could see that it had black mirrors instead of eyes; still, he was sure it was looking at them.

"So, at last," it said, its voice hoarse and throaty, "you have come to the land of the Tecpatl!"

"The Tecpatl?"

"This!" the cat spat at them, and from nowhere a knife, carved from the same black glass as the animal's eyes, fell to the sidewalk. Elliot eyed it, but he didn't pick it up. "It might be yours," the jaguar told him. "You should pick it up and see."

"Perhaps it would want to be used if it were held," he said, once again not knowing where in hell these words were coming from. "And there are only three of us here!"

"It wouldn't be improper," the cat told him. "You know, after all, where you are!"

"Yes," Elliot said. To him, at that moment, a peculiar kind of an equation was obvious; rising, descending, sustenance—all these he'd seen. Therefore, this must be—

"Destruction, deprival," he said.

"Ah, the man learns the way!" the jaguar howled, startling both of them. It came very close to Elliot, its great shaggy head on a plane with his. "So now that you know," it said, its voice coming from somewhere deep within it, "will you, this night, give me what is mine?"

"I will not," Elliot said, though he didn't know exactly what it was talking about.

"Though you are my brother, O Jaguar Warrior?"

"Even so!"

The cat sat down, lifted an intimidating paw, put it on Elliot's shoulder; he sagged momentarily, just from the weight of it. It flexed its muscles, and the claws slid out. Like the eagle's, they were too large even considering the giant size of the animal; and they weren't claws at all, but flint knives. Elliot turned and stared at them as they lightly touched his shirt. The jaguar flexed them a little, and they opened the fabric as if it were tissue paper, but they never touched his skin. "I could take it," the cat purred.

"No, not without a fight, my brother!" Elliot said fiercely, looking straight into its mirror eyes.

The animal dropped its paw, turned and licked itself a few times. "Well, let's see, then," it said. "Let's just see what you're made of! If you are indeed worthy to be called a Jaguar Warrior!" With that, it turned suddenly and bounded away from them, and in less than a second it had disappeared into the dark concrete canyons. The streetlights around them began to flicker on, and Elliot looked around nervously. For some reason, what the animal said frightened him more than its claws, its fangs.

"We need to get out of here," he said to the girl, not caring whether or not she understood him. "Quickly!" He took her arm, began to tow her along, southward. Back to the center, he thought. But would it do any good?

"Elliot!" a voice cried, from off to his right, from, as he stood, the west. He looked up, and there was Nikki, wearing her robe, open in front as usual, except that it was a white robe, not a red one.

He paid no attention to this. "Nikki!" he cried, delighted to see her, and he ran toward her, towing the Indian girl along so fast that she stumbled. But as he got close, he saw something that made him stop short. The hair was Nikki's exactly; but the face—not quite. It was as if a not-too-skilled artist had painted her portrait, made it live: very close, but not exact.

"Elliot, Elliot!" she called, trotting toward them. Her gait was somehow peculiar too, and Elliot looked down at her feet. With a shock, he realized that they were backwards, her toes pointing to the rear. He looked up, his own eyes wide now. She had something in her hands, holding it out to him. Food of some sort, perhaps a pancake. It looked soggy and unappealing, perhaps molded.

"*Mujer Enrededora!*" the Indian girl behind him whispered, pointing. "*Matlacihuatl!*"

Elliot didn't understand any of this, but he did sense that this creature was dangerous, whatever it was; and it certainly wasn't Nikki. As it came even closer, he could see that her hair wasn't right, either; it was not curly, like Nikki's, but wild and unkempt, patted down—or perhaps oiled down—in a semblance of his friend's. She was very close now, holding out the pancake to him.

As he stood there, wondering what to do, the tiny voice in his ear spoke again, telling him to "reach within himself." It seemed to him that he knew what that meant, and he did so.

A moment later, he took the pancake from the woman, bit into it. The woman grinned as he did, turned around so that her back was to him, knelt down. She put both hands into her wild hair, lifted it off her neck; Elliot stared. There, just under the hairline, was a complete set of female genitals. The "vagina" was slightly open, and wet.

He spat out the pancake. "No seasoning," he said and watched the woman's body quiver. Digging in his shirt pocket, he located a roach he'd put there earlier, stuck it into his mouth, and lit it. But he didn't smoke it; he stuffed it, lit end first, into the woman's neck-vagina.

Not surprisingly, she screamed, jumped up, her hands fanning wildly at her neck. What was surprising was that the soggy pancake in Elliot's hand was immediately transformed into moldy leaves, and as the woman fell forward, her form shimmered, vanished. A small grayish snake then crawled rapidly away from them, disappearing into a grating in the sidewalk.

No sooner had the tail of the snake vanished from their sight than Elliot heard another voice calling his name. With the Indian girl still clinging to him as if for dear life, he spun around to confront this new threat, whatever it might be.

This time it was Laura, wearing her oversized dress like she always did, running toward him. He sighed, almost as if he was bored. Laura—or whatever it was—was running on backward-pointing feet. She kept coming as if she would run straight into his arms, but, releasing the Indian girl, he held his hands out in a peculiar gesture, fingers of one up, the other down, the butts of his hands together. The Laura-thing stopped, snarled at him. Now he could see her hair writhing; Medusa-like, it was composed of long, thin caterpillars, each covered with thousands of needlelike spines. Clumsily—her arm seemingly jointed wrongly—she held out a glass of some milky-white beverage to him and grinned sickeningly. He shook his head, pointed. Her face collapsed into a wild and hideous countenance; she jumped up and down on her reversed feet, threw off her dress; from between her legs, liquid matter like feces ran, dripped onto the cement. Elliot's stomach surged, and he pointed again, commanded her to go. Still snarling, she picked up the dress and turned to leave; as she did, Elliot saw that the back of her head was completely hollow. Inside, the features of the face, in reverse, were clearly visible; the eyes looked back at him from inside there as she walked away with her strange, bouncing gait.

"You should be proud, my brother," the jaguar rumbled. Elliot turned and jumped; its face was only inches from his. "We put it there for you to find, but not all can. I do not think we shall bring the third of Ixnextli's daughters out; she would be no challenge for you. Perhaps sometime, though, when you least expect it! Remember, brother. A Jaguar Warrior is always a warrior. Never relax. Never be off your guard. We may be watching!" Silently, it dragged its huge paw across the pavement, sweeping the obsidian knife toward Elliot. "Now, it is yours. Now, you can pick it up. It will not command you."

For several seconds, Elliot looked back and forth between the glossy black knife and the creature's equally glossy eyes. Then he shrugged; instinct had carried him this far in this insane nightmare. He bent down, impeded somewhat by the Indian girl's vicelike grip on his arm, and picked up the knife. He felt a sensation like an electric shock as he did so, but felt no overwhelming urge to use it on himself or on the girl, as he was sure he would have if he'd picked it up earlier. Carefully, so as not to cut the leather, he slipped it into his belt, like a small boy playing pirate. Only its thickness in the center kept it from cutting through anyway; it was sharp as a straight razor. When it was in place, he looked up again, and the giant jaguar was gone.

Now, he told himself, the problem was what to do with the Indian girl. Still terrified, she refused to release his arm for any reason. Keeping to the shadows of the buildings—he felt, at least for now, very much at home in darkness—he led her along the streets. Though in one way he had no idea how to get back to it, in another he knew that Alejandro's restaurant was right around the next corner, as indeed it was. He led the girl inside, down into the bar. As he expected, the tall Indian stood there, waiting for him. He looked at the girl, nodded, took her arm and led her away. Elliot turned and left, ignoring the massive shadowy form at the door, the other patrons, and the Unseen Ones he knew were watching him.

Still keeping to the darkness, feeling like a predator on the prowl, Elliot began to work his way back toward Gerald's apartment. Now it seemed that he had no doubts as to where it was: only a few blocks away, though it had been farther than that earlier. The geography of New York City had been changed somehow, but that didn't seem strange to him, not at the moment. He felt very good, wild, free, and powerful. He only wished that Nikki, the real Nikki, could have been here to share this exhilarating experience with him.

Down in Greenwich Village once more, he entered the

doorway leading to the stairs, which in turn led to Gerald's apartment. A single glance up there told him no one was home at the moment; if they had been, he would have seen their presence through the closed door, smelled them, sensed them somehow.

Occasionally touching his fingers to the step ahead as he went, he bounded up, unlocked the door somehow—he didn't know how—and went in. Just as he opened the door, he heard an explosion of traffic sounds from the street below him, and the normal din of many unintelligible voices wafted up the stairwell. All that frightened him a little, like it was no longer proper; and only when the smell of the city's pollution hit his nose did he realize it had been gone. Rushing into the apartment, he slammed the door, stood with his back to it, eyes taking in every inch of the dark room. He took the obsidian blade from his belt, crept into the bedroom; perhaps he was wrong, he thought. Maybe Laura was home. If so, he'd have a truly pleasant surprise for her, but she wasn't, and a buried part of his mind was screaming and howling at him. He tried to shake it off, but it persisted, and finally he hid the lethal blade in the lining of his suitcase, replacing the steel butcher knife he'd taken from the girl earlier. He stared at it, wondering what to do with it; finally he stuffed it down behind one of the steam radiators, ensured it could not be seen short of a direct search, and left it. Aimlessly, he walked into the kitchen, looked around; he was feeling more and more confused. Staring at the empty teacup that Laura had used, he felt the shell surrounding his mind shatter like brittle glass. His hands went up alongside his head, and he started to utter a mournful, low sound, but rapidly it turned into a scream. His heart was racing, head pounding, and he was convinced he was going to die on the spot; he could not catch his breath.

The full impact of the evening's events washed over him, all the terror he hadn't felt earlier came to him full force now. He wanted to run, hide, get away. He could not even go over the events in his mind; they were just too crazy, too disjointed. Thinking his hereditary heart problems might well catch up with him now, he tried to calm himself, but only partially succeeded.

He decided he ought to lie down, stumbled into the front

room, and collapsed onto his mattress. His face was wet; he was weeping from sheer fright. Then he lost consciousness, more as if he passed out than fell asleep. But he didn't wake that night.

26

In almost an exact repeat of the previous morning, Nikki greeted Elliot at the door very affectionately, wearing, as usual, her red robe. Again, she had coffee on the table, insisted that they sit and talk for a while before doing anything else; today, he didn't have a problem with that. He had convinced himself that the events following his decision to leave the Obsidian Butterfly had simply not occurred; it was hard enough for him to deal with the peculiar illusions associated with the "show." Several times that morning he'd considered looking in the lining of his suitcase, but he couldn't quite bring himself to do it; he was terribly afraid of what he might find there. Besides all that, he felt guilty about Laura. At least he hadn't had to search for her that morning; he'd found her sleeping with him again. He just wished she wouldn't look so damn heartbroken every time he left.

However, Laura and her difficulties were not what he wanted to talk to Nikki about today. Immediately after he'd been seated at the table, he asked her if she was familiar with the shows at the Obsidian Butterfly.

"Of course," she told him. "I've seen a lot of them. Dances from ancient Mexico, mostly. Recreated a bit. Nobody knows exactly how some of them went."

"That's all?"

"Well, except for the special shows, but they don't take place very often. Why do you ask?"

"I went there last night," he told her grimly. "The show—

well, it was just what you said. Let's just say it had a peculiar effect on me.''

"What sort of effect?"

"It seemed," he said, choosing his words carefully, "that I was part of the show, at times. And the dancers—uh— didn't always look the same."

"They changed costumes?"

He studied her face; it appeared open, innocent. Apparently what he was saying was ringing no particular bells with her. He tried to drop the subject, but she didn't let him. She kept pushing, encouraging him, until he told her about his peculiar viewpoint shift while he'd been watching the dance. "Doesn't that strike you as weird?" he asked when he'd finished.

She stretched, clasped her hands over her head. "Yeah, it is a little weird. Anything else happen there?"

"I don't know if I can tell you. You'll think I'm crazy."

"I already know you're crazy, Elliot," she said, sounding quite serious. "Go ahead and tell."

He did, in matter-of-fact terms and with no comments on his emotional state at any point. She listened closely, seemed very interested. But what happened after he left the club, he didn't mention at all. The glowing-eyed giant was bad enough.

"Is that all that happened? You left, went home, nothing else?"

"Uh—yes," he lied. He just couldn't talk about the other things, not yet, at least.

"You sure?" she probed.

"Yes, dammit!"

"You weren't scared?" she asked, ignoring his outburst. "Most people would have been terrified!"

"I don't really think I had a chance to be," he told her frankly. "And this morning, I'm having a hard time believing it happened."

"Well, I don't think you dreamed something like that up! I'm impressed, Elliot. I really am."

"About what?"

"Oh, your ability to hang on to yourself when your world is falling apart," she said with a laugh. "It's a good ability, my friend. You'll find it useful. Some night, we'll go to the Butterfly together. See if anything happens while I'm there."

"You work nights, remember?" he almost growled.

"My schedule can be flexible. Sometimes."

"Not for the past couple of days!"

"No. Things were planned in advance. Tonight, too, I'm afraid."

"Shit. I was hoping—"

"I know, but let's make the most of the day, okay?"

That he couldn't argue with. She guided him into her bedroom again, and the next hour or so was, for Elliot, another spectacular experience, this one highlighting Nikki's oral skills, which, he discovered, were many and exquisite.

Afterward, he waited for her to say that she wanted to go out; she didn't surprise him. But today, she did something quite different. She made a phone call, and they went downtown to meet a girl, a coed at City College, whose name was also Nikki, Nikki Keeler. It seemed that she and Nikki had known each other quite a long time, were close friends. Elliot found it difficult to be around her at first; she suffered from cerebral palsy, was confined to a wheelchair, could hardly talk. But after a while, he became comfortable with her, and the morning turned out to be pleasant after all, though he didn't understand some of the innuendos that passed between the two of them. It seemed that the Keeler girl had something she was going to give Nikki, in the near future. Elliot never did find out what it was, and he didn't feel like it was really any of his business.

"She's in something of the same position as your friend Laura," Nikki told him after they'd left the student.

"How so?"

"She hasn't long to live, and she knows it. There's a difference, though; she knows what is waiting for her. Her illness—it's gone too far. It's a real shame."

"That's too bad. Nothing can be done?"

"No. And it's awful. She's a pre-med student. She would've made a good doctor, too."

"Her doctors have told her she's terminal?"

"No. They think she's stable. But she knows—and I do, too—that it'll flare up on her again, and she won't make it."

"Nikki, how can you be so sure of these things?" he asked her, a little exasperated. "I mean, you always make these absolute pronouncements like you had infallible knowledge of the future or something!"

"No, just some knowledge," she told him. "And some experience. But like I said, she knows it, too. I'm just confirming what she says. You know, Elliot, if somebody believes something like that—really believes it, I mean—then it'll happen. Like Laura—whether the dream had any meaning at all, if her belief is strong, she'll find a way to do herself in. You just watch, you'll see."

"Now that I can agree with," he said. "And in Laura's case, that's what I'm trying to do. Break her away from this conviction. It's silly, but it can be dangerous."

"That's a waste of your time and hers," Nikki told him firmly. "But, look, I've told you all I'm going to about that. You do what you must; we'll talk after it's resolved. One way or another."

"Sounds good to me," he said. He glanced at his watch, saw that it was after one. "You hungry?" he asked her. "I could do with some lunch."

"Yes, sounds good," she responded. "How about Alejandro's again?"

He turned and stared at her, looking for perhaps a smirk in her eyes. But there was nothing there. This is stupid, he told himself angrily. Reyes is a friend of hers; she likes the place; there isn't a reason in the world she shouldn't suggest we have lunch there. But he was extremely uncomfortable about the idea of going there, now or, in fact, ever again. He chided himself, demanded that he disbelieve the previous night's events. Had to be dreams, just peculiar ones, he insisted. Had to be.

"Sure, fine," he croaked, trying not to reveal how ill at ease he really was. "No reason not to, is there? I mean, that stuff I told you about couldn't have actually happened, right? So, no reason not to, I suppose—" He finally noticed she was smiling oddly at him now. Doubtlessly she was aware of his discomfort, but at least he wouldn't have to face Reyes.

"Good!" she said, and his heart sank. "Let's go!"

As she turned away from him, he realized how hard it was for him to deny her anything.

Elliot entered the place with his head down, mumbled a greeting to Juan Reyes, and twice almost fell over chairs getting to the same table they'd had previously. But Reyes said nothing whatever about the previous night; Elliot had expected at least a question about his precipitous exit. For some time after they were seated, he stared intently at the menu, saying nothing. When the waitress came, he flicked his eyes to her brown hand resting on the table. Could be Carlotta again, he told himself. Could be some other Mexican girl. Couldn't be—could it? Nikki was talking to the girl, who spoke softly in response; he hoped she'd call her Carlotta, but she never did. Just wouldn't help him out. Finally mustering his courage, his knees trembling, he glanced up quickly. And breathed out the air he'd been holding all that time. Carlotta. Sweet, pretty, ordinary Carlotta, not the girl he thought he'd seen raised from the dead. He could have kissed her, just for being who she was. Some of his confidence returned, and he ordered his lunch, even trusted himself to glance around the room. There were few customers, none sitting anywhere close to them. And no familiar-looking Indian girl in sight. He grinned weakly, and very gradually his knees stopped crashing into one another.

When they had finished their lunch, Juan came over to their table. "I trust you enjoyed it?" he asked Nikki. He seemed to be almost subservient to her. "And you, Elliot?"

First-name basis, he thought. That meant not all of the previous evening had been hallucination or dream or whatever. But he knew that; he just didn't have a good handle on where reality had ended. Perhaps, he told himself, Juan could help him on that. He asked the Indian to join them, an action that seemed to surprise both Juan and Nikki. Taking charge, he instructed Carlotta to bring them all coffee.

"I wanted to ask you a question, Juan," he began. "About last night."

"Ah. And what is it, Elliot?"

Okay, fine, he thought; now, exactly how do you ask it? Without sounding completely mad. But then he had an idea. "I believe I might have had a little too much to drink," he lied smoothly. "And I wondered: Did anything unusual happen as I left?" He hesitated but forced himself to ask the next, much more critical question. "And did I come back?"

Reyes's eyes were totally unreadable. "You left," he said, "in rather a hurry. I don't know why. I, and my doorman, suggested you stay until the show had ended, but you insisted. Perhaps you did not find it pleasing."

Elliot shook his head. "No, it was very impressive. I just became—uncomfortable. The smoke," he improvised, "it was so smoky in there—odd-smelling smoke."

"Yes, that was copal incense. We always use it, along with some herbs."

Herbs, Elliot thought. Might be an answer there, but somehow it didn't seem like a good idea to ask. "And then later, did I come back?" he persisted.

Juan glanced at Nikki; it seemed to Elliot that something he was not privy to had passed between them. "No," he said finally. "I have not seen you again until now."

Much as he wanted to believe that was true, he could not miss the discomfort in the Mexican's demeanor, as if he were telling a lie he didn't want to tell. And Elliot didn't want to push it; he so much wanted to believe it.

"I hope you will return to the club soon," Juan said after a period of silence among them.

"Of course," he said. "Soon." But only if there was no way to avoid it, he promised himself.

Juan threw down the last of his coffee and stood up. "I must get back to work," he said. He made a peculiar movement in Nikki's direction—a kind of a half squat. Scenes from the dream passed through Elliot's mind as Juan turned and walked stiffly back to the door, relieving the young boy who'd taken his place as host.

"Poor Juan," she said to Elliot as he walked away. "I think he was a little hurt when you left his club suddenly, in the middle of the performance. But don't worry about it. A lot of things like that get to him. The ways of the U.S., New York in particular, are still strange to him. But they were to me, too, when I first came here."

"How long have you been here, Nikki?" he asked.

She was still looking at Juan, her face expressionless. "About a hundred years or so," she said, then almost immediately turned to Elliot and laughed. "Or so it seems sometimes!"

They finished their coffee and left the restaurant, Elliot giving a last glance around at the people there but seeing no young Indian girls except the familiar Carlotta. They'd hardly set foot on the sidewalk when Nikki succeeded in attracting a cab, and soon they were on their way back uptown, toward her apartment. Forgetting about the previous night, Elliot settled back, his body in contact with hers. He enjoyed the anticipation. "Norwegian Wood," he thought, an image of the Beatles drifting across his mind. Interesting pun.

Back in the apartment, as Elliot began to undress, Nikki turned on the stereo again; it appeared that it was going to be another lovemaking session set to music. Her choice this time was the Beatles' untitled album, which everyone referred to as the "White Album." For Elliot, "Mother Nature's Son" and "Happiness is a Warm Gun" were particularly appropriate when they came up. There was an oddity, although he was too distracted to pay much attention to it; both songs had played, yet he knew full well they weren't on the same side of the album. And neither of them had gotten up. He also found himself responding, though negatively, to the song "Helter Skelter"; it seemed to conjure up images of random brutality for him. Violence that had the effect he'd like it to have: repugnance. During the song, he remembered the part of the dream, or vision, or whatever it was he'd experienced the night before. He could see himself stalking through Gerald's apartment, looking for Laura, carrying the savage knife. But it was strange; even though that image was horrifying, it seemed to somehow clash with the other brutal suggestions of the song. Very odd, he told himself; there was nothing violent about a playground slide.

When they had finished, reluctantly separated their bodies, Elliot rolled over onto his back on the soft carpet, allowing Nikki to nestle her head into the hollow of his neck. He was not tired, nor spent; that hadn't happened since the very first day. For quite some time, he lay there looking at the ceiling, just enjoying the utter contentment he felt. When he was with her, nothing else really mattered to him very much. It was as if she formed a world for him.

"What are you thinking, Elliot?" she asked after a time.

"Lots of things," he told her, still looking at the cracked ceiling. "About you. How much I like being with you, making love with you. About the weirdness in my life lately. About your job, or whatever it is you do at night."

"Now, don't start that again," she warned, patting his chest.

"I sort of have to," he said slowly, reluctantly. "Maybe I'm being silly, but I feel like I only half know you. You have another life, at night, that I know nothing about."

"Why do you need to?"

"I need to know everything about you!" he said, turning to kiss her hair. "Your favorite color, lucky number, sign—everything!"

"Red. Four. Scorpio," she said.

"Scorpio, I might have known," he said to the ceiling. "What else?"

"Sun signs aren't that important," she said, her voice somewhat muffled by the fact that she was nuzzling his neck.

"You into astrology?"

"In a way. Not as you know it. In parts of Mexico, there's a kind of astrology, if you want to call it that, based on day signs, day numbers, and rulers of the hours. It's pretty different, but still it gives information about a person based on their exact time of birth."

"I've never heard of it."

"Yes, you have. From me. I mentioned it during one of our discussions."

"Oh, I remember—had an odd name, that I can't remember."

"Well, the calendars are called Tonalpohualli, recorded in books called Tonalamatl. They were once held to be sacred."

"How does it work?"

"Well, there are twenty day signs, and thirteen day numbers. Starting with any one—the first sign is called Cipactli, and of course the first number is one—that day would be Ce Cipactli. Translated, 'one water-monster.' The next day would be two, and the second sign is Ecatl, so the next day would be Ome Ecatl, that is, 'two wind.' And so on, but when you get to fourteen, you go back to one. When you get back to Cipactli, you're at eight already, so the twenty-first day is 'eight water-monster.' See?"

"No. Not a bit."

"Well, like I told you before, it's complicated. More so by the fact that you divide the day into thirteen hours, and the night into nine, and each one has a ruler, whose significance you have to take into account. Then there are the rulers of the weeks—twenty of those in a cycle, thirteen days in this kind of 'week'—and the month rulers, where there were eighteen 'months' in a solar year, plus the five useless days, of course, and—"

"Stop! You're giving me a headache! I can't even follow Jupiter in Aquarius in the Fifth House! About all I know about it is they say the Age of Aquarius has just started—"

"No," she said, quite firmly, quite seriously. "They say wrong. The changing of ages is a profound event, hardly marked by a transitory social phenomenon! No, the age we're in—call it the age of Pisces if you wish, I call it the Sun of Tonatiuh—will end, and the next one will start, in the year 2011. If I'm sure of anything, I'm sure of that! And I'll tell you something else: nobody, but nobody, will be able to mistake the fact that something major is happening!''

He raised up slightly, looked at her with raised eyebrows. ''You're sure?'' he said, grinning.

''I'm sure.''

''It says so in this Tommametal?''

''Tonalamatl. Yes—well, it's implied. You can figure it out, just simple math.''

''Well, we'll see, won't we?''

''Those of us who live that long.''

''No problem! It's only—let's see—forty-two years more!''

''Not a lot of time,'' she said seriously. ''One true generation past yours.''

''You mean ours.''

''Oh, yeah, sure. Ours.''

''One more question, okay?''

''Okay, shoot.''

''What do you do for a living?''

She rolled over off his arm and sat up. ''You have a one-track mind, Elliot, you know that?''

He grinned at her, propped his head on his arm. ''So I've been told.''

''You were told right!''

''You're avoiding the subject.''

''You're right!''

''Don't, okay?''

She sighed deeply. ''Damn. I'm just not at all sure I should,'' she said, as much to herself as him.

''This from the woman who knows when the age ends, who is to live and who is to die?''

''Don't make fun,'' she said, her eyes flashing at him. ''This is serious. Don't make light of it.''

He stopped smiling. ''I'm really not, Nikki. It is serious; it's important to me to know. I can't understand why you're being so secretive about it.''

''I have my reasons,'' she said, looking off into space. For a time she said nothing. Then: ''Tell me, Elliot. From your viewpoint, what're some truly obnoxious ways I could be earning a living?''

"I think you're trying to dodge me again!"

"No, I'm not. Just answer my question."

He put his head back, thought about it. "Well, you've already said you aren't a cop, don't work for the CIA or FBI," he said. "God, I don't know. Contract killer, ransom kidnapper—hard to say. Maybe member in good standing of the Military-Industrial Complex." He looked at her, laughed. "You don't work on Wall Street, do you?"

She laughed back. "No, I'm not a stockbroker!" she said, making a face at him. "Besides, the investment firms aren't open at night!"

"Do I have to guess it to find out?" he complained.

"No," she said, her voice softer. "No, I'm not playing a game with you, Elliot."

"Then tell me, Nikki," he asked her. "Please."

She folded her hands together, looked down at them for a moment, then back up directly into his eyes. "I'm a prostitute, Elliot," she said in a clear voice, no hesitation or fumbling.

He heard what she said, but it just didn't connect, and initially he was certain that he'd heard her wrong. Must have been something else, he told himself, something that sounds like that. He hit upon an idea, seized it. "I thought you said you didn't work for the government!" he said accusingly.

"Huh?"

"You just said, 'I'm a prosecutor,' didn't you? Like a D.A.? That's working for the government, isn't it?"

She stared at him blankly for an instant. "I said prostitute, Elliot," she told him. "A call girl, sometimes an actress in stag films. You know, as in fucking for money?"

Silently, Elliot regarded her. Her face was peaceful; this was no confession jerked tearfully out. "No," he said, "that isn't possible." It was not a question, but a very definite statement.

"It is possible, and true," she told him, leaning forward as if to study his face more closely.

"No—this is a joke, right?"

" 'Fraid not. Remember now, Elliot, you insisted I tell you. I didn't force it on you."

"Do you mean to sit there and tell me—that these past few nights—after I left, guys came up here—and—and—"

"Not these past few nights, no," she said, and he started

to take on hope, clutching it to himself. But just as quickly, it seemed as if his hands passed through it. "We've been making some loops—stag films—and we've been going out to do that—"

"We?"

"A man named Andrew. He makes and sells such things. On the black market, of course, but he's betting that in a few years you'll be able to buy them openly. I think he's right, too. But that really isn't my concern. He pays quite well, and I have the freedoms I feel I need."

"Freedoms?"

"To turn down guys I see as unacceptable. I'm not a streetwalker, Elliot. I don't take just whoever comes along."

"Turn down?" He seemed to be unable to get anything out except these short, nonsensical questions, and he tried to get his mind working again. But he was sort of in shock. This was just about the last line of work he'd have expected Nikki to be in.

"Are you all right, Elliot?" she asked, waving her hand in front of his face.

"Can't be," he mumbled. "You didn't ask me for any money—"

She laughed merrily. "But I like you, Elliot! With you, it's fun, not work! When you were telling me about your psychology experiments, did you charge me tuition?"

"How can you?" he asked, his voice so low as to be difficult to hear. "Isn't it degrading—"

"I don't think so," she told him frankly. "It's just a way to earn a living, and not a bad one, I'd say."

"But—you let men use you—for money—"

"Look. You're a college professor, right? They pay you to teach students about psychology. You get up in front of a class and pour out everything you know about a subject dear to your heart. So they can learn. And they pay for it, they pay tuition. In the end, Elliot, you're selling your mind! All I'm selling is my body. Renting, actually."

"It isn't the same . . ."

"Maybe not, not exactly. Let's take another example, then. Would you have been shocked if I'd told you I was a professional athlete? Say a tennis player?"

"No . . ."

"But if I were, then I'd still be selling—or renting—my

body for money. The fans pay to see it play the game. Or a model, perhaps, a high-fashion model. That's even closer, because the main thing that matters is how she looks, right?''

''It still isn't—''

''Oh, but it is, Elliot! It just depends on how you look at things. This particular culture says that sex is either dirty or sacred, or both. It cannot just be. But in terms of economics, all of us who don't sell a product sell a service, right? And at the bottom line, the service is ourselves. One way or another. Our minds, our skills, our hands on a factory assembly line, or, in many ways—not just in my business—our bodies themselves. Why should this be so different?''

''Everybody knows—''

''What an answer, from you! Everybody knows we just absolutely have to stop Godless Communism in Vietnam, or else they'll take over the world! Everybody knows that smoking marijuana leads directly and inevitably to shooting heroin, and from there to skid row! Everybody knows that sex outside of marriage is evil, sinful, and bound to give you a disease that'll rot off your prick! Everybody knows, too, that men should wear their hair short and shave—and just look at you! Seems to me you pay very little attention to what everybody knows!''

''But—''

She put her hands on her hips, leaned toward him again. ''If you have reasonable objections, let's hear them, Elliot!'' she challenged.

''All the talk about disease isn't just a scare tactic!'' he said, after searching for a moment.

''Never had a problem,'' she told him. ''Never.''

''And it can be dangerous!'' he cried suddenly, remembering the recent string of murders. ''Why, you could hook up with that killer and—''

''I don't expect problems of that sort, either,'' she said softly. ''None that I can't handle, anyway!''

''That kind of attitude could get you killed!''

''But that isn't what we're talking about, is it? Your first reaction wasn't concern for my health or safety. It was moral outrage, right?''

He had to admit it; it was just too damn obvious. But now that he'd thought of the disease aspect, he was trying to discreetly examine his penis, see if any sores had erupted there.

She saw what he was doing, sighed again. "Elliot," she said, "there is no problem of that sort. Please believe that!"

"How can you be sure?" he muttered, checking himself more overtly now.

"Just take my word for it!"

He didn't respond, and after a moment, he got up, started to dress. She watched him from the floor, not speaking either. When he'd gotten all his clothes on, his shoes tied, he looked down at her again. "I have to go," he said in a stony voice.

"Okay, if you must," she told him. But she didn't sound indifferent.

He didn't speak again, just turned and walked out the door. There was just no way, he told himself; no way he could go on seeing a woman who made her living that way. A thousand epithets leaped into his mind: whore, slut, hooker. Even so, he could remember his own high-sounding statements in various discussions, his criticisms of others for these very attitudes. But when confronted with it on a personal level, it was very different, and he did not feel like he could accept it. In his mind, he had said his good-bye to her, to the good times in her apartment.

As he rode the subway back toward the Village, he found that he could not get her off his mind. Trying to stop thinking about her, he forced himself to study the advertisements posted in the tiled stations; it wasn't until he saw one promoting an anti-drug campaign that he remembered that today was Monday, October 20th. In his obsession with Nikki, he'd forgotten all about Dave Jennings, the court hearing. He pounded on his seat and cursed aloud, drawing a few stares from his fellow passengers. Glancing at his watch, he saw that it was after six-thirty; Dave's hearing had been at two. He'd missed it completely.

The next time the train stopped—it was at the Fiftieth Street station, one stop above Times Square—he got off, searched for a phone and started making calls. First he dialed Marcia, hoping she was home. She was, but she told him she still had heard nothing from his friend. Cursing again as he hung up, he wondered what to do now; he debated with himself briefly, then called the police department.

After an hour's time and over four dollars in change—it

seemed to him he'd been referred to more divisions of the police department and the court system than could possibly have reason to exist—he finally put the phone down and turned away. This, he told himself, didn't make any sense at all. No one had ever heard of a person named Dave Jennings, nor a David, nor a D. Jennings. There were dozens of Jennings currently enmeshed in the New York judicial system, but none fit the description at all. He'd also learned that the court Dave had referred to was a traffic court—hardly one that would handle a major drug case. He could only assume that Dave had somehow gotten the charges dropped, had had his name removed from the records, and hadn't bothered to call and tell him about it. Perhaps he'd been confused about the hearing, too. Composing in his mind an acidic speech to be delivered the next time he heard from Dave, he got back on a train and headed to the Village. Unfortunately, with Dave off his mind, he couldn't stop Nikki from returning to it; and he brooded about her for the rest of the ride, and during the walk from the station to Cornelia Street.

His fervent hopes that nobody be in the apartment were dashed; Laura was out somewhere, but Haze and Gerald were sitting at the kitchen table, sipping herbal tea. Across from him, Conrad Weiser again; oddly, he was wearing a blue sweatshirt with the logo "Carolina" on it in white letters. Elliot had seen many of those in Chapel Hill, very few in New York. He looked up from the newspaper he was reading—or perhaps just staring at—as Elliot stood in the doorway.

"Elliot," he said with an ingenuous smile, his mouth hanging open. "See?" He pointed to his chest. "I found it at the Goodwill—thought, well, since I know several people from Chapel Hill, I oughta get it."

Elliot didn't really want to hear about any other people Weiser might know from Chapel Hill; he just nodded, forced a smile he didn't mean.

"I saw you last night," Weiser said, apparently determined to start a conversation.

"Yeah? Where?"

"Oh, just out on the streets. You were just walking along there. Just walking. It was far-out." Now he gave Elliot a closed-mouthed smile; his lips looked like a crescent moon, points up.

Elliot resisted the temptation to ask him why or how his walking along might be "far-out," but decided against it; the term had become so cliched it no longer had any meaning at all.

"You look like you had another piss-poor day," Haze commented.

"I really don't think I want to talk about it," Elliot told him. There was a silence; Haze might accept that, but he was sure it wouldn't sit well with Gerald, who usually wanted to talk about everything.

"You are back earlier than usual," Gerald said finally, a question in his eyes.

"Not much," Elliot said, trying desperately not to get into it. He searched his mind for something to change the subject. "But I did want to ask you something," he continued, concentrating on the weirdness of the previous night. "Have you ever heard of a restaurant called Alejandro's? Or a bar called the Obsidian Butterfly?"

Gerald thought for a minute. "No. Why?"

"I was there last night. A freaky place, I'll tell you! I just wondered if there was any kind of a story there, any talk around about it."

"Shee-it, man," Haze put in. "Ain't nobody talking 'bout nuthin' right now 'cept the heat!"

"The heat?"

"Yeah, man, where you been, anyway?" Gerald asked. "A lot of girls have been killed. One or two a night, every night. Some close to here, too. I knew one of them myself. The pigs are really freakin', man. And as usual, they think it's a crazed druggie. So they're coming down hard on everybody. Things are getting dry out there."

"I haven't seen a paper in a while. There've been more murders?"

Weiser shoved the paper toward him. "Seven, now," he said, his voice showing some animation. It seemed to Elliot that he was upset about it, but that was natural, he told himself. Murders should be upsetting to anyone. Elliot looked at the article:

SEVENTH PROSTITUTE MURDERED

The body of Jeanne Firestone, 24, of Concord, New

Hampshire, was found today in a hotel room on Bleecker Street. A police spokesman said this brings to seven the number of prostitutes slain in the area by the killer who has been dubbed, "the Killer Guitarist," since all of his victims have been strangled with a guitar string. At the present, there are no leads as to the killer's identity. . . .

Elliot stared at the newsprint for a long time, the words blurring in front of his eyes. He had a vivid image in his mind of Nikki thrashing on a bed, a guitar string cutting into her delicate throat, some huge, apelike creature holding her down, pulling on the ends of the string. He considered going directly back up there but was sure he wouldn't be welcome, even if she was there—which she might not be. He was pretty sure she'd mentioned "working" tonight. That led to another explosion of images of a different sort, and he pushed them down. She ought to be safe from this, he told himself almost desperately. These killings were taking place in and around the Village, and she worked uptown. At least it seemed reasonable that she would; he recognized the fact that he didn't know that for sure.

"So, Elliot," Weiser was saying, "you're a psychologist. Tell us about this killer, huh?"

"I was a psychologist, too," Gerald said rather petulantly.

"But he still does it for a living," Weiser persisted, not even glancing at the older man. "What's he like, Elliot? Why does he do it?"

"Maybe he's impotent," Elliot said distantly. "Maybe he hates his mother. Who knows?"

"There's probably some reason he focuses on hookers," Gerald observed.

"Not necessarily," Elliot commented, his voice lifeless. "A lot of killers have chosen prostitutes for victims. Jack the Ripper, for example. Maybe for no other reason than the fact that they're available, vulnerable. By the nature of their business."

"We should legalize it," Gerald pronounced. "Then, you could have houses, protection. It'd be better all the way around. The police never stop it, anyhow."

"No," Elliot said. "No one can stop it."

"Maybe he will," Weiser told them, tapping the newspaper. "Maybe he'll scare all the rest into quitting. You think?"

"People never think it can happen to them," Elliot said, not looking up. "We always think that we ourselves are invulnerable. I'm sure every one of these poor girls thought that. Until it was too late."

"They prob'ly deserved it anyhow," Haze muttered under his breath.

Both Elliot and Gerald looked at him, startled. "What the hell do you mean?" Elliot demanded.

"Well, shit, man," he said, refusing to meet Elliot's eyes. "Nobody oughta be chargin' money for it now, you dig? Oughta be free. Free love, that's the idea, right? Should mean free fuckin', too. I figure the bitches that want money got somethin' bad wrong with 'em—"

"Maybe that's the only way they can get any bread," Gerald told him gently. "You remember, Laura once—"

"Laura?" Elliot snapped. "You mean Laura was hooking?"

"Now, calm down, Elliot," Gerald said, holding his hands up. "She doesn't do it anymore—"

Elliot sighed, held his head in his hands. Laura too; but if she'd quit, what could he say? Gerald might have been right: a young runaway in the city could make more doing that than most anything else.

"Well, look, we gotta get going," Gerald said, stopping the discussion of the murders. "I'm taking Conrad over to see some people about him moving in with them."

"Sure, fine," Elliot said as the other two got up from the table. A few moments later he was left sitting there alone, as he'd wanted it. But the newspaper, with its ominous headline, was still lying in front of him, as if its message was for his eyes alone. It was as if he could see the "seventh" as "eighth," the name of the unfortunate young woman as "Nicole Howard." Thinking about that, he realized he'd never asked her how old she was.

Restlessly, he went into the front room, flopped down in the chair. Once again, his bruised brown suitcase caught his eye, and he stared at it doubtfully. Part of him still wanted to look and see what was in the flap, but another part was afraid to. This evening, the first part won out, and he shuffled over to it, laid it flat, and opened it. Pulse pounding, he cautiously reached his hand into the rip in the lining and breathed a long sigh of relief. There was nothing there. That load removed from his mind, he sat back down, leaned back, then sat upright again. That wasn't right; something should have been there. The big steel butcher knife he'd taken from Laura. Returning to the bag, he rummaged in the lining but came up with nothing. He remembered that in the dream he'd hidden it behind the radiator, and he checked that location. Sure enough, he could see the black handle, a line of silver running down the center of it, peeking up when he looked over the top of the iron heater. Now, that was strange, he told himself. Had he been sleepwalking in some odd way? To the point where he moved the knife, even though he'd obviously had no obsidian knife to put in its place? He must have; the evidence was right there. Briefly he considered trying to go back to the Obsidian Butterfly tonight, but he didn't feel like going out, particularly to some place as closely associated with Nikki as Alejandro's was.

Throwing his head back against the upright of the chair, he mentally cursed the fates, or perhaps Nikki, or whatever it had been that had driven her to become a hooker. Thinking about it, he was quite sure that something, some set of circumstances, must have forced her hand. That was not a choice an intelligent woman would make voluntarily. And yet, with the exceptions of the matters of disease and the risk of violence, she certainly had given him a well-thought-out defense of the profession in general. Sitting there, he began to question his own attitudes; it was certainly true, as she'd suggested, that his horror of what she was doing was apparent before he'd even thought about VD, about the Killer Guitarist. And, since he prided himself on accepting virtually none of his society's mores without having analyzed them, that made no sense. In any intellectual discussion, Elliot would have been the first to trumpet the notion of the absurdity of Western moral codes. Yet, at the root of things, he too was affected by them. Not only by his attitude toward Nikki's profession, he realized, but also by his insistence that Laura Neill was a child, no matter what she thought or how she acted. Neither one was logical, he told himself. Neither could be defended in a debate.

But, on the other hand, how could Nikki's profession not upset him? Here he was, alone, and though his leaving tonight was by his choice, not hers, he was certain that she would have sent him away as she'd done previously. If he stayed with her, that would be his life, unless she could be persuaded to give up her "career." And he would be left with what he was doing now—seeing pictures in his mind of her with some faceless, nameless man. In her bed, on the floor in front of the stereo, on the kitchen table. One after another, the images came: all varieties of men, tall, short, fat, handsome, black, white. All the possible sexual variations, all possible locations. When they stopped coming of their own volition, he found to his surprise that he was encouraging more, and for at least a half-hour he sat there doing virtually nothing except fantasizing about Nikki and her customers. He stopped only when a sense of pressure made him realize that he had a prominent erection, which made his inclined position in the chair uncomfortable. Shocked at himself, he stared down at it. Remembering what had happened when Melissa had told him about her liaisons, it slowly dawned on him that he'd made a mistake.

Digging into his wallet, he came up with a scrap of paper that Nikki had written her phone number on, and he almost lunged for the phone. If she were "engaged," he told himself, she'd probably have the phone off the hook. But he remembered what she'd said at the time she'd given him the number—that she had an answering machine. Fumbling only a little, he made the call.

"Hi!" came her voice after a moment, clearly a recording. "This is Nikki, but I can't come to the phone now! Leave your number, and I'll call you back, okay? When you hear the tone!" There was a second of tape hiss, then a loud beep.

"It's Elliot, Nikki," he said. "Call me when you can, tonight or tomorrow. Or I'll call—" He stopped, having heard the machine disconnect itself. He shrugged, replaced the receiver. There was nothing else he would do right now, nothing but wait. There was only one thing he considered fortuitous: if his VW had been ready, he would probably have already been on the road for North Carolina. He'd been promised the car tomorrow, and it was just as well, he told himself. If he'd come to these conclusions somewhere in Virginia, he would have just had to turn around and come back.

He was still thinking about these things when Laura came in. She greeted him warmly, and he found that he was glad to see her; he was becoming increasingly fond of her, even if he still was not to a point where he could give her what she wanted. She had a package, wrapped with string, canceled stamps in one corner and "Fragile" marked all over it.

"What's that?" he asked.

"From home," she told him excitedly. "Took a while, but I had a girlfriend send it to me on the sly. I shoulda brought it in the first place!"

Discreetly, for future reference, Elliot peeked at the return address: Dayton, Ohio, not Minnesota. "What's in it?" he queried, as she sat it down on the floor.

"You'll see," she said, ripping at the paper with abandon. Soon she had revealed a small, oblong case, covered with black leatherette. Putting it in her lap, she released the two little catches, opened it. With a gentle touch, she brought out several cylinders of bright silver metal.

"I didn't know you were a flute player!" Elliot said, watching her assemble it.

She grinned at him, slid the pieces together with practiced hands. Putting it to her mouth, she played a short bit of "The Dance of the Sugar Plum Fairy," from the *Nutcracker*. Elliot was even more surprised; she was extremely competent with the instrument.

"That's great!" he enthused. "Really good!"

"I was all-state," she said with a shy smile.

"Maybe we can play together some," he said. "I play a little classical guitar—" He glanced at Haze's guitar sitting in the corner; one of the strings, the A, was missing from it. "Damn!" he said. "I guess we can't, unless you know where we can buy some strings tonight?"

"Sure!" she said, bouncing up. "There's a pawn shop, open till midnight! They have strings!"

"My dear, would you accompany me?" he asked. Together, they left the apartment.

In Laura's company, the streets of the Village seemed quite different than they had the previous night, even before Elliot had visited the Obsidian Butterfly. Tonight, she was happy and ebullient, a joyful child who saw something exciting in the most mundane things. She seemed to have forgotten her conviction of her impending death, at least for the moment, and Elliot felt quite sure that when he talked to Nikki tomorrow, things were going to turn out well for him—not that he was resigned to the idea of her working as a prostitute forever. The notion of asking her to marry him, taking her back to

North Carolina, was beginning to play around the edges of his mind. Naturally, he didn't mention any of this to Laura, and she didn't ask. She seemed happy enough just with his company, and again he found her attitude toward him quite flattering.

Once more it was a warm, pleasant evening, and the streets were filled with people, from the long-time locals of the Village to the tourists who sometimes came to gawk at the hippies. Certain kinds of activities that were normal on these streets—such as open dope-smoking—were muted tonight, and Elliot remembered what Gerald and Haze had told him about the "heat." But, mostly, life went on as it always did. On one street corner, a group of Hare Krishnas, heads shaved, danced in their saffron robes. Laura wanted to watch them for a while, and they did. Elliot was gratified, though, when she expressed a certain disdain for their particular cult.

"You aren't into anything like that, are you, Elliot?" she asked him.

"No. You?"

"Uh-uh. Not me. When I first came to the city, before I met Gerald and Haze, I got hooked up with a guy named Nigel. He called himself 'Chingon.' I didn't know it at the time, but he was into one of these crazy things—I believe it was called 'the Procedural Church' or somethin' like that. It was freaky, Elliot, I tell you. He took me to a house on the East Side, where a whole bunch of people lived. And the way they acted, you'da thought I was a long-lost sister or somethin'. At first, it was just good food, good dope, good friends. Not a single word was said to me or around me about this being a religion. But after a day or two, people started talkin' at me, a little at a time. Don'tcha think this, whattaya think about that. Pretty soon, I started gettin' the picture—this was a cult house, and I was their new member!

"Well, I said no, that wasn't for me. I wanted to leave. But they said—can you believe it—that I couldn't, that they were goin' to save me from backslidin' to the devil whether I liked it or not! So I played it cool. I says, okay, maybe you're right, whattaya want me to do? Then they really started gettin' me into it.

"It was craziness, Elliot. Normally, they didn't do any drugs; they just used them as bait. As far as sex was concerned, you screwed whoever Chingon told you to, when he told you to. Nobody else, no other time. I mean, like a lot of the guys weren't getting any at all. And then there were these weird rituals, where they said they were tryin' to drive the devils out of the city. They didn't make any sense at all, of any kind. I thought at first they might be old black magic things, but they weren't. Chingon just made them up as he needed them; they were mostly to keep people in line. Because you could get tied to a table and beaten within an inch of your life if the Chingon said there was a devil in you.

"Anyhow, nobody had any money or any jobs, so I kind of wondered where all the food, the big house, and all that came from. I found out pretty quick. They had about twice as many girls there as guys, and all the girls were expected to turn tricks. Since they tried to pick a lot of young ones, pretty ones, they made a lot of money that way. Also, they were drug-dealers, pretty big-time. Not just grass and acid, but heroin, cocaine, anythin' that would make a buck. And here I was, a little stupid from Ohi—uh—Minnesota, caught in the damn middle of it!"

"But obviously you got out. How long were you with them?"

"About six weeks—too long, I tell you! There's a lot of guys in the city that really dig real young girls, right? So they wanted to get me out in the street real quick. I figured, soon as they send me out, I'm splittin'. So I said, sure, I'll do it.

"But they sent me out under guard, is what it amounted to. Two guys with me all the damn time. We'd pick up a john, take him up to a room in some fleabag, and they'd wait outside the door. I'm tellin' you, some of the guys that've wandered into the apartment ain't been prizes, but there's been nothin' like some of these scuzzy dudes! You just wouldn't believe it! Anyway, I had to go through with it. But in a way, it made me tough; and that's good, isn't it?"

Not for an innocent little flute player from Ohio, Elliot thought. This city, he told himself, can really be hard on the strays. "Um," he said, noncommittally. He wondered briefly if Nikki's story might be similar.

She seemed to take that for assent, went on with her story. "Anyway, things around the house got weirder and weirder. I thought at the time that the Chingon was losing his cookies. He started talkin' about killin' people. Goin' out and catchin' somebody and bringin' him in and killin' his ass. And there was always rumors that people who tried to escape from the group were being killed. But you know, who knows? I never saw any of that, never saw anybody just up and disappear either. But there were a bunch of different commune houses. Nobody knew everybody in the church. 'Cept maybe the top guys—and I don't think even they did. Or do. Anyhow, I didn't wanta be close to that. I managed to convince them that I could turn more tricks, make more money, without these guys hangin' on me all the time, that they were scarin' off a lotta the johns. He bought it, and they let me go out alone. I figured they'd be sorta watchin' at first, so I just played it straight, three days. Then I split. I never saw any of them again.''

"That sounds like a damn terrifying experience!''

"It was. But I learned a lot from it, too.''

"You know, I almost never say that anybody should be reported to the police,'' he growled, "but these people, they really should be stopped!''

"They should be stopped from makin' other people do stuff they don't wanta, yeah.''

"No, I think stopped completely! I mean, you never know— they might actually start killing each other!''

"Well, you know, Elliot, I'd say that's okay by me.''

"I can understand that you don't like them much—''

"No, that isn't what I mean. If they want to do stuff like that—to each other, I mean—then, well, that's fine. Somebody wants to let Chingon kill him, okay, it's his business. All I say is don't drag people in from outside when they don't wanta come! It ain't a lot different from the way some of the regular churches act, though. They wanta tell you what to think, too. And it seems to me that's what Chingon is after, really. A buncha people who do what he tells 'em to. And you know, there's a hell of a lot of people out there that hate to hafta decide for themselves what to do. They just love havin' somebody tell 'em.''

Once again, his respect for the girl increased markedly. "Pretty deep for a kid!'' he said.

She shrugged. "I been tryin' to tell you. I may be just thirteen, but I ain't no kid! One day, you'll figure that out. I just hope it ain't too late.''

That, Elliot definitely didn't want to get into again. He reminded her that they'd come out for guitar strings, and she guided him to the pawn shop, where he purchased a set of La Bellas. Back at the apartment, he strung them on Haze's guitar—an excellent older Yamaha, undamaged by the "artwork"—and they spent the rest of the evening with the instruments. A pleasant time for Elliot, it passed very quickly. Afterward, Laura again insisted on sleeping with him, but again, all they did was sleep.

27

Tuesday morning, Elliot's first order of business was to pick up his car; a quick call to the garage verified that it was ready. Before he went, he called Nikki's number but again got the recording. After leaving another message, he and Laura walked down to the repair shop, where it turned out that the car, was, after all, not quite ready. The mechanic hadn't finished putting it back together yet, and they were forced to wait.

In the lounge, he picked up a current newspaper, felt his stomach surge when he saw the headline:

EIGHTH PROSTITUTE MURDERED BY KILLER GUITARIST!

It was almost physically painful for him to look at the article. But he had to, and his relief was immense when he encountered the victim's name: Alice Jenks. He wished to hell the cops would catch this particular maniac, get him off the streets—before he did see the name he so dreaded under such a headline.

It took almost an hour, but finally, after paying what he considered to be an exorbitant repair bill, he and Laura drove the VW out of the garage. He had to admit it ran much better, better than it had since he'd taken it to Illinois, which seemed like a hundred years ago in ways.

He was lucky; he found a parking place less than two blocks away. Once back at the apartment, he tried to call Nikki again, and this time the line was busy. Too impatient to wait any longer, he decided to leave, go uptown. As he closed the door, he was sure he could hear Laura crying behind him. Vaguely, he wondered where Haze was; he apparently hadn't returned with Gerald the previous night. But that wasn't really his problem, and Elliot put it out of his mind as he worked his way through the traffic, headed north toward Cabrini.

It was already past eleven, and the lunch crowds were on the street. As he searched for a parking place along Cabrini, he found that his luck was still holding; he found one almost in sight of Nikki's building. Nervously, he walked down the sidewalk, forcing himself to go slow, try to keep calm. He didn't think she'd be holding grudges, but one could never tell. It was possible that she'd taken extreme exception to his attitude.

He became even more nervous when there was no answer to his ringing of the bell. He well knew that she went out most every day, and he was prepared to camp on her doorstep until dark, if necessary, to see her. He turned, started to sit down on the low stoop, and she was standing there, right in front of him. He hadn't heard her walk up.

"Elliot," she said softly, though she didn't move toward him.

He put his arms out, and she came to him then. "I'm sorry," he said as they embraced. "I sure acted like an asshole."

"Sure did," she told him from over his shoulder. "But that's not a surprise. It must've been quite a shock for you."

"It was, but I got over it. I shouldn't have stomped out."

"It's okay. You want to come up?"

"Love to."

Once in the apartment, she went directly to the kitchen. "I was going to eat lunch at home," she said. "I never let anything interfere with food! You want some? I was going to make an omelet."

"Yeah, that'd be great."

While eating, he told her briefly about Laura's experience with the cult, with the man she'd called the Chingon. He didn't use her name, or the man's title—just spoke of "a girl

I knew,'' used it as an example of how some women get into prostitution. "I was wondering," he said. "Is that the sort of thing that happened to you? Got you started, I mean?"

She grinned. "You mean, was I driven into it by the cruel fates? Lured and trapped by a vicious pimp? No. I hope it isn't a new disappointment for you, but it was totally different for me. A purely rational decision, the best way I had of solving—certain problems.''

"No, I'm by that now," he said. He wondered whether he should tell her about the way that fantasizing about her working had turned him on, and he decided to at least wait on that. "I was just interested. You mean, money problems?"

"Among others.''

"What?" he persisted.

She put down her fork, swallowed a mouthful of eggs. "Right now, that'd be pretty difficult to explain. You can't exactly call me a nymphomaniac—I certainly get plenty of satisfaction from it!—but I have—certain needs—that are a little outside the ordinary. There just isn't a way that one man could satisfy those. Now, don't let that wound your male ego, Elliot. It's just a simple statement of fact.''

He digested this for a moment, wondering if his ego should indeed be wounded. But in the end, he decided not to push it. "I don't mean to beat a dead horse, but—what about VD, Nikki? And the possibility of running into a maniac, like this Killer Guitarist?''

She frowned. "Yeah, I was reading that he's killed again. Eight, now. But Elliot, you are, for now at least, just going to have to accept this: neither of those things are a problem for me. I told you that yesterday. Sometime, maybe, I'll tell you—or better yet, show you—why not.''

"I just can't believe you're being rational about it. Those problems, I mean.''

Her frown deepened. "You just aren't going to be comfortable about it until you know, are you?''

"Know what?''

"Why VD, for example, isn't a problem for me.''

"If there's a reason—''

She waved her hand, took her last bite of food. "There is," she said around it. "Okay, lover. You become privy to one of my secret tricks of the trade, all right?" She got up, went to her kitchen cabinet, came back with a quart jar filled with crushed leaves. "Damiana," she said, tapping the bottle. "It grows wild in Mexico. And it is absolute protection against any kind of VD. And a lot of other diseases as well."

He looked at the herbs; they looked like marijuana to him. But when he opened the jar, sniffed it, the smell was completely different. "I suppose this is more native lore from your childhood, right?" he asked, rolling the jar in his hands.

"Right."

"How do you know this stuff works? I mean, modern medical science—"

"Doesn't know everything there is to know about medicines, especially herbal medicines."

"I understand that, but you'll forgive me if I'm doubtful? About this specific cure, I mean?"

"Sure. But the fact is, I've been doing this for quite a while, and I've never had the first problem with any disease."

"Maybe you just never encountered it."

"The odds are against that. Gonorrhea can be pretty damn common sometimes. But I've never had a trace."

"I've heard that women can have it and not know it—"

"I've been checked by doctors. I do that too, just to be sure. No problem."

He handed her the jar back, gave it up. It was clear that there was no convincing her that she might be relying on a very suspect remedy, but he promised himself that as long as she continued this line of work, he'd have himself checked periodically. The idea of denying himself her favors never crossed his mind, disease or no; there was always penicillin.

"Well, let me address what is, for me, another problem," he said. "That is, the nights. Sometimes, at least, I'd like to see you at night, spend the night with you."

"Well," she told him, "I don't work every night!"

"What about tonight?"

She sighed. "I told you we were doing a series of loops—stag films. We're cutting another one this evening. But I'll be done about midnight, if you want to wait."

As she said that, he realized suddenly that waiting was not what he wanted to do. But he didn't know how to ask her the question.

She leaned forward slightly, looked closely at his eyes. "What is it, Elliot?" she asked. "Something—"

He became flustered. "Well, I—uh—that is—"

She giggled. "I do believe we may have a voyeuristic tendency or two here?" she asked bluntly. "Could that be so, my friend?"

His face felt hot, and his jaw was working. "I'm not sure I can exactly—"

"But you want to ask if there's any way you can come along? Isn't that so, Elliot?"

"Ah—I—er—"

"Well, that isn't a problem at all!" she cried. "At least, not while I'm doing the loops. With some private customers, of course—"

"Oh, of course, I quite understand!"

"Then, it's settled. Tonight, you come along! You're sure you're up to this?"

He knew his face was still scarlet. "Um-hm!" was all he could manage.

28

As the evening drew close, Elliot became more and more nervous; having never done anything even remotely like this before, he had little idea what to expect. Nikki was no help. She kept giggling at him, teasing him. Worse, she refused to make love with him, saying it would "spoil his appetite." As a result, he was so upset by dinnertime that he only picked at the meal she prepared. An hour later, he felt almost physically sick, but it was a peculiar kind of sickness, like a fluttering of his stomach. It was so odd, in fact, that it was not altogether unpleasant.

It was nearly eight o'clock when the phone rang. Elliot, in a near frenzy, though looking calm, almost fell out of his chair, at the sudden sound, precipitating another peal of laughter from Nikki. She spoke briefly into the receiver, then hung up.

"That was Andrew," she said, though he already knew it must have been. "He said I—I didn't tell him yet I was a we—should come to a motel up on U.S. 9, above Yonkers. I assumed we could take your car. Is that okay?"

"Sure, fine," he said. After a few minutes, he realized that in his eagerness to discuss these other matters, he'd completely forgotten to mention the car. But she'd met him outside; perhaps she had seen him drive up. It had to be that, he thought, and he dismissed it from his mind.

Traffic was not heavy as he found his way out onto the highway, drove through Yonkers. As each mile passed, his jumpiness increased; he glanced over at Nikki, who sat beside him perfectly calmly. Of course she'd be calm, he told himself. She's done this many times before, it's routine to her. Several times she tried to engage him in conversation, but he was not really able to talk very intelligently. After a while, she fell silent, until at last she directed him to turn off the main road to the right. In sight was a large, but not at all fancy, motel, three stories tall, with a big sign out front that proclaimed it to be the Capri Inn. This, she told him, was the place.

Still following her directions, he drove around behind it, parked under a small illuminated sign directing them to rooms 202-302. Room 212, she told him, was where they were going. One flight up by the outside stair, they walked down a narrow balcony to a room halfway down, where Nikki stopped and knocked. Almost instantly, a thin, tired-looking man opened the door, glanced around. His eyes skimmed over Nikki, then fixed coldly on Elliot.

"Who's he?" he said bluntly.

"And good evening to you too, Andrew," she replied. "Nice to see you and all that shit. This is Elliot. He's a friend."

"Friends ain't welcome!"

She shrugged. "Okay," she said. "Let's go, Elliot." She started to turn away.

"Now waitta minnit," Andrew said. "You just surprised me, that's all. You sure he ain't—"

"A cop? Elliot? Last person in the world," she assured him.

Andrew looked at Elliot for a moment. "Awright," he said. "You cause any trouble, you'll get more! Dig?" he paused, glared. Then, reluctantly: "Come on in."

Elliot nodded, followed Nikki inside. For a motel room, it was rather spacious, and they had apparently rented the adjoining room as well, since the paired doors separating the two were open. To Elliot's right was a little kitchenette with a small wooden table; a group of men were sitting and standing around it. On the couch, two more men were sitting; there was no camera equipment in sight. That made Elliot wonder, but Nikki seemed undisturbed.

She glanced at the pair on the couch, nodded as if she knew them. Then she walked over to the group around the table, looked back over her shoulder at Andrew. "Eight?" she said, as if surprised. "Why—?"

"Lookatcha script," the producer said. "You'll see." He handed her a "script," which consisted of a single mimeographed sheet. Not exactly Hollywood, Elliot said to himself, watching her read it.

"Oh, shit," she said after a moment. "This may be a little heavy, Elliot. You gonna be okay?"

He looked back at her, doubtful. "Heavy?" he said. "Nothing—uh—out of the—uh—normal?"

"Depends on what you consider normal," she said levelly. "But it'll be okay. Trust me?"

"Hell, I've come this far!"

"A long way, too. Okay, Andrew," she said in a businesslike manner. She pointed to two of the men, one after the other. "Those two, no good. Sorry, guys. The rest are all right, I suppose." She turned back to Elliot. "As I told you, I get some special privileges. I can decide who's acceptable and who's not. So Andrew always brings more than are needed. In this business, guys are pretty easy to come by."

"Uh, lissen, Nik," Andrew said. "There's sumpin' I gotta ask ya, babe. You sure you ain't got no—disease or nuthin'?"

Elliot went a little cold inside, but Nikki turned on the thin man, her eyes flashing. "You mean VD, Andrew? You know me better than that!"

"No, no. Not VD. Maybe flu or sumpin'?"

She calmed down. "No," she said. "I've been fine. Why?"

"Sumpin' going round, I s'pose. Guys you worked with the last coupla nights, they're down sick. Flu."

"Like you said, something going around. I don't have it. Neither does Elliot here, and he's spent the last several days with me. You look okay yourself, Andrew. And you don't have to be screwing somebody to catch the flu from them, you know.''

''Awright. I just thought I'd check.'' He went over and began to talk to the men in the kitchenette; Nikki handed Elliot the script. He read it quickly, and his eyes got wide. He looked up at her.

''Four?'' he said, disbelieving it.

'' 'Fraid so. That's why I asked if you were okay!''

''Awright,'' Andrew said, ''time is money, people! Let's get to it! Nik, here's yer outfits,'' he told her, handing her a small bag. The two men who had been sitting on the couch got up, went into the next room; in a moment, bright light flooded through the open doorway. ''You gotta go in there, too, if'n you wanna watch,'' the thin man growled at Elliot, starting through the door himself. ''We're gonna be shootin' towards the door.''

Elliot glanced around at Nikki; even though most of the men had not left the room yet, she already had most of her clothes off. He was used to a good deal of casualness about nudity these days, but it still surprised him. It shouldn't, he told himself, considering her profession. She looked around, grinned at him, waved him into the other room.

As he'd seen in the script, the second room had been made up into a facsimile of someone's living room, or den; the bed, dismantled, leaned against a far wall. They would not be using it in these scenes. Standing in the center was a card table, four chairs around it, some chips in front of each station and a deck of cards in the middle. The flimsy plot, a mere excuse, told of three men invited to a friend's house for poker; Nikki was playing the role of the host's wife. As Elliot seated himself behind the tripod on which the camera rested, four of the six men who'd been deemed acceptable by Nikki came in, took their places around the table. Elliot wondered how it had been determined which four of the six would be actually playing the roles; he assumed that they'd somehow decided among themselves, perhaps drew lots. One of them dealt a hand of poker, five-card draw.

''One question,'' Elliot asked the cameraman.

''Yeah?''

''You shooting sound film?''

''Nah. Silent. Super-eight.''

''So there's no need for quiet?''

"Uh-uh. Just don't distract anybody, okay?"

"Sure, okay."

As the men proceeded to play an apparently real hand of poker, betting their chips as if money were actually being wagered, the cameraman started to shoot the scene. The click of the chips and the soft whirr of the camera were, for a few minutes, the only sounds.

"Okay, 'nuff of that," Andrew said after about two minutes. "Nik, yer up!"

Nikki came through the door, a seductive expression on her face; to Elliot, it didn't look phony at all. She was fully dressed, but revealingly; the shorts she wore were too small for her, revealing part of her rear end and pulled up tightly in the crotch, and her T-shirt, also too small, exposed a strip of her stomach. Her breasts were quite visible through the thin material. She was carrying a tray with four bottles of beer, Pabst Blue Ribbon. Circling the table, she plunked a bottle down in front of each man, and each leered at her as she went by; their expressions, unlike hers, looked totally contrived. When she came to the last man, he put one arm around her waist, fondled one of her breasts rather crudely with the other hand. He, apparently, was supposed to be the "husband."

He pulled her head down, whispered something in her ear, drawing each movement in broad strokes for the camera, and she nodded. Swinging her hips much more than she normally did when she walked, she disappeared back through the door. As soon as she was out of sight, the cameras stopped, and the beer—or perhaps it was water—in the bottles was emptied in the bathroom. The next scene, then, opened with a close-up of empty or nearly empty bottles.

In a state of high anxiety, Elliot watched Nikki come back through the door. Again she was carrying the tray with four bottles, but she'd changed her outfit; now she wore only a G-string below, with a tiny white apron tied in front of it. Above, she wore a flimsy tank top, even more revealing than the T-shirt. But this, instead of being too small, was too large. As she served the first beer, she bent over more than necessary to sit it on the table, and the camera zoomed in for a close-up of her breasts, revealed as the top fell down a bit. This time, each man fondled her a bit as she went by, but she smiled and twisted away from all of them until she came to her "husband." He extended one of his legs, and she sat on it for a moment while he stroked her crossed legs, again squeezed her breast. Then, as before, she went into the other room, and the cameras stopped, the beer was dumped. As soon as the bottles were back on the table, the camera whirred once more.

When Nikki came back, four more bottles—actually the first four again—on the tray, she still wore the G-string. But the tank top and the tiny apron were gone. Topless, she approached the table, her high heels clicking on a strip of bare wood between the carpets in the two rooms. She pushed herself close to the first man she was serving, and he responded by taking her nipple into his mouth; the others laughed, applauded. The second and third were equally direct, and when she got to her "husband," he slipped the G-string down off her hips. The other three men got up, the table was pushed aside, and the poker game forgotten.

As this phase of the production began, Elliot drew a deep breath. This was what he thought he wanted to do, and in just a moment, he was sure, he was going to find out if he could stand it. Nikki, naked except for her earrings and her high heels, was being fondled by all four of the men, eight hands running all over her body, four mouths finding their way to very intimate places. In turn, she had her hand on one man's crotch, rubbing him through his pants. The "husband" stepped aside so the camera could focus on her face, and she dropped to her knees, undid the man's belt and pulled his pants and underwear down. Elliot held his breath, and when she took the man's surprisingly still-limp penis into her mouth, he let it out all at once. Staring, he felt the hardest part was now over.

Fascinated in a way he had never dreamed he could have been, Elliot watched them. She was never actually involved with more than two of the men at a time; two were always standing and watching. But the pairings kept shifting around; almost always, she had one in her vagina and another in her mouth, but periodically one of these would leave her and another take his place. His arms wrapped around his stomach, his whole body tight, Elliot watched her face closely. Either she was enjoying herself fully or she was a very damn good actress.

At one juncture, she was sitting astride one of the men, no one at her face; the camera was around behind her, focused on the details of the action. She looked over her shoulder, then back to Elliot, and crooked a finger at him. He got up and came over, his knees feeling weak and rubbery.

"Enjoying yourself?" she asked, never losing the rhythm of her bouncing.

"I think so," he said honestly. "I don't think I'll know for a few days!"

She put her hand on his neck, pulled his face to hers and kissed him. "Always analyzing," she said. "That's a psychologist for you! Doesn't even know if he's having fun until he's analyzed it!"

He tried to smile. "How can you carry on a conversation?" he asked.

"Oh, it's no problem," she said casually. Looking down at the man underneath her, she asked him if it was a problem for him. He just grunted.

"Business, people!" Andrew said.

Elliot backed off, walked around beside them, then behind the camera, and watched the same action it was watching. He realized that not only did he not find it erotic, but he also was able to appreciate what he was seeing in an artistic sense as well. It occurred to him that human lovemaking was, despite many people's dismissal of it as inherently awkward and crude, an intrinsically artistic thing, a beautiful thing to observe. Never before had he thought of it that way.

Trying to get a variety of shots and angles, Andrew and the cameraman instructed Nikki and her four partners to turn this way and that, get into this position, do this. They were professionals, it seemed; everything they were asked to do, they did, with no hesitation and a minimum of lost time. Finally, though, Andrew said it was time for the "wet shots." Though unfamiliar with the jargon, what he wanted seemed apparent enough to Elliot; and that meant the filming was just about over. Elliot was of two minds about this; he wanted to get Nikki home, alone, but he also didn't want to stop watching, either. The psychologist in himself worried about it, about the depth of his voyeurism, but he cheerfully told it to shut up.

"Can you do one from the back?" Nikki asked Andrew. "The same position we were in a few minutes ago?" This was the first time she'd made any comments on how the film was being shot.

"Sure," the thin man said. "I was gonna anyhow."

One of the men stretched out on the floor, and Nikki climbed atop him; their movements were more vigorous now, as the camera moved in very close behind them. Nikki again bent her finger, and Elliot moved close to her face.

"This one's yours," she said, leaving him wondering what she meant. Just then, the man under her began stiffening in climax; Nikki balanced herself on her knees, one hand around behind her, one on Elliot's face. She drew him close, kissed him lightly, and surprised him by exhaling a long breath into his mouth. He stared at her, wondering what she'd just done; he felt very odd. But very good, he had to admit. Her breath was like a cool breeze on a hot day; he hadn't intentionally inhaled it, but he thought he could feel it spreading through his chest. It didn't stop there, either, but continued up into his head, down his legs, out to his fingertips. Lastly, he had the weirdest sensation of the breath running into the hairs of his head, flowing into his beard. He felt invigorated, strong, energetic. Suggestion, he told himself. But he didn't try to push the feeling away; it was far too pleasant for that.

Now, one at a time, the three remaining men were brought to climax, each duly recorded on the film. As the last man disengaged from her, the camera zoomed in for a last close-up of her face, semen smeared across her cheek where she'd intentionally allowed it to run from her mouth. Then the cameraman shut it off, cut the lights as well.

"I'm going to take a quick shower," she told Elliot as she jumped up. "I'll only be a second." She darted into the bathroom, and he assumed she wanted to beat any of her partners there.

But they, it seemed, were in no such hurry. Two of them sat on the couch, one with head back, the other holding his face in his hands; a third man was lying on the floor, just staring at the ceiling. The fourth, Nikki's "husband" in the film, said he was going to shower in the next room, and started to walk in that direction; to everyone's surprise he suddenly passed out, falling heavily on his face near the doorway. Andrew and the cameramen rushed to him, rolled him over, and patted his cheeks. In a moment, he came to, shook his head, and sat up.

"I don't know what the hell's wrong with me," he said, his voice thin. "I just feel weak as a kitten."

The man on the floor lifted his head, looked at the other.

"That's funny," he said. "So do I. I don't feel like I can get up."

"What the hell's the matter with you guys?" Andrew snapped. "We need to get outta here—"

"Why?" asked a man from the couch. "Room's paid for till tomorrow, ain't it?"

"Yeah, but—but—"

"Oh, God, just lemme alone, willya?" the man on the floor moaned. "I just gotta sleep, gotta rest! Shit, I can't drive!"

Andrew turned to the cameraman. "You ever seen anything like this shit?" he demanded.

Nikki came back from the bathroom, still naked, a towel wrapped around her head. "What's wrong?" she asked.

"These guys, that's what!" Andrew told her. "I can't get 'em up, get 'em outta here!"

Nikki looked a little startled, glanced around her at the four men. "Damn," she muttered, rubbing her hair with the terry cloth. "Well, it doesn't matter to you, does it?" she asked Andrew. "Just let them sleep here. Don't worry about it."

"But what's wrong with 'em?"

Nikki knelt down, looked at her "husband," tipping his face up to hers. "I don't know. Maybe they partied before the shoot, maybe some drug. But I think they'll be okay."

"I din do no drugs tonii—" the man said, his voice even weaker than before.

"Yes, you did," Nikki told him. "You must have. Let them alone, Andrew. They'll be fine."

"How can you be so sure?"

"Just take my word for it. How often am I wrong about things like this?"

"Shit, Nik, you ain't never wrong about nuthin'! It's freaky sometimes—"

"Whatever. Just leave them."

Andrew looked doubtful, but finally he shrugged and helped the cameramen pack up their equipment. Elliot followed Nikki into the other room; the other four men had already left, and she started to put her clothes on.

"You sure about those guys?" he asked her. "What you told Andrew, I mean? If they're drugged out, they could—"

"They won't. I'm sure of it, Elliot. I guess it was because you were here. I just got a little carried away, that's all."

That seemed to be a non sequitur. "But—shouldn't we—"

"No. Really, it's okay. Let's go, huh?"

Taking his hand, she led him out the door, started down the balcony toward the stairs. Then she snapped her fingers. "Damn!" she said. "Forgot my money. Just a minute." She darted back inside and came out a moment later with a handful of twenties, which she was stuffing into her bag. About four or five hundred, Elliot estimated.

"It seems to me the money would be the last thing you'd forget," he observed.

"There are more important things," she told him, leading him down the steps, out to the VW.

"Like what?"

"Like you, Elliot," she said warmly, and he felt a rush of pleasure. "Like getting back to my place. I'm not quite finished for the night!"

29

After a nearly frenzied session of lovemaking at her apartment, Nikki and Elliot retired for the evening. For him, it was most pleasant to finally be able to sleep with her; lying in her bed with her head on his arm was almost as pleasant as the lovemaking had been. He could not even force himself to be worried about much of anything; she had prepared him a cup of the Damiana tea, and he had drunk it as she instructed. It had had a slightly bitter, alkaloid taste but was not unpleasant. And he found himself believing her assurance that it was a positive defense against any form of VD. In any event, such concerns would not have kept him away from her, but he would have worried himself sick about it later. He made a mental note to himself to check out the herb later, see if there was any literature on it.

An hour after they'd gone to bed, Nikki was sleeping soundly, while Elliot just lay there, staring into the darkness. He was thinking about how vastly his life had changed, and only in a very few days. In his wildest imagination he would not have projected such an evening for himself, not ever; and even if he had, he would have been quite sure that his jealousies, his insecurities, would have quite utterly prevented him from enjoying it at all. Thinking about Melissa, he reminded himself that he was not so liberated that he felt that fidelity between lovers had no meaning, but only now was he becoming fully aware of how the moral and philosophical loadings on such concepts hid the baser truths behind. The ultimate fear was that another man might be so much better than he that his woman would immediately reject him. But somehow that didn't seem to apply to Nikki. She projected an aura of confidence that suggested that she'd been around, never would do anything she didn't want to, never was unsure of her own motivations and feelings. And that was contagious. Exposed to confidence, and with an implicit expectation by the confident person that one was worthwhile, it sprang up like morning glories in fertile soil. With these pleasantries running through his mind, he drifted into sleep.

But his sleep was disturbed by dreams, vivid and realistic ones. In them, Nikki was being attacked, taken unawares by a john who twined a guitar string around her throat. He seemed to be somewhere watching it all happen but was powerless to interfere. Twice he woke up sweating, saw her face peaceful in sleep, and tried to return to sleep himself. But each time he was back in the nightmare; all that ever changed was the appearance of the Killer Guitarist. Sometimes he was white, sometimes black; sometimes a huge apish man, sometimes a skinny psychopath. Always he was killing Nikki. Once he was even seeing the scene through the eyes of the killer, and that was the most disturbing of all. There was a peculiarity in that vignette as well; in it, Nikki was begging and pleading, but not for her life. Instead, she was telling him—or rather, the killer whose mind he seemed to be inhabiting—that death by strangulation was reserved for criminals, that she did not deserve it. Rather, she said, she should die by the knife, and she presented the glossy black blade he'd seen in his delusional state the previous evening. But the killer was relentless; he kept using the string, winding it around her neck and pulling on both ends.

When he woke from this one, he glanced at her bedside clock, saw that it was just before seven, and decided to forget it. He let her sleep, went to the kitchen and made coffee. There was a thud against the door, and he opened it, saw a morning newspaper lying there. In it, he read about the Killer Guitarist's ninth victim. The story noted that there was a difference in this killing: the victim had been stabbed, though not fatally, prior to her strangulation. Remembering his dream, Elliot felt a little chill, and by the time a sleepy-eyed Nikki joined him in the kitchen, he'd worked himself into a near frenzy of concern over her safety.

Unable to help himself, he almost immediately started in on Nikki. As he saw it, he was merely expressing his fears, his concern; there was no possible way she could have viewed it except as pressure. As a result, the remainder of the day was marred by periodic squabbles between them. He could not let go of the idea that she was in imminent danger from the Killer Guitarist or someone like him, and she, in turn, refused to take it seriously. He wanted her to stop working until the killer was caught; she refused, saying the killer might never be caught, saying there were always maniacs around. He suggested that perhaps there was enough work for her in the stag films to keep her going; she said there wasn't, that she didn't like to do that full-time, and again she refused. He asked her if he could remain in the apartment, perhaps in hiding, while she entertained her "customers"; she said sometimes, not every time. Finally he made a suggestion that she stick with established clientele, men she knew already. Even this, she argued with him about, but, sensing a weakness in her armor, he kept pounding at her until finally, probably more to shut him up than anything else, she agreed to do that for a couple of weeks and see if the police came up with anybody. If not, she said, she'd have to reconsider. But he managed to extract a promise from her that she'd tell him before she resumed business as usual. Clearly, however, she was not terribly pleased about his intrusion into the way she conducted her business, and she was rather cross with him that afternoon. He was wondering if that would extend into the evening, when she told him he'd have to make himself scarce for the night.

"I told you," she said, "that there'd be times you could be around and times you couldn't!"

"Is this an old customer?" he demanded. "How well do you know him? What's his name?"

"Oh, sweet Jesus!" she said, throwing up her hands. "He's an old customer, a trusted one, okay, Elliot? I've known him for years. He cannot bring himself to swat flies or kill roaches! His house is full of vermin, he's just so gentle that he can't—"

"Come on, Nikki, I'm just concerned!" Elliot cried. "I just don't want anything to happen to you, okay?"

"Nothing's going to happen to me except that I'm going to get fucked!" she yelled, her eyes flashing. "You damn well enjoyed that last night!"

He looked hurt. "I thought that was an experience we shared," he told her, his voice much softer.

Her own face softened, too. "Oh, shit," she said, with some feeling. "It was, Elliot. I liked having you there. I got off on your arousal, okay? But I swear, you are driving me to distraction with this. I'm liable to say just anything!"

"Like I said, I don't want you hurt."

"And I don't either. I'm not going to get hurt, Elliot. I can honestly promise you that. The man I'm seeing tonight, I really have known him for a long time. He isn't the Killer Guitarist. Believe me, I'd know."

"I just don't see how you can be so sure!" he grumbled, still not satisfied. Yet he didn't want to create a real rift between them, either.

"I told you before. I have my ways. I'm no newcomer to this business, Elliot. I've been reading the papers, just like you have. Most of this guy's victims are teenagers, runaways. Green. But I'm not. I may not exactly look it, but I am an old pro. I know how to take care of myself!"

"I sure do hope you're right," he told her miserably. He was not looking forward to the evening; it would be a long time before he saw her again. Or at least it would seem that way, he was sure.

"As long as we're seeing each other," she told him pointedly, "this is just something you're going to have to live with. I don't mean to be harsh, Elliot, but I like my life and I have no interest in making that kind of a change in it!"

That seemed to end it; he reminded her of her promise,

and after some haggling, also managed to extract the promise of a phone call sometime during the night; he knew that sleep would be out of the question for him if he didn't know whether she was dead or alive. Although she accused him of being overly melodramatic, she agreed, telling him to be in Gerald's apartment about one A.M., that she'd call then.

With her promises clutched tightly in his mind, he left her apartment about seven-thirty, began fighting the traffic down Broadway. He couldn't stop thinking about her, about the previous night, and he couldn't stop worrying, either. In this frame of mind, he spotted a little shop along the way with a sign advertising "Natural Herbal Medicines," and on impulse, decided to stop in.

"Hi, can I help you?" asked the girl behind the counter. Until she moved, she had actually been rather hard to see in the shop, stuffed as it was with jars containing all manner of odd concoctions. Her plain brown hair and Ben Franklin glasses acted almost as a natural camouflage.

"Yes," he said, peeping at her between two huge jugs of crumbled green leaves. "You ever hear of an herb called Damiana?"

She laughed. "Surely! You need some?"

"Uh—yeah, I guess—" He'd been taken a little by surprise, having assumed that the drug was arcane.

"How much?"

"Couple of ounces, I suppose. What's the price?"

"Fifty cents an ounce," she told him, working her way into a corner, where she pulled a wide-mouth gallon jar off a shelf. It was clearly marked "Damiana leaves," and was about three-quarters full. She brought it over to the main counter, began shoveling the crushed leaf material into a scale. Elliot sniffed it; it was the same, no doubt. At least it smelled the same.

Might as well do this, he thought. He hated to appear stupid under any circumstances, but if he didn't ask her, his stop here would not have served its purpose. "Could you tell me what this is used for?" he asked, his voice wavering just a little.

She glanced up at him meaningfully. "You don't know? Why are you buying it?"

"Uh—a friend recommended it—"

"Oh, okay. Well, Damiana is a—uh—a sexual tonic. It's

supposed to be good for impotence." She colored, looked away from him, and rushed on: "Or just for the—uh—sexual organs in general. Some people believe it makes you more attractive to the opposite sex, too."

"Does it prevent VD?" he asked bluntly, casting his pride away.

"What?"

"VD. Does it prevent VD?"

She stared at him over the top of the little squares of glass that perched on her nose. "If so, I've never heard of it," she said. "Is that what you were told?"

"Uh—well—" The embarrassment was coming back now, much the same feeling as buying rubbers in the drug store at seventeen. "Yes, I suppose—"

"I think that's someone's wishful thinking," she said firmly. "I mean, I'm really up on herbs and what they do, but I never heard that! Besides, I don't see how it could. I mean, there are all different kinds of VD germs and all—"

"Okay," he said. "What do I owe you?"

She quoted a price, he paid her and rushed out, the little bag clutched in his hand. Maybe it did do what Nikki said it did, he told himself. That was no proof. But if it didn't, it called her judgment about other things into question. Such as her safety.

"Elliot!" Laura squealed as he walked into the apartment. "You're back!"

"Hi, kid," he said warmly. She ran to him, jumped on him, and he gave her a hug.

"What's that?" she said, pointing to the little bag of green leaves. "Dope?"

"No, it's called Damiana, it's an herb—"

"Oh, I know," she said breezily. "We have some here."

"You do?"

"Sure. Haze read somewhere it makes you more attractive to chicks. So he drank a whole bunch of it, and maybe it did. I couldn't see it, but I don't know. Anyway, he went out and got laid somewhere, and you know what?"

"No, what?" he asked, but he had a sinking feeling he knew exactly what she was going to say.

"He got the clap!" she howled gleefully. "You shoulda heard him screech when he took a leak! But he went down to the clinic, got some shots, and got over it."

Resisting the temptation to hurl the bag of leaves across the room, he cursed mentally. At least the fates could have gone on letting him believe it was possible that Nikki wasn't wrong about the stuff for one night, at least. But he just had to have a coincidence like this piled on his head. He decided he would believe it anyway, even if it was irrational. Maybe, he told himself, Haze hadn't brewed it right, hadn't taken it at the right times. He was aware that these were just rationalizations, but he just didn't want to worry about it. Not tonight, anyway.

"You didn't come back last night," Laura was saying to him, a hurt tone in her voice. "I missed you."

"Laura," he said patiently, trying to make her understand, "you know I'm involved with this other woman—"

"I know. But you'd been coming back here every night, and I guess I kinda got used to it. I like sleeping with you, even if we don't screw."

"Well," he said, almost callously, "I'm here tonight. Dammit."

For just an instant, she looked hurt again, but then she seemed to remove the expression by an act of will. "Can we play together tonight?" she asked. "I really liked that—"

He managed to grin at her. "Yeah, I did too. We'll do it, okay?"

"Okay!" she said excitedly, started to go get her flute immediately.

"Not right this minute, though," he told her. "I gotta unwind a little."

"You want a joint? A beer? Tea? A blow-job?"

He laughed. "Tea would be good, thanks."

Once again, she made two cups of Red Zinger, and they sat down at the table in the kitchen to drink them. Through the steam rising from her teacup, Laura's face lost the ebullience it had had when he'd come in, became moody. Twice he started to ask her what was wrong, but he thought it probably had to do with her dreams, so he initially resisted. She seemed to become more withdrawn as time went on, though, so finally he did ask her.

"Another dream," she said, confirming his fears. "Last night."

"Laura, I've tried to tell you—"

"Oh, this one wasn't about me, about the fire. It was about you."

"Me?"

"Yeah. Seemed like I was way up in the air, over some jungle or something. It was real dark, but I could see you down below, coming up to a clearing. And there was something in front of you; I knew you couldn't see it yet, but I could. I was afraid it was going to kill you!"

He stared at her, the forgotten teacup hanging in his hand. For some reason, what she'd just said—though there wasn't much to go on yet—reminded him irresistibly of his dream of Nikki and the giant rattlesnake, the dream he'd had back in Chapel Hill. He really didn't want to hear anymore, but he didn't seem to be capable of saying so. "Go on," he said woodenly.

Her eyes flicked up, then down again, and she sipped her tea. She frowned. "This is hard," she said. "I said I was up, but really I wasn't. I thought I was 'coming up.' Does that make sense? Anyhow, I was covered with blood, but I wasn't hurt, and I was comin' up. With somebody important, I was comin' up. That's the only way I can describe it.

"Anyhow, I saw what was ahead of you—a snake, Elliot—a giant snake! It spoke to you—or—or—damn, it made sense in the dream, but now it makes no sense to say it! It was like, maybe, a part of it was talkin' to you—or maybe its ghost or its—uh—its double—was talkin' to you. And you talked back to it. I couldn't hear anythin' either one of you was sayin', though. Then— whatever was talking to you—it was a woman in a red robe—and you talked some more. I knew then that for the time bein', you were safe. It—she, I guess—wasn't going to hurt you.

"But then it disappeared, you were left alone. You disappeared too. For a minute—well, I'm sure it was a minute but it seemed like I knew it was a couple of months—I couldn't see you. I was looking all around. But I found you again, and I was really scared then."

Elliot, frozen in a block of ice, waited for her to go on, but she was just looking at him. Finally he felt obligated to speak. "Why?" he croaked.

"You were sleepin'," she said, her frown deepening. "Looked really peaceful, more peaceful than you look at nights here, when I wake up and look at you. But, Elliot, you was in danger! Terrible danger! You was sleeping with this giant white snake coiled all around you! It was so big, it showed its fangs and they was like swords. It could have killed you just by turnin' its head!''

He leaned across the table, still staring. ''Did it?'' he asked.

''No. Sometimes it'd lift that big old head and that horrible tongue would lick at you. But it never bit, or squeezed. I just knew, I just knew it could, anytime! And there'd be nothin' you could do 'cept die!''

''That's an interesting dream, Laura,'' he forced himself to say, his voice shaky. He didn't want to explain how it linked up with his own dream; it might add fuel to her convictions about her dying—fire dreams.

''That ain't all,'' she said. ''In the dream, I went down, somehow, to the big white snake. An' it could see me. It looked up, and it said, 'Who're you? Whaddya want?' And I points at you and says, 'He's my friend. You gonna hurt 'im?' Then she says, 'Yeah, but he won't mind,' just as cold, just like you'd expect a snake to talk if they could talk. I says, 'Why?,' and she says, 'What do you know?' And I said something real funny—I remember it real clear. I said, 'Nilauralli,' and she says, 'Oh. Okay, then, I'll tell you. He belongs to the Smokin' Mirror.' I said—screeched, I think—'No, he don't! He can't! Why don'tcha let 'im go?' And she says, 'I can't do that. But I'll make it worth it for 'im, don't you worry! I like 'im a whole lot.' Well, I just hung around for a while. I wanted to find a way to stop her, but there wasn't nothin' I could do, but then I had to go, like someone was callin' me. I couldn't say no. She watched me go, and she says, 'Don't worry about 'im.' But Elliot, I am worried! I don't know how I know, but I know that if you belong to the Smokin' Mirror, you gotta die! And anyway, she was a snake! You can't trust a fuckin' snake!''

For a long time, Elliot didn't say anything at all, the information Laura had just given him swirling around in his head. He had not mentioned the dream to anyone; there was just no way in the world Laura could have known about it. Yet she had; moreover, she had implicitly, at least in his mind, associated Nikki with the white serpent, and the hallucinatory experiences he'd been having had made that same identification. In fact, Nikki had directly told him that her *nagual* was the Mexican Diamondback, that day at the zoo. Laura had even used the word "double," for God's sake! His visions, however, had never presented the serpent as threatening, at least not to him. Laura's dream was another matter. And where the hell had she heard the name, "Smoking Mirror"? He'd only recently heard it himself, and he didn't really understand what it meant.

But now, armed with these facts, he was being forced to admit that something unusual was going on—which he had been trying mightily to deny—but what was he supposed to do with them? Discussing the matter with Laura seemed a poor notion; she already had too much confidence in her own dreams. Nikki, he was sure, would know nothing about it, as she'd known nothing about the photographs; but, rather queasily, he was beginning to wonder if she was in fact innocent. She seemed so much the center of all these events. But in spite of his hallucinations, he'd been having a wonderful time. Nikki was everything he could have hoped for, and much more. But a darker notion was beginning to intrude itself on his mind, as well. Accepting the premise that Nikki hadn't been entirely honest with him about some things—like the Damiana, the photos—he had to, he told himself, begin questioning exactly what she did know. His thoughts wandered to the restaurant, to the Reyes family, to the experiences he'd had at the Obsidian Butterfly—the dance, the male dancer in the middle, the Smoking Mirror. He had to find out exactly what that meant. And whether Nikki knew anything about this. But he wasn't sure how to go about it. He couldn't just ask her; she'd just laugh at him. He remembered what she'd said about Juan's ancestry, about her childhood. And the thought crossed his mind: Were they perhaps followers of the Aztec religion? There were one hell of a lot of implications in that!

But even as he had the thought, he told himself it was ridiculous. The fact that the woman believed in a few folktales from the country where she grew up hardly made her a devotee of that nation's ancient religions. And he had no evidence at all that Juan Reyes was into it even as far as Nikki was. Most likely, the Reyes were Catholics, like most Mexicans. If there was going to be a survival of a bloody ancient religion, he told himself, it would be in the secluded mountains of Mexico, not in Manhattan! And even if there were, it didn't explain the oddities, like the synchrony between his dreams and Laura's. In fact, he told himself glumly, there wasn't much of any good way to explain that.

"Are you okay?" Laura was asking him, bringing his attention back to herself, back to the apartment.

"Yeah, sure," he told her, swallowing the last of his tea. "I was just thinking about your dream. It was really interesting."

"It's a warning, I think," she said earnestly. "Maybe you shouldn't see that woman anymore—"

He managed to grin at her. "Maybe you have a conflict of interest there!" he said.

"I ain't sure what that means," she said defensively, in such a manner that Elliot was sure that she did know what he meant.

"Don't worry about it," he said, waving it off.

"But—"

"Laura, I'm sorry. It isn't that I don't appreciate it, but I'm going to have to see Nikki again!" he told her honestly. "I'm not sure I could stay away if I wanted to!"

"I could—"

"No, you can't. It isn't that you aren't attractive, and it isn't that I don't like you. But I can't stop thinking of you as a child! I've told you that, over and over!"

"Your loss," she said sullenly. But then she started to cry. Elliot came around the table, gathered her up in his arms again. She really got into it, wailing into his shirt, her whole body shaking with her sobs. It took him the better part of an hour to calm her down. When she finally stopped, he suggested a little music; she seemed interested, but much of her former enthusiasm was lacking. Nonetheless, she got out her flute, while Elliot went to get Haze's guitar.

30

At just about the time Nikki had said she'd call, the phone rang. Elliot nearly dropped the guitar as he pounced on the phone. He held his breath until Nikki spoke, then relaxed. She was all right, she said; her "customer" had been there several hours, showed no signs of becoming crazed. In fact, she said, she could speak quite freely, inasmuch as the man was currently passed out on the floor.

"You sure do have a devastating effect, don't you?" Elliot said, grinning into the phone.

"You don't seem much worse for wear!" she shot back. They bantered back and forth for a few minutes, then Elliot caught sight of Laura, sitting cross-legged on the floor, her flute in her lap. She looked very dejected.

"Look, Elliot," came Nikki's voice, just as he'd begun to feel bad for Laura, "we better quit this for now. I'll see you tomorrow, okay?"

"Well, I'd like to—"

"No, you're inflicting unnecessary pain, don't you see? Go over and hold that girl. It's what she needs."

He stared at the receiver. "How in the hell did—" he started to say.

"Never mind, I just do. Let's just say I sense it. Remember, you told me about her. It stands to reason. I'll see you tomorrow, okay?" He heard a click, and silence returned to the line. Slowly, he turned toward Laura, went to her, and held her as he'd been instructed to do. This time she didn't cry; she just clutched him to herself.

After a while, they returned to the music. When they ran out of songs both of them knew, Laura put records on the stereo, and they improvised accompaniment to them. More than ever, she impressed him with her musical abilities; she was much better than he was at this sort of thing. When a new song started, she would fumble with it for a few bars, finding the key and the chord sequence, then go right into it as if playing a written part.

"You really ought to get a job with a band," Elliot told her. "You have real talent."

"I thought about it once. But you know, it takes time to work into somethin' like that."

And I don't have time, he finished for her mentally. Still, that obsession coming through, permeating everything in her life, everything around her: Live for now, there's no tomorrow. But the worst of it was that Elliot was becoming a little frightened for her; this new dream, the way it linked up with his own dreams and visions, cast a different light on her other experiences. Still, he refused to believe that she was going to die in the next few days. She looked so vibrant, so healthy. And anything other than sickness, he refused to even think about; he had enough on his mind worrying about Nikki.

They heard the door lock being worked, stopped and looked around. It swung open, and Haze walked into the room. "Hey, guys, don't quit on my account," he said, making for the chair, which he almost fell into. "Ol' Haze likes good sounds, mannn . . ." He grinned at them idiotically, leaned his head far to one side.

"Tripped out," Laura said.

"Yeah, man, Owsley Green," Haze told them, referring to a near-legendary form of LSD, reputed to have been made by the mysterious Stanley   wsley. Elliot had encountered it numerous times; anything in a green capsule or pill was liable to be called "Owsley Gr en." The legends, it seemed, increased the potency. "Oooh, man, you lookin' *black*!" Haze said, pointing at Elliot. "Jesus! You really are!"

Elliot smiled. "You looking black, too, Haze."

"No no no. I don' mean like that. I mean you *black*. Like a hole is black. But you gotta little bit a yella on ya—"

Suddenly, Elliot didn't like this. "Just the drug, Haze," he said, hoping the man would shut up. "Just the drug—"

"I don't know. Never saw nuthin' like that before! Sheeeiit! Teeth and claws an' all, stickin' out every which away! You look like a black egg, Elliot! A big black egg with all kindsa teeth, and tentacles like a octopus comin' outchoo middle.

Man, you fuckin' *horrible*!'' So saying, he let out a piercing screech and buried his face in the cushioned arm of the chair.

"Oh, shit," Elliot muttered. "He's having a bad trip. Give me a hand, Laura; we got to calm him down—"

"Don't touch me!" Haze screamed, looking at Elliot again, his eyes wide with terror. "Don't touch me, don't kill me, oh Goddd—"

"I'll try," Laura said, coming to stand beside Haze. She reached out for his hand, but he jerked it away.

"And you got a skull for a head! You dead, woman! OhmyGod, what'm I gonna do? A monster an' a dead woman, ohhhh—" Moaning, Haze curled up on himself in the chair, drawing his legs up against his chest, tucking his head in between his knees. From inside the fetal bundle, he continued to moan, and occasionally to scream.

"Well, shit!" Elliot said, disgusted. "What the hell are we supposed to do?"

"Let 'im get over it, I s'pose," Laura said philosophically. "He'll probably be okay. It ain't his first bad trip."

"I wonder where that stuff is coming from—"

"From me," Laura said, her voice emotionless. "He's just seein' me as I really am. My fire's out, I'm already dead. I just ain't stopped breathin' and movin' around yet. You, I don't know. Maybe he is seein' you as you are, too. The black, the yellow, all the teeth and claws—somehow that seems right for you. I can almost see you with a big black and yellow cat—talkin' to it—like maybe a leopard or somethin'—" Her eyes started to glaze as she stared at him, evidently caught up in the quasi-mystical mood Haze's pronouncements had created. "No, no," she continued, her voice distant now. "Not a leopard. A jaguar. You are of it, for it. A soldier for it, you were born to it. The Smoking Mirror—"

Jaguar Warrior, Elliot thought. Somehow, Nikki had known, or worse, somehow she'd started all this. In his vision in the streets, the jaguar had called him "brother." Was it possible that somehow Haze was seeing that? If so, what did it mean? And the mysterious "Smoking Mirror"—who was he, what did he have to do with all this? He knew he was going to have to talk to Nikki about it; she was the only one he could think of that even might have an answer—if she'd tell him what it was. But now, he was concerned about Laura; she'd clearly gone into some trancelike state. But just as he started to move toward her, she blinked her eyes rapidly, seemed to return to normal. Both of them then turned their attention back to the black man.

"Haze," Elliot said gently, not getting close to him. "Look at me again, tell me what you see. Is it the same?"

The black man opened his knees, peeped out. "Yes," he said in a thin voice. "And more—"

"What else?"

"I see a snake—over your head, its head wavin' in the air—big feathers, all white—maybe green, blue—ahhhh—" As Elliot watched, his eyes rolled up in his head, and he tumbled out of the chair like a ball, finishing by stretching straight out on the floor.

"Let's get him to bed," Laura said, tugging at his arms. "He'll be okay."

Yes, Elliot thought, but will we?

31

For Elliot, Thursday morning was one of the worst, insofar as leaving the apartment in the Village was concerned. Laura had given up any pretense of being uncaring about his trips uptown; she cried and clung to him. The previous night, after they'd finally gone to bed—together as usual—she had put more pressure than ever on him to have sex with her, but once again he had resisted. In spite of the intensity of his relationship with Nikki—or perhaps, in some odd way, because of it—he was unsure about whether he could continue to push the girl away. The fact was, his attitude was slowly beginning to change. Though he was still aware of Laura's age, and the various ways in which she behaved in a childish manner, she exhibited an emotional maturity, a sensitivity, that made it difficult for him to continue being unresponsive to her.

But, again, when Nikki let him into her apartment, held him in her arms again, Laura was almost completely forgotten. Also neglected were the strange coincidental dreams, Haze's LSD visions that somehow fitted in so well. Once again, he focused on his concern about her safety in connection with the Killer Guitarist, but he managed to avoid starting another argument with her about it. Still, it preyed on his mind, but when she told him she was not working that evening, even that problem vanished, at least for the day. It ended up being a most pleasant time for him, a dramatic contrast to the anxiety-filled evening previous.

A couple of times during the day he had tried to discuss the weird events that had been taking place, but it seemed that the time was never right; consistently his mind was diverted to something else. Her constant wearing of the open-fronted red robe around the apartment was itself an ongoing distraction, keeping him in a more or less constantly aroused state. In fact, the only time it was less was just after they'd made love. With some surprise, he realized that he'd made love more times with Nikki in four days than he had with Melissa in a month. He tried to tell himself that this was only because she was a new lover, and the new was always exciting, but the fact that it was better for him virtually every time belied that. He wondered how far that could go; it just couldn't go on forever, he told himself.

These thoughts were still running around in his head when they finally retired for the evening. But for Elliot this night was different from the previous one he'd spent with her; he fell asleep quickly and easily, and was not bothered by nightmares about her being murdered.

But in the middle of the night, something woke him. For a moment, he could not understand what it might be; he glanced at the clock by the bedside, saw that it was about three-thirty. Not feeling Nikki's body against his, he next looked over at her and saw that she was not there; he was alone in the bed.

Instantly he was fully awake. Sitting up, he listened to the sounds of the city, but all sounds were outside. The apartment itself was totally quiet. He was bothered by an odd conviction that something was very wrong somewhere, but he could not define what it might be.

Silently, he got out of bed, padded barefoot through the apartment, wondering if there was any possibility that Nikki had sneaked out with a "customer." He didn't really believe that, though. She'd been very direct, to say the least, with him about her business; there was no reason for her to go slipping off in the dead of night now. Unless, he reminded himself almost hysterically, she was off with a new customer in violation of her promise.

Outside the bedroom, he moved down the darkened hallway. The bathroom door stood open, the shower curtain drawn back; there was no one there. The kitchen was equally empty, and the only other rooms in the small apartment were the living room and a tiny foyer. He looked in there and swore to himself silently. No Nikki. That meant, he told himself, that she had indeed gone out somewhere, and he could imagine no reason for her to go out at three-thirty in the morning except to entertain a customer. Equally there was no reason to conceal it from him unless the customer was a new one.

Knowing the idea of sleeping was out of the question, he decided to go to the kitchen, make some coffee, and get dressed while it was brewing. He wished to hell he had some idea where she might be. But as he moved out of the little foyer, he caught a glimpse of a reddish, flickering light out of the corner of his eye. Looking around for it, he couldn't see it, but a very odd odor of something—perhaps some incense? —came to his nostrils. Though he could not immediately identify it, the odor was familiar to him, and it provoked an odd anxiety. He turned completely around several times, trying to find the source of the light and the smell, but he was having no luck. Finally, with a shrug, he took another step toward the kitchen. And again he caught the light at the edge of his peripheral vision.

"Now what the hell?" he said aloud, in a low voice. Again he turned around, and again he saw nothing. Then, while he was facing it this time, he saw a little red flash under the door that stood alongside the front door, perpendicular to it. Blankly, he looked at it; he'd never questioned that door, assuming it was a hall closet. But as he came close to it, he realized that the smell was coming from there as well; if it was a hall closet, there was a fire in there! He jerked it open, and briefly thought that his original belief about it was confirmed; there were winter coats and such on hangers, boots standing on the floor. But as he pushed the coats from one side to the other, looking for a possible source of the light and smell, he stopped again, staring.

The closet had a normal back wall, a normal left-hand wall; but the wall on the right side was missing. Just beyond the space of the closet proper, he found himself looking at an unfinished wall, exposed electrical conduits running down it. Continuing on to the right was a narrow corridor, the interior lathing of the walls exposed on both sides. Down at the end, where the source of the soft, mobile red light was, it turned to the left. Not understanding, he just stood there and looked for a minute. It was like some secret passageway in a Gothic mansion, except that it was entered through a normal-looking closet door, not by a rotating bookcase. After puzzling over it for a few seconds, he realized that the area it led into would be the neighboring apartment, the one that was closed off and painted shut.

Cautiously, he crept down the corridor, the smell getting stronger as he did so. When he came to the end of it, he peeped around the corner; he figured he was looking into a room about on the level of the bedroom. What he saw inside he found difficult to believe, and even harder to understand.

The narrow hallway opened into a room larger than any in Nikki's apartment. He could not tell if the walls back here were finished or not; they were completely covered by hanging blankets and tapestries. Straight ahead of him, as he looked in, was a structure he could only assume was some type of altar. It was in the shape of a truncated pyramid, about four feet tall, and on top of it stood a strange artifact. It was a statue of a man, almost life-sized. His arms and legs, and part of his face, were painted black, but most of his face could not be seen, being covered with a red, birdlike mask, the ''beak'' of which was filled with long, sharp teeth. From around this mask curled a long black beard, and atop the man's head was a peculiar little conical hat, made apparently of jaguar skin. He wore an open vest, with an ornament, a cut section of a seashell, lying on his chest, and a kiltlike garment below. In one hand he held a scepter much like a short shepherd's crook, but with a sword handle, blazoned with jewels; in the other hand was a little cloth bag, white with five red diamonds on it in a quincunx pattern. As he looked at the statue, Elliot realized he'd seen one very similar to it before; at Reyes's restaurant, enclosed in glass on the wall. But there were differences; the small one at the restaurant wore only a loincloth, the conical hat, and the mask, plus fur cuffs on his ankles, sandals on his feet. On this one, he couldn't tell how the feet and ankles were clothed, because around the figure's legs, then rising up over its back, was the carved form of a huge serpent. The head, coming out from behind the man just above his shoulder, was adorned with many long plumes, and the tail bearing the rattle was raised between the man's legs. But it wasn't white; it was painted in brilliant blues, reds, and greens. Peripherally, Elliot could see that there were at least two other statues in the room, but right now, this one fixed his attention completely. At that particular moment, it almost seemed to him like the thing was living, watching him come in.

Down at the base of the pyramid, which served as a dais for the statue, a brazier stood, a small fire burning in it, most of the smoke wafting away through an apparent vent situated between two of the tapestries. Atop the brazier were several balls of a black, gummy material that were smoking. This was the source of the incense smell. In front of the brazier, on the floor, a rug or blanket was spread; on the front edge of it was a beautiful polychrome jar, the lid lying alongside it, and some long, thin, white objects visible inside. Beside the jar was a ball that looked like rolled hay, or dried grass, and several straws spread out in a neat row next to it. Just over from that, a stack of small pieces of paper, like thin index cards. And on the back part of the rug, facing all this paraphernalia, was Nikki, facing away from him.

She was quite naked; her familiar red robe lay near the door, almost under Elliot's foot. Kneeling on the rough-looking fabric, her knees spread far apart, she lifted her hands toward the statue. Elliot glanced up at it again; it had jeweled eyes, and they seemed to be moving actively in the subdued firelight. In her fingers, as if being offered to the image, was one of the white objects from the jar. Elliot could see it clearly now; it was sharp at one end, rounded with a hooked indentation at the other. It looked sort of like an awl, but longer and thinner.

He still hadn't moved from the doorway when she brought the object down, put the sharp point against her earlobe, and punched it through. The hook served as a thumbhold. Just as quickly, she pulled it out again, and slid one of the straws that had been lying on the rug into the hole it had made. Working the straw back and forth, she stained it completely red with her blood, then carefully put it back down. The awl was thrust into the ball of hay, and she took another from the jar. Moving his head a little, Elliot saw that there was already a punch in the ball, and that her other earlobe was bloody as well.

His mind in turmoil, he took two steps toward her, wondering if he should speak.

"Don't say anything, Elliot," she said in a clear voice, though she didn't turn around. "There's no harm if you watch, though I didn't mean for you to. But don't speak, and don't interfere. Not until I say you can."

He didn't know how she'd known he was there; he'd been very quiet. But that didn't concern him at the moment. Moving slowly, he came around until he could see her face, then sat down cross-legged on the floor. Holding another punch in her right hand, she gave him a warning glance, then, raising her left arm, slid the point into the fleshy part below the bone, midway between elbow and shoulder. She continued to push on it until the point emerged from the other side, then quickly pulled it out.

Blood flowed out of the puncture, running down her arm and starting to drip; sticking the punch into the hay ball, she put one of the pieces of paper on the rug beneath her arm, so that the blood was dripping onto it. Then she worked another straw through the hole, again back and forth until it too was completely blood-covered; when it was, she took it out, laid it down. Patiently, she waited for her arm to stop dripping blood, occasionally putting another piece of paper there to catch it. The bloody papers, like the straws, were carefully handled, laid out in neat rows in front of her. When the bleeding stopped, she repeated the procedure, in exactly the same way, on her other arm.

Now there was a short pause, during which she stared at the statue as raptly as Elliot was staring at her. But after a moment, she picked up another punch, put it against her thigh, midway between her hip and her knee. Her face showed no signs of pain whatever as she pushed it into herself, kept pushing until the point emerged from her skin. She went through all the same procedures on her legs as she'd previously done on her arms, the straws and the papers. Then, after laying out the last paper, thrusting the sixth punch into the ball of hay, she again paused, a longer period this time. Again taking a punch from the jar, she gave Elliot another warning glance.

It was harder this time for him to keep silent, though he managed to do so. She located the point of this punch up under her nipple, then slid it up and through, the point thrusting out the top. The usual straw followed, and she held a slip of paper, watching to see if the blood would drip, but it didn't, and she proceeded to do the same thing again, using the other nipple. Studying her face, Elliot thought he might be able to detect just a trace of a pained expression, but if so, it was a very subtle thing. After the straw was laid out, there was yet another pause. Elliot was hoping intensely that she would not reach for another of the punches.

And she did not. Instead, she picked up the ball of hay, ran the used punches back and forth through it until they were almost completely cleaned of any blood adhering to them. Then she gathered up all the bloody straws and pieces of paper and loaded it into the brazier. As it burned, she guided the smoke toward the statue, never saying a word or uttering a sound. Then she rocked back onto her knees, letting the fire burn down.

"What are you doing in here, Elliot?" she said after a while.

"I can talk now?"

"Yes. I'm through here. We can go back to the apartment if you like."

He stared up at the statue, glanced at the two others, equally grotesque, standing on smaller pedestals of their own. "What in the fuck were you doing?" he asked her, his voice low and sounding somewhat strained.

"Strengthening Him," she said, dipping her head toward the main statue. "Though he doesn't know it right now."

"Probably not," Elliot said, still a little too shocked to worry much about possibly offending her. "Since he's made of wood."

She turned to him, and, rather surprisingly, grinned. "Oh, you just don't understand!" she said. "And that really isn't all that unusual. It'd be unusual if you did!"

He looked from her face to the statue and back. "I understand idolatry,'' he said in measured tones. "It doesn't offend me per se, because I don't consider myself a Christian. But—''

"That isn't an idol,'' she said, looking back up at the statue herself. "It's what's called a Ixiptla.''

"Different word, but same meaning, I'm sure.''

"Not at all! Idol as a term comes from the ancient Middle East, where the total essence of the God-form was thought to be contained in a statue of some sort. This is different. It's a representation, and through certain procedures, it takes on—damn, how can I explain this easily?'' She stopped, ran her hand through her hair, thought for a minute. "Let's try it like this. When this thing was carved, it was, indeed, just a lump of wood. But by repeated—uh—procedures, it comes to achieve a kind of—connection, if you will—with the—ah—consciousness it represents. Then, it has become Ixiptla. That consciousness can be—reached—via the statue. Fundamentally, though, it's still a statue, an artwork. It's only by what I've done with it over the years that it's anything more.''

"Was this representative of what you've done over the years? Punching spikes into yourself, burning your blood?''

"Yes,'' she said levelly. "Among other things. He's—special to me. For many reasons, I've had to establish a—continuity with him.''

"But that's so—so gross!'' He searched for another word, one that would better express his repulsion for what she was doing to herself. "Barbaric!'' he came up with, finally. "Self-mutilation? In the name of some—some cult?''

"A few pinpricks is hardly mutilation,'' she said dryly. "And cult isn't right, either. Cult implies a lot of things, which have very little in common with what I'm doing here.''

"So what exactly are you doing here?''

"I've told you. Specifically, offering blood—and therefore power, power I've collected—to this specific—consciousness.''

"I have a hard time accepting it.''

"Your intellect does,'' she said, smiling at him again. "But the rest of you has no problems. If you'll think about it, you'll see what I mean.''

Though she'd said nothing that sounded even remotely related, he was sure—he knew—that she was referring to his experiences in the street the night he'd left the Obsidian Butterfly. Events she presumably knew nothing about. But he didn't feel like he could acknowledge it; he felt like that was committing him to something. "I don't know what you mean, no," he said finally, in an almost formal tone.

She shrugged. "Yes, you do. You haven't talked to me about it yet, but you've been—made aware—of some things. When you want to, we can talk. Okay?"

He felt a little tremor, straight down the center of his back. How could she possibly have known about his visions? Yet he was sure she did. "Nikki," he said slowly, dragging out his words, "I think I know, but—you want to tell me? What exactly are you into here? I mean, this goes a little beyond some folklore picked up during your childhood!"

"Yes, it does. What I'm 'into,' as you put it, it's a whole way of life. In the old days, they called it the way of the 'burning water.' Call it a religion if you wish, but it's more than that. And it does indeed come from the Mexico of my childhood."

"Aztec?" he almost whispered.

She nodded. "Very close. As I know it, even older—back to the Toltecs of Tula, to the great city of Teotihuacan. To Chichen Itza in Yucatan, to El Tajin. The Aztec themselves, well, they changed lots of things. Human sacrifice is what everybody knows them for. They were pretty damn excessive about it."

Elliot didn't know half the places or names she mentioned, but he was greatly relieved to hear her denigrate the Aztec practice of human sacrifice. As to the rest of it—well, he didn't know what the rest of it might entail. But in general, he told himself, he didn't like cults. People were far too likely to be fanatical about them. And, he told himself, running spikes into your body to let blood was itself fanatical, after all. "So," he said, glancing back up at the statue. "Who is he supposed to be, anyway?"

"Quetzalcoatl," she said.

Now that name he'd heard. The plumed serpent god of ancient Mexico. "That's who Montezuma thought Cortez was, right?"

"Yes, but the name is Montezuma, as near as it can be rendered in English. But, yes, there was a legend of Quetzalcoatl's return from the land he'd fled to, when he was defeated and shamed by Tezcatlipoca in old Tula. And they did expect him to come back. Or somebody. They sent gifts to Cortez appropriate for him, for Tezcatlipoca, for Tlaloc, and for Xiuhtecuhtli. They weren't sure. And their indecision cost them an empire.''

"I never heard of the others," he said.

"There's a lot more, too," she told him. "Look, I don't feel it's really very appropriate for us to sit around in here and chat. Can we go back out?''

Elliot got to his feet, and by the time he did, she already was near the door, throwing her red robe over her shoulders. He asked her about the still-smoldering fire in the brazier, but she said it would go out by itself, there was no danger. At the door, he paused and looked back; somehow, he thought, the statue looked different than it had when he'd first come in. More majestic, in some way he couldn't define, yet at the same time it was hard for him to tell himself that the difference was not objective. Nikki was calling him, and the fire was in fact rapidly dying, and since it was the room's only light, it was getting darker as well. Reluctantly, he started to follow her out, but then he looked, really looked for the first time, at one of the other statues. This one was familiar, at least in dress; it was dressed exactly like the dancer at the Obsidian Butterfly. The coldly handsome face was painted with broad yellow and black bands, and he wore a dark mirror in place of his left foot. Elliot stopped in front of the image, frozen. He couldn't take his eyes off it. And, though the image of Quetzalcoatl seemed to have lost the illusion of life in the dying firelight, this statue seemed to turn its black-mirrored eyes directly on him.

Nikki was tugging at his arm now, but he resisted her. "Who is he?" he whispered.

She stopped pulling. "Tezcatlipoca," she said. "The Smoking Mirror. Patron of the Jaguar Warriors!''

Frozen in place, he continued to gaze up at the statue; but his mind was in turmoil. It seemed to him that his mind was split into two halves, and one of these now understood the relationships. Nikki and her snake *nagual*, with Quetzalcoatl, the plumed rattlesnake. Himself with the Smoking Mirror, Tezcatlipoca. In that moment, he knew—with a weird, absolute certainty—that Jaguar Warrior was not just a saying, at least as far as he was concerned, and consequently, he knew what his own *nagual* was. But the other part of his mind categorically refused to accept any of it. Once more, because it was easier, he allowed his rationality to pull him away from what he knew was correct. Yet it was still with difficulty that he finally left the statue.

When they'd returned to Nikki's living room, her first suggestion was that they go back to bed. As she logically observed, it was very late. She didn't seem to be very interested in talking much about what he'd just seen, and that in itself surprised him. Most of the time, people who were into cults and such were obnoxiously eager to gain new converts. He had more or less assumed that she'd try to win him over, seeing that he had not run from the apartment screaming. But she wasn't, though she didn't seem reluctant to answer his questions. It was as if nothing at all unusual had happened.

"The bloodletting," he said finally. "That really bothers me, Nikki. I mean, you could get an infection. You might even get hit an artery and bleed to death back in there."

"You can always find something to worry about, can't you? Usually something physical!" she countered, grinning. Then she became serious. "I've told you a little already," she said, "about the concept of the *tonalli*. That's a big part of the—uh—way. If it is in my *tonalli* to hit a major blood vessel and bleed to death, well, that's just something I have to accept. I don't think—from a practical viewpoint—that there's much risk. Infection, well, I just don't have to worry about that, period. I have my herbs."

"Speaking of which, I have some evidence that Damiana is not so very effective in controlling VD."

"Wasn't used right," she said flatly.

"But—"

"Now look, Elliot," she told him, her voice rising just a little. "That, I'm sure of. You complain if you get VD from me, and only then, all right?"

"That'll be a little late—"

"Well, Goddamn it, if you're so worried about that, then we can stop screwing!"

He looked away from her. "I don't want that," he said.

She softened. "I don't either. I really like you, Elliot. I don't want anything like this to come between us."

"I suppose that means you wouldn't consider giving this up? The blood rituals, I mean?"

"You suppose right. But then, I don't do this every night, either."

"I'm glad to hear it! But—"

Far on into the night, they argued the issue back and forth, just as they had previously about Nikki's work and the Killer Guitarist. But this time, Elliot won no concessions from her at all; she was utterly intransigent, pointing out that she'd learned this way of life when she was a little girl, that it was deeply ingrained in her. Even while trying to convince her of the wisdom of giving it up, he found that, except for what he felt to be the inherent physical risks in the bloodlettings, he was not able to object to her practices too strenuously. And he wondered why not. A year ago, he was sure, he would have been stressing the irrationality, the psychological dangers, the probable masochism that underlay the blood offerings. But tonight, he just couldn't do that. Not that he was at all ready to leap right in and join her—he still told himself that what he saw as worshiping an idol was foolish at best—he just couldn't find it in himself to object too strongly. That realization gave him quite a start. In some way, he could see, his attitude was itself due to the visions he'd had, and to his strong reaction to the statue of the Smoking Mirror. With something of a start, he realized that he was making a conscious effort to evade any discussion of that statue. In fact, he didn't even want to think about it. He had to admit to himself that something about that statue, something about that name itself, both attracted and terrified him. He wanted to know more about it, but couldn't bring himself to ask. Thinking about Casteneda's book, he wondered if he, like Carlos, would succumb to the First Enemy, which was fear. Looking at Nikki sitting across from him in the chair, he wondered again how much similarity there was between her practices and the teachings of the old Yaqui; quite a lot, he was beginning to suspect. There was one thing he was sure of; even though he'd never seen Don Juan, or a picture of him, he was sure Nikki was more attractive.

Eventually, of course, he ran out of arguments. When Nikki again suggested they return to bed, he didn't argue with her. He would have liked to have made love with her again, but he was too tired, and he assumed she probably was too. Besides, the long discussion had taken some of the edge off the arousal he'd felt earlier. But the images of her in front of the idol—or whatever she'd called it—came back to him, and he could not deny their erotic force. He looked at her closed eyes and resigned himself to waiting; the images would still be there, in his memory. Besides, he thought, she was probably also too sore.

Before they turned out the light, he looked at her arm as it lay across his chest, and he was startled to learn that while he could still see the puncture wound, it was closed, almost invisible.

She opened her eyes, saw where he was looking. "I heal very fast," she said in a sleepy voice and closed her eyes again.

32

At first, the girl had tried to get away.

Everything she knew, she had tried, but it seemed to her that nothing worked. There had been a sort of a gray inevitability, from the moment he'd reached into his clothes and pulled out an elaborate glove with a guitar string wound around it. She could find it in herself to regret that moment; maybe if she had reacted instantly, run away then, it would not have been too late. But she had not; she had just stared at it, knowing what it meant, but not believing it was possible. Then, in an amazingly swift movement, the string was over her head and around her neck, being drawn tight. She had grabbed at it then, tried to pull it away, but he was much stronger, his strength that of a maniac.

Still, she'd managed to get loose from him, thrashing him with her arms and kicking him. One of her feet had landed solidly against something, and he had grunted and backed off. Then, the string still on her neck, still tight enough to restrict her breath, she had made for the door.

All these thoughts went through her mind as her hand, reaching for the doorknob, began to move backward. His arm was across her upper chest, and he was dragging her backwards across the floor. Still, she fought on, though she was beginning to feel like it was hopeless, but she had gotten away from him once, perhaps she could do it again. She kicked backwards, reached her hands around, trying to grab hair, grab something. She saw his other hand, raised over her; she started to grab at it, but stopped herself.

The hand held a knife but such a knife as she'd never before seen. It looked like it was made out of black glass, the edges chipped and irregular, but very sharp-looking.

Unable to see anything else, she tried to squirm away from the arm holding her, but she couldn't; all she could do was watch the knife descend.

Her eyes followed it down. She knew it was coming very fast, but for some reason, it looked like slow motion to her, the point just floating down through the air until it touched her stomach and disappeared inside her. She heard herself grunt, felt her eyes snap shut involuntarily.

A fiery pain tore through her, and for an instant, she couldn't breath or move. Opening her eyes, she saw the hand come back up, the knife now bloody. She felt herself being hurled onto the floor, and for just a second he wasn't touching her. She lifted her head, saw the terrible wound in her stomach, saw the blood running out. She was out of time, and now she knew it for sure; especially when the pain began to go away, taking her strength with it.

The man knelt beside her, put his hand against her chest and started to pull hard on the free end of the string. In spite of her resigned attitude, she could not, for a moment, stop herself from struggling even more when her air was cut off, but finally her body gave in to the inevitable.

She knew, as a bright light started to form in front of her, that it was just about over. Refusing to allow her assailant's face to be the last thing she saw, she forced her head to turn slightly and focused her eyes on an object that had, in the past, brought her pleasure. She carried its image—and a mental picture of the face of a friend who had become dear to her—into her death.

33

Panting from the exertion, the man with the silver ring withdrew himself from the body of his latest victim and rolled over on the floor.

For a long while he just lay there, his arms spread, looking at the ceiling; he felt utterly satisfied. Turning to his side, he looked at the girl's face, swollen in death. Her eyes seemed to be looking into his, and it made him just a little uncomfortable. He looked away, scanned down her body. Unfortunate that he'd had to stab her, he told himself; this was the second one recently he'd had to subdue that way, and it made such a mess! A little blood around the string didn't bother him, but he always seemed to stab low in the body, and there was that unpleasant fecal odor. Not, he told himself, the most romantic thing in the world.

"I don't understand why you fought so hard," he said aloud, looking back into her dilated, staring eyes. "Didn't you know how good it was going to be, for you?"

"It wasn't good; it was hideous, a nightmare," he seemed to hear her say. He stared at her; her lips hadn't moved, her chest was still. She couldn't have spoken to him.

"What did you say?" he asked, his voice quivering a bit.

"I said, it was a nightmare. I had no orgasm. There was only pain, no pleasure. I hate you!"

He jerked up to a sitting position. She hadn't spoken, he was sure of that. But he seemed to hear her voice in his mind!

"You can't be talking, you're dead," he whispered.

"Yes. I am dead, you've killed me. But my spirit is not yet gone, and I have the strength to make you hear me. And you will hear me, you bastard! Nothing of what you believe is true! You bring no pleasure, you only destroy, and if I can

272

stay long enough, I'll destroy you! I'll eat it from the inside, I'll put worms in your belly, I'll put rats in your brain to chew you from the inside out—''

"Nooooo . . ." he moaned. "I'm imagining this, it isn't happening, that isn't the way it is! All these women loved me—''

"They all despised you. I can feel them all. They would give you death by fire, they would tear you to pieces—''

"No—you're lying—'' He covered his ears, but he could still hear her voice clearly. Ignoring it as best he could, he wiped the girl's blood from his body, dressed himself. Deciding that it was a bad idea to leave the body here, he wrapped it in two green garbage bags, tying them together in the middle. When it was ready, he checked the floor carefully. Her clothes and shoes were in the bags, everything was ready—then he noticed a puddle of blood on the ragged rug. Cursing, he snatched a towel from the bathroom, cleaned it up as well as he could, then stuffed the towel into the bags.

Carrying his burden on the streets made him nervous, but no one challenged him. There was a hotel with a back entrance nearby, one he was quite familiar with. Leaving the body in an alley, he paid for a room, then carried the body in the back way. After he unwrapped it, he didn't stay. He took the garbage bags and left, dropping them in the nearest Dumpster.

The girl's voice, he was gratified to notice, was getting weaker all the time.

34

Elliot didn't get up until after ten that morning. When he finally did open his eyes, he was once again alone in the bed. But this time, it was different. He could hear Nikki moving about in the kitchen, hear the coffee perking. As he sat up in the bed, he still could not shake the feeling that something was wrong. He could not figure out what it might be, and, still not quite awake, he staggered into the kitchen. Nikki greeted him brightly, but he could only grunt, fall into a chair until the coffee had finished perking.

"You do wake up slowly, don't you?" she asked him. He responded with another unintelligible grunt, and she made a face at him, poured coffee into a cup. He looked up at her, her robe open in front as always, and for a moment even the coffee was forgotten, a unique thing for Elliot in the morning. He pulled her to him, examined her arms, thighs, ears, and nipples. Nowhere could he find even a trace of a puncture.

His eyes moved slowly to the closet door. "I think maybe I had the weirdest dream—" he said to her. Like a sleep-walker, he got up, walked to the closet, and opened it. She said nothing as he pushed the coats aside, looked at the wall on the right. He pushed it, first on one side, then on the other, wondering if it would swing open.

"Elliot?" Nikki asked him. "What are you doing in my closet? Are you awake?"

"Like I said," he told her, "I had a weird dream." He wiped his hands down over the wall again. "Real weird."

"Want to tell me about it?"

"No. I'm going nuts. I swear to God I am. There just isn't any other good explanation."

"I don't think you're getting any nuttier than you've been!"

274

"If I told you that dream—and some others I've had lately—you might change your mind. You might throw me out."

"I doubt it," she told him, sipping her own coffee. "Oh, get the paper, will you? Should be right outside the door there."

Still undressed, he went to the door, looked through the peephole; there was no one in the hallway. He unlatched the door, and, keeping it between himself and anyone who might suddenly appear, reached around and picked up the sheaf of newsprint lying against the door. Then he walked back to the table, plopped it down between them, and picked up his coffee cup.

After a sip or two, he realized that Nikki was sitting frozen, her cup midway between her mouth and the table. She was looking at the newspaper with the same expression she might have had if he'd thrown a severed head on the table.

"What's wrong?" he asked her.

"Oh, Elliot," she said, looking up at him, her dark eyes moist. "Oh, my friend—"

He followed her eyes as she glanced at the paper once more. All bad news, as usual, he could see that: fighting in Vietnam, bombing at Haiphong, college riots, inner-city race riots, Nixon. All bad news, none of it personal. "What is it?" he repeated.

"I should have known," she said, "but I guess I wasn't paying attention. Other things on my mind—"

"What on earth are you talking about?"

She flipped the paper over. He had laid it on the table with the bottom of Page One up, and she hadn't previously turned it; he didn't see how she could have known anything about the other side. But she was looking at it, looking sad. He turned it toward himself, saw a headline:

KILLER GUITARIST CLAIMS TENTH!

Still not understanding, he looked back up at her sad eyes. The only real concern he had with this was her safety. But she was safe; she'd been with him.

He looked at the article again when she said nothing, started to read.

Then, without warning, he screamed. Nikki didn't even

jump; she'd known it was coming. Known exactly how he'd react when he saw the victim's name: Laura Neill, age 13.

"No—no, it isn't possible!" he yelled, pulling his own hair. "She wasn't hooking anymore, the guy only went after hookers. She was safe, no, I don't believe it!"

"I'm so sorry, Elliot," Nikki said, a tear running down her cheek. "I know how you're hurting—"

"It can't be, I won't accept it!" he cried. "There has to be some kind of mistake! Maybe it's another Laura Neill—those names aren't rare! Maybe they found something of hers, the ID is wrong! There has to be something wrong!"

"Oh, Elliot—"

"I gotta go!" he said, jumping up. He ran into the bedroom, started jerking his clothes on. "I gotta go down there, make sure she's okay!"

"Elliot, there isn't a mistake—"

"Don't say that!" he screeched. "You can't know! There has to be, somehow there has to be!"

She put her hands on his shoulders. "Go, then," she said, her voice as gentle as her hands. "Do what you must. I'll be here, waiting for you."

He didn't even respond to that, just yanked his shoes on and ran out the door. Viciously, he hammered the elevator button, and when it didn't come immediately, he ran down the stairs, almost falling once. Then he was out on the streets, running. To his car, which he cursed when it failed to start instantly. Pulling out of the parking place, he bumped the car in front of him a little, paid no attention.

It was something of a miracle that he got to the Village without having a wreck, but somehow it happened. By the time his feet hit the stair leading to Gerald's apartment, he had pretty much convinced himself that it was a mistake of some sort. He'd open the door, Laura would run to him like she always did, he'd hold her, he'd find some way to protect her—

He threw the door open, not bothering to knock. No one in the living room. His heart pounding, breath ragged, he went into the kitchen; Gerald and Haze both were sitting at the table. When Gerald raised his face, and Elliot saw that the older man's beard was wet with tears, he knew. There was no mistake. He stopped short in the doorway, threw his head back and howled.

"How did this happen?" he demanded when he had some control over his emotions. "How? Laura was no hooker, Goddamn it! How did she run into this guy?"

Haze looked up at him; he didn't seem too terribly grief-stricken, but Elliot could see a reason why not. He was heavily drugged, probably on reds, and they had indeed put him into a haze. "She was hooking, Elliot. She asked us not to tell you, said you'd get mad."

Elliot was speechless. After all their talks, his warnings—how could she have done it? Repressing the urge to jerk Haze out of the chair and hit him, he spoke again instead. "Why?" he asked. "Wasn't your idea, was it?"

"Me? Oh, no! Shit, no! That's a racist pig remark anyway. Just 'cause I'm black, I gotta be some kinda pimp? No, it was her idea. Gerald and I both tried to talk her out of it, just because of this nut runnin' around. But—it was after you talked to me 'bout her sleepin' with guys who came around, our deal, remember? She said, after that, that she had to earn her keep someway. So she started hittin' the streets again. She used to, maybe she didn't tell you. When she was messed up with that weird cult?"

"She told me," Elliot growled. He waited for the man to go on, desperately looking for some way to blame him, some way to hold him responsible.

"Anyhow, she went back to it. She could make good money at it. She was young, cute. So whenever you wasn't here at nights, she'd go out, make some bread."

"It was only two Goddamn nights! Only two!"

"Bad luck, man. Shit, the other night she only turned one trick, then she came home. She ran into this fuckin' dude on just her second trick, I guess."

Elliot turned, pounded savagely on the door frame. So much he would have done differently, if he could do it over. "When did you find out?" he asked.

This time, Gerald answered, his voice unsteady. "Right after she did the first one," he said. "She came in with sixty bucks. We were here with Conrad, trying to get him to do some dope—he won't, you know. She told us all about it. An old guy, she said. And she told us then never to tell you about it. Said she was in love with you, man. Told us she didn't want you thinking she was some kind of common whore.

"Hell, we told her then, Don't be doing this now. There's a

killer out there, and the pigs are all over the place looking for him. But she said it was the only way she could make good money quick, and she wanted to pay her way around here. She wanted to have some money so if you wanted to take her back with you, she could help pay the way—''

Elliot turned away from the door; he just could not take any more of this. Gerald's words were like hammers, each of them smashing into his skull. But even when the older man stopped talking, the words kept running through his mind, cutting at him. Laura's own words; he could almost still hear her telling him that she didn't have much time, that if he delayed, it'd be too late. Well, he told himself, he had, and it was. He remembered Nikki, urging him to make love with the girl, telling him her dreams were indeed prophetic, pushing him off the phone because she somehow knew it was hurting Laura.

For a few minutes, he stood looking at the beat-up armchair she used to sit in, not in the least ashamed of the tears that were running down his cheeks.

Incredible, he thought; he'd been so deeply involved with Nikki, yet at the same time he'd come to care for that young girl so very much. Like she was his daughter, his little sister, he told himself. But that wasn't true; always, when he'd refused her sexually, he had been doing something he really didn't want to do. It just seemed proper to him. Now, too late, he became aware that he had been reacting to social injunctions, that he was not nearly so free of the demands of the larger society as he'd once believed, and that the learning of that lesson had cost both Laura and himself dearly. So stupid, he told himself. Such an utter waste.

Some of his control back, he turned back to the men sitting at the table. ''Where did they find her—'' he asked, not quite able to finish the sentence.

''A flophouse, about two blocks over,'' Haze told him. ''They done been by, talked to us. We done flushed all our dope. They said they didn't think she was—they didn't think it happened there. Somewhere else, they said. She was carried there.''

''Why do they think that?''

''You sure you want to hear all this, Elliot?'' Gerald asked; he seemed genuinely concerned.

''I feel like I have to,'' Elliot told them woodenly.

"Well, like the last one, she was—stabbed, too," Haze said, and Elliot winced. "And there wasn't enough blood there." The black man looked toward the ceiling. "I heard them pigs talkin' among theyselves," he said. "Said something about same knife or whatever as last time. Said it'd be easy to identify if they found it. That's when they was talkin' about gettin' a search warrant for here. But I guess they decided not to."

"What was special about it?"

"Hey, man, I dunno. They just said it was—what'd they say? Real unusual. Like I said, they wasn't talkin' at me. I just overheard em."

"Anything else?"

"No, man. A guitar string, like all the others."

A vivid image of Laura with a guitar string around her neck leapt unbidden into Elliot's mind; it would not go away no matter how hard he tried to banish it. There was no way, he thought, that he could ever forgive himself for this. If anybody was at fault here, it was Elliot Collins, and there could be no doubt of that. The only thing that could possibly make him feel better was to have the Killer Guitarist in his hands, be able to destroy him piece by piece, ever so slowly and painfully. Briefly he fantasized about this, about hunting down the killer, but he realized that he had little chance of doing that. He was not experienced in such things, and if the police, with an army of men on the case, were not even able to slow the man down, how could he hope to find him?

Once again he turned away from Gerald and Haze; they could not help him any further. Perhaps, just perhaps, Nikki could; maybe she could ease his pain somewhat. He felt a flash of guilt about that; he'd been sleeping with Nikki at the exact moment Laura was dying. Even so, he decided to go back. Nothing, he told himself, nothing could rid him of this guilt, not completely. At least he was moderately well under control.

As he walked through the living room, his mind packed in cotton, he caught a glimpse of a little black case sitting on the plank-and-concrete-block bookcase. Unable to stop himself, he went to it, snapped it open, looked at Laura's precious flute inside.

His control collapsed completely, and he fell onto the floor, weeping like a small child.

At no time did he notice the fact that the D string was missing from Haze's colorful guitar. Or that there was a dampness and the remains of a dark stain on the rug, as if something had recently been cleaned up.

35

As she had promised, Nikki was waiting for him when he finally got himself under sufficient control to go back up to her apartment. The only question he'd had left for Haze and Gerald was the dispensation of the body; he'd been told that the police had already contacted Laura's parents, that after the requisite autopsy, it would be shipped back to her family home in Dayton. Knowing there was nothing left for him to do, he had meandered back uptown.

"My fault," he told Nikki, staring at the table. "I should have made sure. I knew that child had problems—"

She sat across from him, looking rather odd to his eyes in her blue jeans and workshirt; she almost never wore anything that was not overtly sensual. But she seemed to sense that this wasn't the right time for it. "I'm a firm believer," she told him, "in taking whatever responsibility is properly yours. The fact that the girl didn't experience the pleasure of your body before she died, that is your fault, no one else's. That she died isn't your fault. You may have played a part in the how, but that's all. Her dream was profound, Elliot, whether you want to believe it or not. If you had somehow managed to save her from the Killer Guitarist, she would have been run over by a truck, or something. Her road was done, and that's all there was to it."

"I wish I could believe that," he said miserably. "In a way. But if I did, then I made another mistake—one you told me I was going to make. It turned out that way, didn't it?"

Tactfully, Nikki said nothing in response to this. She just looked at him, her brown eyes soft and sad. "I feel so bad for you, Elliot," she told him. "I know how you're hurting."

"Yeah, well, there's nothing I can do about it now, is there? Nothing at all."

"Just to make sure it doesn't happen again."

He looked up at her. "Meaning what?"

"Meaning, don't let social conventions you think you've overcome stand in the way of something you know you should do, deep down. This isn't something I'd say to very many people, Elliot. It isn't true for very many people. But for you, it is. If you can get in touch with your true instincts, and follow them, you won't have very many problems. You understand me?"

"Yes, and I can't deny that with Laura, I was doing what I felt was—I guess—socially right. At some other level, I knew she was not really the child I kept casting her as."

"Then you've learned a valuable lesson."

"That doesn't help me now! And it sure doesn't help Laura!"

"No, there is nothing more any of us can do for Laura, except to remember her. But—and I don't know if a 'religious' idea like this will have any value for you—but according to my beliefs, she will end up in a rather pleasant place. A place my childhood friends called Tonatiuhanchan."

"Heaven?"

"Not exactly. But a nice place, anyway."

"I'm sorry, Nikki, but that isn't really a lot of help. I wish it was. My beliefs are that when you're dead, you're dead. And that is the absolute end of it."

"For most people, that's true," Nikki told him. "According to my beliefs, too. The old man—I've mentioned him before—he used to talk about a four-day sojourn in a dreary place called Mictlan. After that, the consciousness just doesn't exist anymore."

"Then what's the point of the four days? I don't know why I'm asking that. Religious concepts don't have to have reasons."

"Oh, these do! Not that they're always known, of course. But the idea here is that the consciousness is refined a bit before it gets absorbed back into the general pool. Eaten, in a way."

"Sounds sort of Jungian."

"There are a few similarities, yes."

"But that wouldn't happen to Laura?"

"No. She—because of the way she died—she gets four years in a place that's a hell of a lot better than Mictlan."

"Then what?"

"Reabsorbed, like the rest."

"Not a very long time."

"It seems so, to the consciousness. Seems like years and years. By the time the four years are gone, they're tired of existing. It isn't unpleasant."

"That's the best anyone can hope for, in your beliefs?"

"No. There are ways to achieve other states. But only a select few ever reach that level. That gets kind of complicated, Elliot. This probably isn't the time to go into it."

"No, I suppose not," he said, looking down at the tables once more. "I just wish," he said, an edge to his voice, "that I could get my hands on that guy!" In fact, he told himself, he wished he had some idea who the guy might be. For whatever reason, having some concrete face or name to cast the blame on would help, or at least it seemed so to him. The nebulous hulk of his fantasies just wasn't good enough. Not when he felt a good part of the responsibility lay with himself. "I wonder," he said, basically thinking aloud, "if that guy that Laura was mixed up with might be behind this." He recognized it was grasping at straws, but anything was better than what he had, which was nothing.

"What guy are you talking about?" Nikki asked.

Briefly, he explained about Laura's prior involvement with the cult. He couldn't remember the name of the church, just the title, Chingon.

"This Chingon, was his name Nigel, by any chance?"

He turned to her, stared. "You've heard of these people?" he asked.

"Yes," she told him. "A cult church, like you said. They call it the Procedural Church."

"That's it!" he cried. "That's what Laura said it was!"

She nodded. "The leader, the one you mentioned, his full name is Nigel Adams. They are a crazy bunch, that's for sure."

He stared at her again. "You know these people? That well?"

"I've run into them, yes. In my line of work, you run into a lot of weirdos. They certainly aren't friends of mine!"

"How did you manage to run into them?"

"Well, you probably already know that they make their money—most of it—by prostitution and drug sales. For Nigel, it's a neat racket—he has all these zombies running around, and if any of them get picked up by the law, he just tosses them to the wolves. The cops have arrested a whole bunch of kids in connection with that church, but they never could carry it back to the top guys.

"Anyway, some of the better-looking girls—and some of the guys, too—answer ads in the underground press for stag film actors. They've turned up in Andrew's office more than once."

"So he uses them? In the films?"

"Not if he knows who they are, no. A few have gotten by, I'm sure, but just as soon as they mention the church, or Nigel, out they go. See, if they get their claws into you, they want to take over. And they're dangerous. Once you hook in with them, they'll kill you if you try to leave. If they can find you."

"So that, then, is what happened to Laura. What these killings are all about."

She gave him a curious look. "That's a pretty big jump, Elliot. Don't you think?"

"You don't agree?"

"Let's say I have my doubts. All the victims are hookers, all women. Not everyone who leaves worked as a hooker. And some are men. So we should have some male victims, some that weren't working the streets. At least a drug dealer or two."

Elliot stared out the window, at the Hudson River and the Palisades beyond. "I'd like to talk to some of these assholes," he said darkly. "Find out for myself!"

"You can, if you want," Nikki shocked him by saying. "But I warn you, they're dangerous. You can't play around with them."

"You know where we can find them?"

"Sure. Well, there are a lot of them, I don't know where they all are. I don't think they do themselves. But Nigel, I know where he hangs out."

"Where?"

She rested her chin in her hand, a little smile playing around her lips. "The church is down on Forty-fourth, a storefront,'' she told him, ''and Nigel is usually there. What are you going to do, Elliot? Barge right in?''

He considered this. From what he'd heard about the church, barging right in and confronting Nigel was probably suicidal. Still, he felt like he had to do something. Calling the police was not under consideration; he had no proof at all, no evidence to give them, just his hunches, which were rapidly turning into convictions. ''I don't know,'' he admitted. ''Maybe at first, just drive by and look at the place. Check it out. Then I'll decide.''

''Good enough. Just don't get reckless, okay? In fact, I think I'll go with you.''

''No—''

''Oh, yes. Anyhow, how are you going to know where it is? Forty-fourth is a long street.''

''You could tell me—''

''I can show you!''

His shoulders sank a little. He didn't want Nikki in any possible danger; and he suspected that she knew that, was relying on her presence as a check on his doing anything rash. He gave in, and they left the apartment. Half an hour later, she directed him to a parking place along West Forty-fourth street. He protested this, saying he only meant to drive by. But she had laughed at him, telling him that they weren't going to jump out and grab him off the street, after all. In the middle of the day? That seemed reasonable to him, and he followed her instructions, parked the VW, and followed her down the street.

''That's the place,'' she said, gesturing toward a storefront on the opposite side of the street. He slowed, looked. Nothing special, other than the fact that it was in better repair than the buildings around it. Above the doors was a sign with the legend, ''C.D.L.P.''

''What does that mean?'' he asked Nikki.

She shrugged. ''I dunno. Some acronym for their church. What difference does it make?''

''None, I suppose,'' he said, looking unhappy. Standing here, he had no better idea about what to do than before. This, he decided, had not been one of his better ideas. He stopped walking, stood and stared blatantly. He glanced over at Nikki; she too was staring at the church. But weirdly, her eyes were crossed.

"What the hell are you doing?" he asked sharply. It seemed to him she was playing some kind of stupid game.

For a moment she said nothing, then told him in a low voice to look at the door. He did. A rather ordinary-looking man of about forty, dressed in a suit, had come out onto the sidewalk. He looked like some kind of businessman, not the kind of individual Elliot would have expected to be involved in a cult church.

"That's Nigel," Nikki said.

Elliot turned his head, followed the man with his eyes as he went by; he in turn only gave them the most cursory glance. After crossing the street, he started off down the sidewalk. Almost automatically, without thinking, Elliot started to follow him.

"What are you doing?" Nikki asked, keeping up with his long strides.

"I want to see where he goes," Elliot said firmly. "If that's the bastard who killed Laura, I don't want him getting away!"

"Understand me, Elliot; this is dangerous! Besides, he didn't kill Laura. Even if the group is responsible—which I doubt—then all he did was put out an order to kill people who left. He probably doesn't know who Laura was!" But in spite of her words, he had the impression she wasn't really trying to talk him out of anything.

"Yes, he does," he told her. "She told me—he picked her up personally."

"He picks up a lot of young girls!"

"I don't want him picking up any more!"

She was trotting now, as Elliot picked up his pace, closing the distance between himself and the tall, dark-haired man. "You know, under some conditions you could get yourself killed. For no good reason!" she told him. But her tone implied that she was enjoying herself.

"Laura was a very good reason," he snarled. "I failed her when she was alive. I won't now!" Up ahead, he saw the man turn into an open doorway, and he broke into a run to catch up. He was looking at a narrow hallway, doors on either side, and a long carpeted stairway at the end. Just at the top of the stair, he saw spit-shined shoes disappearing, and with no hesitation, he lunged inside, started up the stair after the man.

One landing passed; he could still see the feet above him, and he continued to pursue, hearing Nikki's lighter footfalls right behind him. Beginning to pant a little, he went on to the second landing. Down the hallway beyond, he saw a door opening; the door was between him and the man he was pursuing. He wasn't thinking at all, he just wanted to know if that was Nigel. Almost running down the hall, he came to the door just before it closed. Immediately inside, Nigel looked back at him. Beyond, he could see something he was sure he wasn't supposed to see: piles of bags full of white powder, jars full of capsules. A drug cache.

He only had time to tell himself that he had a problem before Nigel reacted, and Elliot found himself looking into the barrel of a revolver.

Now he knew exactly what Nikki meant about foolhardy. Not only had he put himself in danger by his rashness, but he'd put her as well; she was right behind him.

"All right," Nigel said, his voice calm. "Let's step inside, shall we?"

"Uh—well, we were just—"

"You were just following me! Don't you act stupid on me. I'll blow you and your lady friend to hell and back!"

"Look," Elliot said reasonably. "There doesn't need to be a problem. We'll just back out of here. We didn't see a thing. All right?"

Nigel grinned. "I don't hardly think so," he said. "You two could damn well call in the cops before I could get half this shit out of here. Now be good little children, okay? Go in the Goddamn room!"

Having little choice, they went inside. It was a small apartment, and, seemingly, no one lived there; most of the usual amenities of any sort of a home were lacking. The window, Elliot noticed, was nailed shut, and the room was quite hot. Standing on the bare floor in the front room—the only room other than a bathroom and kitchenette off the side—was a ruined couch and a single chair. The kitchenette was even more empty; no stove, no refrigerator. Just piles and piles of boxes.

"Quite a stash!" Nikki said. Elliot could not understand how she could be so cool, considering the position they were in. It seemed to him she was perhaps irritated about something, but she showed no fear at all.

"I trust you enjoy the sight. Now shut up and sit down." Nigel sat on the arm of the chair, the gun still in his hand, and looked at them, at Nikki especially. "Don't I know you?" he asked her at last.

"Andrew," she said simply.

Recognition lit his eyes. "Ah, yes. Nikki, isn't it? Now, you tell me, what's an uptown whore like you doing with this Goddamn hippie, following me?"

She returned his gaze directly. "He wanted to ask you about someone, that's all," she said. "We aren't with the cops, if that's what you think."

Nigel turned to face Elliot. In the light, the man looked about as totally insane as anyone he'd ever seen. "Who?" he said.

Trying to emulate Nikki's coolness, he answered. "A friend of mine named Laura Neill," he said.

"Never heard of her. Was she a whore, too?"

"She was a kid. She got herself killed."

"You think I killed her?"

"Crossed my mind."

"You gotta lotta balls, I'll say that. Both of ya." He stopped talking, rubbed his chin. "How old was she?" he asked finally.

"Thirteen."

"Well, shit, I might have. I don't even know. Those kids of mine brought in a bunch of chicks in the last month, and we offed a few of them. I don't even know the names."

Elliot stared at the man; he couldn't believe what he was hearing. "Are you telling me you killed some kids, and you don't even know who they were?"

"Sure," Nigel said offhandedly. He walked to the window, looked out. "About five, I think," he said conversationally.

Struggling for words, Elliot finally asked, "Why?"

Nigel didn't even look back at him. "Oh, they was just kids that were brought in, didn't want to join up. We offed them in front of the others, keep them in line."

In spite of the heat of the room, Elliot felt a chill. This man was far more vicious than he'd expected; vicious and crazy. He could not imagine what sort of person would do this, what kind of mental warpage it took. And at the same time, he realized that he and Nikki were truly in deep trouble; there probably was no way to make a deal with him. Stalling, he described Laura, asked Nigel about her again.

"I told you, I don't know!" he snapped, waving the gun around. "Wait a minute. Wait a minute. Laura Neill—I have heard that name. In the paper, the Killer Guitarist, right? One of his victims?"

"Right. The latest."

Nigel laughed. "You think I'm the Killer Guitarist?" he asked.

"Like I said, it crossed my mind."

"Shit, man! I don't do things that way! Anybody we offed got their head chopped off, on a block. Makes a big mess, scares the shit out of the other kids. Especially when the body flops around. Besides, all ours are done over there, in the church! That little whore bitch was killed in some dump of a hotel! You stupid shit! You got the wrong guy!"

Stunned, Elliot looked around at Nikki. "That means you were right—"

"You told him I didn't do it? Glad to see you have faith in me, Nikki," Nigel said with a laugh.

She shrugged. "Laura was a runaway from your group. All I told him is you wouldn't have bothered to do it personally."

"Well, you're right about that, honey. I do tell 'im to off anybody who tries to leave. If I'da known, I'da told some of the kids to off her, yeah. But I wouldn'ta done it. I stay clean from that stuff."

"You bastard—" Elliot snarled, taking a step toward him. But the gun swung up, and he stopped.

"You asshole. You got the wrong guy, and you got yourself and your whore friend here killed," Nigel said coldly. Still facing them, he walked to the window, pulled down the shade, and the room grew moderately dark. "Don't want nobody to see," Nigel said with a strained grin. "Gunshots, well, nobody pays much attention!" He stood in the center of the room. "Stand up!" he commanded. They did. "Now, turn around!" he barked at them.

"No," Elliot responded, with a quick glance at Nikki. She was actually smiling, looked amused; he could not understand it. Strain, maybe.

He judged the distance from himself to the maniac, prepared for a desperate lunge. He knew he had little chance, but it was better than just standing there. Out of the corner of his eye, he could see that Nikki had a rather strange expression on her face; it made him hesitate, wondering why she didn't fear this armed madman.

"Suit yourself," Nigel said, pulling back the hammer and aiming the weapon at Elliot.

"I think not, Nigel," Nikki said coolly. The man paused, glanced at her.

"Why not?" he asked.

"Because I say so," she told him.

He laughed. "Well, we'll just see!" he snapped. The muzzle of the revolver aimed at Elliot's chest, he began to squeeze the trigger; in the half-light of the room, Elliot could make out his finger contracting.

Then it stopped.

Nigel's hand tightened up more, and even more, until the knuckles turned white. "What—?" he said, staring down at the gun. But stubbornly, it refused to fire.

Elliot considered leaping at him, but Nikki somehow caught his attention, and he glanced at her; she was shaking her head. Her right hand was held up in a peculiar gesture, the thumb and forefinger aimed at Nigel, held as if to show the size of something quite small. Something just about the size of the trigger guard on the pistol.

Nigel began yelling unintelligibly, struggling with his gun, but try as he might, he could not get it to fire. His eyes wild, hair hanging over his forehead, he stared at Nikki, pointed the gun at her, clutched it with both hands, tried to shoot. Her normally warm and friendly face wore a cold expression, as if she were smelling something disgusting. As Elliot watched her, not understanding at all what was going on, she lifted her left arm and pointed it at the man in the suit. As she did, Elliot would have sworn that the room got a little darker. Her arm—there was something odd about it, he couldn't tell what. She had it extended rigidly, palm down and fingers together, her thumb tucked under. Then she shook it.

And the way it shook caused Elliot's eyes to go wide, Nigel's even wider. It didn't move as if it were jointed normally at wrist and elbow, but rather sinuously, rippling up and down, starting at her hand and extending to her shoulder.

As if there were no bones in it, or as if there were dozens . . .

He looked back at her hand and became utterly confused. He could still see a smooth, white, feminine arm extended from the rolled-up sleeve of the workshirt, a delicate, long-fingered hand at the end of it. But, seemingly at the same time, the back of the hand was scaly, the fingers had unified to form a snout, glittering eyes looked from beneath armored brows. And a black, forked tongue flickered from the mouth. Then, the reptilian head began to move forward and downward, a golden brown body marked with lengthwise neck bands and black diamonds following, issuing from her shirt-sleeve. Her arm remained, merging in some insane way in his vision; there was only one object, yet there were two. But as it tapered down, the rattle visible in the crook of her elbow, the vision became normal; the rattlesnake, at least eight feet long and a foot thick, was on the floor, and Nikki's arm was still extended.

Keeping her elbow high, she pulled her forearm back until it was touching her chest at the wrist, her hand turned at a right angle, still aimed at Nigel. On the floor, the big diamondback looped the front part of its body into an S-shaped coil, elevated about the front third of itself off the ground; the tongue made long sweeps out, pausing and vibrating at full extension. It was not rattling, but a few harsh snaps from the heavy rattle could be heard as it began to hitch itself toward the Chingon, tightening its neck loop as it went.

"No," Nigel moaned, backing away from it. "No!" He aimed the gun at the golden-brown, triangular head, once again tried to pull the trigger, but only the muscles standing out on his arms attested to his effort. Nikki dropped her thumb away from her palm, and the snake gaped at him, erecting its fangs, showing a clear drop of venom beaded at the tip of each one. And still it moved closer, backing Nigel across the room.

Finally, he tried to move to one side, as if to run for it, but just as quickly, the snake shifted its angle, cutting him off. He moaned, backed away again, but then his nerve broke, and he tried to cut around the other side of it. As he did, Nikki's left arm shot forward with inhuman speed, fingers up, thumb down. Below, the snake's head also jerked forward, then back again; it all happened so quickly that Elliot could not tell what the result was. Then, as he followed Nigel's shocked eyes down toward his leg, he saw.

Midway up the Chingon's thigh, on his pants, were two little spots of red.

"Oh, my God, no," he cried, holding his leg. "Oh, no. I don't wanta die, for God's sake! Help me, please, I need a doctor—" The results of the bite were, based on the little Elliot knew of snakebite, peculiar. Of course, he could not see the man's leg through his trousers, but there didn't seem to be any obvious swelling. Instead, in a matter of minutes Nigel was holding his head, screaming that he couldn't see. His breathing, too, seemed very labored, long deep inspirations accompanied by a sound like a rasp on wood.

He dropped the gun, tried to move toward the door, and again Nikki's arm flew out; simultaneously the snake hit him again. This time Elliot could clearly see the whole thing, the mouth so wide open as to present a flat surface, fangs standing straight out; the actual impact, on the wrist this time, the needlelike teeth piercing the skin like it was tissue paper, then the vigorous working of the bulging glands behind the reptile's eyes. And finally, back to its striking posture. Waiting, watching.

"Oh, God, Nikki, please help me," Nigel moaned, falling to one knee, then to both. "Oh, God help me. It hurts. It hurts. I can't stand it! Get this thing away from me, get me to a hospital, help me, oh God help me help me—"

For what seemed like a very long time he remained there on his knees, his face a mask of agony, his sightless eyes staring into space. As if his neck were broken, his head lolled over to one side, but somehow he stayed up, his hands twitching rapidly, looking like some kind of malfunctioning machine. At last, so slowly it didn't seem possible, he fell over onto his side. His legs stretched out painfully far, one at a time, then pulled up hard. Then, suddenly, his whole body spasmed backwards, bending his head around toward his ankles, his hands flapping on the dirty hardwood floor.

Elliot could smell feces and urine as the snake approached Nigel's jerking form, its long tongue testing his body. For another interminable interval, Nigel just lay there, no longer saying anything, just groaning and twitching, while the snake explored around him. Then, with no warning, the head flew out again, one fang sinking into his cheek and the other into the side of his neck. Once more his body arched backwards, he managed another screech, and Elliot could hear the sickening crack of his vertebrae as his back muscles pulled too far.

Twice more the body jerked violently. Then, it was still.

The rattlesnake left him then, gliding across the floor toward Elliot with surprising speed. Its head came up, and the glittering eyes with their catlike elliptical pupils fixed on his for just a second. He experienced a moment of stark terror, even though he could see that its neck was extended, not pulled into an S, and he knew what that meant. Never slowing down, it turned, crawled to Nikki. She gathered it up in her arms like it was a baby; the black tongue flicked over her face. She turned her body away from Elliot, and when she turned back, there was no snake. But just for an instant, as she turned around, Elliot saw her face. Same pretty features, smooth skin, curly black hair. Same dark brown eyes.

But the elliptical pupils, that was a difference.

36

"We've got to get out of here," Nikki said, the first words either of them had spoken in quite a while. "I have a feeling that the cops have been watching this place. They've probably heard the screaming, and they'll be here pretty soon."

He looked at her face: normal eyes, round pupils. Normal hands, all normal. Then back to the twisted corpse on the floor; not normal. "Cops?" he said irrationally, not knowing what else to say.

"Cops," she said firmly. "Cops that'll cost me more energy if we stay here. Can we go, please?"

Feeling numb, and not knowing what she was talking about, he turned like a mechanical man, opened the door, walked through it. He could hear her follow him, close the door behind her. Down the stair, there was noise, commotion, blue uniforms.

"Shit!" she said vehemently. She gestured with her hands, making a wide circle, and pulled Elliot to one side of the landing as the officers rushed up. He didn't resist her at all, just waited for the cops to catch them. Vaguely, he wondered how they were going to explain Nigel's demise.

Even in his benumbed state, he was surprised when the officers totally ignored them, just rushed right by. Not one of them gave them even so much as a passing glance, even when the first ones in the room started yelling about the body they'd discovered.

"They can't see us," Elliot said aloud, staring at the speeding blue uniforms.

"Or hear us, no," Nikki told him. "Let's go, okay? So I can relax!"

"Hey!" he screamed at one of the cops. "I'm here! Don't you give a shit!?"

The young officer paused, glanced around, as if he'd heard something. But he shrugged and ran on, joining his colleagues in the room with the corpse.

"You like pushing your luck, don't you?" Nikki snapped. "Will you please get your ass out of here?"

He hesitated a moment more, then complied, walking down the stairs slowly, dodging an occasional officer who was running up or down. Still in a daze, he went into the street, started toward his car. Nikki was still right behind him, and he found himself frankly terrified to turn and look at her. But when she got into the VW, she looked perfectly normal. He started the engine, wondering if people in the street would be seeing a moving car with no one driving it.

"No," she told him as if he'd spoken aloud. "You can be seen normally now."

"You can read my mind, too?" he asked her with a quick glance.

"Some—surface stuff. Go."

He pulled out, went straight east on Forty-fourth. Normally he would have turned off, but he couldn't think at all, just kept going in a straight line.

"Where are you headed?" she asked.

"I dunno," he said in a monotone. "I don't care."

She sighed. "All right. Alejandro's. You remember how to get there?"

"I remember."

"Good. Go there."

He had to park several blocks away, and in the end, he left

the VW with a tire on the curb and the rear end sticking out. He didn't even think about a ticket. When he got out of the car, he started walking, zombielike, in the wrong direction; Nikki had to catch up with him and turn him around, steer him toward the restaurant.

"What are you?" he asked, when he'd recovered enough of his shocked senses to frame a question.

"Later," she said. "Just hang on, okay? Don't fall apart on me."

"Why not?" he giggled. "You could put me back together, I'm sure. Couldn't you?"

She glared at him, towed him along faster. He thought people were laughing at him as they watched the woman tug him down the street like a mother would pull her two-year-old. Little did they know, he thought. He looked at the hand holding his and shuddered, felt an urge to scream. But Nikki glared again, and he stifled it. After what seemed like forty blocks, they arrived at Alejandro's, went inside.

Juan met them at the door, looked from one to the other. "What is it?" he asked.

"He's seen some things," Nikki explained. "It was necessary. Let's just say something fucked up, all right? I made a mistake. We need to get him downstairs. Now."

"Si, si," Juan said. He motioned for someone to take his place at the door, guided Elliot toward the saloon doors. It was more brightly lighted now, and he could see the decor; plumed serpents, pyramids, black mirrors that smoked. Not even on his most intense acid trip had he felt so close to having his psyche just shatter. Juan seated him alongside the stage, Nikki following them a few paces back. He stared around wildly, then down at his hands on the table. They were shaking violently.

Someone brought him a drink, put it down in front of him. "Senor Collins," Juan said gently, "drink. Try to relax a little."

Elliot raised his head with a violent jerk and stared at the Indian. "Do you know what she is?" he asked, his voice rising. "What she does?"

"Si. I know. Nikki is very special to us."

"Oh, she's special all right! You sure as fuck are right about that, by God! Oh, shit, I cannot believe this, cannot—" He put his head down on the table and covered it with his hands for a moment. Then he popped back up. "Hallucination!" he said brightly, an idiotic grin on his face. "That's what it was! I've had others, recently! One of them involved you, Juan! But I think I'm much better now—" Still grinning, he threw the drink down his throat.

Nikki sat down across from him, looked at him rather sadly.

"What the hell happened?" Juan asked her.

"I showed him a transformation," she said, as calmly as if she'd been talking about the weather. "Pushed him too far. He didn't handle it very well."

"You couldn't have thought he was ready!"

"Nooo," she said, resting her chin on her hands. "I blew it, what can I say? His friend Laura—that guy that's been doing all the killing, he got her. Elliot thought it was that maniac Nigel Adams. And he was so heartbroken, so filled with a righteous vengeful anger—I just, well, he got to me, okay? I told you I really liked him!"

"Nikki, what did you do?" Juan said softly, rolling his eyes.

She looked embarrassed. "I thought, well, the world would be better off without Nigel anyhow. So I was going to give Elliot a taste of blood, let him be the Warrior he was born to be. I touched Nigel, drew him out, and just like I expected, Elliot went right after him. And wouldn't you know it—Nigel came up with a damn gun! Well, it spoiled the whole thing. Then, I made it worse. I got so mad I transformed, killed Nigel myself."

"You didn't know Nigel had a gun?" Juan asked. He sounded incredulous.

She wouldn't meet his eyes. "I was concentrating on Elliot," she said. "I felt so close to him—"

"In all the years I've known you, Nikki, I've never known you to lose control like this—"

To Elliot's utter amazement, she started to cry, big tears rolling down her cheeks. "I know," she sobbed. "Now everything is in such a mess. I guess I fell in love with him—"

"You fell in love with his great-grandfather, too," Juan snapped. "Or so I was told. And you didn't mess that one up!"

"I don't understand—" Elliot managed to say. He was

feeling like he was in a fog, perhaps watching some hazy movie that didn't make any sense. "My great-grandfather?"

They looked at him. "Yes, Elliot," Nikki said. "And his father before him. And his son, and his son's son. Your father. I knew them all."

"The photos—" he murmured.

"Yes. You were right in the first place. Both pictures are of me."

"Not possible. You'd be over sixty—"

"She's well over sixty," Juan put it. "Her father was one of the original Conquistadors of New Spain—Mexico. She was born around 1510!"

"But—but—"

"Is that any harder to believe than her transformation?" Juan demanded.

"That was a hallucination—"

"No, it wasn't! She is the *nagual*. She has achieved a full union with her spirit serpent, they are one! She can go back and forth as she wishes—"

"Impossible."

Juan's face softened; Nikki just continued to cry, her head down, shoulders shaking. "There are many things you'd consider impossible," Juan told him. "Many things you haven't experienced. You thought your journey to the Four Directions was hallucination. It wasn't. The Black Jaguar of the North claimed you for his own, tested you, found you worthy. He gave you a gift."

"No—"

"Yes. You know who the jaguar is, as well. Don't you, Elliot? What is his name?"

"I don't know—"

"His name, Elliot!"

"The Smoking Mirror!"

"The Smoking Mirror," Juan repeated. "Tezcatlipoca. You are his. Your father was his. Every one of your ancestors for nine generations back has belonged to him. You were promised to him before you were born."

"I can't believe—"

"You know it's true. You are his. Nikki is only delivering you to him. She is not his, she is of the White Serpent, Quetzalcoatl. I am not his. I am of the Blue Eagle, Tlaloc."

"Delivering—?" He sounded stupid even to himself, once more only able to mouth single-word questions.

"Delivering. She touched you, in Chapel Hill. She brought you here. She was readying you. And you'd be ready if you'd followed your instincts."

"But I have—"

"No. You refused one of the four women, the girl called Laura. She was your Fourth Part of four. Don't you remember the dance? So you've only three parts complete. That's why you're so confused. Why you weren't ready to see what Nikki showed you."

"She's some kind of monster—"

He shook his head firmly. "No. She is a woman, a wise and powerful woman who had become a Nagual. She is in touch with the spirits, Elliot—the spirits that control and sustain this Fifth World. The spirits that will, if all goes well, create the Sixth. She is also priestess to Quetzalcoatl, whom she will sustain. But you, you must sustain the Smoking Mirror. As your father did. As your son will."

"I don't have a son—"

"You will. You have to dedicate him to the Smoking Mirror!"

"I'd never do that. Anyway, if all this is true—if Nikki is some kind of priestess—" He paused, turned to look at her; she had stopped crying, seemed more under control. "Then why are you a hooker?" he asked her.

"I told you before," she said with equanimity, "I have needs most women don't have. I need a source of energy to maintain myself. Otherwise, I'd age and die like anyone else. Human beings release usable energy at only two times— when they have orgasms and when they die. So I take energy from men when they have orgasms. Being a prostitute allows me to take small amounts from many men. Usually, they hardly notice it. It's better than killing people, isn't it?"

Elliot shook his head. "I cannot accept this. I don't believe any of it—"

Juan sighed, reached into his pocket, pulled out a little leather pouch. Nikki glanced up at him, her beautiful eyes red-rimmed; she looked as if she was about to protest. "You have a better idea?" he asked her.

She sagged. "No."

"Now what're you talking about?" Elliot asked them.

"This," Juan said. He poured a brownish powder into his palm, held it over to Elliot as if to show him.

"What is it?" Elliot asked, looking closely; it was nothing he recognized.

"An herb," Juan said. Without warning, the Indian blew on the powder, sending it flying into Elliot's face.

He jerked back, coughing and choking. The stuff was burning his nose and throat. It was like he'd inhaled pure fire. Gasping for air, he fell from his chair onto the floor. Instantly, Nikki was beside him, holding his head. His body jerked in wild, uncontrollable spasms, and he was experiencing unbelievable pain in his head, stomach and chest. He was sure he was dying.

"It'll pass," Nikki said. She was crying again, her tears falling on his face. "Just a moment, it'll pass—"

"Why—?" he managed to say. Then his world went dark.

37

He found himself lying on something hard, and somewhere, music was playing; a flute, guitar, drums. His eyes still closed, he seemed to be able to see Laura's gentle face in front of him, her lips cupped over the mouthpiece of the flute. With effort, he tried to lift a hand to reach for her, but she was ethereal as smoke, and the hand was black and yellow.

His eyes opened. Yellow lighting, and he was on a stage. For a few seconds, he couldn't figure out where he might be, just that he was on a stage in some otherwise utterly dark room. Then, piece by piece, it started to come back—he was lying in the center of the stage at the Obsidian Butterfly. Nikki and Juan—for some unknown reason, Juan had blown some kind of terrible poison into his face. But now, he felt good; indeed, he seemed to feel better than he had in a long time. He decided to sit up, and just as he'd made the decision, he was sitting. Looking out at the unseen audience. But then, they weren't unseen anymore; his eyes adjusted, and he could see Nikki sitting just offstage, dressed in her red robes, looking at him.

"How do you feel?" she asked. Her voice was full of concern.

"Good, fine," he told her truthfully.

"Who are you?"

"Uh—I'm not sure—"

"Feel. Don't think. Who are you?"

He paused, trying to do what she said. "The Smoking Mirror," he said. "No, that isn't quite right. I am of the Smoking Mirror. Part. I—I—" he stopped, tried to concentrate.

"No," Nikki told him. "Feel. From your belly. Feel it, tell me. Who are you now?"

He tried to do as she asked. "I am a Jaguar Warrior," he said at length, choosing his words carefully. "My brother is the Smoking Mirror. I stand in his place—"

She nodded, smiled, and he felt immensely good. The lights came up in the room a bit, and he could see Juan, Carlotta, strangely dressed. Both of them were clad only in little skirtlike things. Another figure, a woman, moved from the shadows, and he recognized her as well.

"Eileen?" he said. "What are you doing here?"

"I've been here, Elliot," she informed him, "all along. I'm here for you now, if you need me. My sister and I."

Behind Eileen, Marcia moved into the light. "You need a fourth, Elliot," she said. "Me, if you like."

"Or me," Carlotta put in.

"Or me," came yet another voice. He looked, saw the young Indian girl he'd seen resurrected in the street. Somehow, he was not terribly surprised.

He got up, walked to the edge of the platform and sat on it. His eyes wandered from one of the women to the other; all were dressed as Carlotta was, all of them more than attractive.

"What about Dave Jennings?" he asked Marcia. "Was he involved?"

"He's fine. He's in San Francisco and he knows nothing of all this," she told him.

"He didn't call me?"

"No. Your own mind created the voice, the reason to come to the city."

"Oh. I see. I guess."

"We had to get you here," Nikki told him. "Had to keep you coming back to Cabrini until we could meet. You wouldn't have come just because we asked you to!"

"I suppose not." It seemed to him his mind was extraordinarily clear, in a way it had never been before. "What do you want from me?" he asked them.

"We don't want anything," Nikki said. "Your brother does. We're only helping him."

"Yes, of course. My brother."

"You know what he wants?"

"I know. You want me to give it to him, Nikki?"

She bit her lip. "No!" she gasped, earning a stare from the others. "But I have to ask you to. Too much is at stake. It has to be."

"But you can't force me."

"No. All I can do is ask, beg. As I said, it has to be."

"But I have no sons—and I won't have any if—"

"Nikki worked that out a long time ago," Juan said. "A marvelous discovery. She has ways. Your father did this, before you were conceived, and his father before he was conceived."

"I think I see. They both died at age fifty-two."

"One complete cycle—a grand round. Yes."

"Of 'heart failure.' "

"Yes."

"And so will I."

"Yes. But it isn't without compensation, Elliot. You will have certain—tools—you didn't have before. So you'll have twenty-six more years pretty much guaranteed. How many men can say that?"

"I might have fifty."

"You might have one. Or you might have fifty—years in a hollow, wasted life. The life of a man who didn't fulfill his destiny."

He turned back to Nikki. "You want me to condemn my unborn son to this as well."

She shook her head. "Condemn isn't the right word. Though I understand. Your ancestors all had the same misgivings. If ever the Teotl permit me to have children, even I might feel the same. But that's a response from the *tonal*. Not from where you are now."

He sighed. Somehow, he knew she was right, Juan was right, they were all right. What had to be had to be, and as she'd said, there were compensations. Thanks to Nikki's consummate skill, to her caring nature; she hadn't had to create these methods. "All right," he said. "Do I sign in blood, or what?"

Nikki started to cry again. "Not even ready, but you came through," she said. "Nothing else is necessary. It is done. I love you, Elliot!"

"You should take a fourth," Juan told him. "Carlotta, Marcia, or Bi 'Ci."

He assumed Bi 'Ci was the resurrected girl. But he shook his head. "No," he told them. "Leave it as it is. I wasn't smart enough to accept Laura when she was alive. It wouldn't be right to take a substitute now, for my own convenience."

"It's more than convenience," Nikki told him, her brow furrowed. "When you return to the *tonal*, you'll be distressed. If you're incomplete, it'll be much worse—"

"It'll have to be," he said, closing the subject. "For Laura's sake."

"As you say," Nikki agreed. Her eyes were glowing, and it made him feel immensely good to have her approval. But then she frowned again, and he experienced a brief anxiety. "I have to tell you," she continued, "there's something just a little different about this time. I can't tell exactly what, but something—"

"Something different compared to what?" he asked reasonably.

"Compared to your father—to his father, and on back. You were tested, Elliot. No one else was ever tested. Power does not make mistakes in these things, and there isn't any wasted effort, either. So there's something—something more than what's happening here. I can't tell you what. Like I said, I don't know. But you were tested for a reason, Elliot. Sooner or later, that reason will be clear."

"So? What am I supposed to do about it?"

She shrugged. "I don't know. Just be aware, I guess. Remember your lessons!"

"I doubt if I'll be forgetting any of this!"

She smiled. "You might be surprised. But I just thought you should know. No matter what you forget, you'll know inside."

There was a short pause. "Well," he said finally, looking directly into her eyes, "right now, I suppose we have to consider my brother's immediate needs."

"Yes, that is what should concern us now."

"So when should we do it?"

"Actually, that's up to you. The proper time is the first day of the month of Toxcatl—April 23rd by our calendar. But it doesn't matter a lot. Whenever you want to, it just has to be before your next birthday."

He thought about this. Anticipation, he told himself, would not be good. "Why not tonight?" he asked.

Again her eyes were glowing. "It's fine, Elliot. As I said—it's your choice. Right now, if you want."

"Now is as good as anytime," he said firmly. Standing up, he stripped off his clothing and walked toward a low table set up on the stage. Someone handed him a guitar; he smashed it against the floor, dropped the broken neck. When he'd stretched himself out on the table, they gathered around him, Nikki holding his head. At his side, he could see Juan holding the object Elliot knew he would have.

"I love you, Nikki," he said. And the ceremony began.

38

Moving down the sidewalk toward his car, Elliot felt like he was sleepwalking. There were other people on the sidewalks, cars rushing by in the streets, but he was hardly aware of any of them. It really wasn't that he was distracted, either; his mind had simply more or less shut down, unable to deal with the day's experiences. Passing a police station, he briefly considered going in and telling them about Nigel's death, but he decided against it. What was he going to say? My girlfriend changed into a rattlesnake and bit him? Oh, well, sure, officer;

she was standing there watching at the same time, but the snake was her as well—see, she'd doubled, she's what they call a Nagual. He was quite sure he'd be shown what they call a booby hatch. Besides, they were likely to ask him about the rest of the day, and he had no idea what had happened during the remainder of it. A little part of him clung to rationality, trying to convince himself that what he'd seen down on Forty-fourth was just another hallucination, but he couldn't accept it anymore. There had just been too much. Now he knew; the beautiful hooker he'd fallen in love with was a monster worthy of his most terrible nightmares. The only question that remained for him was how he'd gotten into the middle of it. But that, he told himself, was reversible; he was going to get out. Going to leave, going to go back to Chapel Hill, forget all about everything that had happened since he'd first seen Nikki's photo. Put his life back together.

But he knew it'd never be the same; he no longer could rely on anything being real, anything being impossible.

With a start, he realized that he'd long ago reached his car; he was standing there with his hand on the door, reviewing his experiences. Several people in the street had in fact stopped to stare at him, he was behaving so oddly.

Finally, he opened the door and crawled inside the little car; the VW seemed, at that moment, like such a friend to him, something firmly connected with the reality he'd once believed was the only one. He put the key in the ignition, turned it; the four-cylinder engine spun, chugged as if it was going to start, but didn't. He stared at the key dumbly; he had never been mechanically inclined, and he had a few ideas about how to go about starting the car if it resisted. Moreover, it was not something he particularly wanted to deal with right now. He pumped the accelerator once, turned the key again, listened to it grind. Annoyed, he stared down at the key; it was as if he could see the little rear-mounted engine superimposed on the switch, as if it had been projected there. Not really thinking about it at all, he looked inside the engine, saw the sparks flying between the points of the spark plugs, and also saw that little gas was getting into each cylinder. He traced it up, past the valves, the manifold, up to the carburetor. Inside it, he could see that only a little of the amber fluid was in the bowl, though the floats were down.

Then he saw the tiny needle valve, stuck in its seat.

Smiling faintly, he tugged on it with his mind, watched it fall, watched the gas surge in behind it. Satisfied, he turned the key again, started the engine, and drove away. As he maneuvered the VW through New York's evening traffic, he gave no thought at all to what he had just done.

Luckily, he found a parking place close to Gerald's apartment, swung the car into it, and shut it off. As he walked up the stairs, he was telling himself that there was nothing he could—or should—do about Nikki. He still didn't consider the police a viable alternative—any policeman who tried to arrest Nikki would, he was sure, get a rude and possibly fatal surprise—but perhaps he himself should take some kind of action. Someone had to stop her, someone who understood her terrible capabilities. But he was unable to decide on any course of action, and in the end he just gave it up. Go, he told himself. Just leave the city, get away from all this madness.

Using the key, he let himself into the apartment, but as soon as he opened the door, he could almost sense the presence of another person there. Almost immediately, a backlighted figure stepped out of the kitchen; it took Elliot a moment to figure out who he was.

"Elliot," Conrad Weiser said. "Nice to see you again, Professor!"

"Hello, Conrad," he said tiredly. "And good-bye. I'm leaving. Is Gerald around? Or Haze?"

"No, 'fraid not. You know they flushed all their dope when the cops came to talk about Laura. I think both of them are out trying to scrounge up some more. I've noticed that they can't seem to do without it very long."

"Well," he said, pulling his suitcase out and opening it. "You tell them adios for me, all right? I have to get going."

Weiser plopped down in the chair, gave Elliot a sickly grin. "Back to Chapel Hill?" he asked. "So soon?"

"I shouldn't have come," Elliot told him. He had no intention of elaborating; he was just talking to fill the silence.

"I thought—well, Gerald said—you had a girlfriend up-town," he said. "I thought you were having a blast with her. What was her name, again?"

"Nikki," Elliot said, still paying little attention to the conversation. "Nikki Howard," he finished. "And that is a thing of the past."

"Oh?" Weiser said; it sounded like he was genuinely concerned. "What happened?"

Elliot glanced up at the moonlike babyface. The truth was impossible. "Turned out she makes her living as a hooker," he said. "After what happened to Laura, I just couldn't accept that. That's all there is to it."

"She was a hooker and you didn't know?" Weiser exclaimed. Now he sounded horrified.

Elliot didn't look at him. "Yeah, that's right," he lied.

"Man, what a bummer," the boy commented. "And after poor Laura getting offed like that. Bummer." He tapped on an ashtray with the big silver ring he always wore, making a loud clicking noise. Otherwise, the only sounds in the room were those of Elliot's packing.

Weiser leaned over the side of the chair and watched Elliot stuff his clothes into the case. "I was really worried about you after Laura. Gerald said you were just a wreck! I know how close you'd gotten to that little bitch, too!"

Elliot stopped, a little surprised by the boy's remark, looked up. He was a little startled; Weiser didn't look any different, but Elliot saw him differently. Colder and more intelligent than he appeared. But regardless, he wasn't going to put up with statements like that. "Don't call her that, not in my presence," he said threateningly. "Just don't."

"All right, all right! Jesus, don't go getting violent on me!" he said, throwing up his hands in mock horror, though he was still grinning. "I was just thinking how rough it must have been for you. Having to sit around and think about that guitar string around her neck, about that glass knife in her belly—"

"*Goddamn it!!*" Elliot screamed, jumping up. He grabbed the boy's shirt, yanked him out of the chair, pulled his face close. "Another word," he said quietly, "and I will personally crush your fucking jawbone!"

Weiser opened his mouth, seemed to think better of it, and closed it again. When Elliot released him, he slunk off to the kitchen, said no more. Elliot continued packing.

After he had finally finished, he glanced down at his watch; it was after ten already, getting late in the evening of what had turned into a very long, emotionally draining day. Reflecting on it, he simply could not believe how much had been packed into it; to him, it seemed like months since he had seen Nikki at her grotesque bloodletting, but that had been only last night; like weeks since he'd learned of Laura's death, and she hadn't yet been dead twenty-four hours. So much for one day, so very much. He stared at the suitcase, feeling like it was utter insanity for him to start out driving for North Carolina now; he could barely get out of the city, he figured, before he'd be forced to pull over somewhere, get some sleep. The logical thing to do was to sleep here tonight, start out first thing in the morning. Yet, though he was dog-tired, he wasn't at all sleepy, didn't feel as if he could sleep, not for some time. Too many things running around in his head, and he feared his dreams. It would be better, he told himself, to wait until he was so tired he would pretty much collapse, pass immediately into a deep, dreamless sleep.

Glancing up, he saw Weiser's shadow as he moved about the kitchen, and he sighed; he certainly didn't have pleasant company. He wished Gerald or Haze was there, but they weren't, and he had no idea when they might be back. It only left one choice, really; go back out. Perhaps find some little bar and have a beer or two, perhaps get smashed. Anywhere would do, he thought, except for the Obsidian Butterfly. That place he had no intention of even getting close to, ever again.

A flicker of lights from the kitchen caught his attention once more, and he wondered what Weiser might be doing in there, why he kept moving around. Not that it mattered much; just something to occupy his mind. He was still watching the shadows play when he had the most peculiar sensation. It was as if he were suddenly not being watched; as if someone or something had been observing him for so long it had become a part of his everyday existence, only noticeable by its absence. A faint flicker of light, like starlight on a dark wall, seemed to move across the ceiling, merge with the orange glow from the kitchen lights, and disappear. He stared; momentarily, he had a conviction that an attention of some sort had been shifted from himself to Weiser.

Then, irritated, he dismissed it as an illusion, went back to thinking about his plans to go out somewhere.

39

The man with the silver ring looked up at the cracked ceiling and allowed a broad grin to cover his face. His eyes dropped shut; he was feeling the light of the Lord God, he was certain of it! Telling him what to do, giving him specific instructions, pointing out the next soul to be delivered! Never had God spoken to him so directly. He could hear her voice so clearly—he stopped himself, frowned. Not her voice; his voice, of course. Strange idea. He wondered where that one had come from. But he shrugged it off, listened to the Holy Voice. As it was instructing him, he heard the door slam; but he was only vaguely aware of it. Not even knowing how he'd gotten to it, he saw the phone in front of him, picked it up. This one was important, much more important than any of the others. God herself—no, damn it, himself! had pointed this whore out. He'd go get her. And he'd love every second of it.

40

Elliot's body was still operating on automatic, and even as he realized that he'd made a decision to go back out, he found himself on the stairs, heading down to the street. Much more aware of his surroundings, he moved among the crowds of pedestrians, appreciating their unrelenting normality. He even gave a bum who approached him a dollar, so pleased was he with the fact that the bum was an everyday, commonplace beggar. Less than a block down, he found a very normal-looking little bar and went inside; there was a folksinger on a small corner stage, not too many patrons, and he could see virtually all of their ordinary-looking faces. Involuntarily, he nodded to himself, relaxed a little. When he'd walked into the place, he'd told himself that any hint of the abnormal there would send him speedily back to the street. But there was none. Climbing onto a bar stool, he folded his hands in front of him and waited, listening to the not too talented young woman who was singing in a style reminiscent of Joan Baez.

"Yes?" asked a female voice, and he turned his head. The bartender, a plain girl with frizzy hair, was standing in front of him.

"Beer," he said. "Draft."

"You got it," she told him, picking up a mug and sticking it under a tap that was so close she didn't have to take a step. She put it in front of him, and he smiled at her. In spite of her plainness—or perhaps because of it—she looked very good to him. She seemed to take the smile as a possible come-on, and after checking with the other patrons at the bar, came back and leaned against it. " 'Scuse me for sayin' so, but you look like you've had a hell of a night," she told him with a good-natured grin.

No way you could know the half of it, he thought. "I have," he said aloud.

"Been rough around here, last several days," she observed. "Cops hangin' around, all the girls uptight. That killer, you know."

"Not something I want to talk about," he said, almost coldly.

She shook her head. "Me, either. One of the victims was a friend of mine."

He looked at her with new interest. "Who?" he asked.

"Girl named B.J.," she said. "Came in here all the time. Fact is, I saw her the night she—ran out of luck. She hooked, of course. Used to pick up some johns here. Hey, you ain't a cop, are you?"

"No way," he told her. "But one of the victims was a friend of mine, too. The last one, Laura Neill."

"You know, I might have known her, too. Real young, real cute?"

"Yeah. You've probably seen her. She lived close by."

"I wish they'd catch that bastard!" the bartender said vehemently. "I thought about callin' the cops, but I didn't. Not yet, anyway. Kind of against my nature, but this ain't like a drug deal or anything."

"Calling them about what?"

"About the john I saw B.J. with the night she—" The girl did not seem to be able to articulate the word "died." "She was in here with him, sittin' right over there." She pointed to a table in a dark corner, "Last time I ever saw her."

"What did he look like?" he asked, wondering why he was bothering. There was no way he'd know the guy.

"Young kid," she said. "Straight-looking, sort of. Blank face. Wore a big silver ring—I remember noticing that."

That description rung a bell with him, but he didn't consider it possible. He frowned, asked the bartender if she'd seen these people together near the time of the girl's death.

"Real close," she said, nodding. "That's why I thought, hell, maybe I oughta call the police, just this once. It was just before, man. And she left with him, too."

"You ever see him again?"

"Sure. Just today, in fact. Walkin' by, outside. I've seen him a bunch of other times, too. You know, now that I think about it, I might have seen him with that girl, what's her name, the young one? Just a day or two ago—not in here, though. Outside."

"Anything else you can remember about him?"

"Just that a lot of times he wears a light blue sweater with the word 'Carolina' on it."

Elliot froze, staring at the girl, feeling like he'd just swallowed a chunk of ice. Images were flashing into his mind; as if lit by a strobe light, he could see Purple Haze's guitar, the string missing from it; he'd seen, but it hadn't registered. Remembered Haze telling him about the police discussing an "unusual" knife. And, less than an hour ago, the words: "that glass knife in her belly." He himself hadn't known where Laura had been stabbed, just that she had been; but "glass knife" certainly meant something to him. There was one he'd put in his suitcase, one that had disappeared, even though the one it replaced was where it was supposed to be. Everything was falling into place, and this time, the fit was far better than it had been when he'd theorized about Nigel and his crazy church.

Jumping up from the bar stool so fast that the girl sprang backwards, startled, he made for the door. There was something else he remembered; he himself had just told Weiser, not thirty minutes earlier, that Nikki was a hooker. Not only that, he'd given the bastard her full name! The only question was, did the boy know her address? He was sure it was possible; something mentioned in some discussion with Gerald or Haze, a casual word among trusted friends. Weiser might have her phone number as well, and that too would be Elliot's responsibility. He ran out the door and down the street, heedless of the stares he was getting. Reaching the apartment, he took the stairs two at a time, used his key to go in, and calmed himself; he could see movement in the kitchen. Cautiously, he went in there, glancing at the guitar as he went by; it was missing two strings. Two, he told himself, taking a deep breath.

As he stepped into the kitchen, Purple Haze looked up, a joint in his mouth. "Hey, man," he said, "I finally scored! Want some?"

Elliot glanced around, almost ignoring him. "Where's Weiser?" he asked, waving away the offered marijuana.

"Oh, he left a few minutes ago. You just missed him, in fact." He paused, looked foggy. "At least I think so. Maybe it was longer than that."

"Shit!" Elliot muttered under his breath. "You know where he went?"

"I got no idea, man. There was something about some chick, but man, I can't remember nothin' when I got a buzz on, dig?"

Feeling his insides surge when Haze said that, he sat down in front of the man, held the hand holding the joint down on the table. "Now, look," he said calmly but intensely, "it's real important, Haze. Matter of life and death. What can you remember about what he said?"

"Oh, wow, heavy," Haze responded, automatically. "Now,

let me see—when I came in, he was on the phone. I heard him tellin' some chick he'd be there—no, he said up there, yeah, that's it— he'd be up there in a few minutes. I heard him mention your name, come to think of it.''

''My name?''

''Yeah—like, maybe he was tellin' whoever that he was a friend of yours?''

''Haze, did he call the chick by name?''

''Oh, yeah, he did. Nikki, it was.''

''Nikki? You're sure?''

''Yeah, yeah, I'm sure! At the end, he said, 'I'll be up there in a few minutes, Nikki.' That's what he said, all right.''

Elliot did not wait to hear anymore, though Haze was saying something else; he ran back to the other room, snatched up the phone, and dialed Nikki's number. As he feared, he got the recording; he let it play through, left a rather flat message for her to call him, and hung up. Standing with his hand on the receiver, he considered his options. One, call the police; that was a possibility. Two, do nothing. If Weiser was indeed the killer, now going after Nikki, he certainly was likely to run into a surprise, a surprise Elliot felt he would richly deserve. But something else occurred to him. Nigel, by standing and talking to them, had given them plenty of warning about what his intentions were, plenty of time for Nikki to plan and execute her actions. He also remembered that it had taken a rather long time for her to do what she'd done; and he considered the possibility of her being taken by surprise, not able to defend herself until she'd already been injured, or was being strangled; in that case, she might well be as helpless as any person would be.

And suddenly, he was terrified for her. Regardless of what he'd felt about her earlier, the simple fact remained that she was being stalked by a madman, a man who fully intended to kill her, the same madman who'd killed Laura. And he felt he could not allow that to happen. The idea of calling the police forgotten, his rational frame of mind lost, he rushed back into the kitchen.

''Haze,'' he said. ''Gun!''

''Say what?''

''Gun. I need one of your guns! Quick, Haze—matter of life and death!''

"Hey, man, I don't know—"

"Come on, Haze, don't argue. I haven't got time! I'll explain it all later. Right now, I need one of your fucking guns!"

"All right, all right!" he said, dragging himself out of the chair. "They're in here. Come on." In the bedroom, Haze moved with maddening slowness while Elliot fidgeted; after what seemed like forever, he came up with a Smith and Wesson .38, four-inch barrel. "Here ya go," he said. "This'll do, I'm sure."

"Thanks," Elliot said, snatching the gun and starting out the door.

"Hey! You don't want any bullets?"

Turning on his heel, he came back, loaded six cartridges into the weapon, dropped another six into his pocket. He thanked Haze again, tore out of the room and down the stairs, only barely getting the gun concealed in his pocket before he hit the street.

This time the VW gave him no difficulties; he roared out from the curb, and a van screeched brakes to prevent a collision. But Elliot could not hear the driver's curses; his mind was filled with images of what might already be happening in Nikki's apartment. His fervent hope was that they were still there, that they hadn't gone somewhere else, somewhere he might not be able to find them.

The traffic in New York was not light, and he had to endure several frustrating stops and tie-ups; pounding on the wheel, he savagely cursed any driver ahead who did not move as rapidly as possible. But he realized that, all things considered, he was in fact making fairly good time; it just didn't seem that way.

As he passed through midtown, he found he was having some trouble paying attention to his driving; several times he shook his head, trying to clear his mind, rid himself of what seemed to be distracting mental noise. But it wouldn't go away, and he realized that his concentration was being broken by a peculiar rasping buzz in his ears, a most unpleasant, but almost subliminal, sound. It was enough, however, to prevent him from clearing his mind in the way he knew he should. At the next traffic light, he allowed himself a moment to focus on it.

At first, the odd sounds were just that—sounds. Like rolling surf, maybe; like the sound on an FM radio between stations. White noise, he realized suddenly; he'd used it before in lab experiments, to mask any audio stimulus from subjects. But why, he asked himself, was he hearing it now? Even as he asked the question, though, the sound began to resolve itself into a voice. A soothing, female voice.

"Don't worry about her," it was saying. "Don't. She can take care of the situation. Remember how easily she handled the Chingon? She'll be all right. Go back, Elliot; don't trouble yourself. Don't worry about her."

That, he had to admit, made sense. It was Conrad that was in danger; there really couldn't be a doubt about that. Nigel had been armed with a gun, and she'd killed him so easily. How could he have imagined that a maniac with a fetish for strangling might even possibly cause her a problem? It was just utterly unreasonable.

Horns started blasting behind him, and he glanced up; the light had turned green. Hesitantly now, he drove on northward, unsure of what he should do. It couldn't hurt, he told himself, to go on up there. At last he could be sure that Laura's killer had paid for his crime; at least he could see it happen. He found that he truly relished the idea of watching Weiser die a drawn-out, painful death, and he was startled at his own savagery. No longer could he think of himself as pacifistic, as gentle; when it came to vengeance, he was downright bloodthirsty, and there was just no way to deny it.

"No!" came the female voice again, so clear and strong now that he jumped, nearly losing control of the car. "Go back, Elliot. You aren't needed there. You'll put yourself in danger! Go back—forget about the *ahuianime!*" The last word he knew he'd never heard, but he also knew, somehow, that it meant "prostitute."

"That's right," he said aloud, just as if he were talking to some other person who was riding with him. "I'm not needed there, I should just go back—" Vaguely, he started looking for a way to turn around, but his eyelids and hands felt heavy, and he couldn't see or think clearly.

The voice now began a droning chant, incessantly telling

him to turn back; he wanted to, but he couldn't even figure out how to do it. In a rapidly thickening mental fog, he drove on toward Cabrini, the voice getting louder and harsher as he went. Dimly, he realized he probably wasn't going to make it; he was not able to drive, and soon he was going to wreck the car. The voice was pounding at both his ears, usurping his whole world, ripping his mind apart.

Then, abruptly, it was gone—from his left ear. Still it screeched in the right, but for an instant there was a wonderful silence on his left side that seemed velvety by comparison. It was broken by a male voice, authoritative and deep, a voice he'd heard before.

"You are a warrior!" it said firmly. "Always, every minute! Whether the enemy stand before you with a sword or enters your dreams, you are my Jaguar Warrior!"

"Yes, my brother," he mumbled, seeing a fleeting image of yellow and black fur. "I am a warrior—always—Jaguar Warrior—" But as the female voice returned to his left ear, he knew he'd already lost this battle. It was too late, he was too far gone already.

He saw a city bus stopping in front of him, and he lifted his foot sluggishly, aiming for the brake pedal. He got to it, but his shoe slipped off the side, and the VW banged into the rear of the bus. He wasn't going fast, and it was a minor collision; but his head flew forward and cracked hard against the windshield. The voice was instantly gone, pain filling his head in its place.

As his body rebounded into the seat and the initial violence of the pain diminished, he experienced a remarkable clarity of thought, but it had been the pain, not the blow, that had effectively knocked the voice—and its effects—from his mind. Reacting swiftly, he threw the little car in reverse and whipped around the bus, leaving its driver staring after him in consternation. But now, though the female voice tried to come back, he was having no trouble fighting it off.

Pain, he thought; sometimes a warrior had to inflict an injury on himself.

He thought about Nikki and her bloodletting ritual in front of the statue of Quetzalcoatl, and believed perhaps he understood a little better. But he had no time to think about that now; weaving in and out of traffic, sometimes reaching sixty miles an hour, he raced toward her apartment. His mind, his intent, was clear and focused; the distracting voice faded and was gone.

When he finally arrived in front of Nikki's building, he double-parked the VW, jumped out and ran to the door. Out of breath, he stood there for just a moment before realizing the problem he had, something he'd forgotten about—the outside latch. If she was occupied, she would have, as he knew, turned the intercom off, and she wouldn't hear it. Even if she did, she might not be able to buzz him in. Fists clenched, he stared at the button, not even trying it. Almost crying in frustration, he backed off from the building, looking up, but then remembered that her apartment faced the back side—the back side, where the fire escapes were! To the right of the building he saw a narrow alley, and he darted down it.

Around back, a narrow strip separated the back of the building from a wooded hillside that fell away below it. Once on this strip, he could see that he might be frustrated again. Each of the escapes terminated in a movable ladder, and, obviously, all the ladders were up. So that burglars, dangerous people, could not use them to break in, he told himself cynically.

He could see Nikki's apartment window, see the low light inside, but the ladder was far out of his reach. In a rage, he cursed it, willed that this not be so, and was only a little surprised when the catch holding it up moved just a little. Squeaking on rusted rails, the ladder fell straight down, banging on the ground; and in a moment, he was on it, headed up.

He was just coming off the ladder onto the first landing when he noticed that the lights from the George Washington Bridge, so obviously visible from this vantage point, seemed to flick off and on, as if something large had passed in front of them. He looked; the lighted parabolas of the suspensions were steady, there was nothing unusual there. He shrugged, started to resume his ascent; but he stopped cold when something heavy crashed onto the landing above him.

Glancing up, he saw that the heavy steel of the fire escape was bowed in by the weight of whatever was up there. He could see movement but could not make out a shape; then a headlike form looked back down the stairway directly at him.

Despite his previous experiences, he could hardly countenance what he was seeing. The other creatures had been animal-like or humanlike; this thing would have been shocking in his worst nightmare. Glaring down the short flight of stairs at him, it caused him again to doubt his sanity.

Its soft-looking, lumpy head was split vertically, the jaws opening and closing slowly, as if it were breathing. The teeth inside—if they could be called that—looked like pieces of broken glass and flint, varicolored and randomly placed. A thick slime, bright blue in color and phosphorescent, dripped steadily from them, piling up on the stair and beginning to flow with the slowness of a glacier. On each side of the head were fleshy tubes, more on one side than the other; these were focused on him, and inside them lights like yellow flames flickered. The remainder of the head was covered with pits and pores of indeterminate function.

It moved toward him, slowly but gracefully, drumming its feet on the steel landing. Its movements were almost like some kind of dance, the body swaying lightly as it came; there was no questioning its agility. As its legs and the remainder of its body came into sight, he could see that the body itself appeared to be made of stone, perhaps chipped flint, but covered with a sparse, spiky reddish hair. The eight or so spindly, spiderlike legs each terminated in a crablike claw, though the claws also looked like some kind of rock. Long thin wings like slender obsidian blades covered its back. Overall, it looked as if it had been assembled from spare parts, but as it took another step down the stair, Elliot noticed that it was bending the metal up with its claws as it gripped them.

After just a moment's paralysis, Elliot's hand flew to the .38 in his pocket, but as soon as he caught hold of the handle, a spray of yellowish fluid from one of the pores on the thing's head splashed against his arm and trousers. The stuff dried rapidly, forming a kind of glue; he found he was unable to pull his hand out.

"You cannot use your gun, Jaguar Warrior," it said in a soft voice, a voice that seemed to echo around inside it several times before coming out. "I think you'd better leave this place. Leave while you still can!"

He stared at it; a fat pink tongue moved around inside the mouth when it spoke. "What are you?" he asked, not knowing quite what else to do. He couldn't leave if he wanted to; there was no way to climb the ladder one-handed.

"I am Tzitzimeme," it informed him. "Does it make you feel better to know?" It emitted a hacking laugh. "I am not like the puny creatures Tezcatlipoca tested you with, warrior. You have no chance against me!" As if to emphasize this, it grasped one of the steps with a claw and tore it free from the stairway, ripping the metal as if it were paper.

Elliot was close to panic; he felt there was nothing whatever he could do. His hand was stuck in his pocket, he couldn't fight, couldn't run. All he could do, he told himself, was die. But even as he thought this, he remembered Nikki telling him something—telling him to "think from his belly," to act from there. Desperate, he tried that, focusing on a spot immediately behind his navel. After a second or two, he felt an almost orgasmic rush, as if something was moving from his genitals and head simultaneously, centering on that spot. In fact, there were seven rushes; five more between his head and groin. As they converged, he saw the monstrosity tip its head sideways and stop advancing.

"Run, warrior!" it snarled at him. "Save what is left of your miserable life! The Nagual is dead already. My mistress has so ordained it! For this she has released me from the spells of the witch Tlazolteotl—"

"Your mistress?" he managed to ask, though he didn't really care about the answer. He just wanted the time to focus his strength on tearing the gun free—

"My mistress Tzitzimitl, Tzitzimitl the long-dead! Murdered Tzitzimitl, who returns in dreams to take her vengeance on the Plumed Serpent and the Smoking Mirror! Tzitzimitl who shall bring peace to this miserable world!"

Elliot was only half hearing the words; he was concentrating on allowing the energy he had collected in his abdomen to flow to his right hand. When it felt strong enough, he jerked with everything he had; the hand snapped free, but the gun remained glued to the fabric of his pants. He decided against trying to get it—likely the muzzle was plugged, and it'd be useless anyway. Knocking the remainder of the cement off his fingers, he turned his attention back to the horror he was confronting.

"You cannot win, warrior!" it cried, its voice rising in pitch. "You cannot defeat me. Run, save yourself!"

"If you're so sure of that," he said coldly, "why don't you just kill me? Why do you keep talking?" He felt his mind sliding sideways, moving into some different place, a place in which he was not Elliot Collins, psychologist. He was indeed a Jaguar Warrior, he had the strength, the agility, the fighting prowess and cunning of the big spotted cats. And he was afraid of nothing, not even this thing. Exhilaration burst over him like a sunrise; he felt strong, he felt capable, he was ready for this fight, ready to kill this thing or anything else that stood in his way!

The creature backed up a step, tore some more metal free from the fire escape. "You cannot!" it shrieked. "You cannot win!"

"I disagree," he said calmly and lunged at it with only his bare hands. Peculiar, he thought as he moved up the steps—peculiar how his hands seemed so large, seemed to have obsidian claws—

The horror emitted a high-pitched squeal as he struck at it; a shower of sparks flew from the contact, raining down on the alley below. The misshapen head darted at him, teeth clacking, but he avoided it easily, springing up onto the rail and coming around behind it. He ripped at the wings, tearing one of them free; and now he had a weapon. The wing was like a sword, balanced in his hand like one. Jumping down beside the thing, he lifted it over his head, prepared to strike at the soft-looking neck.

"No!" it howled, turning to stare at him; he thought he could see fear in the burning eyes. "No, you cannot save her. She killed you, don't you see—"

"Doesn't matter," he said, and he brought the blade down. It slid through the slimy neck with almost no resistance at all.

As the body sprawled on the steps, the head bounced on down, making a wet, sloppy sound each time it hit. As he watched it go over the edge, he saw it become less material; he could see the trees through it. The blade in his hand, too, was becoming intangible, and after just a few seconds, the only evidence that remained of the thing's presence was the bent and twisted metal of the fire escape. Pulling the .38 from his pocket, he saw that the yellowish glue had disappeared also. But he had no time to dwell on this; the thing had cost him precious time, and for all he knew, Nikki was already dead. He spun around, ran up the steps; his mind was in transition, returning to normal from the odd state it had been in during the battle.

On the stairs again, he took them two at a time, moving as fast as he could. As his thoughts returned to normal, it occurred to him to wonder if his heart would take the stress. After all, he reminded himself, he couldn't do Nikki any good if he had a heart attack. And both his father and grandfather had died of sudden heart attacks—

At exactly age fifty-two—

Standing on the third landing, one floor below Nikki's apartment, he stopped, his head spinning. Suggested by what the Tzitzimeme had said, it all came rushing back; all the events that took place at the Obsidian Butterfly after he'd seen Nikki kill Nigel. And he was no longer in the strange state of mind where it seemed that these things didn't matter much. He could see events for what they were. Juan, Nikki, Eileen, Marcia—they had murdered him!

Desperately, he tried to reject it; they couldn't have torn out his heart; he was standing here, he could feel it beating in his chest! Yet he knew it was true. Just as they'd murdered his father and grandfather; the fact that the victim didn't die for twenty-six years made it no less a murder. And the memory was now vivid. The incredible pain of the knife biting into his chest, Juan cramming his hand into the hole, his still-beating heart held aloft. Offered to Tezcatlipoca, the Smoking Mirror: human sacrifice. And he had been so under Nikki's spell that he hadn't even resisted, he'd just lain there and let them do it.

He didn't know what else had happened, but he did know Nikki had repaired him somehow, allowed him to go on living, for her own purposes, so that he could sire a son who, twenty-six years from now, would provide the next feeding for the Smoking Mirror! His rage flared. She forced him to dedicate his own son, not even yet conceived! As he'd been dedicated, as his father had!

His mind reeled, but he knew it was true. And it changed his plans. He had a unique opportunity to protect his son-to-be from her, rid the world of the menace of her, avenge his own murder and who knew how many others—simply by waiting. Waiting until Weiser had done what he came to do. Then he could go in, avenge Laura. And if, by chance, Nikki defeated Weiser—then Elliot would have to kill her himself.

When he reached the landing in front of Nikki's window, he took the pistol out of his pocket once more, prepared to break the glass with it if necessary. But he was able to concentrate on the latch, cause it to move, allow the window to swing open perhaps a quarter of an inch. That done, he watched the drama unfolding inside.

He was not too late; he had arrived with time to spare. Weiser was just getting undressed, though Nikki already was. He watched as the boy put his hands on her shoulders, as they went to their knees.

"I'm glad you came back, Elliot," Nikki murmured, startling him. But when he examined her face more closely, he saw that she was not looking at the window, she was looking at Weiser!

"You're crazy, lady," Weiser said with a grin. She didn't seem to hear him at all; she just smiled and caressed his cheeks, his neck.

Elliot did not understand what was happening here. As he had done with the latch, he let his mind extend, let it go toward the woman, felt it touch her. His vision doubled, he was seeing the scene twice as his eyes involuntarily crossed, but then he was seeing through Nikki's eyes, seeing from her viewpoint! And from the , he was not seeing Weiser; he was seeing himself undressing in front of her.

He could feel her emotions as well, feel her affection for him, feel her arousal, feel her regrets at having done what she knew was necessary with him. Somewhere above her, he sensed a little light, like a distant star. Exactly, he told himself, like the one he'd seen move from himself to Weiser back at Gerald's apartment, except that it was perhaps a little fainter. He focused on it now, drew his perception close to it. The light resolved to a form, a deformed human skeleton. He knew, then. Knew the light was a projection of Tzitzimitl, knew what she was doing, knew how she was using Nikki's love for him to keep her guard down until it was too late for her. But he could always see that the projection of the dead crone was weak; it had taken a lot for her to free one of her monsters from Tlazolteotl's spell, the spell cast three thousand years ago that held these celestial demons in check.

Just as well, he told himself bitterly as he withdrew into his own body; otherwise, the maniac would have no real chance with Nikki. He didn't think he would either, not even in his warrior persona. But this would stop her, this would avenge him. He continued to watch, but his eyes became moist; he could not prevent a little part of his mind from calling out to hers, telling her that it was not Elliot Collins who stood before her.

Her body stiffened just a trifle, her eyes went just a little wider; for a moment he thought she might have heard his mental warning, pianissimo though it was. But she apparently hadn't, since she immediately returned her attention to the boy, acting as if she found him very attractive, as if he were Elliot.

Then they were on the floor in front of the stereo, where Elliot had been so many times. But Weiser did not enter her; instead, he produced an elaborate glove with a loop of guitar string hanging from it. In a flash, the guitar string was around her slender neck. There was a lump in Elliot's throat, and part of his mind screamed at him to do something, to stop it. He might have considered it, but their facial expressions stopped him. Nikki was calm, perhaps smiling a little; Weiser looked bewildered. The end of the string was still wrapped around the glove, he was jerking hard on it; but Nikki just looked back at him, unconcerned. Her face was not red, her breathing not labored. It seemed to Elliot that there was a tiny space, maybe a quarter of an inch, between the string and her neck, all the way around. It was not really touching her.

"What the fuck?" Weiser muttered, yanking on the string again.

"Having a problem?" Nikki asked, her voice level.

"Goddamn it! There's more than one way!" So saying, he lifted his hips as if to pull away from her, but they only rose perhaps an inch or two and stopped. His head dipped, he stared down between them. Somehow, his penis had gotten inside her. "Fucking bitch!" he yelled. "Let go of me!"

"No," she said quietly. "You're mine, now. All of you."

Straining himself, he pushed up, lunged backwards, but he could not seem to pull out of her. Twisting his upper body to one side, his hands found his clothes, piled on the floor nearby. He fumbled with them for a moment, then pulled out Elliot's obsidian-bladed knife. With no hesitation, he slashed at her with it, and Elliot gasped, thinking this was it. But there was no mark on her body. Weiser stabbed the blade downward, aiming it directly at her chest, but as it came close, it veered to one side, swept harmlessly away. Nikki's smile broadened as he tried again and again, with no luck at all. "Now," she told him, raising her head a little, "it's my turn!"

Instantly, the confused expression on the boy's face turned to one of shock, followed quickly by agony. He shrieked, dropped the knife, and pounded at her with his fists, which could not find their way to her body either. As far as Elliot could see, not a thing was happening to him, but he seemed to be in great pain. Poison perhaps, he told himself. Repeatedly, the boy surged up on his arms, trying to extract his penis from her, but he could not seem to do it. As he did, Elliot noticed something peculiar; each time his body came up, he appeared to be a little thinner.

His eyes were rolling, bulging now, as he tried again and again to get loose, his teeth chewing into his own lip. Beneath him, seemingly impassive, Nikki just watched his contortions; he could not touch her in any way, could not move her body from its supine position. As he twisted sideways, his arms fanning out wildly, Elliot could see that it was definite now; his stomach was collapsing beneath his rib cage, his wrists and ankles growing slimmer. Finally, he managed to grab the leg of the couch with a hand, and with a strength born of desperation, ripped himself loose.

As his body flopped backwards on the floor, Elliot's stomach surged; he controlled it with effort, transfixed by what he was witnessing. The boy's penis was more than erect; it was grotesquely swollen, and at the end was folded open like the petals of a flower. Out of this opening spewed an inch-thick stream of blood, pieces of tissue, and bits of bone. Weiser floundered on the floor, trying to regain his feet, spraying parts of his body around the apartment.

And Nikki reacted. With incredible speed, she lunged at him; Elliot had a brief glimpse of her fingers, which now terminated in massive talons. Her dark eyes again had vertical pupils, and her lips were very red. It was as if she had heavy lipstick on, but otherwise her mouth did not look abnormal. Until she opened it, and Elliot could see the rows of needle-like, recurving teeth in her lower jaw.

In some way he could not describe—but certainly not an ordinary way—she sprang onto the boy, her arms wrapping around him, the great talons sinking into his back, his buttocks. He howled again as she took him down, swung him into position, and closed her mouth over the spouting penis. Her throat worked so rapidly that its motion reminded Elliot of the wings of a hummingbird; and the boy's shrieks rapidly turned to groans. His body collapsed quickly onto the bones, then the bones themselves began to fall apart, to disappear from beneath the graying skin. The whole process only took a few minutes; finally the skin itself was being sucked up, leaving his head and body hair behind on the floor. The last bit disappeared into her mouth, and she put her hands, no longer taloned, out on the floor, pushed herself up to a kneeling position. Her brilliant red lips parted again, and an enormously long, shiny tongue, black and forked, licked out. It flicked lightly over her body, picking up every trace of blood and tissue that had escaped during the few seconds the boy had been free. This too took only a few seconds; then she stopped.

In a trancelike state, Elliot wondered what she'd done with him; she was no larger, no fatter than she'd been. But the only traces of Conrad Weiser that were left was the pile of his clothes and the hair scattered over the rug.

She opened her mouth again, and it looked quite normal now; human teeth, human tongue. Her lips, too, had faded back to their usual color, red but not scarlet. All that remained were the elliptical pupils, and she looked at the hair on the floor like any woman might look at a mess on her rug. Then she glanced up at Elliot, gave him a brief smile.

"You might as well come in," she said. "No sense standing half in the window and half out!"

He pushed the curtain aside, stepped into the room. She was still kneeling, facing him, nude; her eyes were in transition from reptilian to human. He walked toward her as if in a dream, thinking that never in his life had he seen a woman more attractive than she was at this moment. She gave him a curious look in return, but no smile. As he approached her, she did not move.

Standing beside her, looking down at her, Elliot fixed her gaze with his own; for just a moment he was unsure of what he had to do. Then, like a mechanical man, he lifted the .38 and put it against her head. Her dark eyes, fully human now, were steady. He could see no surprise there.

"Murderess," he said, no emotion in his voice at all. "You murdered me, murdered my dad, my grandpa. Who knows how many others?"

She continued to look at him unwaveringly. "I wouldn't call it murder," she said. "None of them—yourself included—were unwilling. Yet you are right, Elliot. I have, in my lifetime, murdered many men. And women. Even I don't know how many. Thousands."

In spite of what he knew, the statement gave him a pang. "Why?" he asked her.

"A lot of reasons. When I was younger—back in the sixteenth century—just because I hated so much. I'm not proud of that."

"You don't sound very remorseful!"

"That'd be a waste of time. I can't bring them back. All I can do is not make the same mistakes again. That's all any of us can do."

He stopped talking, fixed his eyes on her head, where the gun was touching her. "I have to kill you," he said simply. "I thought Weiser might do it. But you murdered him, too."

"Why should that bother you?" she asked curiously. "You were going to kill him, weren't you?"

"Because," he said in a low voice, "you are a monster. Even though he was too—at least he was a human monster. And monsters have to be destroyed. I mean, that's what people do to them!" He looked back into her eyes; he couldn't seem to help it.

She nodded slowly. "Some do, yes."

There was a long pause, the two of them staring into each other's eyes. "How?" he asked finally, not moving the gun.

"Power," she said. "Energy. I take it, from men. When I make love with them . . . but I told you that before. It's why you were so tired, that first time. Most guys—like those in the film—I take just a little. They hardly notice. I can take it all. As you've just seen."

"You took something from me—?"

"Yes. And as you must know by now, I gave you something in return. Far more than your father got, Elliot. You couldn't have defeated the Tzitzimeme without it."

"Am I supposed to thank you?" he almost shouted. "I had to die for it, Goddamn it! I'm fucking dead, and I'm walking around!"

"I know."

Keeping the gun pressed tightly to her head, he wiped his face with his other hand. He was aware that he was putting off the final moment, but he couldn't help it. "That— Tzitzimeme," he said. "It was trying to delay me. So that Weiser could kill you." It wasn't a question.

"Yes."

"But—what's the connection? I mean, Weiser was just crazy, he had nothing to do with—"

"That's true. But Tzizimitl found him, and she used him. He was her agent, her tool. She may have been aiming him at me for quite a while. I don't know."

"Who the hell is this Tzitzimitl, anyway?"

"Let's just say, an old enemy."

"Why would she want you dead?"

She flicked her eyes away from his for an instant, then back. "Because I provide Quetzalcoatl and Tezcatlipoca—among others—with what they need. Because of what I'll do for them in the future. Because of my destiny. A lot of reasons. She may well try again when she's strong enough. Maybe she'll even succeed. It isn't something I can afford to worry about."

"What will you do for them in the future?"

Again she looked away briefly. "Believe me, Elliot, you don't want to know the answer to that. Given your own part in these matters, it's just better that you don't know."

He digested these words for a moment, then listened to a voice deep inside himself that told him not to pursue it. There were other matters of more immediate interest, anyway. "Me, my ancestors," he asked, shifting the subject, "why do you kill us?"

"Because it is your destiny. You are promised to Tezcatlipoca—the Smoking Mirror—from before your birth! Elliot, I tried to tell you before: a man who doesn't fulfill his destiny can't have much of a life! It's true, yours will be cut a little short, but believe me, you will understand, even if you don't now, that it was worth it!"

"Platitudes," he snarled, his finger tightening on the trigger a little. "How the hell did all this get started, anyway?"

"It began a long time ago. To keep Tezcatlipoca strong—and you just cannot imagine how important that is. We had to sacrifice someone every fifty-two years. And that was absolutely minimal. The Aztecs used to do one each year. Back in the eighteenth century, I met a man named Kevin Collins, in Ireland. He was a practitioner of what was then called the 'Black Arts,' so he was more open than most to new ideas. It really was his idea, to double up the frequency of the sacrifices, and to dedicate the sons, each generation down, as the Ixiptla. I had to develop some techniques to make that possible, but . . . anyway, we've accomplished things the Aztecs didn't dream of. Thanks to his sacrifice, and to the sacrifices each Collins man has made, down to the present time. I think it has to do with the nature of the giving—"

"You made me dedicate my own son!"

"Yes. Though by the time his day comes, it might not be necessary; Tezcatlipoca is even now in the world. But if it is, I will help him find his destiny, too—"

He didn't really understand all that, but he knew what he could do to stop it. "Not if you're dead," he told her coldly.

"No. Not then."

Again he paused for a moment. "I really do have to kill you anyway, you know. It's my duty, to other men. You're a vampire of some crazy kind—"

"That's your choice, Elliot. You have to make it. You saved my life a few minutes ago—so in a way my life is yours, to do what you will with. Fair, isn't it? I took yours, now I give you mine. But really, you already had it. Nothing has really changed for us, nothing at all."

He stared down at her with some consternation; her easy acceptance of her own death was profoundly disturbing to him. "But how can you—?"

She smiled at him. "Easily. Because I really do love you, Elliot. Don't you remember, back at the zoo? I told you then that if you knew what my nagual was, you held my life in your hands. You still do, Elliot. I'm a woman who—"

"You are no ordinary woman! That's why I have to kill you—"

"No, I'm not ordinary. But there is something I'd like you to do."

"What's that?"

She pointed to the obsidian knife. "If you do decide to kill me, use that, not the gun. For me, it's much more appropriate."

He followed her gaze to it, remembering his dream. The blade glittered in the light, seemed to draw him somehow. But he was able to resist. "I can't," he told her after a long pause. "It's too—too intimate."

She grinned once more, briefly. "You've pushed other things into my body, Elliot!" she said.

"I can't," he mumbled. He looked down; a curl of her hair was wound around the blued muzzle of the gun where it touched her head, as if holding it in place. His hand trembled as he pulled the hammer back, cocked it into place.

She shrugged, almost imperceptibly, lowered her eyes, and seemed to wait for him.

"You could stop me, couldn't you?" he asked in a whisper.

"Yes," she said.

"But you aren't going to?"

"No."

He pulled the trigger halfway back, watched the hammer move just a tiny bit. A little more pressure, that's all, just a little—she looked straight ahead still, her eyes completely calm, her hands on her knees . . .

Just a little squeeze . . .

He caught the hammer with his thumb, lifted the gun away from her head, and let it move gently back. Then he dropped it into his pocket, started to turn away. She looked up at him, a faint smile on her face as he walked to the door, pausing on the way to pick up his obsidian knife.

"I'm going back to Chapel Hill," he said in a clear voice. "If Melissa is still waiting, I'll marry her."

"I know."

He put his hand on the knob, turned to look at her again; she was watching him, hadn't moved. He started to say something, didn't. He felt as if his mind was shifting again somehow. There was an image of high-tide seas rushing out.

"Know that I do love you, my Jaguar Warrior," she told him.

Still silent, he opened the door, stepped through it, but paused. One more glance back—

"I promise you, Elliot," she said, leaning over a little to look at him, "when your son comes to me—if he must come—I'll treat him gently. As if he were my own."

Images raced through his mind: their first day together, the film, the death of the Chingon, the death of Conrad Weiser. It seemed to him that his mind was in two layers, a conscious one, which had little understanding, and another beneath, which was not at all confused, but which he was not fully in contact with yet. He thought about what she'd said, looked at her eyes. At last he found his voice again.

"I know you will, Nikki," he said with a smile, and he closed the door.